This sequel to *The* the Von Rahmel family and their continued fight to save Berlin from the Russians, just as they fought with such fierce determination to save their beloved city from Hitler's abuse. The Berlin Wall is erected, dividing families and preventing travel by anyone Russia wants to keep for its own purposes. The Von Rahmels invest money, resources, and their lives with their own resistance group to help those who need to escape East Berlin: journalists, scientists, professors, and those imprisoned for speaking openly, as well as Christians no longer allowed to practice their religion. In the background are Cousin Peter, with MI6, and the professional Israeli assassin Grigory.

Katarina Von Rahmel is brought back into the circle in a web of espionage while she fights her own memories from the war and deals with the ongoing fears caused by dark secrets and running away from the men in her life. The demons follow her everywhere she goes, and Father Anthony, her brother, is the only one she believes can save her.

With all their wealth and station in life, this family will have to make peace with the past while their private worlds erupt around them, Katarina at the core of it all—Katarina, who tries to crawl out of the darkness into the light and restore the hope she once had as a prima ballerina. Through the torment, there still remains one person they had all thought dead—a man determined to avenge his brother's death and destroy Katarina and ultimately her loved ones. Who will save her? Who will bring her to the light? Or is she forever doomed?

Praise for Evelyn Turner's Books

"Evelyn Turner's riveting book *THE STAR AND THE CROSS* left us thirsty for the hidden chapters of the astounding and tragic life of Germany's famous prima ballerina Katarina Von Rahmel during WWII. Infused with alarming truths based on Turner's personal memoirs of her German family and the secrets, lies, and loves of her mother, ...the electrifying sequel, *CRAWLING OUT OF THE DARKNESS*, will quench that thirst!"

~Libby Belle, author

~*~

"*CRAWLING OUT OF THE DARKNESS* is a story that needed to be told. ...a vivid picture of what life was like for the Von Rahmel family. ...their pursuit of justice far outweighs their shortcomings. ...We need more books like *CRAWLING OUT OF THE DARKNESS*, a reminder that if we don't face our past head on, we are bound to repeat the casualties of our lives."

~Tiffany Murphy, Emmy Award-winning television news anchor

~*~

"If you have read *THE STAR AND THE CROSS*, then this sequel is a must-read. The pages seem to turn themselves as you fall into the calamitous upheaval of the Cold War. Part spy thriller, part family drama, *CRAWLING OUT OF THE DARKNESS* brings life to history; a strikingly emotional portrait of a sister and brother, separated by miles, faith, and tragedy. ...Heartbreaking!"

~Ryan Kennedy, television and film producer

Crawling Out of the Darkness

by

Evelyn M. Turner

a sequel to
The Star and the Cross

This is a work of fiction. Names, characters, places, and incidents are either the product of the author's imagination or are used fictitiously, and any resemblance to actual persons living or dead, business establishments, events, or locales, is entirely coincidental.

Crawling Out of the Darkness

Contact Information: info@thewildrosepress.com

Cover Art by *Rae Monet, Inc. Design*

The Wild Rose Press, Inc.
PO Box 708
Adams Basin, NY 14410-0708
Visit us at www.thewildrosepress.com

Publishing History
First Mainstream Historical Edition, 2019
Print ISBN 978-1-5092-2891-1
Digital ISBN 978-1-5092-2892-8

a sequel to The Star and the Cross
Published in the United States of America

Dedication

To Jerry Olson, my husband,
a man of great faith and honor to all who know him

Acknowledgments

Huge thanks to Tiffany Murphy of Fox 6 KFDM for my first TV interview and for her kindness and continuous support for both books. Thanks also to Greg Saleme for starting the journey for interviews and to Ryan Kennedy for his belief.

As always, I thank my friends in Texas, Delaware, and Pennsylvania.

A shout-out to the acclaimed author Rod Davis.

I thank Travis Knotts for the technology rescue, and Mike Pollinger for technical assistance on weapons and operations; also thanks to Gail P. and Gail S.

Love to my sister in Berlin, Monika, and to Rudi and my nieces, and I give special thanks to Shawn Banks, my beautiful and kind sister by another mother. Thanks to my godchildren for being in my life, Sara and Nick, and to Katie, Hannah, Tony, and Andrea.

I give special thanks to my dear friend Libby Bryer, a writer of witty and quirky short stories soon to be published in four books by Libby Belle. She was my second pair of eyes for envisioning the final shape for *Crawling Out of the Darkness*. Her honesty and love for the history of my family were the perfect ingredients. We should all have friends like Libby, who dove into this project with unadulterated enthusiasm and faith for its bright future.

For all those who fought and are fighting the cause for freedom and Christianity.

Chapter 1

Italy, Lucca, Piazza Napoleone, 1964

Sipping on a cappuccino, a porcelain cup held delicately in both hands, she eyed the tourists walking by with their Italian sun-soaked tans, a stark contrast from her own alabaster white skin. She wore fashionable black ankle-length pants with a light pink sweater. A large beige, floppy hat angled perfectly on her head not only protected her face from the sun but conveniently hid any facial expressions she wished not to share. The blonde hair peeked out from under the hat the minute she looked up to place an order for another coffee, but it was the violet eyes that one would notice first.

From the café she watched him exiting the Duomo di Lucca, Cathedral di San Martino, the seat of the Archbishop of Lucca. Dressed in black, except for the stark white collar and the crucifix hanging from around his neck, his six-foot frame, bronzed skin, and thick salt-and-pepper hair still cut such a handsome figure that heads turned whenever he was present. As it was said so many times in the past, her brother Anthony was a beautiful priest.

They shared the same high cheekbones, but his eyes were blue with flecks of green. Now, as he approached Katarina's table, his smile broadened at the sight of his sister. She had not expected to see that welcoming expression after their conversation on the phone two days earlier when he had given her quite the scolding. Not in the mood for another lecture, she was relieved and offered him her sweetest smile in return.

When he reached her, she stood, and before she could stand fully erect, he wrapped his arms around her and gave her the biggest bear hug; the patrons all around curiously watched a "man of the cloth" openly displaying affection for a beautiful woman. Katarina pulled from his embrace and said sheepishly, "I didn't think you would come, after our conversation."

Anthony, brow furrowed, gave her a look she had known since they were children. "Do you think that *one* phone call could keep me away, especially since you have been in Vernazza for what, two weeks now, and not one word from you?"

"Well, I…" Katarina looked down.

Noticing her discomfort, he changed the subject. "I have business here, instructions of the Vatican. I also promised Father I'd look into the estate. But for now, let's order some lunch. I'm starving!" He signaled for the waiter and pointed to specific items on the menu.

When Katarina removed her hat, the hair tumbled down around her face. Anthony looked pleased to see she had gone back to her original silver-blonde color and let it grow out again. He had disliked the heavily dyed dark hair she wore after leaving Berlin in 1948 to live in the United States; the chin-length severe cut designed to fit the latest American styles had hardened her face, unlike the flowing shoulder-length hair she now wore.

"How is your Italian, Kat?"

"Well, not as good as my French and English, but I'm getting by."

"We'll make good use of speaking it often and relearn together."

Several hours later, after shopping in the market, they were on their way by train to Vernazza, where cars were not allowed. The weather was perfect for the small hike they would need to take to their parents' estate. The hypnotic movement of the train allowed Anthony a moment to close his eyes and reminisce. He loved Vernazza, the house set in the hills, his father's gift to his mother after falling in love with the area while on their honeymoon. It had proven to be a profitable investment, the land and climate ripe for producing olive oil and wine, the bottles proudly stamped with their own family label. Although the war had set them back, their loyal staff had taken care of their summer home and the grounds all through World War II.

Overlooking the colorful harbor, he remembered as a child he and his brothers had pretended they were pirates, stumbling wildly as they climbed the green hills alive with grapevines and farms, imagining themselves conquering the outcrop of rocks leading to the imposing Doria Castle. He recalled their mother always stopping at the Santa Marta Chapel along Vernazza's main street, Via Roma, and instructing her strong-willed boys to confess quickly if they had done something wrong for the day.

Their favorite time was spent on the beach, and many days they played on the northwest side of the fortified town belonging to the Obertenghi family, of Italian nobility, since 1080. They approached the town by train from either Milan or Lucca—mostly Lucca, where the train stopped, leaving them to walk the rest of the way.

When Katarina was born, they continued their wonderful visits to the sea, carrying her through the sunshine and hills of Cinque Terre, watching her squeal with delight as the ocean waves swept over her. Her brothers would marvel at their baby sister's eyes, so brilliant, like the sparkling water before them. Times were simple then, filled with so much love, and life was so much easier. Anthony looked over at Katarina with a deep sadness of longing for those days. How life had changed.

Chapter 2

They were walking to the house, groceries in tow. The air was light, and so seemed their moods, although Anthony sensed that Katarina had more to say.

"Mother says you have been here for several weeks. What have you been doing with your time?"

"Oh, I spent many days just walking. I was indulgent with food. I would sit at the trattoria and let the sun sink into my being after I stuffed myself with mounds of pasta, and then I'd just walk it all off again." She paused to reflect. "You know, Anthony, this place is still magical. Memories are good here. It holds a warm feeling, nothing with anger."

"I do hope you have found some happiness in being back here."

Whatever was in Anthony's tone triggered something deep inside Katarina. She stopped and sat on a large rock and allowed the tears to fill her eyes. "Anthony, he came to Corfu. I knew the minute the shadow draped over me it was him. I always know when it's him. He told me he will always be able to find me. That's what Grigory does, finds people, as you know."

She wiped the tears off her face. Her voice was a whisper, "Anthony, why do I destroy the things I love? What happened in Berlin? Why didn't I die?"

He knelt beside her and took both her hands in his,

"Because Heaven, my sister, was not ready for you."

"But my heart aches all the time. I hurt Grigory, I hurt John, even Francis. I have hurt all my children. No one has escaped my anger. And now, well, now I would not know what to do if you ever left me. I'm certain I'd fall into the abyss."

His own eyes were moist with sadness. He knew in his heart that she would always be lost. The family had tried to help her, her husband John had tried, and all had failed. She was forever running.

Even now, looking into her brother's loving eyes, Katarina felt helpless. She loosened his grip, picked up the grocery bags, and started walking. He rushed to catch up with her.

"So what did you think of Corfu?" he asked casually, wanting to lighten the conversation.

"It's beautiful, Anthony, similar to here. Mountains dotted with homes of all different colors. Old villages untouched by war. It's very Venetian, idyllic beaches and small villages everywhere. There's a castle called the Angelokastro, and it's at the highest peak of the island. I went there alone, and from the top I could see miles of turquoise water, so still and never-ending. I wished I could fly and sail over it. I've never felt that free. I may never again."

She let out another sigh, one of many Anthony was used to hearing. "I think, after a while, I will return to Paris to be near you. Seems we always have someone staying at the apartment. Their visits keep me sane."

"Oh, look who's here." Anthony smiled, pointing straight ahead.

It's Giuseppe." Katarina's eyes lit up.

Waving, a large grin on his weathered face,

Giuseppe pulled the miniature donkey toward them, the empty wooden cart bouncing as it rolled closely behind. Anthony and Katarina met him half way.

Giuseppe greeted them both with warm hugs, insisting that they unload their packages into his cart. "Father Anthony, what luck. I was just going over to the neighbors when I saw you in the distance. You certainly can't hide from us in all that black." He chuckled. He was like one of the family, respected by all, as it was he and his wife Marie who managed the estate, harvested the olives and vineyards, and kept the house in tiptop shape.

Katarina felt a sudden chill and put her sweater back on. They watched the countryside go by as they walked alongside the cart, Anthony kindly asking after Giuseppe's large family.

Soon they came upon the two-story home, surrounded with healthy gardens and inviting patios. They entered from the back door to the kitchen. Anthony stood at the threshold and looked behind him into the distance. No tourist had yet discovered this paradise. They all ventured to the Amalfi Coast. As much as he loved Paris, he hoped someday to have a parish in Italy before he died. With all its wonderful art and music, and the cute Parisian cafés, even the "city of love" could be lonely. He also felt the lingering apprehension toward Germans, but as long as he spoke French he was well received. He stood a little longer and inhaled scents of the lemon trees, olive branches, and the clean ocean breeze. Yes, his dream was attainable, and he would pray about it. The aroma of freshly baked bread lured him inside.

Katarina grabbed a cookie as she walked through

the kitchen into the open villa, with its vast windows, polished tiled floors, rugs and tapestries scattered throughout, large sofas and overstuffed chairs in soft spring colors. When Katarina's parents had purchased the place, it was a rundown, century-old villa, and they had painstakingly restored it. Many a Christmas was spent there to get away from the cold of Germany. They were fraught with worry during the entire war that it would be destroyed, but it was miraculously spared.

Marie entered the kitchen and screamed with delight when she saw Anthony. "My sweet boy!" she still called him, cupping his face in her hands. She shoved him back and stood looking him up and down, her hands determinedly placed on her hips. "You're much too skinny! We will make a feast tonight to celebrate your homecoming and fatten you up! Giuseppe, my husband, quick, go into the cellar and bring up some good wine." She gave Anthony another tight squeeze and ruffled his hair.

Hearing the commotion, Katarina made her way back to the kitchen and was standing at the door, nibbling on the cookie, smiling at Anthony, who now looked like a little boy who had just had his cheeks repeatedly kissed and pinched by an eccentric old aunt. She turned, and from the hallway she yelled over her shoulder, "Get out of that priest outfit and wear something relaxing for a change."

He turned to Marie, and his childlike smile dropped, a look of concern in his eyes. "How is my sister doing?"

Marie clasped her hands together, shook her head, and crossed herself. "She cries so much, and she has terrible nightmares. We will find her sometimes downstairs drinking herself to sleep." Upon hearing his wife's response, Giuseppe turned from the door and stood behind her, silently agreeing, his head bowed. "She has lost so much weight, Anthony. When Katarina cries, it can break the angels' hearts."

"Thank you for sharing. I know this is hard on everyone. Please continue watching her, and keep me informed. I am here for her."

He walked out to the terrace, where he found Katarina drinking a glass of wine, looking in the distance at the emerald sea, sails and fishing boats stippling its surface. He stood quietly beside her in respect for her moment of peace, until she loosened her gaze, suddenly aware that he was close by.

"Kat, in quiet moments like this, what are you thinking?"

She managed a weak smile. "I think of every year of my life, and I think so much of Grigory, how he loved me all those years and how he protected me, even with all my sins. I look back, and it seems there were more bad times than there were good." She tugged playfully at his collar. "Enough talk. Go and change your clothes, sweet brother. I feel as though I'm in confession every time I look at you."

Walking up the stairs, he knew she was fighting battles within herself every day. She is broken, he thought, but now she could be free.

An hour later, the clang of the dinner bell was heard throughout the home as it had been for years, notifying them that they had only fifteen minutes until dinner. Katarina was on the patio, freshly made up and dressed in a blue cotton empire-line dress, silver strands stitched tightly high above her waist, accentuating her breasts. The table was set, fresh bread in the basket, and homemade churned butter nearby.

Anthony had changed into an oxford blue shirt and chino pants and entered the patio barefooted. With Katarina's hair pulled back into a ponytail, at a glance they looked like teenagers sitting lazily in silence, innocently watching the sun set, anticipating a good meal.

Marie came in and lit the candles on the table. Giuseppe followed with bowls of pasta, fresh lobster, shrimp, and meatballs the size of golf balls. There was enough for ten people. For this special occasion, Katarina had insisted that they use the Italian Majolica and the Austrian Riedel wine glasses.

As they gathered at the table, Katarina giggled like a child. "Dear brother, I warn you, do not walk around Paris or Rome looking the way you do now. Mothers will kidnap you to marry their daughters."

As always, they asked for Giuseppe and Marie to join them, and as always, the humble couple declined and retreated to their cottage on the premises. Anthony took his sister's hand and said a prayer over the meal.

"Tell me, brother, did you ever regret not having a family?"

He looked at her, surprised at the seriousness of her question. "Where in God's name did that come from?"

"Just seeing you right now, comfortable in everyday clothing."

"No, I knew at a very young age that I wanted to be in the presence of God and serve him to the best of my ability."

"But Mother said you had a woman before the seminary." A mischievous look gleamed in her eyes.

"Well, yes, I did. I didn't go into the seminary as a virgin, but in the end my soul belonged to my church."

"Glad to know you were a sinner, just a little bit." She laughed.

They dug into the mass of food, and Anthony ate heartily, while Katarina picked slowly through the food piled much too high on her plate, her eyes bigger than her stomach. When they finished, they moved to the living room to let it digest in the cool of the evening. Coffee and cookies were waiting for them on a table. Anthony chuckled. "Giuseppe and Marie are like the elves and the shoemaker, so quick and efficient."

Passing up the refreshments, he poured a brandy and lit up a cigar. "What did Grigory want in Corfu, Kat? It is a long way to go for him to seek you out."

A sad smile crossed her lips. "He asked me to stop coming to Israel. He needs to be free of me. I'm afraid we didn't part on the best of terms. I guess he'll spend the rest of his life trying to find vengeance and save Israel."

"Do you think you will ever see him again?"

"I'm not sure. When he is away and has the strongest need for me, he looks for me. I am forever imprinted in his brain, I know that. The problem is we can't forgive each other." She shrugged and shifted uncomfortably in her chair. Grigory would always be her biggest regret, and she and Anthony both knew it hurt her to talk about him. "So, tell me, brother, how is Paris treating you?"

"It's difficult teaching at the university. So many don't believe in God any longer, and the students are angry with the politicians, the politicians angry with the students. The *Union Nationale des Etudiants de*

France, or rather the National Union of French Students, is much more vocal than at other universities. They won't be brainwashed like so many students or the youth in Germany. The women we teach are more open to theology. Fifty percent now attend. I'm caught between the old order of elite morals and the teaching of philosophical views, which are hard to understand for many. They meet at my church, where we discuss humanities and social justice."

"They meet at your church? So how does the church feel about that?"

"They don't know."

"There you go, being a bad boy," she scolded.

He threw his head back in the chair and laughed.

"Did you ever tell your students how many people you got safely out of Germany and how many you protected when the wall went up?"

He shook his head. "No point."

She stood and reached for the brandy decanter and poured him another. "We never did really talk about what happened after I first left Berlin. There are years of gaps while I was in Hawaii and California. I know Mother in her letters was beside herself with worry."

"The short of it is, Europe was savage—refugees everywhere, borders changed, spoils of war—and Jews were treated just as badly as we did at the beginning. The Soviets took their stronghold, and the Cold War had just begun."

Anthony inhaled a long drag of the cigar and gently let it flow from his mouth. "I know you dislike our sister-in-law, Gertrude, but she suffered terribly. Her hometown was destroyed. Thank God she was in Berlin with us when her parents were murdered in

Nemmersdorf. The Red Army killed every soul in that town as they marched through…including children and babies." He saw Katarina wince.

"Go on, Anthony." She hoped if he talked it out, the haunted look might leave his eyes.

"You know what the Russians were like, just the brief time in Berlin when they called it the rape of Berlin. Women, children, babies—they murdered them as they did in most of the eastern provinces of Germany. They crucified women in our churches, calling it the spoils of war."

She leaned over, took his hand, and squeezed it. "I'm sorry."

Even though he knew Katarina deeply suffered with her own ghostly memories, he needed to share with her, for if anyone could understand the hell they had come through, it was his own sister. "Does it matter? We are still fighting, and there is no real peace from Poland to Prague to Budapest. When I was in Eastern Europe with the church after the war, I witnessed such savagery, women killing their own babies so the Russians and others wouldn't torture them or rape them. We said many a prayer over dead children. This was why we fought so hard against Hitler. Eastern Europe had their own ethnic cleansing of Germans."

Anthony let the cigar rest on the ashtray, no longer savoring the smoky taste. "Revenge is powerful; that's why you saw me always with a partner. I could have been killed many times over. And you saw the revenge toward me in Berlin. No law and order existed. It was madness."

She had to ask, "I know every scar you got in the

war, but your hand, it looks like a knife opened it up."

"I was lucky. Your boy Grigory saved my ass. How he continuously found us is a mystery to me. He helped me find my way to the Austrian border tucked in the back of a car with diplomatic plates. The church was being attacked by every person in power."

Before he could complete the story, they were interrupted, hearing Giuseppe humming his way toward them. "Aw, and here comes one of our little elves, right now."

Giuseppe brought in a plate of cheese and olives, with a pile of sausage. "Here, Father, a good-night snack."

Katarina laughed. "Food is the answer to everything here."

"Giuseppe, we are going to roll out of here into our beds if you keep feeding us like this." Anthony held up the crystal glass. "Great brandy."

"Ah, yes, Ahyesi Barone Ricasoli sent it up to us for thanks…hmm, for something your Father did."

Katarina popped an olive in her mouth. "So fresh, and right from our own land," she murmured.

Anthony let the brandy slide down his throat as he looked up at the beautiful tiled ceiling, while Katarina fingered the old Irish linens on the armchair, feeling the knots put there by her mother or Marie as they mended the fragile material every so often.

"Enjoying the brandy over wine, are you?" Katarina asked, catching the satisfaction now back on his face.

"I have had my share of wine over the years. This is a nice break. You would have enjoyed the little trip my seminarian and I did last week. He took me to

Henokiens where they have been making wine since 1495, the finest Viogniers and Cabernet Sauvignons. We traveled all over Avignon. Ah, the breathtaking beauty, and that is where some good eating is."

"You sound like a travel magazine, Anthony," Katarina remarked. When Giuseppe walked away, she asked, "Do you still want to talk?"

"Not much more to tell." Anthony rose from his chair and moved toward the terrace. The stars above shone as brightly as the village lights below, each twinkling messages of peace. A reminder that God was ever present, he assured himself.

He came back in, closing the double French doors behind him, a signal that the evening had come to an end. He could now smell a hint of the Osso buco alla Milanese, fresh bruschetta, and Cicchetti tapas being prepared for tomorrow's meal. Katarina had placed classical music on the stereo. She was obviously not ready to retire.

"Where did the scar come from, Anthony?" she asked again.

"Not tonight, my dear. Maybe tomorrow. Tomorrow you and I are going to go to Siena and several other towns. I left the car at the church in Lucca. From there I need to travel to Buonconvento. I'd like you to come with me."

"I don't know Buonconvento."

"I think you will enjoy it. It means 'Happy Gathering Place.' It's Latin."

"Sounds like fun. I haven't ventured out past the village since I've been here. I hope it's a nice car, not something that will break down."

He walked past her and ruffled her hair. "Go

upstairs and pack a bag for tomorrow. I think it's time for me to head for my own bed."

She entered her bedroom with the four-poster bed. The floral wallpaper had seen better days, slightly peeling. Her father hated the wallpaper. It was too busy, he said. He wanted the walls to be pure yellow or white. Outside was where the real beauty was displayed, and he expressed with deep concern that no mere human should try to duplicate God's nature on something as insignificant as bedroom walls. The temptation to start peeling the paper off the walls nearly overcame her. Instead, she took a long, leisurely bath with lavender petals picked fresh that morning.

The bed had been changed with crisp, cool linens, and she sank into the softness in a simple T-shirt. In earlier years, she would have worn the finest silk sleeping gowns. She would not allow her mind to go there and depended on the large amounts of wine she had consumed to keep the ghosts away. Particularly that one ghost, the one that refused to leave her side. She had been told that Grigory had killed Frederick Spitz's brother, and knowing that had brought her comfort, for a while. It was so hard for Grigory later to break the news to her that the man was still alive. Grigory felt defeated and Katarina felt cursed, both of them always looking over their shoulder.

****

The sun came peeping through the thin curtains and gently woke Katarina to a new day. Marie must have come into the room while she slept, as fresh water with lemon and a small bouquet of flowers from their own gardens were now on the nightstand. Remembering that Anthony had planned a special day, she took one swig and hastily dressed.

She wore pink capris and a black sweater when she tiptoed downstairs, stopping to listen to the happy voices in the kitchen. When she entered, she saw her brother at the table having coffee, but surprisingly dressed as a priest. “Why are you dressed like that?”

“I had mass earlier, in town. You should have come, sleepyhead. You know, church will not kill you.”

“I’ll let you say all the prayers you want for me.”

“Did you pack?” he asked.

“Yes, I packed, but first I’m going to sit here in the silence and have my coffee, if you please.”

He hit her over the head with the newspaper. “I’ll meet you down here in one hour. Be ready.”

As planned, they went on the train to Lucca. Once again, they took in the beautiful countryside, until Anthony went to task reading church articles. Katarina picked up her own book but couldn’t concentrate. She closed her eyes, deep in thought. She needed to know how Grigory had found Anthony in Budapest and what took place. Any news of him might assuage the unbearable days of missing him. There had been nothing she could do to persuade Grigory that things could be different between them. Still he was lost to her in so many ways.

Chapter 3

He closed the folder and raised his arms above his head in a quiet stretch.

She opened her eyes. “We left the conversation last night for later.”

“Oh, yes, we did, didn’t we?” Anthony placed the folder by his side and pushed the things he had been reading out of his mind. “After you left, the church was fighting for survival. Stalin was trying to hold on, but he came up against Josip Bvoz Tito, who didn’t need Stalin. He knew how to dispose of his enemies. He was his own killing machine. Stalin became more paranoid, especially when the blockade failed in Berlin. He needed a propaganda tool, so he blamed it on the churches, and soon the clergy ended up in concentration camps. Once again, we became the enemy to everything Stalin and his newfound Communist countries believed in. Soviets were worse—they didn’t waste time. Catholic or Lutheran, they were bent on destroying them all.”

“How did you fit into all of this?”

“I had to save my church. I was sent over to see what I could do.”

“You’re always saving your church, Anthony.”

“I wish I could have saved more. Communists feared the church and the morals and the belief that there is evil and good. They recognized that we, the church and our schools, were teaching reading and writing for the masses and promoting our youth groups, so we were being terrorized and jailed. They shut down our seminaries and our charity—Caritas—our soup kitchens and orphanages. They tried to demoralize us by imprisoning the priests, forcing them to say they were only loyal to Stalin. Some priests gave up the fight and turned to Marxist teachings just to save their church. The Communists killed hundreds of them. Many died in their concentration camps. Bishop Miklos Beresztocz was brutally tortured. Too many broken souls, Kat."

"But yours didn't break, brother. Tell me exactly what part you played," she urged.

"I went into Hungary, to get our own priests out, with papers they would need to cross the border. The one priest we thought we could trust to deliver those papers we found out—or should I say, Grigory found out—was working for the secret police. We wanted to get out Father Mindszenty before they killed him, but we did not make it in time. Wyszyneski got me letters to take back. He worked so hard not to confront the Russians, he wanted a conciliatory peace, but then another list came forth that he shared with me. Father Niemans and I were on that list to be arrested and executed, no trial. I spent three days in jail."

There was a gasp from Katarina. "You never told me."

"You asked about the scar." He lifted his hand. "They pushed a knife through my hand, hoping I would give up our other priest." Balling it into a fist, his jaw clenching with the memory, he placed his hand back in his lap. "I thought for sure they were going to send me to their concentration camp when I would not talk, but by God's Grace, they let me go. When the secret police showed up at the rectory, I fled with the other priests through the tunnels that were so narrow a piece of iron slashed through my hand, opening the wound that was not yet healed. Of course that led to an infection later on. We walked for several miles, until a car pulled up alongside us. We thought this was our end, but there he was—our savior, Grigory—ordering us to get in, throwing a change of clothes at us as we hid in the back seat. Before we got to the border, we switched cars again, this time with diplomatic license plates and Hungarian flags. Two other priests were dressed like Russian generals, but because I was the most wanted, they stuffed me in the space below the trunk."

"Grigory always shows up, doesn't he, Anthony?" Katarina held her hands to her heart, unaware that she had been holding her breath.

"He always will. He's like a phantom of some sort, appearing out of nowhere. I pray for him. But I understand that he does well in Israel. The Mossad is his life now, as you well know."

Anthony blew out a harsh breath of resignation. "Forty million people died in this war, and still there is no peace."

"All right, enough sad conversation. We still have lovely Italy, we have our homes, we have kept people who worked for us and their families safe."

"Yes, you are correct. We have done our share before and even after the war. God will always lead the way."

It was a relief when the train came to a halt. The tempo changed, and they quickly hailed a taxi into

Lucca. Once they arrived in the walled city, Anthony walked so fast Katarina could barely keep up with him.

"Anthony, where is the fire? Why are we suddenly in such a rush?"

"I'm sorry. I have to go to the church and pick up the car, and there is another matter I must take care of."

"If you don't mind, I'll just wait here on the corner at the café."

"You can't possibly be hungry again."

"I'm always hungry." She patted her tummy and grinned.

The town seemed empty; all the tourists had started to leave. She ordered an espresso with a slice of cheesecake. She had just taken her second bite when she saw Anthony walking toward her, looking anything but happy.

"What is wrong? You look like you are ready to kill someone—not that you would."

"Kat, when do you think you might be going back to Paris?" he asked hurriedly, ignoring her remark.

She looked at him questioningly. "Well, I had not planned to go back for a while."

He kicked the chair.

"Goodness, you need to tell me what's going on, and right now!"

"Listen, I'm going to meet up with a woman named Lucina. I phoned Giuseppe. He will bring her to me, and from here she'll be put on the train to Paris. I sent a message to Christina to expect her. She can do the legal work."

"Has my brother taken a lover?"

"Not funny." He frowned.

"Sit down and share my cake."

"This is serious, Kat. You need to help me save this woman. I want you to go across the street and buy her some clothing, including a very large hat to cover most of her face." Scaling his sister's body with his eyes, he surmised, "She is about the same size as you."

She drained the last of her coffee. "So just what am I saving her from?"

"Just go and buy the clothing, I will meet you at the back of the church, last pew."

He left in a hurry.

Katarina did as she was instructed and bought a simple blue dress with a white collar. To be on the safe side, she chose a size larger than her own, thinking, what would a priest know about women's sizes. She purchased the biggest hat she could find to match.

When she arrived at the church, Anthony was in the last pew with his arm around a woman—hardly a lover, as her eye was swollen shut, her lip split, and bruises covered both arms. When she handed him the clothing, Anthony told the woman to go in the confessional and change.

"What are you doing, Anthony?"

"This poor woman has been beaten every week by a drunken husband."

"You're interfering with the church's law that a wife should submit to her husband, aren't you?"

"Yes, I'm going against it. This is the fourth woman we have rescued. We get them to Paris and Christina finds them places to stay. Then we find them work and help them start over. This woman is lucky. There are no children we have to move with her. No one has the right to do abuse like this."

"Anthony, you can be excommunicated."

"They will never know, trust me. I must follow my heart on this. Of all people, Katarina, you should understand, especially after what happened to you in East Berlin."

She shuddered, thinking of that time, and felt a surge of sympathy for the woman who at that moment walked out from the confessional, with head bent, in a dress that was too large for her. Katarina had been wrong about the size, but that certainly was of no concern to anyone at the moment. They might have a laugh about it later. Anthony told her to hide in a dark corner with the woman while he brought the car around back.

Katarina put her arm around the young refugee and whispered, "It will be all right, with my brother's help, but you must never, I mean *never* mention his name." Transfixed by Katarina's stern and penetrating eyes, the woman nodded with humility.

The Fiat pulled up, and they drove her to the train station, Anthony giving her instructions along the way. After boarding the train, the frightened woman timidly waved from the window at the excited people below, while Anthony and Katarina pretended they were just sending a family member on vacation to Gay Paree.

As soon as the train began rolling out of the station, they turned on their heels, dropped their fake smiles, and hurried back to the car. "Who got you into this, Anthony?" Katarina had to know.

"A young seminarian came to me and told me the husband had beaten his sister to death. The authorities didn't even prosecute him. Katarina, when I saw what happened to you, I swore no man would ever do that to a woman again if I could help her. Not under my watch.

This happened frequently in Paris, especially after the war. Women who even looked at the Germans were shaved, tarred, some even murdered, hung in squares, or paraded down the streets naked. A horrible punishment."

"When will you stop being everyone's savior, Anthony? Do you not realize you did enough by saving so many lives during the war? You and Hans did your share."

"As well as you, Kat. But *you* know I'm right."

"Let's just drive. I don't want to talk about this anymore."

"You never want to talk about your past, but I know you dream about it."

The drive to Siena was eighteen miles of silence to the southwest of Buonconvento, a pristine medieval village. They drove through it and moved on to spend the night in San Giovanni, where they looked forward to a fine meal.

Settling into a quaint hotel, they made their way to a highly recommended restaurant, where they enjoyed grappa-infused truffles. Later that day, they waded up to their ankles in the hot springs nearby. Anthony went to talk to old friends in Castello di Ama who were helping his parents transport the wine from their vineyards to Munich. After that they traveled for four days, Anthony stopping at various churches to check on their needs. They kept the conversation simple the entire trip, just enjoying being together and dining on good food. For Katarina, shopping in Rapolano Terme was a highlight.

Their trip was coming to an end as they made their way back to Florence. Anthony had one last church to visit, while Katarina went to the market. She was planning to bring Giuseppe a treat to fix for them. She so enjoyed cuttlefish, and the preparations in Venice were always exceptional, combining lots of capers with soft pasta, the black sauce preserved from the ink sac prepared just right and drizzled gently on top. The sauce had the saltiness of the sea and the pasta absorbed all of the flavors. To some, this dish did not look very appetizing, but for her it was one of the most delectable dishes she'd ever eaten, and her mouth watered just thinking about it. She bought all the ingredients, including freshly made mozzarella, parmigiana cheese, and sweet strawberries for dessert.

Engrossed in planning the meal, she thought she heard her name being called. Looking around, she saw no one. A shiver ran up her spine. Then she heard it again, loud and clear, "Katarina!" Not her brother's voice but an evil voice she had heard many times before. She suddenly felt very cold and stood instinctively still like an animal sensing a predator nearby. Willing it not to speak again, she jumped when a hand touched her shoulder.

"Hold on there! I didn't mean to startle you. I thought you saw me coming." Anthony placed both hands on Kat's tightened shoulders.

"Anthony, did you call for me several times?" she asked, her eyes wide with fear.

"No, I knew you were coming here and just tracked you down." He raised his eyebrows. "You look like you just saw a ghost."

"No, I think I just heard one."

He kept one arm on her shoulder as they continued down to the other stalls. "Come, there is some plump shrimp to buy at a stand farther down."

"But I already bought cuttlefish."

"Oh, well…um, let's just add some shrimp to it."

"Not a cuttlefish fan, I see."

They spent a little more time walking the market before heading back to Lucca to drop off the car.

"Anthony, have you heard anything about the young woman?" Katarina thoughtfully asked.

"I called from the church, and Giuseppe said she is now in Paris," he said proudly.

Katarina could not help but feel proud herself.

They reached home and entered through the kitchen. Giuseppe was making bread, and Anthony held up the shopping bag. "Look, we have a surprise for you."

Giuseppe peeked into the bag and clasped his hands with delight. "This I will prepare for tonight."

"I'm going upstairs to take an indulgent long bath," Katarina said, pouring herself a glass of wine to take with her.

Anthony cocked his head and gave her a disapproving look. "It's a bit early."

"For the bath or the wine?" she asked, turning on her heels. "Not to worry, big brother, it's just one glass."

As always, the bath was soothing, as was the chenille bath robe she wrapped around her body. She braced her hands on the bathroom sink, leaned forward, and studied her face in the mirror. With her hair pulled back, she could see that her skin was completely flushed a dark pink from the warm bath and the wine, and the violet eyes were staring back at her in judgment. No happiness in them, she thought, and the crow's feet are now deepening—youth has deserted me.

She couldn't find Anthony anywhere, not even outside where the breeze was soft and warm. She finally found him in the library. He was writing. She put her arms around him. "I love you, Anthony."

He patted her hands, "You will always be loved."

"I had a great time walking around old churches and museums with you."

He leaned back in the overstuffed chair and set the pen down. "I will only be here for two more days. Rome is next, then Paris. What are you going to do?"

She walked around the desk and sat down opposite him. "I think I'll just stay here a while, for the peace. My life has not exactly worked out as planned."

"But will you find your peace here?"

She opened her mouth to respond, but the dinner bell interrupted the moment. She chose not to answer, but just smiled and walked out.

Anthony didn't come immediately to the dining room. He walked down to the olive trees to meet up with two of Giuseppe's sons, who were talking with a vendor. He was away twenty minutes before he returned.

"Giuseppe, looks like a good crop."

"Yes, Father," he said, very pleased with Anthony's report. He had brought a cheese platter and a decanter of wine out to the patio. "Dinner is behind. The cuttlefish has been long time since I make."

"We have nothing but time, but don't forget the shrimp." Anthony made a face at Katarina.

She stuck her tongue out at him. Still slightly annoyed with his last comment in the library, Katarina spouted, "I just want you to know, I *do* find peace here."

"I'm sure you do, as well as I. I just hope you can find happiness again."

"I doubt that will happen. But if it'll make you feel better, I will promise to meet our brother Hans in Paris, and we will all have a good time then."

They spoke little over dinner. Anthony had no wish to annoy his sister any further. He just knew in his heart that she could not find happiness until she turned the horrible past and her sins over to God. He believed she knew that, as well. She left the dinner table with a bottle of wine and escaped to the terrace. He went back to the library and worked well into midnight. He found her still on the terrace, the empty bottle of wine next to her as she slept in the lounge chair. He woke her gently and escorted her to her bedroom. When he suggested that she'd had too much wine, she explained to him that the wine kept her from fractured sleep, kept her from waking up in a sweat with a pounding heart. Although her family and even John had tried to help her, she refused to see a therapist. The wine was like an old friend to her, and she would not give it up.

****

She woke with a pounding headache from the sun's rude and uninvited entry, cursing at the curtains left open overnight. The shock of the cold tile on the bottom of her feet and a splash of cold water on her face got her attention. She slowly dressed into white shorts and a sleeveless blue blouse but decided to go downstairs in her bare feet.

Anthony was at the parish church and not there to lecture her. He would not have liked to see her pass up, because of a hangover, the big healthy breakfast laid out on the table. She took a cup of coffee and a croissant filled with chocolate out to the patio that faced the olive grove. From there she was entertained by Giuseppe making all sorts of animated hand gestures to his three sons. She was glad he was training his boys to take his place when the inevitable retirement would come. Her parents were right to donate a parcel of land to build a home for his oldest son in preparation for taking his father's position on the estate. Watching them now, one would have never known this close family had lost a brother who had been shot and killed by a Nazi in the village simply because he did not salute an officer. The thought of that humbled her, and she retreated to the dining room hoping to catch Anthony.

She knew she had to learn to compartmentalize her feelings better, but she was having a hard time protecting herself from dark moments. She would apologize to Anthony. He and Hans were the reason she was alive today. Still, deep inside she would never understand why she had been spared.

When Anthony joined her, across the table, Katarina sat sheepish and apologetic. "Thank you for getting me to bed last night. I hate when I fall asleep outside on the terrace."

Before he could say anything, they heard shouting. They dashed outside to see what all the commotion was about, and what they saw made them laugh out loud. All three boys were chasing the dozen goats which had broken out of the pasture and headed straight for the olive groves and vineyards. Joining the chase were two dogs, their tails wagging as if it were a game. The Saint Bernards, in their clumsy attempt to play, kept jumping up on the boys, knocking them down and keeping them from corralling the goats. Katarina and Anthony doubled over with laughter as they watched the scene unfold. It was good to laugh, a hearty laugh from deep within them.

Chapter 4

There is nothing like a belly laugh, Anthony thought, and he was thrilled to see the smile remain on Katarina's face. "Why don't you and I go into town and have dinner, give Giuseppe and Marie a break. I leave soon. Let's have a little fun. There is a small orchestra playing in the park. It's classical music."

"Oh, let's do! We could visit that sweet gelato place after dinner."

"I'm curious, Kat. Why is it, with this incredible appetite of yours, that you do not gain one ounce? It's amazing, and actually unfair, you know."

She shrugged and knew right then that she wanted to hold on to him as long as she could. She dreaded being alone, even though she told him she wanted the peace.

He saw a trace of panic in her eyes. "The Paris apartment is always open. Don't wait. Come soon. I think it might be healthier for you. There are theater and ballet performances, cafés—plenty to keep you busy. I promise no one will bring you harm there."

She knew Anthony's plan made sense, and there was less chance of the darkness and fear entering into her soul as it did when she was totally alone. If she remained in Italy, she had the memories of her childhood filled with love and laughter, but without him here, the loneliness would follow her. He gave her the strength she needed. "You might be right. When you are leaving Rome, let me know, and I will take a train to Paris."

"I'm glad to hear your decision. In the meantime, let's go down to the beach for my last time. I need a little sun and salty waves."

"I'll be right back. Let me go change into my bathing suit, and you do the same."

It was a gentle sun that greeted them when they sat down on a blanket, picnic basket nearby. As it did Anthony, the sea mesmerized Katarina, and they sat in silence, gazing upon it with their own private thoughts. He was pleased to see that many of her scars from the torture had healed and were now just faint white lines. She would always be a striking woman.

Still looking ahead, Katarina said, "Anthony, would you forgive someone who confessed a horrible past like mine?"

He thought she was seeking an answer from a priest and not her brother, so he chose to quote what was written, "Matthew 6:14 says, 'For if you forgive others when they sin against you, your heavenly Father will also forgive you. But if you do not forgive others their sins, your Father will not forgive your sins.' "

He looked at her for a long time until she turned and looked at him, "Well?"

"Kat, I forgive you because you are my sister, and I love and understand you. You are always forgiven by God if your intentions are honest. There is nothing he does not know. He knows your heart, and there is nothing he won't forgive, if you ask. Luke 17:3-4 says even if they sin against you seven times in a day and seven times come back to you saying I repent, you must forgive them. And too, Ephesians 4:31-32, 'Get rid of all bitterness, rage and anger, brawling and slander, along with every form of malice. Be kind and compassionate to one another, forgive each other, just as in Christ, God forgave you.' Katarina, God has forgiven you. Just repent. We as man have no room to judge, and neither I nor anyone else can throw that first stone."

Her voice was almost a whisper. "I do ask for mercy and understanding."

"You cannot lose faith. If you do, the enemy—the devil—will enter and corrupt and take you away from God."

"I do not plan to let evil come to me. But why did he spare me when so many in the concentration camps and prisons, and so many children, were killed? So many who could have offered so much good in the future on this earth. Look at how I have treated all my children, how I treated John. Will God forgive me for that after he let me live?"

"That is not for me to know, but I promise he hears every cry, every prayer. It's his plan and path for us. Though I must ask this: Your daughters are growing up thinking their mother never loved them. Do you, at all? So many times I saw Alexandra and Natalie reaching out to you, begging you, and you pushed them away, allowing Gertrude and others to soothe their tears and rock them to sleep. Kat, you must know those little souls needed their mother…needed you."

She thought for a long minute. "I don't think I truly loved them, not completely. When they were born I marveled at the miracle of their life, so helpless, and yes, they needed a mother, but I also needed the attention and love they craved. I just couldn't have them near me. It was too much to give. I was filled with remorse when I unleashed my anger on Natalie, but that didn't stop me. I resented Alexandra in many ways, and when she was born, my heart cried out to save her, so helpless, so innocent, but she came from the devil himself. It was better to just leave her with Father and Mother, and to leave Natalie also, till she returned to the States when John retired. They have the love of our parents and family."

They went back to silence as they walked the beach. She was relieved he did not bring up again her relationship with John—or that with Grigory, both men who loved her but, in the end, had given up on her. Life might have been different with John, if Francis had not exposed her secret. John was filled with a mixture of hate and sorrow. It had taken him two years to thaw, and now he no longer asked for the divorce, and neither did Grigory.

They left the beach close to dinnertime and changed to go out on the town. A fun evening was spent dining and listening to music, just two people enjoying life, and no more talk of the past.

That night, soaking in the tub, she thought of their conversation again. Anthony didn't understand, as much as he tried, how every man she loved turned away from her. Yes, she knew it was mostly her fault, but when Grigory left her, it shattered her soul. He had fought to save her, risking his own life, and he would disappear but always show up again. She let her body slide down until her head was completely under water. Ah, the quiet, the peace. No wonder she was always drawn to the ocean. But once she rose to the surface, she was reminded that she would always be damaged by the secrets, the fear, the worry. It was so tiring. Would the good days ever outweigh the bad? The East Berlin incident had shaken her to the core, and not knowing what became of him scared her still. It could happen again.

Meanwhile Anthony sat in his armchair with his own memories, trying to sort out what she had said. He remembered seeing the fear in little Natalie's eyes whenever Katarina approached her; she was only nine and always cowering behind her Aunt Gertrude. It was that terrible phone call from Sister Agnes at the boarding school that he remembered vividly.

Sister Agnes, the Mother Superior, insisted on seeing Anthony immediately, and it was by sheer luck that he was in Berlin. She explained to him, facing the window, that Katarina had come to visit Natalie in school, unannounced. The last time she had promised to pick up Natalie from boarding school, the child was never picked up, waiting and waiting. But on this visit Sister Philomena saw Natalie's mother strike her over and over again, until the child fell to the ground. Even then she continued pounding on her until the child couldn't breathe. Not one cry did she make, but the defiance in Natalie's eyes upset Katarina even more. The sisters confessed to Anthony that they had never seen so much hate for a child. "The brutality was out of hell itself!"

Natalie always held back her tears and would only cry to her Aunt Gertrude, which explained why Gertrude held such contempt for Katarina. There were more of these awful incidents, too many, in fact. Anthony put those aside for a moment to remember how beautiful his niece was when he first set eyes on her in 1955 at the age of three. She had light brown hair filled with curls, streaked in gold, that swirled loosely around her cherub face. An exquisite child, skin like a china doll's and eyes like her mother's only soft and hazel. Gertrude, caring for Natalie while Katarina was in Paris, had so wanted another child that she fawned over Natalie. She was frequently Natalie's caretaker.

As the years passed, the time Natalie spent with Katarina was less and less. Natalie always returned from those visits with a bruise or two, and the excuses were that she had fallen or hurt herself on the bicycle, "a clumsy child." The child said nothing and let her mother lie. Natalie did confess in the later years how she feared her mother's rage, which mostly happened when she drank.

But in the loving care of the family and the church, Natalie warmed everyone's hearts, and she grew especially fond of animals. She and her grandfather were thick as thieves, and they would spend hours in the stalls. His granddaughter had inherited his love for horses, and when he had taught her everything about riding that she needed to know and how to care for them, he bought Natalie a pony.

Another terrible memory came to Anthony's mind. Outside the stall one day, her grandfather found Natalie sobbing so violently she couldn't even speak words. She was kneeling before a little cross stuck in a mound of dirt. Gertrude was in the garden with Anthony when they heard Jona calling them. When they approached the scene, they heard Natalie crying, a rare sound, as she had always been a stoic child. When she saw Anthony, she ran to him and clung to his waist.

Anthony looked over at his father. "What happened?"

It was Natalie who answered, "She killed Luke!"

Luke was the kitten Anthony had given to Natalie, a black-and-white baby abandoned on the side of the road. Knowing her love for animals, he knew she would nurse the kitten back to health, which she did, and the two were inseparable. Over her mother's objections, the cat slept in Natalie's room and in her bed, and the nuns had allowed her to bring it to boarding school.

Anthony lifted her tearstained face up to his. "Who killed Luke?"

"My mother… She hates me so much! When I said I didn't want to go to town with her, she grabbed me by the arm, and I said I was going to tell Grandfather if she hurt me. She screamed at me. She said I was a terrible child and then…and then, she picked up Luke and threw him against the wall!"

He let her cry until the trembling subsided. "She left the room, and left me with Luke. Uncle Anthony, I held him for a long time, hoping he would come back to life, but he didn't."

Anthony saw the outrage in Gertrude's eyes. He knew she wanted to say what they couldn't. They gathered around the small grave in silence. Natalie searched their eyes for an answer before she announced, "I never want to see her again!"

Gertrude looked over at Anthony. "I'm calling the States. I'm asking her father to give us temporary custody, until he can come for her. Enough is enough!" Alexandra and Hans were standing at the end of the stalls, listening. The truth was out for all to hear. Alexandra took the anguished Natalie into her arms and told them she would take her home with Helena and keep her safe until everything settled.

Later that night, Anthony waited for his sister to return. He was seething and could not quiet his rage. When she finally arrived, bitter words were exchanged, and Anthony, not able to make her see sense or reason, shook his sister until her teeth rattled, and shoved her to the ground. Even then he couldn't shake the devil out of her, and it pained him to know his own sibling could be so abusive to her children. Hans heard the commotion and came between them. Katarina packed her bags and left for two weeks without one word of where she had gone.

At the time, Alexandra was entering the university, at sixteen, having excelled beyond the high school curriculum. She was a beauty like her mother and could pass for Katarina's twin at that age. She had been raised in the loving care of her aunts, uncles, and grandparents. Hans was particularly close to her. Over the years, Alexandra had stayed silent and turned the other cheek. But Natalie would never forgive her mother.

Anthony retired to bed with a heavy heart, knowing that tomorrow he would be leaving his tormented sister behind.

It was a tearful goodbye the next morning. He said a silent prayer as he walked away, asking for Katarina's protection.

Chapter 5

She was lonely. He was gone. Everyone was gone, and the house was silent. Anthony was right, she should go back to Paris.

How did it all go so wrong? Katarina closed her eyes.

She had thought she wanted to open a ballet school right in the village. Even as she went to sign the papers with Anthony, she realized she couldn't teach something she loved knowing she herself would never dance again. The failure of wanting something yet not following through, her fears always crippling her, of being in one place, where she couldn't leave, couldn't run. What if *he* returned? There would be no Grigory there to help her this time. Giuseppe and his boys would defend her to their own death, but why chance it? If Grigory could find her in Corfu, couldn't *he*? Would she ever be free from this ghost and all the dead ones before him?

Anthony was right.

****

She fell asleep nightly with a bottle of wine after spending the days walking aimlessly through the village. Often, she sat in a trance, observing the bees crawling in and out of the flowers, their short lives so busy, productive, not wasting time as she did. But Anthony would be on his way to Paris soon, and she would meet him there.

A letter from the United States had been forwarded by her parents. John had written. A simple note, perfectly written as if carefully thought out, asking how she was doing, no longer mentioning the divorce but clearly reminding her that he wanted Natalie to live with him as soon as he retired. He had stopped asking her to come back.

She held the letter up to the sunlight as if she could find some meaningful words hidden between the lines. So much had happened, never discussed and never forgotten.

Chapter 6

Hawaii, 1952

She was sitting alone, holding her stomach and wondering how she could have gotten pregnant so quickly after their first child was born. Katarina counted the months in her head—only a fourteen-month difference in their age. It would be like a landslide tumbling down if John knew she had hidden the first pregnancy from him and given up their child for adoption. She expelled a breath, exasperated. She needed to get off the island. Her deceit and lies could catch up with her here.

She needed to be free, free of Francis, away from Hawaii, where he could easily expose her. It was his fault everything had gone wrong. John's baby had been a bargaining chip to him. Put the baby up for adoption, Francis demanded, and he would give her a divorce at the same time. No one but them would know the truth. She signed the documents and never looked back, leaving Douglas, the child she had with Francis, to be raised by him and his lover, Maria. She had let go of two of her children in one year. Wasn't that enough torment for one human being? Not for Francis; he continued to torment her. He had his way of putting fear into her heart, and as long as she remained on the island, she could never find peace.

John came into the room with a box of baby clothing. "Why is Francis sending us newborn baby boy clothing, and how would he know you're pregnant or what you are having?"

Katarina's heart nearly stopped beating as she looked at the box in his hands. *Good God, what is Francis up to now?*

"I don't know, John, maybe these are items left over from Douglas, and he thinks we might want them." What John didn't see behind the innocent look was the fear racing through Katarina like a storm.

There was a note in the box. John read it aloud, "Maria and I saw you and John in our favorite restaurant and thought you might like the baby clothing you left behind, seeing that you are pregnant."

Katarina turned away and pretended to be stacking some books.

"Hmm." John looked puzzled. "You had Douglas in Germany, didn't you?"

Frustrated with the stupid question, she answered, "Yes, John, you knew that."

"I'm sorry, Kat, it was silly of me to question that idiot's intentions. Sour grapes on his part."

He gave her a comforting hug and softly patted her stomach. "But you know, I wouldn't mind one bit if we had a boy."

She couldn't look in his eyes, nor could she stop her body from trembling inside.

"Are you sure you will be all right here, all alone? I should be back in three days, unless the admiral makes a detour. I really think next week it would be a good idea for you to stay with Lydia and her family in the cottage up in Santa Rosa."

She had rebuffed the idea early on when he suggested it, but living on the North Shore, at seven months pregnant and with Francis lurking in the background, she quickly changed her mind. "John, I think you are right. When you get back, why don't we make the arrangements. Since the child is going to be Lydia's godchild, she might like to see the baby when it's born."

She started removing the clothing from the box, as if it were a nice gift given by anyone but Francis. She tried pushing aside the uneasy feeling until she spotted a second note tucked inside a tiny gown. Tossing the clothes quickly back into the box, she held it to her chest just as John pecked her forehead with a small kiss on his way out the door. When she was certain he was out of sight, she read the note:

Should you be slightly curious, you were under the impression you gave birth to a daughter, but in fact it was a boy. You were so sick with fever and only held the child for a few hours, it was understandable that you might have missed it on the adoption papers you signed. Now you know. It clearly stated a baby boy.

Her hands were shaking when she folded the note and hid it in her purse. She was sick with confusion and worry. A boy? John's boy. If John had seen this message, what would have happened? She was horrified. Why would this man not leave her alone? Tension gathered at the base of her neck, and she felt a wave of nausea. She sat down and held her face in her hands. She had found contentment with John, who was so easygoing. There was rarely any drama in their lives. She was in love, in a good place for the first time in years. Francis could ruin it all by telling John everything, and if John had seen the note, Francis would have already accomplished it. Her life with John would be over.

John had been so excited about the pregnancy—their firstborn. "He can't know. He just can't know," she cried. The voices in her head were like muffled screams, suffocating. Francis still had control over her.

She shook the thoughts from her head. "Yes, I'll go to California!" she said out loud and jumped when at the same time she heard a knock at the door.

Lydia floated in, as she always did when on a mission. "My God, woman, what is wrong with you? You look so sick. Is it the baby?"

"Just another round of nausea. I'll be fine. What brings you here?" Katarina sat up straight, relieved to see John's dear friend, the dynamic Lydia, so strong, so wealthy, with her determined eyes and always smelling of gardenias.

"I came as soon as John called me at the hotel about you coming back with me. You are *not* staying here, and I won't let you change your mind. I will arrange for our plane to come back early, and we're getting out of here today!"

There was no arguing with Lydia. The only child of wealthy Texas oil tycoons, she had married a man who later made rear admiral and retired to California. John had dated Lydia before introducing her to her current husband, with whom she'd produced four boys. They had remained close friends ever since. She had stood by Katarina's side through her divorce from Francis, never understanding fully why Katarina went back to the island and stayed for nearly six months during that dreadful time. She never asked, but assumed much of it was to be near her son, Douglas. It remained a thorn in her side that Katarina had refused Lydia's offer to sign on some hotshot attorneys to fight for custody and then allowed Francis to take him. With all the energy she put into Katarina, John was her primary focus, and if it were not for him, she would never have befriended his wife.

When they first met, John told Katarina that he had adopted his own nephew, Philip. Lydia thought since Katarina had lost her son to Francis, perhaps this child could fill the void. Philip was a lovely nine-year-old, and John adored him. The boy had been born of a teenage pregnancy, the mother dying at childbirth and the father—John's brother—only sixteen and certainly not ready to raise a child. John, with everyone's blessings, wanted to give Philip stability and officially became his adopted father. The grandparents, living on the East Coast, helped him raise the boy.

A handsome, blue-eyed blond, Philip was more mature than other boys his age, capable of adult conversation and able to keep up with them. John's love was all he knew, but Lydia took notice that stepmothering would not come easy for Katarina. She observed their first meeting when Lydia picked up Philip in California in her private aircraft and brought him to Hawaii. Katarina was distant and treated the child as if he were a stranger off the street, making no attempt to hug him or greet him with enthusiasm, and later, no effort to get to know him except when John was present. Philip would be able to rely on only John's love, nothing more.

"Kat, you look worried. Trust me, you'll love California, and we will pamper you to death till the baby comes. After all, it is my first godchild."

"Lydia, I'm not worried, just lacking in energy. But John is right. I don't think it's wise to be here alone."

Katarina enjoyed being around Lydia, who was always upbeat, her first real female friend since Anna died in the bombings. Her life had consisted of only her brothers and parents after the war, and then, for a brief time, Francis.

Lydia went into the bedroom and emerged with suitcases. "We will pack, and then you and I are going to lunch. Tonight, we'll be on our way to beautiful Santa Rosa."

Lydia drove the Cadillac with the top down, singing along with the radio, the breeze lifting Katarina's spirits. She wore a scarf over her hair, which she had let grow to the middle of her back, but the wispy bangs blew wildly in the wind. Even now, her natural beauty rarely went unnoticed.

Lydia knew Katarina was not eating well, and that she'd had a difficult delivery with Douglas. She wanted to assure her that this time all would be easy, different from the swelling she experienced on the hot Hawaiian island. The sweet California mountain air would do her good. They stopped at a country club for members only. Katarina was uncomfortable in public in her simple sleeveless dark blue smock and seersucker stretch pants. To add to that, her feet were aching, and she wished she could walk barefoot. She couldn't wait to sit down and kick off her shoes.

Lydia said hello to several people on her way to the table. Katarina thought the woman should run for mayor, with all the people she knew. When seated, Lydia observed Katarina studying the menu. She thought the poor woman rarely showed any sign of happiness unless she was at John's side. She knew enough of her past to know of her sorrows, but as a mother of four children herself, Lydia could never contemplate leaving even one of them. Having no idea what it was like to walk in Katarina's shoes, it still was hard not to judge her. But, as long as she made John happy…

"Kat, I had one of my crew go to the house and pick up your luggage. They gave me a message at the front door that the plane is ready whenever we are. Don't worry, your house is closed up, and after lunch we are leaving. No time to think about anything."

Katarina looked so surprised, it made Lydia laugh. "Dear woman, when I make up my mind, it will be done."

For the first time, Katarina gave her a genuine smile. "Lydia I'm so relieved and happy. We need to tell John."

"I sent him a message. He will make the arrangements with the Naval Hospital for the birth. Since the baby is due in September, that also leaves a good month before school starts, so there will be a good time with Philip. John will be so excited." Lydia caught a sudden flash of something unkind in Katarina's eyes. "What's the matter, Kat?"

"I just thought John and I would spend our time alone, and Philip could stay with his grandparents this summer. This firstborn child is important to him."

Lydia was taken aback by the statement. "Philip is his son just as much as any biological child would be. You won't be able to do much that last month, so just enjoy the time of pure relaxation. Philip spends a lot of time with my boys anyway, so he won't be around *all* the time."

Katarina didn't want to anger Lydia. "I'm sorry, it came out wrong."

Determined not to fall into an argument, Lydia said curtly, "It's fine. Let's just order. I'm starving." This was a side of Katarina she did not like, and she'd seen it before—the unnecessary arguments when Philip was coming for Christmas and Spring Break. Lydia had always bitten her tongue, but this statement had to be addressed. It was bad enough the little boy was in a military school at Valley Forge in Pennsylvania. She could never send her boys away, although in this case it was Philip's decision to say no to living with John and Kat full time. He felt unwanted and even told his father so. John refused to accept the excuse but still allowed him to remain on the East Coast.

Katarina felt justified. Why would she want John to bring Philip, since her own son was being kept from her and raised in Kauai? Sensing Lydia's anger, she mustered up another apology. She did not want to make an enemy out of this powerful woman, even if she had to lie.

"Lydia, it's just my hormones. I'm being completely selfish, it's not like I can go fishing or hiking with them, so why don't we make a pact and go shopping. I will need new clothing after the baby is born, and then next we can go and buy baby clothes."

Lydia smiled. "Yes, we will leave the men to their own devices, and you and I will go out on the town."

Katarina went in for the kill. "I just ache for my own son when I see Philip. It's my fault. I'm sorry I didn't..." Lydia, not listening, was staring at the entrance with a hardness in her eyes.

"Kat, don't turn around. Francis just walked in the door with another couple. Damn, I forgot he's a member here, too."

Katarina's insides were shaking when Lydia, her eyes widening, reached across the table for her hand. She knew he had seen them.

He had the couple seated, excused himself, and boldly walked over to their table. "Hello, Lydia, Katarina. You both are looking well." Francis placed his hand on Katarina's shoulder. She flinched.

"I should bring my guests over. They adopted a little baby not too long ago. Perhaps you can give them a little advice on the matter." He spoke with pure bitterness.

Katarina moved his hand from her shoulder.

That did not stop him from speaking further. "They were very fortunate to have found a white baby. Imagine that, on this island. No doubt it was from one of our military boys impregnating some poor brainless island girl." Francis kept his eyes on Katarina, pounding the words in like nails. He saw the fear in her eyes, and he enjoyed making her miserable.

"Oh, Lydia, how are your boys? Healthy, I hope?" he said, his tone changing, but with the spiteful look still in his eyes. Turning back to Katarina, he leaned close to her face. "I do hope the baby clothing arrived. I'm sure it will be of good use." Stepping back, he looked over at his dinner guests, who were watching the whole scene. He swept his finger across Katarina's cheek. Just that slight momentary touch revolted her.

"Francis," Lydia said, having heard enough, "please leave us. Your table is waiting, and this conversation has come to an end."

"Well, perhaps you're right. I must get back to the Kaufmanns—a business deal awaits. Good day, ladies. I hope the baby brings you a great deal of happiness. Yours and John's firstborn—how excited he must be. I know how I felt when Douglas was born. I guess you're not interested enough to ask how he is doing without his mother. Not to worry. Maria is taking good care of him." With that final nail in the coffin, he turned and walked away.

Heads turned as he passed tables, women always taking notice of him. Even Lydia had to admit he was an incredibly good-looking man, broad-shouldered, an equal blend of Hawaiian and French ancestry. His speckled gray hair made him even more stunning, although his eyes seemed cruel. But that wasn't the reason she remained civil toward Francis—they had done several business deals together in the past, and Lydia suspected they would be across the table from one another again in the future. She would keep that to herself.

Katarina felt the room spinning in circles, her face ashen. Relieved that he didn't expose her—and he could have easily done so—she couldn't shake the guilt for how she'd treated him and left him for John. Maybe she could have had a happy marriage, but her demons kept her from loving him unconditionally. She looked at this handsome man, now smiling, pretending to be happy without her, a man at one time she did love in her own way. He had been her salvation. She had trapped him with pregnancy to take her from the rubble of Berlin. They both were at fault, and maybe they could have been happy if only he hadn't tried to control her, keeping her a prisoner in all his wealth, and even keeping her from her brother,.

Lydia left to find the waiter to have her car brought to the entrance. She knew, with the look on Katarina's face, that lunch would be impossible.

Francis caught Katarina's eye from across the room, and beheld the face he dreamt of every night, the woman he could not stop loving, and the woman who was responsible for his gaping wound. Like always, after he'd twisted the knife in her, he asked himself why. He couldn't make her love him again, but he could destroy her happiness in one fell swoop if he chose.

She rose to leave, but she couldn't stop herself from looking back at the couple sitting with him, wondering if they were the ones who adopted her baby. They held each other's gaze.

Katarina remained quiet on the way to the airport.

"I'm sorry, Kat. I never thought he would show up there." What power he has over her, Lydia thought, seeing the lost, forlorn look etched on Katarina's pale face. "I find it strange he would be celebrating someone's adoption. Seems odd, don't you think?"

"Lydia, let's just forget the encounter. All I know right now is that I'm looking forward to getting off this island."

"Look, I've offered this before. I have lawyers who can fight just as dirty as his. We can still go for custody, Kat. I will match him dollar for dollar."

"I don't have it in me to do battle with him. Maybe in time he will come around and change his mind." She could still see Francis sitting next to her, his head on the bed while she dealt with a difficult pregnancy, tears rolling down his face, hoping she would not go through with the divorce. Her freedom meant more to her than he did, or their child. She had no hope of any reconciliation.

What Lydia didn't know was that Francis and Maria had planned to tell Douglas that Katarina had died in a car crash. The boy was so young they counted on him forgetting who she was and would remove all evidence that she ever existed.

Francis had wanted her and the baby, unlike her first husband, who ordered her shot while eight months pregnant. It was a miracle she had been spared. It was pure luck that the man had removed himself from all responsibility, changing the papers to a concentration camp instead. Nobody would ever know that her first child was born from evil.

Chapter 7

California

After landing in San Francisco, they drove an hour to Santa Rosa. Acres of trees lined the lane to the house, pastures on one side with horses and cattle, the house enormous as they pulled up the winding drive—twelve rooms, six of them bathrooms, plus two guest cabins each the same size as her house in Hawaii, all within distance of a peaceful, flowing river. The main house was full of activity—maids, cooks, hired help just for retrieving their luggage—and most beautiful of all, in the near distance, the stables and the vineyards.

The interior had been designed with two large living areas, the centerpiece of one being a gorgeous Steinway piano. Three sets of French doors each led to a separate patio. Plush oriental rugs in exotic patterns covered the floors. Tromping over them with wet boots came four boys toting fishing gear, with George, Lydia's husband, leading the way. None seemed to care about the furnishings as they dropped everything and ran past their father, racing him to their mother's arms. Philip followed slowly behind.

"Kat, we thought we would surprise you and John and have Philip here earlier," George proudly announced.

Katarina could barely hold her disappointment

when Philip reluctantly came over to her and shook her hand.

"Good Lord, child, give her a hug," Lydia encouraged. Katarina bent down and offered her cheek and received a kiss that barely touched her skin. No love there, Lydia thought. This child's heart was as pure and loving as John's. She hoped someday Katarina would start to feel something for the boy with such a gentle smile and easygoing laugh. But not today.

Lydia's oldest boy, who was twelve, felt the tension and immediately came to Philip's side. "Come on, Philip, let's get the fish ready to cook, and then we can see what the horses are up to." This would not be the last time he would encounter this cold woman in their home, and he immediately disliked her.

Lydia showed Katarina to her room; the maid was already unpacking her luggage and placing items in the closet, and iced tea and chocolate cookies waited for her on the table. She flung her tired body onto the bed and felt the baby kick unusually hard; sitting right under her rib cage, the child made it difficult to catch her breath. Calming the baby with a soothing rub, she realized that she wanted this baby more than the others. Her thoughts went back to Alexandra, reaching hungrily for her mother's milk, and when there wasn't enough, how the other women in the concentration camp would let the baby latch on to their own breasts, helping to keep her alive. She swore to herself this baby would never go hungry.

She spent the week taking long walks in the woods, and sometimes Lydia would join her. The raucous boys had the house in constant turmoil, and dinner was like a free-for-all with long stories of the day, each one trying to outdo the other. Lydia was in her glory surrounded by her children, and she was careful to keep Philip in the conversation and involved in all the boys' activities. Katarina never invited him to walk with her until one day, in front of all the others, she asked him to join her. His eyes lit up when she asked.

It turned out to be a pleasant walk. Philip easily shared, and talk of his school was the main topic. Then, with clear eyes, he told Katarina how much he looked forward to meeting the new family member, and at that point, the conversation came to a halt, and the walk was shortened, Katarina suddenly needing to rest.

Finally, John arrived late one evening while Katarina slept. He woke her from her sleep with a sweet whisper. Crawling into bed next to her, he placed his hand on her belly and took in the smell of her skin. He smoothed out her hair and gently kissed her cheek. Katarina tried to turn over, with little success, and they both laughed and fell into a deep, comforting sleep.

He was already downstairs having a hearty breakfast with Lydia and George when she woke. She dressed quickly, eager to see him in the light in his striped blue short-sleeved shirt and black shorts. He ran to her when he saw her watching him from the doorway and led her to a seat at the table. His eyes shone when he looked at her; no one could miss the love in them. A patient man, he made her feel complete. After breakfast, they sat on the porch and caught up on everything.

****

In the middle of the night, her water broke. It was the last day in August, and by the first day in September Katarina and John's baby was born. She came into the world with a small cry and a head full of dark blonde curls, her eyes dark as coal. The labor had been easy, and by the time the sun rose, John and Philip were charging into the room with flowers and a teddy bear larger than the baby. Mesmerized, John couldn't take his eyes off the infant, while Philip stood by simply in awe. Later Lydia came by with the children, everyone oohing and ahhing, taking turns holding the newborn. Philip held her the longest. Watching him, Katarina thought of Anthony and how he had shared with her that he was sixteen when she was born, and he would hold her for hours and just look at her.

She was not the only one watching Philip's attachment to the baby. Lydia and John were whispering together, smiling and nodding their heads toward Philip, obviously pleased to see the smile spread across his face as the baby held tightly to his finger. The nurse entered the room and attempted to take the baby from his arms. He reluctantly let go. Handing the baby over to her mother, she encouraged her to try breastfeeding, but Katarina did not want to show the scars around her nipples where they had burnt her in the concentration camp. Nursing with that memory would be unbearable. Katarina asked for privacy, and everyone respectfully left the room. She explained to the nurse that this baby would be bottle fed and there was no room for argument.

They named her Natalie. John loved the actress Natalie Wood, and he thought the baby reminded him of her. Katarina could see no resemblance to herself in the child—the baby was all John. John laughed at that statement; she had time to look like her mother. And she would.

After four days in the hospital, they made their way back to Lydia's. Philip gave up the guest room, which was set up as a nursery so the parents could have their privacy. He was fine being with the boys and sleeping in their rooms.

John had leave for four days. Katarina, as always, tried to convince him to retire so they could be together all the time as a regular family. He let it go in one ear and out the other, dedicated to his job. But when he was home, his dedication to his family was just as strong. Katarina seldom got up during the night because the minute the baby cried, he was in her room rocking her to sleep. She had plenty of time alone with John, as Lydia and the boys took the baby on long walks and picnics where they would spend all their time holding and kissing her. Philip gave her the most attention—their eyes locked, as if they already had an understanding.

John always waited until Natalie slept before dashing off to fish or ride the horses with Philip. He was careful to balance his time with everyone, but always made sure his wife and baby were first. It seemed a blessed chapter in their lives, but soon Katarina began showing her resentment for the time everyone spent with Natalie, as if she herself did not exist.

Chapter 8

Four months went by quickly. Philip had gone back to school and returned again for Christmas break. He was becoming spoiled by Lydia's insistence that he fly home on her private plane so he could have the time with his family that he would otherwise have spent on the train. Christmas at Lydia's was hectic—so many presents to buy and wrap, and neighbors continuously stopping by for good cheer. Lydia with her infectious laugh adored people around her; the more the merrier was her style. And they, too, enjoyed her sparkling and generous personality, but everyone knew better than to take her on in the boardroom or in a business deal, for that was when her hidden claws came out. She was a shrewd businesswoman, and her husband basked in her shadow.

In the spring she took Katarina to San Francisco for shopping. "Time for new clothing, my dear, and definitely time to throw away those unflattering maternity dresses!" Reserving the finest hotel, they stayed overnight in luxury. Katarina was thrilled to get away. Lydia made sure the baby was in the capable hands of a highly recommended nanny, one she had hired earlier when she'd told John in strict confidence that it was not time for Katarina to be all alone with the child on the North Shore. He trusted his dear friend's instincts completely. Katarina had no problem accepting the gift when she and the baby returned to live in Hawaii after Christmas.

During these early stages of their life as a family, Katarina felt John's need for her, coming to her aroused, eager to pursue their delicious lovemaking. Life was bliss for the first time, and she even felt she would be okay with Philip for the summer. He adored Natalie, who at seven months was quite the handful, and having him there would give her the breaks she needed. The child was taking on a very strong personality, the priest had observed during her christening; he could see her will to fight back tears even then. Her little hands reached out often for Lydia, and of course Lydia was touched, having so wanted a baby girl but sensibly giving up after the fourth boy. With her amber eyes, speckled with green, and that marvelous head of unruly hair they were constantly trying to tame, Natalie was a bundle of joy.

Yet with everything seeming to be right, the discomfort of living so near Francis weighed on Katarina's mind, and along with that she was beginning to distance herself from Natalie. She pleaded with John over and over to put in a transfer to California. He assured her he was trying.

Lydia was in and out of Hawaii with her business and had flown in for a meeting to check on the low production of her sugar crop. While there visiting Katarina and John, she noticed changes in Katarina toward Natalie, and that she left the child with the nanny more than necessary. Lydia's affection and love for this child grew with every visit, and she had a growing concern for Katarina's moods. She would convince her to let her take Natalie to California on occasion.

Lydia kept from Katarina that she had met Francis at her business meeting. He had told her to look out for the little girl because Katarina was not capable of loving her children. Lydia had not objected to his comment, nor had she replied, which confirmed she had already witnessed this flaw in the mother. She stayed on the North Shore and found a new house for John and Katarina, closer to Diamond Head, still on the beach but larger and more convenient for the nanny. As usual, she arranged the packing and the move.

Katarina devoured the letters from her brothers and parents. They loved the pictures of Natalie she had sent and were looking forward to a visit. It was shortly after they got settled in the new place and Lydia had returned to California that she decided to venture out to Waikiki Beach with the nanny and Natalie and a picnic basket all piled into the car.

Natalie was crawling everywhere, and the blanket they had spread out on the sand could not contain the determined child. The nanny had her hands full and finally decided, after collecting her every time she headed toward the water, to take her to the water's edge and play. Katarina was too busy re-reading her letters to notice she was gone. Engrossed in the words from her family that made her feel as though she were home, she was startled by the warm breath next to her ear.

"Katarina, I'm so surprised to see you here. This is not your usual place," his voice spoke softly.

She looked around for the nanny, who was nowhere to be seen, and pulled her knees to her chest. "How is it that you are here at the same time, Francis?" she asked, eyeing him warily in his white shorts and

Hawaiian shirt.

He sat down beside her, too close for comfort. “I always know where you are, and a little birdie told me you might be here, not far from my office, it seems.”

He looked into those exquisite eyes, a slight tan forming around the spaghetti straps of her dress, her face flushed with color, when the last time he’d seen her she had looked quite the opposite. He ran his fingers down her arm, and when she started to get up, he pulled her back down and held her with a firm grip.

“What do you want from me?” she asked in a hoarse whisper.

“I just want you to realize you will never be out of my sight. You will never get away, regardless of where you go.” His face was now next to her face; his lips could have touched hers. He smelled her hair. She froze. Slowly he released her arm and lightly touched the back of her neck, slightly pulling her head back with her hair. “You are still the most beautiful woman I have ever had.”

“If you don’t let go of me, I will scream for help,” she declared.

“I wouldn’t do that. I will scream your secret to your precious husband, the naïve John, who knows nothing about you.” His hand slowly moved up and down her leg, pushing the dress up to her thigh. “I saw your daughter a few minutes ago. She is quite lovely. How long will it be before you desert her, I wonder?”

He left his hand on her bare thigh and moved the other along her arm until it skimmed the side of her breast. He brought his lips to her neck and then suddenly let go.

Her heart felt as if it would jump out of her chest as

he abruptly stood and brushed the sand from his legs.

She stood with him, stretching up on her toes to meet his height. “You’re a vile, pugnacious ass!” she said, as her hand moved to strike him. He caught it in midair.

“Surely you must think of me sometimes,” he scoffed.

She pulled from his grip. “I never think of you.” Her voice was surprisingly steady and her intense stare unwavering as he pulled her suddenly in and kissed her hard on the mouth.

“John will never be enough for you,” he said, turning to walk away.

He stood on the street and watched her. He never would get over how she had shattered him. He hated her equally as much as he loved her. Maria was no substitute, but she was consistent, and she cared for his son, now his main purpose in life. The child would grow up nothing like his mother.

****

She sat there for a long time, just looking out at the waves rolling in, and suddenly remembered what Francis had said about a little birdie telling him where to find her. She heard Natalie’s laughter and turned to see her coming toward her with ice cream all over her face. She felt no desire to greet the happy child and insisted that they go home for the day. How long must she live with her secret? A move to California could not come fast enough.

Chapter 9

Chesapeake, 1955

"Please, John, don't be sad. I won't be gone that long. I must visit my family. I miss them. I promise we won't stay long. Berlin is in a much better position now. My family moved back to the old estate while they decide what to do with the land and the home in Munich."

"Why not wait till Natalie is older? She's only a toddler, not even quite three. The travel will be too much for her."

"John, she will sleep most of the time. Please, I really need to see my daughter Alexandra."

"Really? If you recall, I wanted to adopt her, and you were steadfast against it. You didn't even want to go there to visit until now."

She stammered and thought about her next words. Her family was on the verge of adopting Alexandra. She had been living with her grandmother all these years, and Alexandra had made it clear that she never wanted to come to America. "Berlin is all she knows," is all Katarina could muster up. After that, she surrendered and let the subject die until later.

It took a week to convince John, but a stipulation came with the agreement. Now that he was on standby duty, she would go with him first to meet his parents, and they would spend a month with Philip on the East Coast. His parents' home was on the Chesapeake, on the eastern shore, in a little town called Oxford, overlooking the bay. John grew up in an idyllic childhood setting on the beautiful bay, his father a country lawyer, his mother a fifth-grade school teacher. There was nothing his father did not teach him, from fishing to sailing. His sisters were already in high school or entering college when he and his brother were born.

Philip, it was always Philip, Katarina silently protested. He and John would go frolicking off to Hawaii to fish off the beach, or taking long, adventurous hikes. If Philip wasn't with John, he was underfoot chasing after Natalie. Philip was robbing her once again of her own time. She cried to John about his lack of time with her and how unfair he was being. His usual response was, "We have been through this before."

And indeed, they had, as John's determination to protect Philip had increased when he overheard Katarina telling Philip that he was a biological relative, not a firstborn like Natalie, and that is why his father loved Natalie so much more. Philip was so deeply struck by the painful remark he cried openly and apologized profusely as if it were his fault. He begged her not to take Natalie from him.

The incident broke John's heart and he and Katarina had a serious argument. In a rage, he reminded Katarina that she had been raised by her aunt when her own biological mother had given her up to the family because she had not wanted children. The comparison to Philip upset her deeply, and she apologized through tears. When she cried, he always gave in, and would find himself giving in more as the arguments began to happen more frequently.

During his free time, waiting to be called back to work, he spent the bulk of it with Philip and Natalie. Soon came the time to travel to his parents' home. The flight had them stopping first in California, where they met Lydia, who offered to fly them to the East Coast. To Katarina's disappointment, John declined the offer, due to all her previous help. He felt she had done enough for his family.

It was late when they finally arrived. John's father met them at the airport, and his mother arrived in a second car because of the amount of luggage and the number of people they needed to accommodate. Philip and Natalie rode to the house with their grandmother, while John climbed into the front seat of his father's vehicle, seating Katarina in the back, where luggage took up one side. Frustrated, Katarina huffed in silence, forced to listen to father and son talk about sailboats and crabbing until, so tired from it all, she fell asleep.

In the other car, following close behind, Natalie had fallen asleep in the back seat while the grandmother made quiet conversation with Philip. She looked back several times, smiling at her grandson holding the little girl's head on his lap, her little thumb stuck in her mouth, the soft curls swirling all around her face. It was a beautiful scene, and the grandmother took note to share it with her husband later that evening.

John looked back at his sleeping wife, softly snoring, her head awkwardly leaning against a piece of luggage. He was grateful she was not talking in her sleep as she often did. So many times she'd wake up screaming, drenched in sweat from the recurring nightmares that had started up again. When he'd ask her to talk about them, she refused. He suggested a therapist, which she also adamantly refused. Her moods shifted with each day. Charming and cordial with the other military wives and husbands, she came off as a balanced and happy person. Yet without any warning, she'd go off the deep end and slip into a depression that not even he could pull her from. As he looked at her now, so peaceful in the dark of the car, he was sure the new climate and views would help get her and even him back on track.

He shook her gently awake to see the sun just setting over the bay beyond the beautiful white house trimmed in green, surrounded by a lush lawn, a long driveway carving its way to the garage, where they unloaded their bags.

They entered the home and walked down a broad hallway that led to a friendly living room with wall-to-wall windows and French doors opening to a sunroom. The bedrooms were all upstairs, and Katarina, anxious to find hers, was about to ask John where it was when the grandfather clock in the hallway chimed, and as if on cue, a tall, lean woman came dashing out of the kitchen, and behind her a robust woman wearing an apron.

The woman with the stark facial features shrieked when she saw John, "Oh, brother, you are here!" This was Elizabeth, who ran to him with hugs, and when she saw Natalie in Philip's arms, she said with a broad smile, "Oh, how precious is this little girl, and this must be Katarina." She reached out for her hand.

The sister looked nothing like John, Katarina

thought when they shook hands. In fact, she looked more like a man, with her hair pulled back in a bun so tight she could see the tiny hairs breaking at the temples. The red lipstick had been drawn on beyond her thin lip line, making her mouth appear larger, and the shorts, bare feet, and short blouse tied at her midriff convinced Katarina that John's world was quite different from what she had thought.

Before they could unload their luggage, Elizabeth made everyone sit, including her parents. "Dinner is almost ready. We have crab cakes, coleslaw, hush puppies, sweet tea, and pineapple upside-down cake!" Philip's mouth watered, and John raised his eyebrows with delight. "Cook and I have been slaving away at this meal, and oh, yes, we added a soup."

Outside they heard barking. "John, go let that wretched dog of yours in," Elizabeth ordered. John went out to the sunroom and opened the door to a very large German Shepherd that stood on hind legs to put front paws on John's shoulders. Greeting him feverishly, tongue all over his face, the dog stopped suddenly, sniffed the air, and ran straight to Philip, nearly knocking him down while licking Natalie's feet, to her delight.

Elizabeth clapped her hands loudly for all to hear. "Let's all get the luggage upstairs, so everyone can freshen up and come down to dinner."

John turned to his father. "She's in drill sergeant mode again, Dad."

"I heard that, John." His sister laughed behind the playful scowl.

His father, Frank, and his mother, Bernice, helped with the luggage, but Philip, having had to listen to his stomach grumble long enough, disappeared into the kitchen. He didn't know until later that they had set up a makeshift crib for Natalie in his room because they'd heard the boy talking nonstop about the child.

Katarina realized how hungry she was and slipped out of her slacks into shorts that accentuated her tanned legs. John teasingly called her long, slender legs with their defined calves race horse legs. Dancer's legs, Katarina thought every time he said it. She slipped on a T-shirt with one simple word, "Navy," on the front. No makeup, a tinge of pink lipstick, and she'd fit right in at the table with John's sister.

John sat on the double bed, which was draped in a chenille bedspread and too many pillows to mention. He looked around the room painted a soft yellow, its windows rolled out, opened prior to their arrival to remove the stuffiness from its lack of use. She saw him smiling while looking across the room at a wall of shelves, as he said, "My room was never painted this color. It used to be a simple white, but look, they kept my football trophies from high school."

Downstairs was alive with conversation and laughter. When they entered the sunroom, they found Philip and his grandfather having an active talk. This was not the child who was mostly quiet and stood in the distance observing. It was clear that he knew he was loved here. Natalie, too, had completely surrendered to her grandfather's arms, rubbing her eyes, fighting the urge to sleep. They had prepared a special meal for her ahead of time—eggs, toast, applesauce, and strained peas—just in case the toddler's taste buds weren't quite developed yet for the main course.

The conversation at the table was mostly about the

Chesapeake and how much they loved it. Activities were planned—a barbeque with the neighbors and every day something new to do while they were there. Katarina's head was swimming with so much information, and she was too tired to absorb it all. Philip naturally finished eating first, and he excused himself and told them he would take Natalie up for a bath and put her to sleep.

Elizabeth shook her head. "That boy just loves his little sister."

Katarina bit her tongue. It wasn't *his* little sister, she wanted to yell out.

****

The next morning, after a much-needed sleep and a brief moment of intimacy, John and Kat walked out on the porch to view the sailboats moving across the bay underneath a solid blue sky. An unexpected surprise started the day off in the wrong direction. Company had been invited to breakfast. John's childhood friends Marybeth and Erick Cassidy, siblings from a family of nine, were seated at the table. Kat learned within minutes of meeting them in casual conversation that Marybeth had been more than a friend, and in John's senior year of college, they had been engaged. Marybeth's eyes never left Katarina's when she recounted those spirited years in every detail. She expressed her love for children, watching Natalie eating eggs with her fingers, and moved on to sharing stories about her kindergarten students.

Katarina sat in a silent irritation, eating her breakfast slowly and listening to the woman ramble on. She noticed that John was uncomfortable with the conversation. He sighed with relief when they left.

It was when they walked to the water he turned to her, "Listen, Kat, she was out of place talking like that about our past. Yes, we were engaged. I went to the Pacific, my best friend went to war in Europe, and when he came back wounded, she married him, end of story. He and I have never spoken since. And I don't even like talking to her, but she has tried to be friends, and as you saw, I'm cordial."

They sat down on the large rocks, their feet in the water. "I'm fine with it," Kat said, casually. "If you wanted her, you would have married her."

This was not the answer he expected. Relieved, he gave her a long kiss. "I found the person I wanted to marry."

"She was your first love?"

"Yes, she was. Did you have a first love?"

"I did. It was the person who turned me in and had me put in prison and wanted me shot. That was my first love." She managed to get her sting in after all.

"I'm sorry. I didn't mean to bring up bad memories." He gave her his hand and helped her off the rocks.

The next morning, John collected Katarina with exciting news. "We are off. I'm going to show you the beauty of sailing today. My sister and mother will have Natalie all day. The boat is in our slip and ready to go, and we have a basket full of food." Katarina finally had her husband all to herself.

The week was filled with sailing and fishing, and they drove over to the Naval Academy, as well. John filled her with stories of his childhood. They topped it off with a night spent on the sailboat anchored in the Choptank River, watching the moon rise and the stars popping out like fireflies. They made love as if they were just starting their life together.

One morning, Katarina walked in on John and Philip in the sunroom. This was the second time she had seen Philip cry, and now he was in his father's arms, explaining that he didn't want to leave him and Natalie, asking his father why he didn't just leave the military so they all could be together. John reassured him that Christmas was right around the corner, when they would be together again.

The scene brought her back to a time when she remembered asking her brothers to stay, to not leave her, begging Anthony to quit the priesthood so he would be near. She understood Philip's cries and allowed herself a moment of pity for the boy. Slipping quietly back into the hallway, she let them have their time together.

Outside, Katarina spotted John's father in the shed with their friend Father O'Brian. She leaned against the shed and overheard Frank asking the priest what he thought of Katarina. Father O'Brian shared that he felt John was a good father, was raising the children well, and he could see that he was madly in love. Careful with his words, he said that he thought there was something not quite right with his wife's love; Katarina's affection for John did not seem to come to the surface, and he was concerned with why she didn't show it, if it was even there.

Katarina moved in closer, careful not to be seen. The visitor continued, "I know of her brother, and as a priest, he is one of the finest, strong in his faith. I met him at the Vatican once. He was healing from wounds that were inflicted on him during the war. I understand his sister experienced her own troubles back then, as well. I do feel she might be capable of breaking his heart, but it's just a feeling."

"I feel the same way too, but my son has a good head on his shoulders, and he will move heaven and earth to keep his marriage in one piece. I shouldn't judge her too harshly. This family can be overly affectionate, and just because she is standoffish doesn't mean she doesn't care. What troubles me more is her lack of affection toward her children. She never hugs Philip or even Natalie, and she doesn't seem to care that everyone else is taking care of her children. She seems to be at peace with it."

"My friend, we can only pray, and I think it will all work out fine."

John's father was silent for the moment, and just before Katarina turned to walk away, he said, "You know, O'Brian, she has terrible nightmares. I heard it last night, and John took her outside at three in the morning to get her some air. He told me he has tried to get her to see a therapist to help her come to peace with whatever she is suffering from. He says she can barely recall it all, much less talk about it, but it surfaces in her dreams."

"Well, then, Frank, we must pray harder for her. I will see you at your home for dinner tonight."

Katarina walked away furious. How dare they pass judgment on her like that! She loved John, and just because she didn't show it every moment of the day did not make it untrue. And how dare John share her nightmares with his family! Her jaw was set in fury and her eyes blazing when John found her sitting on the swing hanging from the oak tree. He pushed the swing from behind and startled her. When she glanced back, his face was lit up with an impish smile.

She inhaled deeply and decided not to tell him what she had heard. He pulled the swing to a stop and kissed her on the lips. "I'm going sailing with Philip. Do you want to come?"

To her own amazement, Katarina answered, "Yes, I would love to come with you two."

They sailed for hours that afternoon. It was the most relaxing time she had ever spent with Philip, but then he was in his element—the boy sure knew how to sail. She was fascinated as she watched them work the sails with the wind, while the soothing sound of the water kept her negative thoughts at bay.

They were home in time for dinner. Philip's eyes were shining with happiness from the day. When she and John got to their room, they were like teenagers in love, showering together, and then a quick round of sex, and he told her over and over sweet things that every woman wants to hear.

Late for the start of the meal, they entered the dining room with flushed cheeks. They were sure everyone noticed. Katarina made it a point to greet Natalie first with a hug and a kiss. She flashed a fake smile at Father O'Brian and Frank as she told Natalie how she'd missed her that day and how much she loved her. She was not going to let these two men judge her. They knew nothing about her life or what she had gone through.

Preparing for sad goodbyes, they packed the cars and drove to the airport. Katarina and Natalie would be boarding a plane to Berlin, as John had promised. Philip held Natalie close and repeatedly told her he loved her.

Once again Katarina recovered a memory of Anthony telling her the same when she was a child, just before he had to leave her.

John held tight to both of them and told them how much they would be missed. Within seconds, Natalie's whimpers escalated into sobbing, as she latched on to her father's neck. Katarina snatched the child from his arms and took her to the side. "You will stop this and stop this now," she growled, practically jerking her off her feet. Philip stepped boldly in front of her and pulled Natalie from her grip. John stepped in between them and lifted the child now gasping for her breath; the marks on her arms quickly turning red, becoming bruises right before his eyes.

"Kat, maybe you should consider going by yourself and leaving her with my parents." His voice was hard like his eyes. He whispered in her ear, "Don't you ever touch her like that again." The passionate farewell kisses he had just given her seemed to evaporate. Philip looked at her with contempt; it was not the first time he had seen her do this.

Katarina's heart was beating erratically. "I'm sorry. I'm just frazzled about leaving you. I will miss you so much, John. Last night I even considered changing my mind." The words seemed to soften him but not Natalie, who was clinging to him desperately with her whole body.

"I want to stay! I want to stay with you, Daddy, and Philip," she said with her tiny voice, reaching out for Philip's hand. The final call to board caught them all off guard. Katarina tried to soothe Natalie, to no avail. The flight attendant allowed John to walk them to the plane so Natalie would stop crying.

Katarina locked eyes with John. “I will be back before you know it,” and she and Natalie disappeared into the PanAm aircraft.

Chapter 10

Berlin

The trip was exhausting, Natalie fussing the entire time, crying continuously for her daddy. The staff took turns entertaining her in their free moments to give Katarina and the other passengers a rest. She explained the child was needy and missing her father. But the minute the flight attendants fussed over her, she calmed down.

They were landing in Tempelhof, so very different from 1948, but even yet, through the window, rubble was visible, buildings half rebuilt, a gray cast of death in the air. On the ground, a large gathering of family met Katarina when she exited the aircraft. Her brother Hans and his wife, Gertrude, and Elvia with her husband, Dietrich, her parents—Jona and Lisa—standing behind them waving. She and Natalie were greeted with hugs and kisses, and praises for their good health. But how pale everyone looked to her, except for her father, who obviously was spending time outside.

Hans noticed her looking past them for someone else she had expected. "He couldn't make it, Kat. Anthony is now teaching theology in Paris. He will try to make it next week."

"I didn't realize, but obviously I'm disappointed. The main thing is, I will see him soon."

As they worked their way to the car, baggage in tow, she felt him before she saw him. He was standing in the distance. Their eyes locked, and she gave a cautious wave. In his leather jacket he was as rugged-looking as she remembered. His hat was shoved back, the hair somewhat longer, his face still beautiful. She wished she could see his eyes closer. Grigory.

Hans caught the wave. "Katarina, he's like a ghost, in and out of Berlin. He is still working with the British but as an outside agent from Israel, and Peter—we never see him. I doubt you will see him either. It's dangerous work moving into the East. We are two different worlds now, West Berlin, East Berlin. We know the East is worried about so many people fleeing to the West. They come across to work every day and some do not go back." When Katarina looked back, Grigory was gone.

They picked up the luggage and loaded it into her father's van. Hans pulled the Mercedes around for the passengers. She heard a loud bang and automatically she ducked and scanned the area. Too many memories—escape routes, bombings, air raids. Her mother's warm hand took hers. How foolish she felt, and then she saw, straight ahead, a young girl who had blossomed into a beautiful teenager, her daughter Alexandra. Lanky and tall, long blonde hair cascading over her shoulders—Katarina thought she was looking into a mirror, seeing herself at that age. But the moment she was able to see closely her large blue-green eyes, she was reminded of Alexandra's father. Why must she have the eyes of Frederick Spitz?

"Hello, Katarina," Alexandra greeted her. "Helena apologizes for not being able to come." Alexandra didn't call Helena "Mother" even though Helena had legally adopted her, another secret Katarina had kept from John. Nor did Alexandra call Katarina "Mother." Alexandra looked at her as if she were any other relative. The teenager turned abruptly and scooped up Natalie. "May I ride with you and your little girl?" Natalie instantly relaxed in her arms, calmly playing with Alexandra's necklace.

"Yes, that would be nice." Katarina gave her a weak smile. Gertrude climbed into the front seat with Hans, and Alexandra got in the back seat with Natalie still in her arms. Katarina reluctantly sat next to them. Hans made small talk on the ride home. Gertrude said nothing, except to ask if Natalie was hungry.

Natalie fell asleep, while Katarina looked out the window at the city slowly coming back to life: cars going places, military jeeps zipping by, a new energy from the people, food stores with their flowers and vegetables once again outside there storefronts, movie theaters open, bright lights luring the patrons. It was too much to behold. She closed her eyes for the duration of the ride, until Hans hit a bump and announced cheerfully that they were a short block away.

Natalie had kept her head on Alexandra's chest the whole time, her eyes now open, looking curiously at the pendant between her tiny fingers.

Once through the iron gates, they drove slowly toward the house. The first thing Katarina noticed was that it had been painted and the single doors replaced with large double doors. The windows, tall and polished, trimmed in a light blue, were open. No longer boarded up, it was now full of life, with its fourteen rooms, six baths, and the guest house where she and

Francis had once stayed. Originally the place had once looked like a small castle, but when it was restored after the bombings, the façade had been changed to a more modern theme. Still, it was their home, and if it could speak, it would have wept.

Everyone gathered together in front of the home where they had shared a happier life in a happier time. They expressed their relief that this place had survived. A Nazi colonel had occupied it for a while, taking with him all the art and the first edition books her father had collected, including an original Renoir that he was still trying to find. The odds were he'd never see it again. They had saved a few sprigs before the vineyard was scorched, and her father was working diligently to bring them back to life.

The first words from Natalie, pointing wildly across the pasture, were "Horsie, horsie!" A dozen horses were in the field, and two goats came running out of the barn. Natalie squealed in delight and wriggled out of Alexandra's arms. The dogs followed the goats, with Franz running close behind. He was trying to round up the goats, which kept running in circles, Natalie and her grandfather now also in pursuit.

Franz had been with the family as long as she could remember. He had remained on the premises while the family stayed in the apartments in Kreuzberg close to their factories and their tenants. They had taken with them canned vegetables, buried underground for safekeeping, and a goat, which they kept in the kitchen to feed milk to the hungry children. If they had lived in the Russian zone, the goat would have been taken, as well as any food. The horses were left behind with Franz. He and her father had built a bunker large enough to hold three of the finest horses, to protect them from the bombing raids and from the Nazis at the end of the war. When the horses and the dogs were moved into the bunker, it had been amazing how they instinctively knew to be still and quiet until Franz opened the door, signaling it was safe.

Natalie ran her little legs off after Franz and the dogs. Alexandra stayed outside to watch her, while Katarina walked up the six steps and entered the hallway with the glistening oak floors. Paint was needed on the dull walls, but pictures were hung to cover the flaws. The dining room to the right was already set for lunch with the best china on the table, and even with the cracks and chips they were still beautiful. The valuable German Meissen chandelier that hung overhead had been brought back from Munich.

Everyone rushed to wash up for lunch while the help took the luggage upstairs. Platters filled with pork filet in red wine plum sauce, sauerkraut, cheese, dark bread, potatoes, and salads were brought in. Katarina's distraught mother, being a vegetarian, always had issues with preparing the food and had left the meat to the cook to do with what she pleased. Outnumbered by her four carnivorous boys and her husband, the hunter, she tried not to show her disdain for the dead animals covered in sauce on the table. Her husband's ongoing joke was that if she would stop giving the farm animals names, she'd be able to handle it better.

Katarina continued touring the home and followed the hall to the library. She peeked in the door and was saddened by the mostly bare shelves. Opening the door wider, she saw Helena at the writing desk, looking out the large bay window. Katarina cleared her throat.

Helena slowly turned, and they looked at each other without expression, clearly still estranged.

Helena spoke first. "Katarina, I see you got here safely." At that moment, a man came from the side door that led to another small reading room. "This is my husband, Helmutt."

A tall man of approximately six feet, completely bald, with a round face that didn't quite fit his lean figure, wore a most pleasant smile as he walked over to Katarina and gave her a warm hug. "We have heard so much about you, young woman. We look forward to learning more in the week of your stay. You must join us for dinner at our home in Charlottenburg. It's not all that far from here."

Katarina saw Helena shake her head and frown, as if Helmutt had stepped out of line.

"Thank you for the invitation. I will have to see how the schedule goes." Katarina welcomed the sudden laughter in the hallway, and her French sister-in-law, Elvia, peeking into the library to announce that lunch was being served.

During the war, Katarina's brother Heinz had married Elvia, and after he was killed, she was brought from France to Germany with their child, Sarah. Dietrich was like a brother to their family, and he married Elvia and they raised Sarah together. Elvia and Katarina were very fond of one another and spoke French together as often as they could. Now Katarina was looking forward to sharing the language again with her.

"You must come now. Everyone is starving, including these girls." Elvia stepped back to reveal Alexandra and her daughter Sarah, the image of Heinz, with perfectly chiseled cheekbones and the darkest black hair. Unlike Heinz, however, the hair flowed down to her waist and the full lips belonged to her mother. The adults followed the younger generation to the dining room, Katarina taking note that Sarah had legs like Alexandra's and they even matched in height, both moving down the hallway like models, arm in arm, laughing all the way.

Elvia noticed her observing them and took Katarina's hand. "They are the best of friends—couldn't be closer if they had been sisters. They spend most of their time here on weekends, just riding with Jona, and he teaches them the best horsemanship. You must know, they started boarding school together and are constantly in trouble. At least once a week the nuns call. You can see they have their secrets, as they are whispering and giggling even now."

"Does Helena mind Alexandra spending so much time here?"

"Not at all. She thinks it does her good to be with family. Helena and Helmutt are mostly on their own, traveling a great deal. Also, it's good for Sarah to be with someone her own age. Plus, now that Sarah is older, she wants to know more about her father and see pictures of him. Your parents are wonderful about sharing Heinz's life with her."

Katarina was caught off guard at how quickly her eyes filled with tears as she remembered her beautiful brother. "As she should. Heinz so loved you."

"Well, the best thing is, he still lives through her."

Katarina thought further on Elvia's remark as they walked to the dining room. She didn't want Frederick Spitz ever to live through Alexandra, but so far, she had not inherited any of his genes, other than his eyes. Alexandra could pass easily as Sarah's sister, except Sarah had more of an olive complexion compared to Alexandra's skin, the color of white gypsum. They were equal in beauty.

Her mother was now fussing for Sarah to take off her muddy riding boots and leave them in the hall. While removing them, Sarah rolled her eyes and thoughtlessly left them at the entrance to the dining room. As soon as everyone had been seated, the room was silent as they gave thanks and after, they burst into conversation, chattering all at once. Talk of horses, land, factories—it seemed like everyone's life had moved on, and Katarina felt oddly like a stranger, not even aware that Gertrude was feeding Natalie in the high chair, giving her kisses on the cheeks and smiles between bites.

"You have a lot of luggage, Aunt Kat," Sarah noted. "I saw them on the landing, so many."

Katarina smiled. "Well, yes, I have lots of presents for everyone, including pants and skirts for you and Alexandra. But seeing both of you have such long beautiful legs, the hems may need to be let down."

"Yes, Aunt Kat, we have been told more than once that our legs are similar to yours." A smug smile crossed Sarah's face. It was almost said with a hint of venom in her voice—or was Katarina imagining things? She had not been around teenage girls enough to know.

Helena spoke up. "I think Alexandra has plenty of clothing. Not only that, she wears a uniform in school, so we do not need charity from the United States."

There was a gasp from Lisa. "Helena, please, Katarina brought gifts, not charity. That was ungrateful.

Let her give them to the girls."

Helena's thoughts were unkind as she glared at her sister Lisa, who always stood up for Katarina as well as everyone else. Thank goodness Anthony wasn't here. He would most likely put a princess crown on Katarina's head; he thought she was so perfect. Helena knew the real Katarina very well. After all, she was her own flesh and blood, and she might have done the wrong thing by letting Lisa raise her child as her own, but she knew Katarina was not perfect either. She saw the other side of her, too much like herself. That's why she knew her for who she was.

There was a moment of silence by all. Alexandra turned to Helena. "I'm still staying overnight with Sarah. Grandfather has it arranged for us to ride in the forest tomorrow." The child's expression was nearly one of panic, as she clearly thought Helena would now change her mind. "We never see each other—our classes are different, and we don't even stay on the same floor."

"Do not exaggerate, child," Helena scolded. "You two are thick as thieves and see each other often during the week and almost every weekend with those horses."

Normally a silent man, Jona's voice boomed from across the table, "The girls will overnight together, and tomorrow is planned." He turned his attention to Katarina. "You are welcome to ride with us. I wish little Natalie could, but we will put her on a pony first thing when we come back from our ride."

A strapping young man entered the dining room, rushed breathlessly over to Katarina's mother, and kissed her on the cheek. "Grandmother, I'm sorry. Football practice ran late." He was Gertrude and Hans's son, Ernst. Katarina thought to herself, What is with these children? All so striking, and tall, blue-eyed beauties every one of them. She did not realize that none compared to her own radiant violet eyes, spellbinding to look at even now she was older.

"I brought company." He stood before them, pointing to the window. Necks stretched to see Katarina's cousin Peter outside talking to the stable help.

Peter took the steps two at a time and entered with a big smile and immediately pulled over an extra chair next to Ernst. "This looks so good! I'm starving. I hope Cook made dessert, too." He piled his plate high with large servings of everything present. "Aunt Lisa, my mother says she misses you and Helena and hopes you two will visit England soon. Brighton is such…" He stopped, suddenly noticing Katarina. "Oh, my goodness, I knew you were coming but had no idea it was today." He dropped his fork, rose from his chair and reached around her from behind.

Katarina looked up at him. He was older now, not a trace of German in him, as all his looks leaned toward his father's British side: sandy brown hair, the sloping nose, a slightly slanted forehead, and wrinkles around his eyes that surfaced when he smiled, a lazy smile that revealed small white teeth. Still married to Claire, a strong marriage with their five children alive and healthy, Peter was the picture of happiness. His parents, Marta and Albert, were still living in the country, as in love as ever since they first met on the beach in Brighton, England.

He went back to his seat, and once again the conversations went in different directions. She saw the look pass between Peter and Hans. Katarina knew that look well. They had secrets between them only.

Ernst was drawn to Natalie as Gertrude was, pulling his chair between them, wiping off Natalie's sticky hands, talking to her as if she understood. When Gertrude saw Natalie's eyes drooping, she swooped her up from the chair and announced she would take the child back to the guest house, where there was a crib set up and she could stay while Katarina had a good night's sleep. Before Katarina could object, she was out of the room, with Ernst dutifully following right behind her. She knew of Gertrude's obsession with girls, as she could never bear one. She didn't know that, at that moment, Gertrude secretly hated her for being blessed with children she did not want.

Chapter 11

Lunch ended slowly, and Cook entered the room to clear the table while everyone disbursed elsewhere. Hans and Peter moved to the library. Katarina knew Peter was still with the British Intelligence and had been working with Grigory. She would find out more. When her mother and Helena invited her out to the garden, she declined. The girls went outside with her father to the stables, and Dietrich and Elvia went into downtown Berlin. Just before they left, Dietrich pulled her to the side and whispered, “Kat, a lot has changed. Hans and Peter have been working hard against the East German Regime. Don’t get involved.”

Katarina was heading upstairs when she heard Hans in a heated discussion with Peter. She looked over the railing and saw Hans pacing past the open door to the library. She stood in the hallway and listened. “Peter, Ulbricht is the worst of all Germans. He touts the Russian agenda, he moves up the ladder in authority, and there are more informers now from the East than we have from the West. They are listening, as you well know, to what the Americans and British are saying. It seems they are always one step ahead of us. We have got to find out who the main informers are that are living and working right under our noses.” Hans ran his hand through his hair.

Peter sat in the overstuffed chair while Hans

looked in frustration out the window at a happy scene, his father walking in the pasture with a halter in his hands, the girls dancing around him. He must never know the danger his son was now in. They had seen enough in the war.

"Hans, we are trying. We just have to set the date and find two people who can pull it off. We have someone on the inside who can give us names, and then we play them, give them bad information, and get what we need."

He turned from the window. "What about *him*? Is he still moving in and out of the East like a ghost? The man has more passports and false papers than any human being I have ever known. He still has the safe house, the small apartment, but he is seldom there. If he is not here, he is in Africa, Brazil, on the hunt to kill. We saw him from a distance today at the airport."

Katarina inhaled. They were talking about Grigory.

"Listen," Peter said, "we can make further arrangements after I see Anthony in Paris next week. He now has one of the best forgers working with him. The man forged enough false paperwork to get many a person out of Paris during the war."

She heard her mother's voice coming from the kitchen. She quickly scaled the stairs and was almost to the top when she heard Helena's voice and then saw her eyes like daggers piercing hers. "Kat, don't forget to give Alexandra the gifts you promised. She doesn't need any more disappointments from you."

"Helena, was that necessary? You have got to let go of this animosity. It's been too many years. We have all learned to live with each other's decisions." Katarina cared little about what Helena thought of her. Helena had given her up when she was born and was trying to make up for it by raising Alexandra. On the other hand, Katarina had long ago given Alexandra up. How ironic! They were two peas in a pod and hated each other for doing exactly the same thing. The only difference was that Katarina did it openly and honestly, while Helena lived the lie that Lisa and Jona were Katarina's parents, and her cousins were her brothers. Nothing could ever change that now, as Katarina knew only their love and her deep love for them. There was no room for Helena in her heart, and her brothers and parents would always be hers without question.

Helena turned and walked briskly back to her room. Katarina stood on the steps and waited for her door to shut. Peter and Hans came out of the library. She braced her body against the wall.

"One more thing, Hans. The safe house was compromised. We are changing it to Kreuzberg on Nostiz Strasse. For now, Anthony has arranged to hide him in the church. We'll work on getting Doctor Stein out when I get back. I will have the identification papers from Anthony. Time is of the essence. Once they identify him as one of the best experts in nuclear coding, they will find him at all cost. He can also name those men now working on nuclear weapons in Russia."

Katarina leaned over the banister. "So much for the quiet life."

Peter and Hans both shook their heads. "How much did you hear?" asked Peter.

"Enough to know I can help you," she whispered, rallying them back to the library.

Hans threw his hands up. "I don't believe that is your place now. You are here to visit."

She cocked her head to one side. "Really? How much do Father and Mother know about this?" She saw the look between them and watched them squirm like children.

"Come clean, gentleman," she demanded, her hands now on her hips.

Hans sighed. "Father will stitch someone up for us once in a while, when getting them out has gotten a little rough, as it does sometimes. We tell him nothing. It's better that way."

Peter looked at Katarina sternly. "You cannot say a word. Do you understand? The less you know, the better. The Russians are making the East a German police state. It is being run and trained by the Russians one hundred percent. Those in authority are puppets to the Russians, with their terrible prisons set up for torture, just like Hitler's. Here in the West, people are disappearing right off the streets."

Hans let out another long sigh. "Kat, it's another dictatorship. It's the unimaginable evil we fought, all over again. If we don't fight them, we will be another part of history, another piece of land that falls into the hands of the Russians. Berlin right now is a city of split personality, schizophrenic, two separate Berlins. The people in the East live in shattered dreams, coming here every day for work, for food, a taste of the better life, before they return to their hell. Can you blame them? University professors, judges, lawyers, writers—they all want to be here."

Peter snapped his fingers and let out a long whistle. "This can work, Hans! Damn, I know now how to solve our problem. Kat can go into the East as a reporter for the French magazine. She speaks fluent French, and they would never suspect her. She will know the code word and can collect the information we need."

Hans was vigorously shaking his head. "No, no, no! We cannot send her over there. If they catch on…"

"No, listen! I'll be the driver, and we will take one other agent with us as a Swedish reporter working on the new regime of the East and how they are schooling reporters and their writing. I will get Anthony to make the false information. I have friends at the magazine who will have vouched for her as one of theirs. This can work. I'll be there to pull us all out if something goes wrong. She speaks French, for God's sake—the perfect reporter."

"Peter, I don't think Anthony will go along with this. You know how he feels about Katarina doing anything dangerous. She did her time."

Katarina cleared her throat. "Excuse me, if either of you are interested, may I speak? First, I don't think I can get in without a passport. I only have my U.S. passport."

"Not a problem." Peter was prepared with an answer. "We will have the French passport, the press badges, and an address in France where you lived, where your parents came from. Everything will be in order. You will have to memorize everything, for they will try to trick you because no one is trustworthy. But they are trying to promote the Communist party in France, so they will gladly share information to spread the word. We know someone there who will pass to you the informers' names, and from there we will proceed to the church and get Doctor Stein out."

Hans, still unhappy with the idea, said, "'Peter, do you forget what happened to Dietrich? By the time we got him out of the East, he nearly bled to death, and we almost took another husband from Elvia."

"The difference is, I will be there. Do you really think I would let something happen to her?"

"Gentlemen, I'm still here in the room." Katarina tapped her foot in annoyance.

Hans took hold of her hands. "This is not a good plan. You have no idea what they are capable of. They execute people, they torture them…"

She placed her hand under his chin and smiled. "Hans, I have so many times been in a silent darkness reliving the past, there is not much that can scare me anymore."

He understood. He wished he didn't. "All right, but you promise—any indication of fear or backing out, you just tell us, and it's called off."

Peter thrust his fists in the air, then grabbed them by the shoulders, pulling them in to form a circle. With their heads bowed, he whispered, "We will not tell Anthony right away, not until it's time to prepare your French identification."

They broke off their talk as Alexandra and Sarah stood at the door, looking quizzically at them.

Chapter 12

"Oh, back from your ride already?" Peter broke away from the circle and easily switched from his serious mood, giving the girls his full attention.

"Uncle Hans, Sheiba did great. She gave us some good cantering today," Sarah said. As they walked out into the hall, she took Hans to the side. "Something strange happened while we were riding. We saw a car parked in the forest, and one of our stable help was talking to someone we didn't know. I just found it odd that even the other helpers didn't know who the stranger was. I thought you should know."

"What a keen eye you have." He winked, moving her toward the kitchen. "I'll look into it. Thank you for letting me know. Oh, I smell pastries. Go see what Cook has made for the two of you."

Peter and Katarina went outside. They had their own private conversation. Katarina had to find out about Grigory.

That night the house was so quiet, Katarina tossed and turned. Natalie was with Gertrude. That was fine; she could smother her all she wanted. Katarina decided to go downstairs to find some brandy, something to settle her stomach. Agreeing to help the cause gave her more anxiety than she'd expected. A light was coming from the library. She glanced at the grandfather clock, which at that very second chimed out two a.m. She entered the library and found her father hunched over papers.

"Father, what are you doing up at this hour?"

He turned in his chair, his eyeglasses perched on the edge of his nose. He removed them and rubbed his eyes. "Well, I should ask you the same, my dear."

She walked over and sat next to him. "Father, you look so tired. It's late. Go to bed."

She saw folders spread across the gigantic oak desk. They were labeled 1939 Berlin Zoo.

"Katarina, you know I'm helping out at the zoo in veterinary capacity. I also want to find the original stockholders, who were Jewish and forced to sell their stock at a loss. They should be paid for their losses. I know many perished, but some escaped." He opened one of the folders and sighed with sorrow. "It was such a wonderful zoo, since 1844, first aquarium 1913, the first animals given were from Frederick William IV, king of Prussia. Do you realize only ninety-one of more than three thousand survived the bombings and the Russians, who ate them? I'm hoping the zoo will commission to find these past stockholders or their descendants or relatives. I'm only doing the preliminary work, as you see here."

"Father, it looks as if it is slowly being rebuilt," she said encouragingly.

He couldn't stop the tears. At his age, there had been so many, they came easily now. "So many animals destroyed! They had no one to help them."

"Father, you can't take the blame. You did everything you could. You put yourself in danger during every bombing. Look how you saved the two lions, and the Asian bull elephant. You talked the

Russians out of killing them."

Outside it was a full moon. He had decided to leave the horses out in the pasture and not confined to the stalls. Katarina walked to the window and pointed. "Why, look, Father, you have three horses that you saved from the Poland Riding School. You risked your life with Wolfgang Kroll, your veterinarian friend, and helped the American Army save the Austrian purebreds."

He stood beside her, looking beyond the field, lost in memory. "It's true. We even tried to save one of the greatest thoroughbred racehorses of our time, Alchemist, but the Russians shot him. My girls out there are from the most valuable horses in the world, from Hostau. The Nazis tried to keep this race of horses pure, just like they did with humans, while the Russians would have thoughtlessly slaughtered them for meat. It took one German officer, who risked being shot and went to the Americans in the last days of the war, to save the horses from the Russians. I know him. I have spoken with him. He gave up his country to save these amazing creatures. He had the respect of Colonel Reed, an American officer who also wanted them saved. I recall the escape route, moving the broodmares and their offspring across fifteen hundred acres of land…"

"Father, you went there without telling us?"

"Yes, I was there."

"You were gone for so long Mother was frantic. She thought you had died or were in an enemy camp."

"I know, but look—I have one of their offspring, Sheiba. Look at his black coat, almost blue under the full moon. And now Stern has her foal. Look at her being nudged by her baby for milk. She is from the

Janow Podlaski stud farm in Poland."

Katarina thought she had opened the floodgates. She was not alone with her secrets; her father had the need to share his, so she listened with intent.

"I remember the connection Anthony made in Poland to bring back the purebred Arabians. When your brother saw one of these colts born, he saw fire in his eyes, a kind of fierce spirit like his own, and he knew then how special they were. You did, too, and Franz, who is still here with us, so dedicated to care for them. We tried to rescue more from Poland, but the conditions were so bad, and we lost so many of them. Like our losing so many of our loved ones, so did they." He turned to his daughter. "I know, my child, the war haunts you, as well."

"Father, I have had my happiness. But you, you amaze me, all that you did to help the others, to save the horses, and now you are looking for stockholders. I'm very proud of you." She flung her arms around him and hugged him tightly. "Now, you must go to sleep. Tomorrow early, just you and I will ride."

She left him still sitting at his desk, and her stomach ached more than ever.

****

Katarina did not sleep well. Even the brandy didn't help. She kept seeing, in her sleep, horses running away from fire, Russian guns, and as clear as day, a gun being held to her head. She woke up feeling physically sick.

It was six a.m. when she looked at the clock and opened the curtains and viewed the gardens below her room. She wanted to smell the roses of every color that were blooming by the hundreds, so she opened the window and stuck her head outside. Her mother was already out attending to them, her pride and joy. It wasn't long before melancholy morphed into motivation, and within minutes she was dressed in her old riding pants, a soft yellow sweater, and her favorite riding boots that her father had thoughtfully cleaned and left outside her bedroom door.

She walked toward the kitchen, tying her hair in a ponytail, and ran into her father just heading upstairs to get her. He was dressed to ride. "Well, my daughter, I guess we are both ready. Have a cup of coffee and a nibble, and we'll be on our way." She kissed her father's cheek and wondered how spry he could be after their talk and barely any sleep. Then it occurred to her—like father, like daughter—and she laughed inwardly.

As always, food magically appeared in this household, Cook being the magician. Hardboiled eggs surrounded with cheese, a stack of croissants, and blackberry jelly—she wasted no time wrapping the pastry in a cloth and pouring a cup of coffee to take outside. She looked around to say something to her father, but he was gone.

"Hello." The young voice startled her, and Katarina jerked and spilled some of her coffee. "I'm sorry I startled you, Aunt Kat. I was just looking for a bracelet I thought I left here yesterday."

"Isn't this early for you, Sarah?"

"Not really. Alexandra and I usually are out riding before the sun comes up. We go over the hill and watch the sunrise."

"Did you by chance see my father on your way in here?"

"I saw him going into the tack room. Why don't you wait for me and Alexandra, or is it too much to expect her mother by blood to ride with her?" There was a challenge in her eyes, and Katarina did not like the tone.

"I think it's complicated, and you are too young to understand."

"I'm not too young to understand that you let her be adopted by Helena." Another smug remark came easily with this child.

"I'm not sure what you know, little girl, but I would stay out of it."

Sarah shrugged. "I know a lot more than you realize." She walked away, and Katarina heard Natalie calling to her, holding out her arms, begging to be held. Sarah gathered her up and kissed her face. Gertrude walked out of the next room and joined her. Katarina watched them disappear around the corner with her child. She would make it a point to see Natalie later.

Katarina found her father out in the round pen, lunging Sheiba. The other horse, Stern, was saddled and ready for Katarina. Her father's face lit up when he saw her.

"What kept you? Have you changed your mind about riding?"

"Father, I would never turn down riding, especially with you."

They rode till late morning, laughing as they turned the corner and entered through the back entrance near the garden. Gertrude was pushing Natalie in the tree swing.

"Katarina, go see your little girl," her father encouraged.

She dismounted and hesitated before she called to her, "Natalie, come see Mommy." As she approached them, Gertrude stopped the swing and took Natalie's hand.

"Come see your mommy," she tried again, and suddenly Natalie burst into a tantrum.

"No, want to swing!"

"Come here, Natalie."

"No!" the child answered with several stomps on the ground.

"You should never answer me like that!" Katarina's voice raised as she grabbed the child by the arms and shook her violently. Gertrude stood there too stunned to say anything. She hadn't expected Katarina's actions.

A hand sternly pulled at Katarina's arm. "Never do that again." Her mother spoke loud and clear.

Natalie was crying and ran to show Gertrude the marks on her arms. "It hurts, Aunt Gertrude."

Katarina was so furious she was shaking, but she did not want to come up against her mother. "Mother, I did not realize I had such a grip on her, but Natalie needs to learn she cannot talk back."

Gertrude spoke up. "She is just a little girl. You could have just given her a tap on the rear or tried to explain to her with time out."

Katarina apologized, which was difficult for her, and she glanced over at Natalie with ice in her eyes and turned to leave.

Gertrude caught up with her as she was walking away. "Katarina, you left a mark on her arm. It's not the first bruise I have seen on her."

Katarina stopped quickly and faced her. "Stay out

of it, Gertrude. Raise your own child!"

"You don't deserve to have children, the way you leave them like crumbs on a path!"

Katarina saw her mother coming toward them with Natalie and decided this was not the time to unleash her fury on her sister-in-law. They had both hated each other from the very day Hans brought her home to meet the family; Katarina hated her for trying to take Anna's place, and Gertrude hated that Hans and his brothers lost all reasoning when defending Katarina.

To avoid an argument, she turned and walked back to the stalls, where her father was showing a stable boy how to clean the horse's feet. His name was Max, and she had seen him before and knew exactly where by the numbers on his wrist. Her parents had taken the boy in as a refugee. With their help, Max would get all the necessary papers to immigrate to Israel, with the Schoemans sponsoring him.

During the war, the Schoemans had lost their daughter—a horrible memory that would forever keep them from returning to Germany. Their daughter Rita and Katarina's brother Edwin had fallen in love, unable to marry because of their religions—she was Jewish, and he was Catholic. Anthony provided false papers making her Catholic, married them, and put the Schoemans in hiding until they were able to get them safely to Switzerland. If Katarina had not married Fredrick Spitz, Rita would not have been sent to Ravensbruck, the largest concentration camp for women in the German Reich. Katarina felt she was the cause of their deaths, even though Frederick had sent her to prison, too. But theirs was a true love story, and like Romeo and Juliet, Edwin and Rita died together, but at the hands of the enemy.

Her father slapped Max on the back. "Good job, my boy. Now you know the smell of thrush and how to clean the hooves. It's harder with shoes, but since our horses run bare, it will be easy for you."

They saddled up a pony with a child's saddle and a lead rope. Father was taking Natalie for a ride, and now she came running into the stables. Gertrude was behind her, still in a bad mood. The grandfather scooped Natalie up in his arms, and Katarina could see her father admire her beauty. She could not help but do so herself. Why did she get so angry with this darling child? Gertrude and her mother were right, she was just an innocent little girl. Seeing her plump legs that ran so quickly dangling from each side of the saddle reminded her of herself at that age. While she was reminiscing, Gertrude stood right beside them, nervous as a cat. Unlike Katarina, she was like a mother worrying for her child's safety.

Katarina walked over to Max. She knew his story—her father had found him in East Germany, severely beaten by the Russians, the only survivor of seven siblings. She smiled up at him. "By the time you arrive in Israel, my father will have taught you everything you need to know about a horse, and you will be able to find a job quickly in any of the stables." The young boy in the six-foot frame smiled at her reassurance. She noticed his hands were red and chapped; the too-short shirt sleeves exposed his numbers. He tried to pull the sleeve down, but she stopped him, placing her hand on his. "Let it show. It's nothing to be ashamed of. I know what you have been through." Their eyes met, a silent comprehension between survivors of hell on earth.

She watched his posture stiffen when Wilhelm came around the corner, another young man her parents had taken in. It was on their earlier ride that her father had explained his situation. He had claimed he was a German refugee from Poland, forced to leave when the Poles took back their land. They were trying to reeducate Wilhelm from the Hitler way of thinking, believing he was humble enough to learn. They had caught him tormenting Max, shaming him as a Jew working for a Christian family. It seemed the tension between them had not changed, as Katarina witnessed Wilhelm giving Max a cold stare as he disappeared into the tack room. She could have sworn the look was meant for her, too.

Still, she felt compelled to comfort Max and help him to understand Wilhelm. "My father is trying to reeducate this boy, to help him realize his hate toward a group of people was the Hitler way, not the German way. It can be maddening, but this has been going on for hundreds of years, this kind of inhumanity. The hate lies deep in the soul, the devil's will against God as we are always being tested. I hope God is collecting every tear we have shed and gives us goodness in man once again."

"Fräulein Katarina, I struggle with God's thoughts on our suffering. It seems our Jewish culture has suffered for much too long."

She patted his rough hands. "Let's hope those days are over."

She saw Hans pull up in the Mercedes, surprised to see him home so early; he usually stayed in town at the factory the whole day and even slept there sometimes, from what her mother said. She caught up with him in the hallway.

"Hans, is everything okay?"

"Katarina, hello." He kissed her on the cheek. "I have to get some paperwork and some blankets. We got out a professor from the East, just one of the thousands who are escaping, but he could be snatched up again. They released him from Sachsenhausen, where they primarily imprison political figures, but he was there because he was helping a democratic youth group. He was the one who informed us of Professor Geist, who has knowledge of the nuclear development. We moved the safe house, but we don't have blankets. Walk with me to the attic. We have some stored there."

"Haven't you learned yet not to follow Hans?" A familiar voice came from behind.

Katarina's smile spread even before she turned to see him. There he stood, her brother, never more beautiful in his collar and cross. "Anthony!"

Hans came down the steps with blankets and dropped them on the floor. He waited respectfully for their embrace to complete and then hugged his brother tightly, lifting him in the air. "You are a sight for sore eyes. Why are you here? Did you meet up with Peter already?"

"In a bit." Anthony nodded, placing his finger on his lips to shush his brother. His mother and Gertrude were coming down the hallway. Hugs and greetings went all around, while Natalie hid behind Gertrude's skirt.

"Well, isn't this fun, a little one running around in the house again." Anthony opened his arms to Natalie, and she allowed him to pick her up. The cross around his neck got her attention. She lifted it and said, “Heavy.” They all laughed, except Katarina, who knew now that she would have to wait to spend time with Anthony. She hated sharing him.

“Where is Father?” Anthony asked.

Katarina took that opportunity to grab his elbow. “Come with me. He’s in the stables.” She tried pulling him to the door. It wouldn’t be long before Sarah and Alexandra would be coming straight from school, and Alexandra was staying over. She would never be able to get his attention then.

“Mother, I brought back some gifts, your favorite perfume, and it’s all in my suitcase. We can sort the gifts out later.”

Katarina was now pulling him harder. “Kat, have patience. I can only go so fast.”

They saw Jona out in the pasture, bringing in two horses. Anthony waved and waited for his father. Max was there to take them into their stalls. “My boy, you have come to visit, I see.” Their hands met in a forearm handshake. “Has your Mother seen you?”

“Yes, I just saw her. Father, I see my horse Capri is out in the pasture. She is looking healthy.”

“I still don’t like the name, Anthony. An Italian city is not a befitting name for such a fine horse.”

“She answers to it, doesn’t she? And she is as sweet as the flowers and lemons of Capri when I think of her.”

While Anthony was saddling Capri, Katarina saddled a little mare. She turned to Max, who was helping her with the cinch. “Who is Wilhelm talking too?” He was at the outer edge of the forest speaking to a man, and with him was Alexandra.

Max looked over. "Fräulein, I'm not sure who that is. This has been happening for over a month now, off and on."

"Is Alexandra always there?"

"No, sometimes it is just Wilhelm."

"I didn't realize he had friends. Do you think it is someone Alexandra introduced him to?"

"I'm not sure, but he comes back sometimes very angry, and I have seen him also talking to a man in the village."

Anthony looked long and hard at the scene, and a worried expression crossed his face.

"What's the matter?" Katarina asked.

"I'm not sure, but it makes me uneasy."

"Should we ride over there, Anthony?"

"No, look. She is on her way back."

Alexandra was trotting back when she saw them coming toward her. Wilhelm was lagging behind on foot. They stopped her in midpasture. She acted as if she had not been spotted and had just come in from a quick ride.

Anthony spoke up. "New friend, Alexandra?"

A blush rose to her cheeks, and she stalled before answering. "It's just someone we were giving directions to." They knew by her hesitation that she was not telling the truth.

Katarina couldn't help herself. "It seemed like a long conversation for simply directions, and were two of you needed to give them?"

Her demeanor changed, and her eyes went straight to Katarina's. "I don't think you have any business questioning me, considering you are not my mother."

Katarina opened her mouth to respond, but

Anthony moved her along. He gave Alexandra a look that said, “We will talk later.”

After a few hours’ ride, Katarina entered the stables first and saw Wilhelm sitting on a haystack reading a magazine. As she dismounted, she asked him to take the horse, unsaddle him, and wipe him down with cool water.

Wilhelm turned to Max, who was just entering the stables. “Let the Jew boy do it. That is what he is being trained to do.”

Katarina was startled by his comment and rude tone, but Max without a word took the reins and began placing a halter on the horse.

A thunderous voice came from Anthony. “Max, give Wilhelm the halter. You”—he pointed to Wilhelm—“take my horse as well. I think Max has done enough work today, and I can see by your clean appearance and your magazine that you haven’t done much of anything except take my niece out to give directions to a stranger.” He dismounted and handed Wilhelm the reins.

They could see Wilhelm’s eyes boring into Max. His glare moved Max to speak. “Father, it’s all right. I enjoy taking care of them. Let me take them, please.”

“Wilhelm, take the saddles to the tack room,” Anthony ordered. Both horses were handed over to Max, and when Katarina and Anthony were walking out, they heard Wilhelm under his breath say, “Jew lover!”

“Katarina, I do not trust that young man,” Anthony said.

“Neither do I. Will you talk to Father about him?”

“Yes, before I leave, but first, Cook has made

strudel and real whipped cream, and that is where I'm going before *you* get there and eat them all."

"Surely with all the wonderful pastries in Paris you didn't come home to eat Cook's simple recipes."

"Nothing better than homemade!" he shouted, picking up his pace and leaving Katarina behind.

When she caught up with him, they entered the kitchen together. Cook raised her chubby arms and smothered Anthony with a big hug. He noticed that she had gained a considerable amount of weight and decided it must be from the many strudels she baked.

"Well, look who else is here!" he sang, when Cook finally released him. Natalie was banging her spoon on the table, her mouth covered with cream, while Gertrude attempted to wipe her face clean. When he picked her up, the determined child tried to feed him with the spoon. Anthony laughed and went along with the game, until she missed his mouth and hit him accidentally in the eye. Then he gently pulled her arm away and took the spoon from her hand.

"Ow," she cried, showing him the bruise on her arm where Anthony had placed his hand. "Boo boo," she said, pointing at another one on her other arm.

Katarina looked at Gertrude, but both remained silent.

"I will kiss it, and it will be all better. How is that?" Her shiny curls shook when she nodded a yes, and he kissed both arms. She in turn gave him a hug and a kiss on his chin. He didn't want to put this precious child down, but Gertrude insisted she needed to take a nap.

Natalie started to cry. "But horsie." She pointed to the back door.

Gertrude rolled her eyes. "Jona has had her on the pony today, and now all she wants to do is ride."

"Well, the genes are in the family, it seems." Anthony smiled over at his sister and handed Natalie to Gertrude.

Anthony made up a tray of strudel and coffee and took it outside to a small table under an old oak tree, one that had escaped being used for firewood during the war. It had to be at least two centuries old, its trunk so wide he remembered as a child hiding from his brothers behind it and not being seen. Their father and Hans had managed already to replace some of the trees that were cut down. They were fortunate to be in the American Sector, so that those in the forest remained.

They sat in silence; only the chirping birds and barking dogs could be heard.

"Kat, I'm sorry for not writing as often as I should have."

"It's fine. I know you are busy in Paris, and your parish has grown so large."

"If I didn't speak French fluently, I doubt very much I would be there. So far the students have not noticed that it's not my native language."

"I completely understand. I still speak French in the United States, and I speak all three languages with Natalie. I see Alexandra doesn't speak English. I thought the schools were teaching all German children."

"Don't let her fool you. She does, but she has no real interest to speak it, and prefers Italian and French. I think she is rebelling against the English side."

He moved on to a more important topic. "First, I'm not happy that Hans and Peter recruited you to go into

East Berlin. With that said, we have slowly been getting important people out that might be stopped at the border or who are watched by informers. It's been easier to hide them in the church until the time comes to move them, the church being so close to the West. We have been lucky."

"Do Father and Mother know what you are doing?"

"They do, to a point. Father has stitched up a few people for us, ones we felt should not be seen by local doctors. We tried once before to get information on who are the informers or double agents, and we got close, but our own spy either was one or didn't show up out of fear."

"Well, I feel secure in my part in this, Anthony, especially knowing Peter is right there with us. Do you know who the contact is with the information on the informer?"

"Yes, he is actually from Sweden. His name is Leonard. He's been working with the Swedish press and has taken on the cause with much dedication. The article you will be claiming to write about is for the French publication and will be titled 'The Free Berlin.' You will talk to them about how free the East is and how open their newspapers are and how journalists don't have their hands tied behind their backs, and how much the churches, too, have freedom. They will make themselves out to be a free society, but, of course, that is nonsense, and we know better."

Anthony continued, "Peter said that a few months ago Leonard's friend was captured. He was a writer and was not heard from again. We have been trying to track him. He was writing about the Politburo. He wrote of the location of the Soviet Ambassador, Vladimir

Semyonow, which was his first mistake. They found him and arrested him on Unter Den Linden, right at the Friedrichstrasse, just as he was sending information on Soviet T-34 tanks rolling into East Berlin. Radio Free Europe is helping the best they can. The radio terrifies the Russians because they can't stop it. As you know, martial law has been imposed several times."

Katarina shuddered just thinking of those captured and where they might have ended up. "What else has Peter told you about this mission?"

"He has it set up like this. You will visit the ministries of communication, posing as a French Communist, and someone will get to you a book or magazine. They might question why you work for a German and French publication."

"What do I tell them?"

"It's reciprocal, and you're trying to build up better relationships." He patted her arm. "Peter will be there, and we have other people who can move you out quickly."

He leaned back in the chair and was looking up to the heavens, as if talking to God. "I can't tell you how many priests and journalists have disappeared, never to be heard from again. Probably working in the mines, most likely in Russia, if not dead." Then he turned to Katarina to be sure she understood. "The Stazi and Soviets are as evil as any Nazi. They spy on the population through a vast network of citizens turned informants. Sadly, they are building momentum and terrifying the dissidents to the point of breaking them down psychologically not to speak out again."

They both turned at the same time, suddenly aware that Wilhelm had been standing nearby, apparently eavesdropping.

"Just looking for Herr Jona's dogs," he explained and turned back toward the stables.

"Do you think he heard anything, Anthony?" Katarina's eyes widened.

"I don't think so, but there is something very off about that young man."

They rose and followed Sarah, Alexandra, and Natalie into the kitchen.

"Look," Natalie said, holding out a stone for Katarina and Anthony to see.

"That is a very pretty stone, Natalie." Katarina held it up to the light like it was a precious jewel and then handed it back to her daughter.

Pastries were on the counter, and the girls were already cutting into them. Alexandra gave a full report. "Uncle Anthony, Cook is making all your favorites—*Baumkucher*, rich chocolate torte, *rote Grutz* with red berry compote, vanilla sauce, and tonight a pork roast."

"Ah, she knows the way to my heart, that woman does."

"So, Uncle Anthony"—Sarah turned—"when are we allowed to visit Paris?"

"When your mother thinks you are old enough to be wandering the beautiful streets of Paree." He blew her a kiss.

Sarah smirked. "I think I am quite ready. How about you, Alex?"

Alexandra looked down in disappointment. "I can't even stay here tonight, much less walk the streets of Paris," she huffed.

"Helena won't let her stay." Sarah rolled her eyes.

Alexandra took Natalie by the hand and led her out

of the kitchen without a word. Sarah followed.

Katarina looked at Anthony, her smile waning. "Helena won't let her stay because of me."

"I don't think you can blame her, Kat. I don't mean to be mean spirited, but since 1948 until now, almost seven years, you wrote her maybe two letters and sent her a few items of clothing."

"Anthony, I just felt it was better. I didn't want to confuse the matter. Alexandra seemed to be happy here, and she made it clear that she didn't want to come to the States."

"You didn't try very hard." Her brother's face saddened, as he spoke the truth.

"That's not fair!"

Perfect timing, Anthony thought, waving at Gertrude, who appeared at the back door.

"You're right, it wasn't," he said, hoping to keep Katarina's spirit up as everyone filed into the kitchen, ready to carry platters of food to the dining room.

But the words stung, as Katarina watched these happy people gathering together under one roof. Their lives seemed settled, almost ideal. She had wanted this kind of life before the war—a nice home, a ballet school, children, all under different circumstances. Her life now was nothing of what she had wished for. She felt like a stranger in the very home she grew up in. Conversations flowed between them, questions involving the girls about music, teen idols, and school. The adults talked about Lisa and Jona's gardens and Hans's business and the horses. They asked Anthony a dozen questions about Paris. Katarina sat in silence, looking over at Natalie, who sat between Gertrude and Katarina's mother, happy as a clam. She had never felt so isolated among the people she loved.

That night, with everyone tucked in bed, the house was quiet, and again all by herself, she wandered downstairs, badly in need of a glass of wine. Her nerves were gradually unraveling. She walked right past Hans, sitting in the corner of the living room in the dark. She turned on the lamp and was startled to hear his voice.

"You just missed Anthony." He held up his glass of brandy. "He went to bed, and I decided to stay here and have another brandy. Pour yourself one and join me."

She pulled her silk robe tight around her waist. "Don't mind if I do."

Hans, like the rest of the family, thought she was much too thin for a woman who ate as heartily as they had observed since she arrived. "I sit here often and just think, in the darkness, in case you're wondering."

"That does not sound very promising, when your wife and son are living in the guest house."

"I can't think over there. When Alexandra is here, the girls play cards with Ernst. Sometimes they stay up till dawn. They're like the three musketeers. Remember when we used to have that energy?"

"Yes, I do. I see Alexandra spends a great deal of time here. Does she ever ask questions about me or her father?"

"She has, but we don't know what to say, so we move the conversation elsewhere. She voiced her thoughts to Ernst, telling him that we won't share, and the deep dark secrets are bothering her. Ernst asked me about them, and I told him the same thing, we just don't talk about it."

She slowly drained the glass of brandy in one long

drink. She needed the courage to talk to Hans about these kinds of things.

"I hope she never asks me," she said sullenly. "I don't ever want her to know what he did."

"It won't come from us, that I can promise. I have to say to you, thank you for letting Gertrude spend so much time with Natalie. She has wanted a child for so long, especially a girl, and this means a great deal to her. I also have to say, I am also smitten with your darling child."

"It seems my child has that kind of charm for everyone."

Hans laughed. "Yes, she does seem to wrap everyone around her little finger. Reminds me of you at that age." He drained his glass and rose to get another. "Have you heard from Francis about letting you see your son? Francis sent our mother a letter on the subject."

Astounded by his comment, Katarina blurted, "Did he tell her of the circumstances?"

Hans saw the concerned look. "Do not worry. John will never hear it from us."

"Pour me a glass of wine while you're at it, please, Hans."

"Brandy and now wine?"

"I need it to sleep," she said resignedly, and now that her mother and Hans knew about her situation with Francis, she felt drained.

"Still having those nightmares?"

"All the time, and I never seem to find the answers, always crawling out of the darkness, it seems…the light never comes."

The clock chimed an hour past midnight. "I have to

be at work by six," he reported.

"How are the factories doing, Hans?"

"Well, we have no shortage of laborers, as long as the Russians and Ulbricht allow the workers to keep crossing over. If the time comes when they are not allowed to come and go, there are some, you can be sure, that we'll help stay here. I know Anthony is more concerned about his church than the factories, having to keep peace by becoming compliant. It's their only way to survive right now. I know it causes him a great deal of stress, since his church will soon be closed, and you know about his protecting the priests. Even though he has ownership in the factories, he doesn't ask about them."

Hans stood and stretched. "I think I'll just stay here in the main house and use my old room. Goodnight, dear. Sleep well."

Katarina found that odd, when he only had to walk across the lawn. She looked down at some paperwork he had left on the side table. It was a proposal to the German government. He was trying to establish a monument for the Resistance fighters of Berlin and elsewhere in Germany during the war. She thought how her mother used to call it "a time of silence," but there were always those working in silence. She thought of the Rosenkranz circle and their friend Manfred Bonhoeffer. Voices that were not silent.

Chapter 13

The weekend was upon them, and Anthony and Katarina had another pressing matter to take care of before they met Hans the following Monday at the safe house where they would execute their plans.

Helena and her husband had chosen this weekend to spend time with Anthony and Katarina, since they would be bringing Alexandra there for the weekend anyway. Lisa and Helena were discussing going to Paris, since the apartment was available, and after relentless begging, they would finally take the teenagers along. Gertrude decided to stay at the house with Natalie for a special one-on-one while everyone else went different directions.

Katarina and Anthony were standing out in the pasture, thinking about taking a short ride, when they spotted Alexandra on horseback trotting toward someone standing at the edge of the forest. They covered their eyes from the glaring sun to see who she was rushing over to. A chill ran down Katarina's spine when she saw it was a male, and most likely the same person she'd seen before.

The siblings looked at each other questioningly, and Hans appeared next to them. "I have noticed this, also, and I am concerned. Wilhelm has joined her several times to meet this stranger."

"Shouldn't we confront Alexandra?" Anthony

asked.

"Not yet. I'm trying to find out more information."

"I don't think I will wait, Hans. Let me see what I can learn."

"Anthony, do not spook her. There is something more to this, I'm certain."

Alexandra came into the stables. Her face registered surprise when she saw Anthony. She obviously had thought everyone was in the house.

Anthony took hold of the reins as she dismounted. "You are late for dinner, and you know how that upsets Lisa."

She stammered, unprepared with an answer. "Time just got away from me. Living in the city leaves me such little chance of riding."

"Alex, how many times have we told you not to ride alone? It's too dangerous."

She forced a smile and slid from the horse.

"I'm curious, Alex." He cornered her. "Who are you talking to out there? It's not the first time."

She looked anxious. "It's just a friend of Wilhelm's." Her expression turned fearful.

Anthony tried to sound casual. "Is this an old friend of his?"

"I'm not sure. He *is* older and has a car. Wilhelm says he is like a father to him."

"Alex, you should know Wilhelm has told Father and Mother that he has no friends and is all alone."

She didn't know how to respond to that, so she nervously unbuckled her helmet and tried to act casual, caressing the horse's mane. "You…you won't tell anyone about this, will you?"

"No, I'm not planning on that. But maybe you

should talk to your mother about it."

The response was sudden, and it was said with sarcasm. "Which mother, Uncle Anthony, my real mother who gave me up, or her mother who gave her up?" She turned and walked away.

Max appeared to take the horse. "Father, it is none of my business, but every time she comes back from meeting this friend of Wilhelm's she seems angry and sometimes in tears. I just thought you should know."

"Thank you, Max, we will get to the bottom of this. Just keep this to yourself. You haven't said anything to anyone, have you?"

"No Father, just you, but I do think Wilhelm has another agenda. Remember that man I told you he sees in the village?"

"Yes, what about him?"

"He has the evilest eyes, the kind I saw in Auschwitz."

"Describe him to me," Anthony nearly ordered.

"He is an older man, light brown hair, smaller than Wilhelm, maybe five-feet-eight, a birthmark between his chin and neck."

Anthony froze. His voice now held an urgency to it. "Tell no one, Max. I will tell Hans. I am grateful for your information."

Max looked long at Anthony, who was in a hurry to go see Hans but had still taken the time to kiss the horse's nose. He had grown to love this family and their home—Jona especially, as he was teaching him to become a farrier. Max was proud to have shared with Anthony his concerns, but the horse's snort warned him of someone nearby. He turned, and right behind him stood Wilhelm, who had crept in without a sound. The look on his face told Max that another uncontrolled outburst was about to happen. He acted casual, but his knees felt weak.

Wilhelm clenched his hands. “What did you say to the priest?”

“We talked about horses as we always do. I have much to learn.”

“I heard you telling Herr Von Rahmel that you have registered with the Jewish Community on Oranienburger Strasse. More and more Jews are coming out of hiding, even now. I hear they’re also looking for living relatives.”

Max knew this was a stab because his family had all been murdered. “I have to go back to work.”

“Well, are we not the lucky ones to work for a family that hated Hitler and fought against their own country.”

Max knew only to walk away as Wilhelm kept spewing his ugly words of hate. He was now even more certain this man was more than just a refugee from Poland.

****

Anthony pulled Hans from the comfort of the sitting room. The children were working on a puzzle, and everyone was talking about the future of Germany and how they needed to make decisions about their homes in Paris and Italy, even though the olive production was in its best year.

Anthony was explaining what had happened with Alexandra when they saw Helena and Katarina in a heated discussion. They didn’t want the afternoon being spoiled, so they walked over to disrupt them and heard Katarina asking why she was sending Alexandra to boarding school.

The answer came back with a frosty edge. "It's the same one we have all gone to. Sarah is also there with her, and they come home on holidays."

"But why not send them to the one right here in Berlin? It's smaller and run by the same sisters. I would have chosen it for Natalie if I lived here."

"Who knows, Kat, Natalie still might end up here, the way you leave children behind."

When Katarina raised her hand to slap her, Anthony knew he had to defuse the situation.

He caught her fingers just in time. "You two get a grip!"

Gertrude looked up and saw the anger on both women's faces. She had no sympathy for Katarina and continued to draw Natalie's attention to the very large playhouse her father-in-law had brought down from the attic, filled with little figurines and tiny furniture, a girl's delight.

Katarina stormed upstairs and didn't show her face until the next morning.

****

By Monday the technicalities had been ironed out and the timing had been synchronized with their own informers who worked in the ministries. Hans and Katarina left very early that morning while everyone else slept in and proceeded to Kreuzberg and the safe house. When they arrived, everyone involved was there: Peter, Anthony, and Dietrich. They introduced her to Leonard, a shy, innocent-looking man. The atmosphere was different—no Gestapo lurking nearby, no one checking papers, no curfew. The mission was nothing like the ones they had encountered in the war, but still there were consequences if it did not go well.

Questions were answered and clarified to make sure everyone was on the same page. Katarina was prepared. She was to be a journalist working for the French newspaper *La Monde* (*The World*), which was revived after the liberation of France by the request of Charles de Gaulle. An outfit had been laid out for her—a dark blue Chanel suit with a simple white blouse, a small hat, and a brown wig with black-rimmed glasses.

"Is this going to fit?" she held up the skirt.

"The measurements were taken from one of your dresses," Anthony informed her with a wink.

"How embarrassing for you, Anthony. One might think you were having an affair." The ongoing joke between them never ceased to make Anthony blush. Of course, everyone laughed at his expense.

She left the men to try it on. She had brought a pearl necklace to wear and a pair of black low pumps with stockings. The suit fit perfectly, and she knew she looked sharp in it.

"Do I have to return the suit?" she asked, modeling it for her partners in crime.

"No, it's a gift to you," Anthony answered, pleased with his sister's look and her attitude.

Peter looked her over. "You know, you can still back out."

"And miss all the fun? I'm fine as long as you are part of it," she held his chin, offering him reassurance with her smile.

"All right, then, let's go to Kempinskis on Ku'damm and have you picked up there. If someone is watching, you have articles you have written for the magazine about the young Communist society in this briefcase."

Hans gave her one last look at some papers. "You will be meeting the head of state security, *Ministerium für Staatssicherheit*, MFS. As you know, the Stasi is the state security for the German Democratic Republic of East Germany." He paused to express his disgust. "Democratic, what a joke!" Everyone in the room nodded. "You will meet with Erich Mielke, former deputy to William Zaisser, first minister of state security. It's the most effective and repressive intelligence and secret police now, over there. The Stasi have their complex in Lichtenberg. Everything they do smells of KGB."

Anthony took her hands. "One more time, Katarina. You must understand, Erich Mielke was—or is, I should say—the Stasi's longest-serving chief. We do know you are not meeting with Markus Wolf."

"Do not talk to anyone, even if they take you to another building," Peter stated.

Dietrich interjected, "Every building has their own *Volkspolizei*, Vopo, and they tell on their own mother and father. You and Leonard will take a taxi from here, and Peter will act as your driver and pick you up at the café. You do remember what your discussion will be?"

"Yes, Peter, we will have a quick discussion on whether or not they allow freedom of the press, and we will keep the conversation light in order not to cause a conflict. In other words, lie right along with them."

"Whatever you do, don't come off as a hard-ass. You have to play them. They will check your notes before you leave. They're suspicious of everyone," Hans commented.

"I wouldn't come off as a hard-ass, just telling the

facts."

They taxied to a café, where she and Leonard sat casually at a table. They would appear to be simply two friends chatting over coffee. Eventually Peter pulled up, and he opened the door for them as they entered the car with the French flag waving from it. They slowly made their way into East Berlin, where the Vopos checked their papers at the Brandenburg Gate. Katarina took notice of her slightly shaking hands as the guard probed the car. She let her skirt rise, hoping to divert his attention. He stopped and took a long look and then passed them through the gate.

A memory flashed before her: 1947, and they were at this same place stealing papers. They almost got Hans killed.

They passed the Soviet Embassy and the famous Hotel Bristol, no longer in its glory, arriving on time at the press publication building, where Erich Mielke was there to greet them.

"*Fräulein* Dubois, I believe." He offered his hand with his greeting and led her from the car. "And Leonard Meile. Two representatives from two opposite publications, how exciting. We are honored that such a prestigious magazine would like to understand more about our own freedom of the press, which the West has lied so greatly about with the untruths of how we handle our own journalists."

Eyes turned and looked her way as Katarina walked through the building to his office. Even with the dark hair and glasses, she could not hide her beauty. The interview lasted a full grueling hour; a ludicrous pounding of the merits of Communism and the lies that accompany it. They moved on next to the School of

Journalism. When they were directed to ride in the car with Herr Klein, Katarina's throat tightened.

"Oh, but we have our own driver," she explained.

"Yes, yes, we shall see," he said, opening the door for her.

"We will afterwards have a visit with the Catholic priest, and my driver will need to take us." she said, trying not to sound nervous. Leonard did not say a word. She knew he was suddenly scared, as she was. Getting into that car might mean the end of them both.

The two military men spoke and made a call to the Ministries office. Their guide returned with instructions. "Your car may follow us. But tell him to drive closely behind, and he must stay with our car."

Upon arrival, they met with Herr Mueller, a fat-faced, burly man with a red complexion. His uniform was badly fitted, and too small for his rotund body. Katarina thought facetiously that he certainly didn't look like any of the East Germans who weren't getting enough to eat. The disgust must have shown on her face, for the officer remarked, "Mademoiselle, you do not look so well."

Before she could answer, he demanded to see the notes they had written. They handed over their notebooks.

"We do not wish to have falsehoods written in your notes. We will check again later." They were interrupted with coffee being served. Herr Mueller was grinning. "There is no poison in our coffee. Please have some."

Leonard was afraid to offend the man, so he accepted a cup as Herr Mueller went over their paperwork.

"Mademoiselle Dubois, we see that you began writing for your newspaper right after the war. Where was your hometown and birth?" He raised his full bushy eyebrows, so thick they covered his eyelids.

She politely smiled. "I came from Saumur, France. Unfortunately, we had to move often because of my parents' unpopular viewpoints about Lenin and Communism."

Mueller leaned across his desk, his large belly keeping him from leaning closer, and studied her face. "What are *your* feelings about Communism?"

"I have no thoughts one way or the other," she claimed, catching Leonard wiping his sweating hands on his pants.

"Mr. Leonard, and you?"

"As a writer I only care to write the truth, so in the future I hope I can teach in Sweden in our university."

Herr Mueller shook his head in acknowledgement. He scanned over some of the articles they supposedly had written. "Well, the two of you might not be aware of our true facts about communications, so we will go over and show you how we teach. Strange, I have not seen these articles before." For a man of his build, he moved more quickly than she expected, and when he stood, his chair nearly flipped over. Katarina almost dropped her coffee in her lap.

As they moved on, she became increasingly nervous. No one had yet to approach either one of them, nothing was handed to them, and it occurred to her that this was all a mistake and Peter had been misinformed. Moving from one building to another, Leonard whispered in her ear, "We could suddenly disappear in one of those buildings."

She frowned and whispered back, "You need to control yourself, or they will see the fear on your face." Herr Mueller was watching Katarina's every move. She deliberately dropped her bag as a diversion, and he bent down to pick it up. As he did, he allowed his hand to brush against her leg. What a pig, she thought.

"Mademoiselle, have you ever been in Germany before? There is something so familiar about you." He was struck by her brilliant eyes and dark hair against her pale skin, and his flirting unnerved her.

"No, this is my first visit to Germany, but I'm looking forward to learning so much on this trip." She turned to pretend interest in a painting on the wall, wishing at that moment she could scratch the itch underneath the wig. She felt her head sweating, and it was making her uncomfortable.

They walked slowly to the next building. She knew Peter was parked outside, watching every move as they crossed the street. She had no need to indicate to him that they were in distress, not yet. When they came out, a car came screeching to a stop, Peter right behind it. Herr Mueller ordered Leonard to sit up front and signaled for Katarina to sit in the back seat with him. Her heart was pounding so loudly she thought for certain he must hear it. He moved right beside her, so close the door handle poked her in the side. There was no more space left, and she imagined herself falling out the door—anything but being so close to this grotesque man! As if he'd read her mind, he casually reached across her chest and jiggled the handle to make sure the door was closed, leaving his arm lingering on her breasts. She held in the deep breath she would expel as slowly as possible, hoping it wouldn't reveal her nervousness. As if they were acquaintances, he chatted on about the goodness of Lenin, while he patted her knee and finally took the liberty to squeeze it.

Peter followed, with one of Herr Mueller's men occupying the seat next to him, looking straight ahead without a word, concentrating only on following the car.

They approached the journalist building. Mueller kept glancing at Katarina's face with a perplexed look, the question tugging at him of where he had seen her before.

They were received warmly by a small man who seemed to be excited about their visit. She thought for sure he was their contact. They were hopeful—until they caught a glimpse through a window of a man punching a woman in the face; the blinds quickly lowered as they passed. They pretended not to have noticed, but their fear returned. The small man turned away and led them down another hall. Two writers were on their way out of a room and nodded a welcome. Each casually handed a copy of the latest book written on the true story of Lenin to Katarina and Leonard.

They thanked Herr Mueller and expressed enthusiasm about reading the latest book. He informed them that he must go back to his office, and after shaking hands with Leonard, he kissed Katarina's hand, leaving a slimy residue for good measure.

After their notes were once again checked, they were allowed to return to their driver. They walked slowly to their car, not wanting to show an eagerness to leave. When they got in the back seat, the bodyguard, who had been sitting next to Peter all the while, reached over and snatched the books from their hands and shook them upside down, thumbing through the pages. Satisfied, he handed them back, slammed the front door, and stood watching them drive away. Katarina and Leonard were finally able to look at each other with relaxed certainty that they had in their possession what they had come for.

During the drive, they made random conversation, being sure to mention several times their appreciation for the books, still using caution with their words, even in their own car. Peter now knew where the information was written, and he wanted desperately out of the East; every second here put them in more jeopardy.

Saint Michael's Church was only a few blocks from their exit to the West. The once magnificent church dedicated to the Archangel Michael had been nearly destroyed by air raids, when nearly a thousand airplanes flew over the city, inflicting serious damage. Half of the church was now merely a carcass of what it was before the war, yet much of the front section had survived, along with the mosaic depicting the annunciation.

The paperwork for the priest was hidden in a sewn pocket between the automobile's seat cushions. Katarina pulled at the string to unravel the stitching and retrieve the envelope. She placed it inside the pocket of her jacket, and she and Leonard walked up to the church. She grasped the heavy door handle on the massive wooden door. The rustling of pigeons from above made them look up as the door creaked slowly open to darkness.

Father John came out of the shadows. His eyes shifted suspiciously from side to side. This priest was bald, with scaly skin, not the young priest of thirty with a full set of hair that Anthony had described. Katarina was hesitant to speak.

"So good to see you. I've been looking forward to your visit." His cold, sweaty hand took hers, and she immediately withdrew it.

"Why don't you both come with me to a small café down the street, where we can have a nice visit."

"I'm sorry, Father, there is no time," Leonard responded. "Our driver has strict orders to keep to a time frame."

"Then go tell your driver I would like to spend more time with you two." Leonard reluctantly left Katarina and went back to Peter to relay the message.

"Get back in there now!" Peter growled. "There is something wrong. Father John would never ask to visit a café!"

Leonard sprinted back into the church. His attention was diverted by a banging in the confessional booth. He opened the booth door and out stumbled a young priest, his mouth gagged, a stream of blood running from his ear. Leonard quickly removed the gag. Their eyes held on each other's when they heard Katarina squeal, confused about what direction the sound had come from. The next thing they heard was a booming voice as it yelled, "Stop!" Out of nowhere appeared Herr Mueller to their left and Katarina, to the right, being held in a tight grip by the man impersonating a priest.

"Mademoiselle, while in my office, a long-lost relative regretted he missed your visit. When I described you, he said you must have changed your hair color." Katarina tried with all her might not to show her pain nor her anxiety at his words. The priest, if he was that, twisted her arm tighter behind her back.

"You will need to come with us and answer a few questions." Mueller pulled out his weapon and pointed it at Leonard and Father John. "I'm disappointed in you, Father John. I thought we were getting along so well. I had hoped we could keep your precious faith moving the way you wanted." He motioned to the three of them to move toward the back of the church.

"I'm not going anywhere with you two assholes!" Katarina yelled, and with that, the sallow priest slapped her hard across the face. She dug her nails into the thin skin of his arm, and the blood poured from his easily torn flesh. She tried kicking him repeatedly, until he swept her off her feet. Mueller kept his gun aimed at Leonard and Father John. "Get her moving, you idiot," he growled through the spittle gathering around his fat lips, a fury in his eyes. Out of the rubble, a figure could be seen slowly moving toward them. She had seen him first as he slipped between the columns, empowering her to fight or flight. The phony priest turned to see the figure emerging out of the dust, working determinedly toward them. He dragged Katarina back into the shadows as Grigory stepped into view, holding a Luger now pointed at Mueller's head.

Mueller fell backward and threw his hands up wildly, his gun releasing a bullet that caught Leonard in the side. His eyes fixated on Grigory and Mueller, while the man holding Katarina was unaware that Peter had crept in behind him. In a panic, he locked his arm around Katarina's neck and tried to drag her farther away. His only hope now was to keep her hostage. When he looked behind him and saw Peter, it was too late—the stone came down on his head so forcefully, it cracked his skull. His grip on Katarina loosened, and she jerked from his hold as he fell to the floor, blood squirting from his mouth and his nose. Mueller suddenly came off the ground like a wild boar. Grigory grabbed him by the shoulders and pinned his body to the column. Mueller twisted violently under the pressure of Grigory's hands. They heard one final gasp from Mueller and then they saw the blood—Grigory had sliced his throat open. Katarina shrank back in horror.

Peter ran quickly over to Leonard and checked his wound. Grigory let Mueller's body drop, wiped the blood from his knife, and walked over to Katarina. He lifted her up and held her like a child. "This was not the way I was planning on greeting you, my dear." She could no longer contain the tears, and the sound of his voice pushed her into his arms. Father John said the last rites over the bodies.

"Grigory," Peter grunted, lifting Leonard's body, "Mueller must have a driver."

"He was taken care of. Go, now. I will handle this mess. As far as they know, Herr Mueller suddenly defected with his driver and this friend, whoever he is."

"Father John, you must also leave now. The less you see, the better."

Katarina grabbed Father John's hand and followed Peter. When she looked back at Grigory, he was scratching the stubble on his face, looking down at the carnage and considering how he would dispose of it.

Peter went back in to help Grigory pull the bodies to the side alley. He left Katarina and John in the car, wrapping Leonard's wound with the silk slip she had worn under her skirt.

When he was back in the driver's seat, Peter explained that Father John would stay with his church and hold on to the paperwork he would need to help Professor Stein when crossing over to the West. Katarina didn't want to leave Father John behind, as she watched him stand idly on the broken steps of the church. He appeared to be in prayer. When they pulled away, she looked up at the statue of Michael. The angel's eyes seemed to be watching over them.

Peter slowly followed three other cars at the crossing, each one of them being searched, trunks opened, underneath checked, no stone left unturned. When it was their turn, the guard looked in their car with a flashlight, as Peter handed him the papers that showed they were under French diplomatic protection. Katarina's hands were shaking as the guard asked what was wrong with the young man slumped over in the back seat, his head resting on her shoulder.

Peter laughed. "This little wimp could not handle your schnapps, especially on top of the vodka." Poor pale Leonard, his eyes slightly opened, managed to give the guard a thumbs-up, accompanied by a slow hangover groan.

The guard laughed and moved them through.

Katarina hung over the front seat to talk to Peter. "How in God's name did Grigory know where we were?"

"I'm not sure, but when it comes to this family, there is little he does not know."

"Surely one of you told him about this plan."

"Not this time. I knew he wouldn't want you in the middle. The man is not the same one you knew. He goes hunting, as he calls it, around the world, and works for his government now."

Leonard groaned in pain, and Katarina realized the bleeding was worse.

"Are we taking Leonard to the hospital?"

"No, we have a doctor on standby, or your father will stitch him up."

"He has a bullet in him. I don't think Father could do this."

They pulled into the street of the safe house. Hans carefully lifted Leonard out of the car. Peter immediately handed the books over to another man, one Katarina did not know, and he left with them.

Leonard was very much in pain as they laid him on the sofa. Anthony went out and looked down the street, wondering what was taking the doctor so long. Rain clouds were moving in.

Anthony and Hans were choking with questions, but they would have to wait. There was a knock on the door.

"Doctor, so glad to see you." The doctor raised his eyebrows at the silly formality.

"When are you all going to stop this? How many have I stitched up so far this year?" He threw his hands up in the air. "Just take me to the poor soul."

Peter gave Hans and Anthony a detailed account. Katarina was quiet until in a whisper she asked, "Does anyone have any idea what Mueller meant when he said a relative stopped by?"

"Yes, I heard him say it also. What relative?" Peter asked.

"Maybe it was a code for informer," Anthony answered.

"Well, someone told someone, and if I had money to bet, I would say it was our stable boy. We must find out now who Wilhelm is speaking with and why Alexandra is there with him."

Katarina looked down at her skirt. "I'm so sorry. I guess this very expensive suit is for the trash. The blood and tears make it impossible to wear, but I think I can still wear the jacket."

The men looked at each other and wanted to laugh, but held it in.

Chapter 14

Grigory stood across the street, waiting for Anthony and Katarina to emerge from the apartment. He watched Anthony put his arm around her shoulder in comfort as they walked to the car. His own heart felt like it had leapt from his chest. He had to see her.

They arrived home exhausted. They tried not to be seen or heard, removing their shoes to walk the stairs quietly.

"Katarina, Anthony," Dietrich's wife called from the library, "come here now, both of you."

They stood before Elvie, quietly waiting for her admonishment. "They roped you into this, and I told Dietrich specifically not to involve you." She scolded Anthony, "And you, you should have known better." Grabbing Katarina's hand, she winked at her as if she was secretly proud. "Come, Kat, let's get you upstairs into a nice hot bath."

Katarina's entire body ached, and she saw the bruises on her arms and wrists where the man had twisted them. Elvie helped her undress and told her she would dispose of the skirt. Katarina had forgotten she still had it on and had left her own clothes at the safe house.

Elvie disappeared for a while and returned with hot tea and a cheese sandwich. Katarina realized she was hungry, and that simple sensation felt good. "I could have gone downstairs," she lightly protested.

"It's best you remain here. The boys are around the table talking about what happened and what went wrong. Hans has the look of the devil in his eyes. He is so furious. A lot of anger smoldering in that kitchen. Kat, I also brought up the letter that was on the table from John. You can take your time reading it up here."

"Where is everyone? The house is so quiet."

"Lisa and Jona are at the opera, and Gertrude, Natalie, and Ernst are at a movie."

"It's late for a three-year-old to be at a movie."

"It's fine, Kat. Be glad she's not here right now. You need some time alone. I'll check on you later."

In the meantime, Anthony was trying to figure out who the relative was that Katarina had mentioned earlier. He went down the list and cancelled out all the possibilities except Wilhelm. They had, after all, caught him eavesdropping on them, among the other things that bothered them about his actions. Hans was so angry he banged on the table. "God forbid when we confront him!"

Anthony raised his hand for quiet. "Hans, we have to go gently with him. There is more to this. I can feel it." The description of the man Max had seen in the village was of a typical German type, but the birthmark was not. He wasn't about to mention to anyone who he thought the man might be. Katarina had been let down once before; it could not happen again.

"Well, I know Peter is not going to let it lie when we could have lost both books and Leonard."

Hans was now plotting, and he suggested, "We have to get Helena to agree to bring Alexandra out here again. This is the only way we can see who they are communicating with, because this stranger seems to know when Alexandra is here."

Hans snapped his fingers. "Wait, I've got it! Easy! We are having a going-away dinner as Mother always does for Anthony, and he would like for them to attend. She won't say no to Mother."

"Tomorrow when I check in on Leonard, I will talk with Peter." Anthony spoke through his yawn. "I am tired. I'm not going back to the church tonight. I will sleep in my old bedroom."

The three of them dispersed and would see each other in the morning.

While the men were in discussion, Katarina read John's letter and felt a pang of guilt. He wanted them back home and missed them, and he had taken on flying extra hours so he wouldn't feel so lonely. He wrote that Philip was back in school. He told her over and over how much he loved her, and the best part was that he was considering applying for a transfer to California, as she had asked. He hoped by the time she came back to Hawaii he would know more.

She folded up the letter and hoped for the transfer to be real. She had to get away from Hawaii and Francis. But tonight, she would revel in their victory, and try not to remember the scene in the church, except for the part when Grigory held her in his arms.

****

Lisa rang Helena on the phone and invited them for dinner, since Anthony was leaving and he wished to see Alexandra. Peter and Anthony made sure Wilhelm was aware they were coming this weekend and that it might be a while before she would come back to the house because of school.

Katarina decided she wanted to go to Ku'damm and do some shopping. She ordered the car around. As they were pulling out of the driveway, she reached down for her purse and looked up when someone knocked on the window. Her expression froze when she saw his face just inches from the glass, and she quickly rolled down the window. "What are you doing here?"

He unexpectedly opened the door and took her hand, "Come with me. My car is across the way."

She didn't hesitate and told the driver he was free for the evening.

Her legs were unsteady as he helped her into the Mercedes, and all she could do was look at him—the face that never left her memory. Grigory's face.

With her fingers, she lightly brushed the hair from his brow. "Where are we going?"

"The last time you left, I promised that when you returned, I would take you out to dinner."

"Oh, look at me! I'm dressed to do some serious shopping. This is not dinner attire."

He just turned and smiled at her. "I have to keep my eyes on the road, not on you, but we will eat and drink at Kempenski's, and there is a little new French café that just opened several blocks from there. He looked down at her long legs stretched out. He loved how they looked. She wore no stockings, which was unheard of by most women her age. Her shopping outfit included a black headband stitched with small pearls, and she smelled like lavender, as he always remembered.

"Katarina, I took a chance, I know. If you hadn't come out, I was ready to walk up to the house, regardless. After last night, I had to check and see if you were okay. Now, I see you are."

They drove in silence, and he found a parking space. He noticed men and women turning their heads as Katarina walked by with such fluidity and grace, her eyes straight forward until they reached the café.

Her eyes were bright as they sat in a corner away from anyone. He held her hand. She soaked him up, noting the changes were few, his hair still touching his collar, his shoulders broad, his face rugged, and she still got lost in his deep blue eyes. The leather jacket over a dark blue sweater and the American jeans with boots accentuated the fine figure of a man. Even through the sweater, when he removed his jacket, she could see the curve of his biceps.

"You have not changed," he said, caressing her arm, "and you are more beautiful than ever." He curled a strand of her hair around his finger and gently pulled her to his lips. It would have been a deeper and longer kiss if the waiter had not appeared. He brought her hand to his lips and kissed it.

"Where have you been?" she asked.

"I've been watching out for you since you came back."

"Were you watching out for me in the East or there chasing someone?"

He sighed. "The details I cannot tell, sweet woman, but I had to eliminate a soul by sending him back to hell. I knew you were at the journalist school, so I watched and waited. I was furious that your family would put you in the middle."

She sat back against the padded chair. "How did you know?"

"Peter, ha! I knew he was up to something. We

have worked too closely together for me not to get a read on him. I overheard him talking to Hans."

She lifted her finger and traced his face. "Anthony said you are now living in Israel."

He was relaxed and couldn't take his eyes off her. "What did he tell you?"

"Just that you were a hunter now. What do you hunt?"

"Ah, your righteous brother, trying to save my soul." His silence was loud and clear. He couldn't share with her that in 1947, as he immigrated to Israel, he had begun working with a new division. At that very moment, thinking of his duties made him instinctively feel for the Beretta in his coat pocket and the knife he knew was in his sock. He was always looking over his shoulder.

"Okay, then, let's talk about you saving Anthony in Hungary," she said, her eyes full of curiosity.

"Once again it was luck I was there, Katarina. I'm everywhere from Africa to South America. I'm not sure day to day where I will be. And now I am here…with you."

Champagne was opened at their table. "Listen, I'm sorry about your divorce. I admit I never liked the guy, but why didn't you just go home and not remarry so quickly?"

"I didn't want to come back here. I wanted a new start. It was just the timing—meeting John, getting pregnant with Natalie. I have too many demons to fight, and coming back here, they would just be constant." She shook her head. "Let's not talk about the past. Let's just enjoy each other today."

"Katarina, your face is forever imprinted in my

mind. I thought of you so often—you were in my dreams, I saw you around every corner, in every room, at every sunset. When I am with others, I still see your face."

She took his hands in hers. "I'm going to Paris. There is plenty of room for you, or you can sleep with Anthony in the Rectory and sneak out and come to me."

They both laughed at that childish thought.

He leaned forward again to inhale her skin. She welcomed his lips on her neck and pushed her hair to the side. He whispered, "I will be there."

She tingled from his touch, as his lips moved from her neck to her cheek. Once again, John was the furthest thing from her mind.

"I think the Champagne is having an effect on us," she cooed.

"You are the effect. It is not the drink."

Over dinner they spoke of life and where it might be leading, just small talk. When she asked how he felt about living in Israel, he replied, "There, I am home."

It was late when they walked back to the car. He couldn't make himself start the engine. The passion he felt was overwhelming. He needed to kiss her longer. He turned to her and rested his forehead on hers. Then he kissed her eyes, her cheeks, her lips, and tenderly took her mouth into his, searching for her tongue with his own. Katarina moaned when he caressed her thigh.

His mouth moved to her ear, and he whispered, "I wanted to kiss you that night I stayed and watched over you, so many years ago. I left aching for you." He kissed her hard now, and she responded with equal passion, and then she pulled away.

"I can't," she said.

He held her face in his hands. “I understand.”

“No, you don’t understand.” She grabbed his hands. “I wanted you back then and still do, but so much has happened to keep us apart. Why did the gods never smile on us?” He kissed the tears as they dropped on her cheeks.

“I denied women. I would not let them in my heart because of you. Katarina, you took part of my soul. Your absence in my life is killing me.” He put his head on her shoulder as she stroked his hair.

“I’m sorry, Grigory, I just don’t seem to give anyone all of me, not even John. I seem to have this innate way of hurting people that I love, and I don’t want you to be another one.”

“When you left, I couldn’t understand why you wouldn’t come back. I would have traded everything for you, but then I heard you remarried.” He rested his head against the seat and closed his eyes.

“Grigory, I don’t think I could have made you happy, I can’t even make myself happy. Just come to Paris. Let’s enjoy life a little.”

He drove her home, and words were lost for them. She left him with a simple kiss on the cheek. He watched her walk through her family’s estate gate, and once again she disappeared from his life. He knew he could slit the throat of anyone and feel nothing, but this woman tore open his heart. He could not walk away. He beat on the steering wheel. He had to make her see. This time she must stay.

Light was coming from her father’s study again. He was still trying to find the stockholders, or a horse that needed a home. She slipped silently upstairs to her room. She had no strength left for him or even to undress. Exhausted, she crawled on top of the down cover, and let out the deep sobs that came from within her.

****

The next morning, Anthony raised his eyebrows over the Bible that he was reading. He had been to church and was dressed in his priestly garb.

"Kat, I hope last night was worth it. I had to reassure Mother, when the driver came back, that you were fine. Thank goodness Grigory had contacted me to let me know he was going to try to connect with you."

"Anthony, no judgment, please. It was just two friends."

He coughed at her flippant remark. "I think not. He is more than a friend, and you know it as well as I do. The man is haunted by you."

"I was honest with him. Nothing happened—we both have our demons, we both had to claw our way out of the darkness. Look what he does now for a living, and look what I did just this week."

Anthony realized there was nothing more to say. "I went to my old church this morning and said Mass."

"How difficult was it for you?" She poured herself a cup of coffee.

"Except for seeing the cross where I buried the collie and her pups, it was fine. I can look at the past, but I can also let it go and move forward."

Katarina didn't digest the words he had just spoken; she owned the sins of the past and couldn't let go. "To think I was married in that church to the devil himself!"

He refused to give up on her, now and for as long as they lived. "I pray all the time for your mind to rest and be at peace. We have so many unspoken words in this house, all kept within, and no one wants to talk about anything. I just want to shake Mother and Father and tell them to scream, cry, something! They just say they don't want to talk about it."

"You can't blame them, Anthony. They lost two sons, murdered, not even killed in war."

"I think, in spite of what you feel, you have angels around you, Kat. They protected you, and I believe they still do."

She felt the dark curtain falling down over her thoughts again. "Yes, and the devil is always standing behind them, knocking to get in."

"But he didn't get in, did he?" A hug was needed, for himself and for her, and he bent over his sister and held her tight. He needed to rest. He was so tired; he had not been feeling well but would not tell anyone. He was leaving Katarina when the house phone rang. No one answered, so he picked it up on the fourth ring.

Katarina perked up when he said hello to Helena. She listened as she prepared a croissant with butter.

"Yes, Helena, I am so glad you are coming and bringing Alexandra, too. No, let her bring her riding clothes, she so loves to ride, and Sarah will want her to ride with her, as well."

He hung up and looked over at Katarina leaning against the counter, peering at him over the hot cup of coffee. "Anthony, you must be careful how you handle this. Alexandra could be in harm's way and not even know it."

"I'm quite aware of that. We will use the utmost care. And to think that after all Father has done for Wilhelm...he could have gotten all of you killed. If he is the one feeding someone information from the East about this family, we must find out this weekend."

"What do we do meanwhile?"

"We already set the trap, several days ago, when we deliberately left the French doors open to the sun room. Wilhelm saw Peter enter the house and Dietrich watched him creep up to the house and put his ear to the door. We also made sure he knew that Alexandra would have her last visit here for a while, which means whoever they are talking to will also know."

Katarina would spend the day with Natalie, as her mother and Gertrude had to go in to church for their weekly meeting and they didn't want to take Natalie. She went to Gertrude's place, where she and Francis had at one time decided they would start their new life. It was beautiful now, all fresh paint, clean windows—nothing like before. It gave her a glimpse of hope.

Natalie and she went into town, had ice cream, visited a small petting zoo and park, and spent the rest of the day at her parents' home, drawing and baking cookies. Natalie was a good girl, always happy, always ready to smile.

When Gertrude came back that night, she gathered Natalie in her arms and kissed her as if she had been gone for weeks. Katarina, felt a pang of sympathy for her, knowing she had wanted more children but had only one. She let Gertrude take Natalie back to their house. Natalie was happy to go along.

Chapter 15

Friday was upon them. Alexandra was thrilled to be back, glad that Helena had accepted the invitation. Alexandra called up the steps to Sarah, but there was no answer. She went into the library and found Anthony writing and reading his Bible. She ran to him and gave her favorite uncle a warm hug.

"I'm so upset that you are going back to Paris. Can't you ask anyone in power to transfer you back to Berlin? We miss you when you're not here."

"Sweet girl, who will show you around when you visit Paris? I know all the best places to shop and eat." His eyebrows lifted, knowing the way to a young girl's heart.

"Uncle Anthony, Sarah is not here, and she doesn't seem to be anywhere around. I was really hoping to ride, so I think I'll ask Wilhelm to ride with me today."

Anthony's ears perked up. "I think she is in the village with a young man who came to take her for ice cream."

Alexandra crossed her arms. "Really! She did not tell me a thing!"

"I'm sure she will. Now run along, and have a good ride," he said, knowing full well that, under the circumstances, he would rather have locked her in the closet. She gave him a quick kiss and practically ran to the stables.

Wilhelm was in plain view, waving to her. Anthony followed and watched from the window. They had a rapid discussion, and then Wilhelm put his hand on her back and hurried her into the stables. Before Anthony could reach them, they were off on horseback. Wilhelm saw Anthony and his back stiffened, and a worried look crossed his face. Pretending he didn't see him, he gave his horse a swift kick and took off, Alexandra right behind him.

Anthony ran out to the pasture waving and yelling for them to stop. He yelled even louder to make sure that Peter and Hans had heard him, the signal that the plan was in motion.

Alexandra heard him and turned her horse around. Wilhelm stayed a safe distance behind. Anthony, now a bit out of breath, composed himself. "Alex, I forgot to mention, please ride Capri a little slower today. Her front leg is still a bit sore from a little spill."

"Oh! Of course." She patted the horse's head. "I will be careful."

Wilhelm stole a quick glance at the edge of the forest. He turned the horse toward the pasture and said, "Let's go!"

Alexandra looked from Wilhelm to her uncle. "Be back in a while, Uncle Anthony," and she followed him.

From behind the tractor, Peter saw the black sedan enter the narrow stone road along the edge of the forest. Few people utilized that road other than the adjacent property owners and the hikers who parked along it. He watched the driver get out and open the door for a man in a long leather jacket, his hat tilted far enough forward to hide his face. He walked over to the fence as

Wilhelm approached him. Alexandra slipped off her horse and tied him to the tree. She immediately approached the man and gave him a hug over the fence. When Peter recognized the man, he waved frantically to Hans, who was hiding in the forest. Anthony saw and knew this was not a good sign.

Hans moved cautiously from tree to tree. When he was close enough, he saw what Peter had seen, and his heart quickened.

Wilhelm saw Peter first coming toward them, his gun now drawn. Wilhelm yelled out, "Colonel, quickly, back to your car!" The colonel gestured wildly for Alex to climb over the fence and come with him. He reached for her arm and she refused, pulling back from his grip and falling to the ground. Seeing Hans approaching from the woods, the man climbed back into the car and ducked. The driver pulled his gun and shot at Hans, who was now running toward them, before he turned the car around, backed up erratically in the small space, and took a second shot at Peter. As the bullet whizzed past his ear, Peter dropped to the ground and fired at will as the car screeched down the road.

Realizing the colonel had left him to defend himself, Wilhelm fell to the ground and pulled Alexandra with him. He placed a knife against her neck and held her tightly.

"Wilhelm, what are you doing?" Alexandra screamed. "I thought you were my friend!"

Wilhelm didn't know where to go or what to do, he was in such a panic, looking from left to right at Peter and Hans slowly closing in on him. As he pressed harder, the knife pierced Alexandra's skin, and a trickle of blood flowed down her neck. He had not realized

Anthony was behind him until he was hit hard on the side of his head with a tree branch. The blow knocked him back, and the knife flew from his hand. Alexandra broke from his grip and ran to Anthony.

Peter lifted Wilhelm's limp body from the ground and shook him violently. "Who the hell are you?"

Wilhelm, still conscious, raised his head and said with a sick smile, "We know about you, and the Communist Party will win West Berlin back, no matter how hard you try."

Peter threw him to the ground, and Hans grabbed the knife and stepped behind Wilhelm, barricading him in. Alex screamed at her uncles, "You all chased him away. He said you all were family, that he was going to come forward once I spoke with you. He is my uncle, like you are!"

Wilhelm laughed and looked up at Alexandra "You're a stupid girl. He wanted to take you over to the East as a bargaining chip."

"What are you talking about, Wilhelm?" she cried, tears running down her tormented face. She now saw a different man, not the one she had come to know. Evil had filled his eyes. She was confused and held on to Anthony. He walked her toward the house.

Peter made Wilhelm get to his feet and pushed him forward.

Helena and Lisa and the rest were in the stables, watching helplessly from the distance. When Helena gathered the sobbing girl in her arms, Alexandra jerked away and stood back from all of them, and the words flew rapidly from her mouth. "You spoiled everything! He wanted to visit. He had pictures of my father. He told me how you all lied about my father, that he was not to blame for how my mother was arrested, and he was being framed by this family. He was going to prove it to all of you. He wanted me to come visit him in East Berlin, to learn more about my father, his family, my family!" She was nearly in hysterics.

Katarina arrived just in time to hear it all. She took her by the arm and squeezed. "Who is this you were talking to? What is his name, Alexandra?"

Catching her breath, Alexandra glared at Katarina. "He was my father's brother. He said my father loved you and would never have done us harm. It was all lies, and you made it all up because you wanted a divorce. This family killed him!"

Helena's eyes closed, and her chin dropped to her chest. She had never taken Katarina's side, but this time she knew she must speak up. With a stern voice she ordered Katarina to let her talk, and she waved her aside. She stepped directly in front of Alexandra. "Look in my eyes, Alexandra. You must know the truth. *He* is the one who lied. This so-called father ordered Katarina shot, with you in her womb, and he had your uncle's wife thrown into Ravensbruck, a horrible concentration camp where your uncle and his wife died together. He ordered Anthony killed. He wanted us all dead, and so we fled to Switzerland. This man, his twin brother, is the one who is lying, and his intentions are not pure. He means this family harm."

Alexandra swallowed hard and looked over at Anthony. She knew Anthony would not lie. "Is this true, Uncle Anthony?" He nodded a solemn yes.

Peter was leading Wilhelm to the car, his hands tied. This young man was going to jail. Wilhelm yelled over his shoulder, "The colonel will find and kill all of you, when you least expect it!"

Helena and Katarina stood watching Alexandra, while Gertrude cleaned the cut on her neck and bandaged it. The young girl was still unsatisfied. "How do you know he wasn't trying to befriend us?"

Katarina snapped, "You're being ridiculous! He is as evil as his brother. Do you not get it? He wanted you and me dead. Did you not hear Wilhelm just now?"

Anthony reached for Katarina's hand. "Let's all stop this and go back in the house."

She pushed it away. She wasn't finished; she had much more to say. "I couldn't get down the steps, I was so pregnant with you. I saved your life when they tried to kill you in the camp. I took beatings so they wouldn't lay a hand on you. I prostituted myself to save you, and this is how you answer? You want this evil man in our life, his brother who wants me dead? He tried to kill me in 1947—ask Hans and Anthony. Ask them how he held a gun to my head and was going to shoot me, but Grigory saved me. You have no idea what you're asking for, NO IDEA!" She was screaming, the veins on her forehead were pronounced, and her hands were balled up in fists of rage.

Hans pulled her back, and her head dropped to his shoulder. She nearly choked on her sobs. "You must make her understand, please, you must all understand…"

There was silence throughout the stables. Even the horses were still. Anthony took Alexandra back to the house; her crying had stopped, and her head was bent with fatigue. The rest followed, except for Hans, who stood holding his sister as she wept. The ghost in her nightmares and in the shadows had come to life.

“Hans, he is out there, he is close, and he will strike again. I am forever haunted.” The tears were subsiding, but now her heart palpitations were escalating.

“Katarina, I promise nothing will ever happen to you. I promise.” He led her inside with that commitment.

Alexandra had gone upstairs. Sarah had just arrived, not knowing what had transpired, and she went upstairs to console and talk to Alexandra as only teenagers could do. Gertrude decided to leave the conversation and remove Natalie from the scene. She didn’t care for Katarina, but she loved Alexandra, and anyone who aimed to harm this family was despised by her. She also knew the story of Frederick Spitz and how he had caused the deaths of Edwin and his wife. She left with Natalie as Katarina entered with Hans.

The room was filled with a stirring whirlwind of emotions brought about by the pain caused by the surfacing of this man, twin brother of Frederick Spitz.

Helena looked at Anthony. “You do realize Alexandra will never be the same, and she will have nightmares like Katarina.”

“A small price to pay compared to what it would be like for her if we had not stepped in, Helena. Alex might have disappeared into the maze of East Germany, and God only knows where he could have sent her. He tried to take her today. Is that the reality you would rather have faced?”

She knew Anthony was right and gave in to his reasoning. “You are right, but it’s so upsetting that this is still happening. I will make sure Alexandra realizes that if anyone approaches her she must tell us. She will have to be put on guard. Poor child, and now she must go back to school with this horror in her head."

Katarina sat quietly in deep thought, and Helena's words did not affect her. No one would say his name out loud—Frederick Spitz, the man who did nothing when a guard kicked her in the side while she was eight months pregnant as she boarded the train to the concentration camp. The man who told the Nazi to riddle her with bullets. The memories were now appearing sharp and clear, no longer in fragments. Even now, with Hans's warm hands rubbing her tense shoulders, she could not relax, knowing the evil twin brother was out there.

Katarina awoke to the conversation when Helena, still unable to let go of her anger, addressed her. "Did you have to be so harsh with Alexandra? You know as well as all of us in this room there is no one to blame but you. Everyone told you not to marry him, but you married him anyway and dragged us all down with you."

Anthony cleared his throat. "That's not true, Helena. No one is to blame here. Let's get that straight now. He would have come after us regardless. There is much you do not know."

Katarina needed air. She didn't want to look at Helena. She went outside and sat in the garden under the large oak. Anthony walked out a few minutes later.

"Katarina, this will all go away, once everyone processes what happened."

"I have committed my share of sins, but Helena has no right to judge me, especially since she gave me to her own sister and let the secret stay hidden for years. I would never have known the truth if I had not found her letters. She can't throw the first stone."

"None of us can, Kat. We have to move on and make a new life, including you. You have to go back to the States. This is not a good place for you. Go home and be happy."

"Do you really think that's all it takes, brother? Don't you see it doesn't matter where I am, it's the same nightmares, the same fears, and now I know for certain Frederick's brother is still out there."

He sat next to her, wordless.

It was beginning to rain. Both stood and walked slowly back to the house. He kissed her cheek before she walked up the stairs.

Chapter 16

Paris

Katarina left a letter for her mother to mail. She didn't want John to see it had been sent from Paris. She told him it would not be much longer before she returned. While watching the world pass by, she re-read John's letters; three more had arrived that week.

Gertrude had been more than happy to keep Natalie, and Katarina was overjoyed to have left Berlin. She so loved Paris and was relieved that it had not been bombed. The apartment Anthony had prepared for their arrival was two blocks from the Champs-Elysées. She was excited to be in a place that she loved, to sit outside and have coffee, and to savor the delicious cheese and pastries.

Elvie had come along on the trip, determined to find out where her two brothers had disappeared to, living or dead. They decided after settling in they would meet at Café Tournon, two steps from Luxembourg Gardens. The café was famous as a favorite of the likes of Duke Ellington and James Baldwin. Elvie was home in her own country and she had tears in her eyes. With her dark hair framing her pure white complexion and full puckering lips, she fit in Paris much better than in Germany.

Katarina nearly danced up the steps after the cab

dropped them off. So excited, she almost jumped into Herbert's arms when he answered the door. He had stayed in the apartment in a little parlor room and bedroom set up for him and his wife. The family was blessed to have had the same loyalty here as they had in Italy. The apartment had eight rooms, with three baths, opulent for its day. It smelled of vanilla.

The women had traveled light, since they wanted to shop for new clothing, with so many boutiques to choose from. From the balcony in the living room they could hear Paris. They were shown to their rooms and unpacked quickly to change, as they had tickets to see the summer collection from Givenchy Couture. Katarina chose a suit from the house of Givenchy for the occasion; a deep black fabric, embroidered, with pearl buttons, the jacket tapered to her small waist and the skirt pleated. She would wear black flats, as they would be doing much walking.

She and Elvie settled into their seats. It was Givenchy who spotted her sitting in the front row, and he immediately invited her backstage, where he twirled her around, admiring how her long slender legs enhanced an original from his own collection. It was the thrill of a lifetime when he asked her to model some of the dresses. Elvie stood on the sidelines and beamed with pride. Katarina outshone every model there with her grace and beauty, and the applause overwhelmed her. It had been a long time since she'd been onstage, and she didn't want the show to end. They were given an open invitation to the next event. Katarina left with the dresses he'd asked her to model.

For three days they shopped, their shopping punctuated by meals in the best restaurants, and on the afternoon of the third day, Dietrich and Hans joined them. They met Anthony at Café Procope, 13 Rue de l'Ancienne Comedie, a street near the Seine, off Boulevard Saint Germain. The café had been there since 1686. Anthony brought along a fellow priest who had become a good friend. He was a young priest, about thirty years old. To their delight, Peter and Grigory walked in together. No one asked what function both men had with their secret service organizations. They would never tell anyway. Grigory did not hesitate to position himself next to Katarina. It annoyed Anthony, but they were adults, and he was tired of trying to convince Katarina not to see this man. They were like bees to honey, inseparable. And the truth was, Anthony was grateful to Grigory for all he had done to protect the family over the years. He prayed fervently for Grigory's soul.

They were finishing up a glorious lunch and planning to walk to another café when Elvie excused herself and went to work further on her task of trying to find her brothers, who had fought against the collaborationist Vichy Regime. They had gone underground to work with the French Resistance and were members of the Maquis. Living in remote areas, they were able to provide firsthand intelligence information and helped maintain escape networks for allied soldiers trapped behind enemy lines, as well as for Catholic priests, liberals, aristocrats, lawyers, and the media when the Nazis began rounding them up. The last she had heard from her brothers was during the invasion of Provence, known as the Atlantic Wall, when they reported that they were almost caught when a fellow classmate, a priest in the seminary with

Anthony, was identified as part of the sabotage on the electrical grid. The Germans caught the young priest and murdered him after he refused to give names of his accomplices.

Her brothers hated the Vichy, the French who collaborated with Germany and joined the Pro-Nazi *Milice Française,* and the French men who joined the Waffen SS. They were the ones who had betrayed Heinz, and they were a horror at Vassieux-en-Vercors, when in July 1944 Wehrmacht forces executed two hundred women and children as a punishing reprisal of the Maquis armed resistance. Their family friend, the writer Jean Cassou, would not accept the idea Hitler would win. And if he did, Elvie's brothers would fight to their death.

Peter had met many times with Heinz when he was with Special Operations Executive (SOE) in 1940. Elvie's brothers respected the Von Rahmel family, and they made sure she was sent to Berlin to be safe, knowing she would not be until the war ended. Safe all these years, she would not give up looking for them and headed to the ministry for any information that could lead her to their whereabouts.

Grigory and Katarina sat next to each other at the table with nothing to talk about. It was enough just being in each other's presence on such a beautiful day, at a sidewalk café in Paris. They had just ordered coffee and pastries, while Dietrich and Hans celebrated with wine. Father Damien, a guest at the table, had connected them with a winery that would help them restart their own in Munich, and the deal was struck, thanks to him.

Their orders had just arrived when Grigory felt

Katarina's nails dig into his thigh. The look on her face was one of panic. He followed her gaze across the sidewalk to a table where a man sat, his beady eyes peering over his glass of wine directly at Katarina. He was an ugly man, pock-faced and thin, with white eyelashes that outlined his evil eyes. Katarina had recognized him—the animal that had tortured her and the woman shackled to her, who had died by his hands. He had violated Katarina with the dead woman still cuffed to her body. The dark memory surfaced, and not even in her dreams did she remember this so vividly. She put her hands over her ears, and she tried to drown out the echoes of boots. Pale as a ghost, she whispered in such a broken voice they almost missed what she was trying to tell them. The tears were choking her.

Grigory and Peter did not need to hear any more. They rose at the same time and sat at the man's table. Dietrich stood behind him as he tried to stand, and with one quick shove, the man was back in his seat. Hans stayed close to Katarina.

"Who are you, and how dare you interrupt me here at my table!" His French was heavy with the sound of German ringing through it.

Grigory sat closer and held a gun to the man's ribs.

Father Damien came over to look at the man. He had been tortured as a young priest, when part of the French Resistance. Anthony rushed over and firmly put his hand on young Damien's shoulder. "Let them do their business, Damien. We need not be involved. They will take care of the situation as they see fit. It's not for you to impose justice."

Katarina stood up and walked over to Anthony with a resurgence of anger. "But for me, it is." She stood across from the man. "Do you remember me?"

He shook his head no, and while he muttered some objections, she interrupted him with a loud bang on the table and reminded him of the prison. He had been the colonel there. Once again he refused her accusations, pretending to know nothing of what she had to say. His alibi was that he had lived always in France, especially during the occupation.

"I remember you. Your face burns in my memory."

Anthony hastily paid the bill and urged Father Damien to go. "Father, let's go back to the church. I'm sure they will take him to the authorities."

Father Damien agreed, but before they left, he walked over and whispered in Peter's ear, "There is an abandoned flower shop a block away, just east of here."

Anthony and Father Damien left, and neither looked back at the family, who were now escorting the man away from the café.

They walked him to the flower shop, where Dietrich shimmied the door open. There was a coldness in the room that merged with their ferocity, and wind was blowing through the cracks of the door like spirits rising to speak. The blood had drained from the man's face as he was pushed down the stairs. He knew he was now trapped like an animal in a cage.

They bound him to a chair, and he still refused to admit to any wrongdoing, whimpering and slobbering his innocence. Grigory cut into his face with the tip of a knife; he would have preferred to kill him right on the spot, but questions needed to be answered.

Katarina caught up with them, panting heavily as she entered the shop. The scene was surreal, and she had hoped to find him dead. The devil was tied, and now was her chance. She flung her body at the man and tried to strangle him, yelling out all the horrible crimes he had committed in that prison with all those women. The wrath came from the depth of her soul, and she knew if she'd had the strength she would have broken his neck. Grigory grabbed her from behind and pulled her away. She jerked from his arms and lunged at the man again, this time toppling his chair, his body hitting the floor in a thud. She stood over him and turned to look at each man in the room individually. "One of you give me your gun, and I will kill this piece of filth myself."

"Who do you think you people are?" he screamed. "Do you really think the authorities are going to believe this crazy bitch?"

Hans wanted to kill him right then and there, but it was Grigory that kicked him hard in the head.

"Katarina, you need to leave. We will take care of this, trust us," Hans said, grabbing her by the arm. "Dietrich, take her out of here."

"Katarina," the man said groggily upon hearing her name. "Yes, the wife of Frederick Spitz."

Everyone in the room stood silent, staring at Katarina. "Kill him," she repeated and allowed herself to be led out by Dietrich.

****

A thin strip of light came from under Anthony's office door. Slowly opening it, Katarina and Dietrich found Father Damien hunched over the coffee table, a glass of wine in his hand, reading over parts of the Gospel. Anthony sat across from him, his hands folded together at his heart, his eyes closed in prayer.

The two newcomers entered the room, and both of

the men in collars looked their direction. Father Damien knew Katarina's tortured soul, as his own had spent many agonizing hours in the same hell. They both had seen the face of evil, and Father Damien also had confessed this to Anthony just minutes before their arrival. Katarina, in a state of shock, sat down in a chair and began rocking back and forth, her arms tightly wrapped around herself. Father Damien sat next to her and rocked with her in the rhythm of their kindred spirits.

Hans was the first to return to the rectory. Anthony stood up behind the desk. "Did you turn him over to the authorities?"

"No, Anthony, we needed to get more information from him regarding the others who settled in France. There is a nice little group of them, some high up in the military, some not. I left Peter and Grigory to make that call."

Anthony looked disturbed. "Tell me, please, you did not kill this man."

Father Damien was looking at Hans, anticipating his answer. Hans knew Father Damien did not care about this evil man's demise. The scars were deep on his body, never letting him forget his own torturers. He gave Hans the look of approval.

"Anthony, the police won't be able to identify him. That's all I'm going to confess."

Hans saw the frustration in Anthony and understood.

"Say your prayers, Anthony." Hans stood over him, clarifying their decision. "But they are wasted on him. He killed small children and women in his first prison. He laughed when he told us how the mothers murdered their own children so they would not be inflicted with torture. Pray for *their* souls, Anthony. Think of the lives they could have had. It should have been them sitting in the café enjoying the day, not the likes of him!"

Grigory had entered the room and stood rooted near the door. He kept his eyes on Katarina, her hair spread across her back, her lips trembling, as she leaned over, trying to collect herself. He turned to hear Anthony's next words.

Anthony was shaking his head. "You should have let God give him the judgment and let the authorities do their job."

"The authorities will have plenty to do rounding up the rest, trust me."

Katarina looked up at Anthony in puzzlement. "Anthony, you can't possibly think that man deserved a trial and jury. He deserved whatever fate gave him."

Hans reached for Katarina's hand. "Let me take you back to the apartment. We all need a good night's sleep."

Father Damien's face lifted. "Yes, I know I will sleep better now."

Anthony stood. "Father Damien, you need to confess. Those feelings do not belong here in church."

Hans looked straight at Anthony. "Anthony, you yourself have killed to save others, and you have found a way to live with it."

"Yes, I have lived with it, and I confessed to my God and asked for forgiveness. I will not escape his judgment."

Katarina now looked at her brother with sadness. "Anthony we will *all* be judged, and I, too, will sleep better knowing he is gone." She looked over at Father Damien and gave him a tearful smile.

She had thought she would sleep better, but it was Elvie who held her in her arms when she heard her screams that night. Katarina clung to her as she shivered, and kept telling her in a sleeplike state how dark it was, how cold. She kept mumbling, asking her to give the baby some clothing, until she fell back to sleep. Elvie left the room with a deep sadness and no answers. What horrors was she reliving, and why couldn't she talk to someone?

****

The next morning, the newspaper mentioned two bodies found dismembered in a brutal crime, parts of them floating in the Seine. They had yet to be identified. Also in the news was information that authorities, in a raid, had arrested a dozen Germans. These murderers had never left France after the war, settling in Paris as if they had not committed any crimes.

Katarina only smiled, handing the newspaper to Hans at the breakfast table. Hans acknowledged her smile; no words were needed. He left to see Anthony.

Elvie and Dietrich had left early to follow a lead on her brothers. Elvie wanted to stop first at the rectory and tell Anthony about her brothers and about Katarina's episode the night before. Grigory and Peter were there, and Grigory was looking at Anthony with patient amusement, but they had never seen Anthony so furious. It was clear he had been yelling at the men, his face reddened, his jaw clenched.

"You two have performed unimaginable violence in my church basement. I know you brought another criminal here and tortured him. Don't deny it—I saw the blood on the basement floor!"

Hans put up his hand, like a child with the answer to a teacher's question. "In all fairness, the basement is perfectly sealed for sound, and he had to see with his last breath the crosses on the wall. We couldn't question him in his apartment, which by the way is only a block down the street. You could have passed him every day, or he could even have been part of your church."

Anthony sat down at his desk and put his hands to his face. His voice was barely audible. "What was his crime?"

Grigory sat on the corner of Anthony's desk and leaned toward him. "He went into a Catholic orphanage and killed twenty nuns and nearly a hundred children, including newborns. He gave the order and then he watched. Is that a good enough reason, Father Anthony?"

Peter came around the desk and placed his hand on Anthony's shoulder. "I'm sorry, Anthony." He loved this man as if they were brothers instead of cousins. "Let me ease your mind. We did not kill him down there, I promise."

"Where is he now?" Anthony looked up at Peter. "Please tell me you didn't bury him here in the church cemetery."

"We couldn't do that. He didn't deserve to be buried. He was responsible for many atrocities, and in the end, he gave us many names to go after, both here and outside of France. They may be scattered, but I assure you we will find them."

Out of the corner of his eye, Grigory saw Katarina

had slipped unannounced into the room and was sitting quietly listening. She had seen Elvie in the church in prayer. Elvie did not want to hear the details of the men's conversation. Grigory couldn't help but notice Katarina's elegant attire—gray slacks and a dark blue sweater with silver-threaded butterflies woven into the fabric. He tried not to let out a deep sigh at seeing her there.

Anthony, however, did give a sigh, although for a different reason. "I guess your governments will think of you only as good agents."

Grigory stepped back, looked at Peter, and they both said in unison a resounding, "Yes!"

"Anthony, Israel will not stop until we find every man and woman who killed Jews and others. We will hunt them down all over the world, and they will pay with their lives if need be."

Father Anthony knew Grigory meant every word he spoke. "Well, I will pray for both of you every single day."

Peter had to add sarcasm, as family often does. "Anthony, if it gives you any comfort, we asked those men nicely several times. They were given the choice to talk or not."

Grigory hid his laughter, and Anthony waved them off, biting away a smile. "I have a class to teach on humanity; it's such a lovely time to teach the subject."

Outside on the street, they all said their goodbyes. Peter was going back to London, Grigory back to Israel. Katarina stood on the bottom step of the church, inhaling the sunny day. Grigory came to her and took her hand to walk. They walked in silence toward the park, where they sat on a bench. Katarina spoke first.

"So you are leaving. Will you come back?"

"I'm not sure how long I will be gone this time, Katarina." He loved saying her name, moving her hair from her face to see her brilliant eyes, as he now did. He drew her in and held her close and kissed her with a deep passion. There was no resistance on Katarina's part; she fell helplessly into the kiss.

"Katarina, let's go to Berlin, pick up Natalie, and go back to Israel together. My aunt and uncle have a lovely home by the sea; it's where I have been living. They are my only surviving relatives. They saw the writing on the wall and left Europe in thirty-three, returning to their roots as merchants. They have a thriving business."

There was a long interlude of silence as people and traffic zoomed all around them. With all his extensive life experience, she was the only one with whom he could not control his emotions.

She looked at his pensive face, and in her eyes he saw the answer was no. He turned his head. He had committed her face to memory, and this look he chose not to remember. She was the force behind his cause, the one who kept him from giving away his heart, the face he saw in every woman he had taken to bed, calling out her name too many times. She was his forbidden fruit. He once again buried his face in her hair and moved his lips to hers. His hand cupped her breast, and then he slowly let it drop. She could read his mind as he begged with his eyes; he wanted to take her some place and make love.

She tore from her own lust and returned to the subject at hand. "I can't, Grigory. My daughter needs her real father, and he is a good man. There is no drama in his life. He is all goodness. Trust me, he is nothing like Francis." She held his face in her hands. "Go home to your roots, my love."

He kissed her tears as they flowed down her cheeks. He would add the taste of them to his memories.

"How will I learn to let go of you, Katarina? I have pictured us together for too many years." There was benign resignation in her silence.

They embraced for a long time and then walked slowly back to the church. They held each other close, lost in the rhythm of their own heartbeats. He ran his hands down the length of her body one last time and savored their farewell kiss. With a soft stroke of her cheek, he turned and walked away.

Chapter 17

The next day Katarina was on the train back to Berlin; from there she would return to the States. She had promised John. Her mood was melancholy, and she cried often, looking around for Grigory, hoping he would show up at the last minute, but she knew he would not. Elvie thought she was crying because she would be leaving Berlin. Only Hans knew the real truth, as they said goodbye at the train station. He had reinforced her decision to go home and do the right thing for Natalie. Hans knew she had given up John's baby for adoption, and he encouraged her to tell John, who had the right to know. She said nothing. That awful truth would never be revealed as long as she was alive. It would be an unforgivable offense to him. Hans's final words stung her the most: "Grigory will be your biggest mistake, and it is time to let him go."

Two days later, they were at the Tempelhof Airport saying goodbye. Gertrude didn't want to let go of Natalie, who cried nonstop. There were no tears from Alexandra; she only wished Katarina well on her journey back. Once again Helena did not show up at the airport.

Looking down from the clouds at the Berlin she was leaving behind in the year 1955, Katarina did not know if she would ever return.

Chapter 18

Hawaii, 1955

In Hawaii, John was anxiously waiting for them on the tarmac, flowers in hand, as they deplaned the United Airlines aircraft. He took notice of how much paler and thinner Katarina had become, but in a month's time Natalie had blossomed. He held them both tight, smothering them with kisses. Natalie was thrilled to be back in her daddy's arms. She looked at John with the eyes of an old soul. "We missed your birthday, Daddy. Let's have a party with Philip." He looked at this precious child, who already had the capacity to think of others before anything else. He loved her sincerity.

"Philip is in school, sweet girl, but he will be back for Thanksgiving," He put his arm around Katarina's shoulder as they made their way to find their luggage.

"I have a surprise for you, Kat. My transfer has been accepted. It will probably take a year before we know where we will be stationed, but I pressed for California."

Katarina's face was beaming. "Thank you. I so hope it happens sooner."

Settling back into their home was easy for Natalie, but not so for Katarina. Even though the place was quite comfortable and pristine, as if John had never spent any time there, the first thing she did was pour herself a glass of wine. Natalie was heard screaming in delight from her room, finding all the familiar toys she had left behind. There was a brand-new one, wrapped in a large ribbon, sitting on the bed. She ran to find her parents to show them. She stopped and stood silently watching her mother pour the wine. Even at four she associated her mother's drinking with yelling at her and sometimes hitting her hard enough to leave bruises. She went back to her room and unwrapped the present by herself.

The transfer came sooner than expected, and they were moved to Moffett Field, California, near Sunnyvale. At first Katarina seemed to be a happier woman, and with Natalie in kindergarten, she had more time to herself, and they would frequently spend weekends in the mountains with Lydia. On those visits, Lydia also noticed the bruises on Natalie, and Katarina's excessive drinking. She heard her often screaming at Natalie when she thought no one was in earshot.

Lydia knew John's marriage was not picture perfect, and despite the geographical change, Katarina seemed to be always on the verge of tears or angry about something. She knew John had approached her about seeing a therapist for the nightmares that seemed to be on the increase. She was her happiest when she spent her days at an equestrian center and volunteered to teach dance for the high school plays. As long as she was kept busy, she was easier to live with, and Natalie was spared her anger.

Letters came consistently from Hans and Anthony. Gertrude would send cartoon books to Natalie to read and to keep up her reading ability in German and French. Katarina spoke all three languages with the child, impressing everyone when Natalie responded in those languages. Her brothers would write of the difficulties the East was causing for the refugees, and how they were constantly seeking housing for them. Father John had to leave his church and was now in Anthony's old church. It was becoming increasingly more dangerous for the clergy in the Communist part of Germany. The East's regime made no bones about everyone now following the Russian way.

Then the days of light came to darkness in May 1961.

Chapter 19

Hawaii, 1961

John had a layover in Oahu, and he and a group of pilots went to the Monkey Bar in Pearl Harbor. He had missed living on the Island, but he had seen in the past six years that California made Katarina much happier. He hoped in time they might be able to return. As he sat there pondering, while his buddies flirted with the ladies nearby, it was by sheer chance that he saw, in the far corner, Francis Lee with two men in business suits. A fire burned in his stomach just looking at the man who had taken his wife's son away from her and would not allow her to bring her daughter to the States. He hated the fact that this man had so much power and made his wife's life hell.

John ordered another drink and told the bartender he would be back for it. As he made his way toward Francis's table, the men were shaking hands and saying goodbye. Little did they know that the next few minutes would shatter the lives of those they loved.

"Well, John Malloy, how is your pretty daughter these days?" Francis asked the second his guests left the table. "I heard your wife spent a great deal of time in Berlin. And I heard that she met up with some old friends while there. In fact, a nemesis of mine, Grigory…maybe she never talked about him to you."

John was clenching his fists. The man wasted no time getting his digs in. That name, Grigory, had never been mentioned. Francis caught the momentary confusion in his eyes.

"You shouldn't worry, John. She came home to you. By the look on your face, it seems you really don't know your wife, do you?"

"You never knew her yourself. That's why she left you."

"I can tell you this." Francis took a casual swallow of his drink. "I do know I could not compete with her brothers or certain other men in her life."

"I don't care about her brothers. I'm completely aware of her closeness to them. I came over here to talk to you, man to man, about letting her see her son."

Francis looked at this young man and felt a tinge of sadness for him. He appeared sincere, something he himself had been at one time, long ago.

"Francis, it's not right you kept her son from her and wouldn't let her bring her daughter over."

Francis raised his eyebrows and took another sip of his beer. "Is that what she told you?"

"Well, yes. I don't see her son visiting her yet."

Francis contemplated his next words. Should he tell him? Should he tell him about her and Grigory? He had pictures of them in Paris, damaging pictures of them embraced in a passionate kiss. His men kept tabs on her always. He had also learned of Fredrick Spitz's twin brother still living in East Germany, a dangerous man, he was told. When his thoughts faded, John was still telling him how cruel he was and fighting for Katarina's rights.

Francis looked hard and long at him. It was not his

intention to hurt this man, this soldier, this family man, but he couldn't stop himself. "John, why don't you go back to California and ask your wife about your son?"

John looked confused. "My son is at school in Pennsylvania."

"No, the one she gave up for adoption on the same day she signed the divorce papers. You were not together for those months, so you would never have known."

John felt like someone had just hit him in the gut. "You're lying. You're so jealous that *I* have her now."

"Sadly, I am not. I have the paperwork she signed. It was a closed adoption. She did put you down as the father, but you won't find him."

John lost all color. "I don't believe you."

"Then go ask her. There is no reason for me to make this up." Yes, he was jealous. Yes, he was hurt. Why should John escape the truth that he had to live with? "Why do you think she wanted off this island? She lived in constant fear that I would tell you. While you're at it, go ask her about her friend Grigory. I can easily produce some pictures to show you exactly how friendly they are with one another. Don't worry, she didn't sleep with him, not like she did with you when she was married to me. Is it possible she now has scruples?"

He finished his drink and walked away from John, leaving him utterly stunned. This could not be true, he thought to himself, but why would Francis tell him this? In the background he could hear Roy Orbison singing "Running Scared."

He did not sleep that night, asking himself over and over the question that now ripped his soul. Did she give away his son? She wouldn't have done this. She had issues, yes, but this is something she could not have done. Only someone evil could do such a thing.

He was almost afraid to go home as he landed in California, not knowing what to say to her, how even to approach the subject. He feared the truth.

When he arrived, the house was dark and the car was gone. He guessed that Natalie was most likely with Katarina. He sat in the chair in the living room, pondering his next move. Someone knocked at the door. It was the neighbor who frequently babysat Natalie.

"I saw you come home. I can keep Natalie longer, or do you want her home now?" She herself had six children and one more in her house was no big deal, she would often say.

"Do you mind keeping her a little longer until I call you? I would deeply appreciate it."

The neighbor sensed John was not his usual self. The man was always happy and couldn't wait to see his children, the joys of his life. "John, why don't I just keep Natalie overnight and get her off to school tomorrow? She loves staying overnight."

"That would probably be good. I thank you so much."

The house was dark when Katarina entered. She stood still when she saw John sitting in the living room chair with no greeting, no hug, no smile.

"Glad you could make it home." His voice was flat and cold.

"Where is Natalie?" She knew if Natalie were here, she would be in his arms.

"She's staying next door overnight. Seems she's

there often."

She hesitated to step forward. She could see through the dimness of the light that he was angry, a rare look for a man of his gentle temperament.

He stood up and walked over to her. "I want only one answer." He grabbed her arm, his face just inches from hers. "Tell me yes or no—did you give up my son for adoption?"

She tried to remove his fingers from her arm, his nails digging in harder as she squirmed. "You don't understand. I was desperate. I wanted you, but I couldn't have you if I didn't have the divorce. It was a price to pay, to be with you!"

His anger was mounting. "We could have tried to find him. I would have understood what you did, but we could have had time to find him. They would have had to give him back."

"Please let go. You're hurting me." The plea was meant for someone else. She could no longer see his face. The blackness shrouded her thoughts, and it was the prison guard she now was pleading with. She screamed, "Let me go! I'm not going back to that cell!"

He let her go, and she ran to the corner of the room, sank to her knees, and shielded her body with her hands. He touched her shoulder, and she bleated as if in pain. The sobs came in heaving waves. John didn't know what to do, but he tried again to touch her. She pulled her arms around her head and whimpered in the voice of a child, "Please don't beat me."

He thought to call Lydia. She would know what to do.

When Lydia arrived, she was horrified at what she was witnessing. "My God, John, what's wrong with her?"

"I'm not sure. She seems to have slipped back to another time, her time in prison during the war, I believe. I can't reach her mind. She won't let me."

"Okay, okay, let's think this out. I know a doctor and a small hospital we can move her to. It's private. It's not uncommon for military wives to have nervous breakdowns. I'm sure they can help her. But I don't think anyone should know about this, including the Navy." John trusted this woman with all his heart and was willing to do whatever was necessary.

Lydia was able to approach Katarina and put her in her car. John ran next door to make the necessary arrangements for Natalie's care. The neighbor was eager to help.

The doctors believed she was reliving a tragic memory and kept her medicated for several days. A therapist was scheduled to talk to her when she had calmed down. John had to leave, and Lydia promised to keep tabs on the situation, but when she went to visit, the doctors explained that she needed time with only the therapist and sent her away. As she was leaving the hospital, she saw Francis Lee coming down the hall. She turned the other direction. She did not want the confrontation.

Katarina saw her former husband through a haze of medication, as he whispered he was sorry to have caused this. He didn't want this for her, and he hoped she had heard him. Francis walked out of the hospital that day less a man.

In her dreams, devastating events surfaced; some she was able to share with the doctor. She spent a month in his care and grew stronger by the day. Her anger returned in full force when she learned what had transpired while she was away. John planned to file for divorce and go for full custody, as well as trying to find his son. Lydia had offered her lawyer for the cause, and Katarina knew they had joined forces, as usual.

There were no words spoken when he finally took her home with the medication prescribed to help level her moods. She threw it in the trash, claiming it made her tired. John slept in the guest room and would look in on her as she lay confined to her bed. He would see her stir, sensing he was in the room, but she would not turn to look at him. Her face remained drawn on most days, and she muffled her grief in a pillow. Upon the doctor's recommendation, he would not discuss divorce again. He probably would never know about the man named Grigory that Francis had mentioned; he would have to keep that to himself also. Nothing could be more devastating than knowing he had a son somewhere out there. Natalie continued to stay with the neighbor and Lydia until John felt it was time for her to see her mother.

When John left for the naval station and Katarina knew he would be gone for several days, she waited until she heard the door lock click into place before she climbed out of bed. In the closet she opened a shoebox that held enough money for plane tickets and a diner's card for meals. The rest of her money was in a bank in Switzerland. She arranged a flight with Pan Am airlines, packed as much as she could, and went into town, where she sent a telegram to Hans that she would be arriving in Berlin the next day.

She took the time to write a long letter to John, explaining that she did not want a divorce, she wanted to work it out with him and would wait for his anger to pass. When that time came, she and Natalie would return. She would agree to regular counseling in the hopes for reconciliation. She apologized for what she had done and explained again that she only did it to be free of Francis so that she could be with him. The ultimate sacrifice, she called it.

She went next door and told the neighbor that she would be taking Natalie back to the house. The woman hesitated, but it was her child, and she had no business questioning. Natalie was difficult to deal with, that evening; her constant questions nearly unraveled Katarina until she finally squeezed her arm so hard the girl ran to her room and cried herself to sleep.

Early the next morning, she had a taxi take them to the Los Angeles airport, and soon they were on their way to Europe. She had spent the money for first class tickets, something that John would never have allowed. Natalie was sullen and apprehensive the entire trip.

The date was March eleventh. Spring would not have arrived yet in Berlin. Katarina shivered, thinking of the cold.

Chapter 20

Berlin

Katarina was thrilled to see that Hans was not the only one meeting her—Anthony was standing next to him. Their smiles were bright and unworried as she waved to them, compared to the frown on Natalie's face. She embraced her brothers while Natalie stood next to her with sadness. Hans and Katarina went to retrieve their luggage.

Anthony wiped away Natalie's tears. "Sweet Natalie, what is wrong?" he asked, now down on one knee.

"I want to see my daddy. Mother didn't leave food out for my kitty, Jinx. He's black and white."

He had taken out his handkerchief to let her blow her nose. "I'm sure your Daddy will take care of the kitty."

"Well, I'm sure he will, but I miss my kitty and my horse. He will wonder why I'm not there to give him carrots. Mr. Blake is what we call him."

He pushed the damp curls back from her face. "Sweetheart, we have horses here, too, remember. I will send your daddy a telegram to remind him to take care of them and tell him you are worried, and I will also find you a special kitty here."

With that thought, she gave him a little smile.

"Come sit with me over there while we wait, Natalie." He led her to a bench.

She now noticed for the first time he was in black, with his white collar and cross. She took the cross in her hand. "Our priest is dressed just like you at our church."

"You visit a church?"

"Oh, yes, my father makes sure I go to Catholic church and school. If my Daddy isn't home, my neighbor takes me. Mother does not go to church." She giggled, as if she were telling a secret. "And our priests are very, very old, not like you. My daddy says they are as old as God himself." Anthony laughed with her. Her happy demeanor changed when Katarina and Hans approached with the luggage.

Katarina practically threw Natalie's coat at her. "Here, put this on. Don't you know it's cold outside?"

Anthony took the coat and helped his niece. When he pushed up the sleeve of her dress, there was a large black-and-blue bruise wrapped around her forearm. Natalie pulled the sleeve down and would not look at his face.

"How did you get the bruise, Natalie?"

Fear entered her eyes. "I fell," she answered, looking straight at her mother in defiance.

He was desperate to ask Katarina what really happened but would not do so in front of the child.

They arrived at the house, which looked even more beautiful than on her last visit. It was freshly painted, the stables had been extended, and there seemed to be more horses in the pasture. Her parents and Gertrude came rushing down the steps toward the car. Dietrich and Elvie were in France. Elvie had found her lost brothers; separated for years, they were finally reunited.

Gertrude instantly went to Natalie first and gathered the child up in her arms, smothering her in kisses, openly admiring her beauty and how much she had grown. Natalie was too young to recall her time there in 1955, and she was overwhelmed with so much affection, something she had only experienced with her Aunt Lydia and her father. Her mother rarely kissed her, and when she did it was only on the forehead. The transition was difficult for her, but she liked Gertrude immediately, and she felt comfortable asking again in one long breath, "When will I see my father, and who will ride Mr. Blake, and will my daddy forget to feed Jinx?"

They were all talking at once as they entered the house, Hans following with the luggage. Gertrude would suggest later for Natalie to come to their home, but until then she wanted to show her upstairs, explaining that her cousins Sarah and Alexandra were in boarding school but would be home for the weekend to visit with her. She showed her the room she'd be staying in, connected to Sarah's.

"I will let you settle in this nice room. Maybe take a little nap until lunch?" Gertrude urged.

Tears welled up in Natalie's eyes. "Aunt Gertrude, can you stay with me till I fall asleep?"

Gertrude's heart swelled. "Of course, Natalie. Let's prop up these pillows, and I'll lie down right here next to you."

They removed their shoes and climbed into the soft bed. Within minutes, Natalie, staring up at the ceiling said how she felt. "Aunt Gertrude, I want to go home."

"Natalie, it's just a little vacation, just like when

you were three years old and you came to visit us for a while and then you went back home. You will go home soon, I'm sure." Gertrude held her in her arms and was surprised at how quickly Natalie fell into a deep sleep.

As she lay there, Gertrude had her own thoughts of what was happening. She was certain this was not going to be a just a small vacation. Katarina had most likely caused a problem again. She knew the child needed to be enrolled in school, so she had taken the liberty of arranging it with the Sisters the minute she heard Katarina and the child were coming. She also knew that it would be only a matter of time before they would send Natalie to the boarding school in Munich. Even though the child could already speak three languages rather fluently, she would need time to adjust.

Downstairs, everyone was preparing lunch in the kitchen—smoked pork with sauerkraut, a simple white wine, and *Schlagsahne*, a whipped cream plopped on top of strudel. Hans couldn't stay, and he went back to work, while Anthony joined Katarina in the library, where she sat near the window, looking at the leaves just barely popping out for an early spring.

"Anthony, what are you doing here?" Katarina sat opposite her brother. "I can't tell you how thrilled I am to see you."

"I'm back and forth these days, still looking for informers. The Russians are up to no good, and we are now trying to find their nuclear threat and keep the Allied forces here. We fought too hard to be left to the Soviets and their Communist ways. So many refugees are coming in, and the Vopos arrest them by the dozens. Berlin seems to be the flashpoint of a good-and-evil scenario. We have had mysterious disappearances of three of our priests, but no one is talking." He shifted in his chair, realizing that he had gone straight to the dark side, when he should be telling her all the good that had happened.

"But on the lighter side, you must know, it's changed a great deal since you were here last. There are even more elegant shops, and hundreds of old cafés have come back to life—it's like your Fifth Avenue and Champs Elysées rolled into one. Those crossing over from the East to work are in amazement at the rebuilding and the food that is available, everything that the East is not providing. But we can talk another time, Kat. I have to leave for Kurfurstendamm for a meeting in a little while."

"Can little sister tag along?" She batted her eyelashes and gave him that irresistible look that had easily melted his heart when she was a child.

"Well, let's not insult Mother, but we can eat quickly and then leave, if you are sure you're not too tired. You could shop, while I attend a meeting concerning our peace movement. Khrushchev is threatening the United States again with thermonuclear conflict."

Before they left the house, Anthony had a phone conversation in the library. He seemed excited as he wrote down a name. George Kennan, one of the most perceptive American foreign policy thinkers, was going to talk with him.

Katarina ran up the stairs and changed into gray slacks and a cashmere sweater, with beige leather boots and gloves to match. She tied an emerald green sweater around her shoulders. Their mother was upset at first that they hastily ate and disappeared out the door, leaving Natalie to Lisa and Gertrude. "Things clearly have not changed," she said to herself.

In the car, Katarina took a moment to study her brother. Now in his late fifties, he had aged since the last time she was here, with more salt-and-pepper streaks in his hair. It reminded her of Grigory's hair, but his was much longer than Anthony's. The dark circles under his eyes were new, and she noticed his collar was looser around his neck, revealing a protruding Adam's apple she had never seen before.

"Katarina, do you mind if we stop at the factory first? I have to give Hans some information."

"I would love to see what has been done to the factory. I would actually like to see the new veterinary office that Father built, too. Maybe we can swing by later."

"Father doesn't have to work, but he felt compelled to do what he does best, take care of animals. I think it keeps him going in spite of Mother's objections. He does put in a lot of hours."

"Anthony..." She looked down at her hands, almost afraid to bring up the subject, but she knew sooner or later he would ask. "I did have a good marriage, up until he found out about his baby. I still want to work it out, but living there now, I don't have a chance. He needs to cool down and start thinking in terms of making this marriage work. Right now, all he wants is to divorce me and take custody of Natalie. I tried to get him to reconsider." She let out a long sigh. "I guess the only good that came out of this is that Francis no longer has anything on me now. That fear has lifted, but it's now replaced with another one."

Anthony looked briefly over at her. He wanted her

to see the seriousness in his eyes when he gave her his advice. "Kat, if you really want this to work out, I would suggest you stay away from Grigory if he shows up. The odds are he will. He has this uncanny ability to find you. I think maybe, after some time, you can figure it out with John, and maybe the two of you can look for the child." He patted her hand with affection, but in his heart, he knew she would not miss any opportunity to see the love of her life—Grigory.

She sucked in her breath and held back her thoughts. Looking for the boy she had given up was the last thing she was going to do. She had accepted the baby was gone, and Natalie was quite enough for her.

They arrived at the factory. It had been rebuilt, and almost everything inside had been replaced. They had lost the other two to the Soviets in East Berlin. Hans's office was large, with wide-open windows that viewed parts of the city. There were people all over, busily walking back and forth. She excused herself after a hug from Hans and took the liberty to look around. Down the hall she came upon a glass door that said Law Department. Through it she could see a woman bent over a desk, giving instructions to someone most likely a secretary. When the woman turned, what Katarina saw made her step back from the door, and her hands began to tremble. Her lips whispered, "Anna."

She was a striking brunette, with large blue eyes that appeared almost translucent. Slender, in a black suit and jacket accentuating her slim hips, about five-feet-five in heels, she had lovely legs one could not help noticing. She was nearly the exact image of Katarina's best friend Anna—Anna, who would have been Hans's wife if she hadn't been killed by the bombings. Hans still grieved for her, and so did Katarina. They had been friends since they were five years old; Anna was the only true friend she had ever had. Kat shuddered, recalling how she had dug her out of the rubble. This woman, in the same bright red lipstick that Anna had worn, now caught her staring and opened the door, smiling.

"May I help you?"

"No," she stammered, "I just, you, well, you just…"

The woman smiled. "My secretary can help you if you're lost."

"I'm not. My family owns this factory. My brothers are down the hall."

The woman held out her hand. "I'm Christina Martine. I just started today as a contract lawyer for your brother. I was actually just going to take these contracts to Herr Von Rahmel's secretary to give to him. I know where his office is, but I have yet to meet him."

"I'll walk with you, if you don't mind." Katarina couldn't take her eyes off the woman, a doppelganger if she ever saw one. She had to force back the tears.

Katarina stopped her just short of Hans's office door. "Miss Martine, would you mind waiting?"

The new attorney wanted to say something but held back. After all it was Katarina Von Rahmel about to barge into her brother's office. She stood in the hall.

Hans and Anthony were just finishing up their conversation when she took Hans's hand. "Come with me. I want you to meet someone. She's a lawyer here."

"I know all the lawyers, Kat."

"Not this one. She just started."

He let her pull him to the door, and he was even more puzzled when she shoved him through it.

The woman was standing in the hall talking to his secretary when Katarina pointed to her. He stood there motionless. No words came. The woman looked over and smiled at him. Katarina saw the look of astonishment on Hans's face, and the same now on Anthony's, as he stood staring at her from the threshold of the door.

Katarina opened the conversation. "Hans, this is Ms. Martine, your new contract lawyer."

He stepped forward to shake her hand. "Anna," slipped out of his mouth.

She took his hand and looked at him with confusion. "I'm sorry. My name is Christina."

He held her hand longer than necessary and was reluctant to let go. This thirty-year-old beauty was his Anna, the only woman he had ever loved. His brain felt on fire, and he was struck with a sudden desperate hunger for all he wanted to feel again and had sorely missed.

Anthony cleared his throat and broke the spell. Hans turned to him, still holding her hand. "Oh, yes, and Fräulein Martine, this is my brother, Anthony."

"It is lovely meeting you," he said, seeing his brother refusing to let go of her hand, "but Hans, we do need to complete our meeting."

Christina gently pried his hand from hers. "Yes, of course, I need to get back myself." She handed him the papers and headed back to her office. Anthony and Katarina watched Hans's face as he gazed at her walking down the hallway. She turned and smiled at him just before she went around the corner.

There was a look of hurt in his eyes when he turned back to his siblings. They knew what he was thinking, and the three of them embraced each other in a group hug. "Glad you are back for a while, little sister."

Anthony and Katarina drove in an awkward silence to Café Kranzler. Before they got out of the car, Katarina said, "She could have been Anna's twin."

"Yes, and from the way Hans looked at her, I think he needs to move her to another office, one not just down the hall from him."

She smirked. "So we are worried, are we?"

"I'm not worried about Hans. He is a grown man, but losing Anna nearly killed him. He has never loved anyone like he loved her. I have always felt bad for Gertrude. She married him knowing that, and she has never received the same love from him."

Katarina knew that Anthony, with his amazing ability to read people, was right on target with this one. She relished the chance to have a coffee and a slice of *Baumkuchen* and would wait in the café while he went to his meeting.

She knew before he even sat down, sliding quietly like a ghost into the booth with her, that he was nearby. After nearly six years, she could still sense him, and the intensity was the same. How much more handsome he had become—the depth of his eyes, the peppered hair flipping up on the back of his collar. The lines around his mouth looked deeper but accentuated his smile, and he still sat tall, his shoulders broad and strong.

"Grigory, it's foolish to ask, but how did you know I was back, and how in the hell did you find me this time?" She shook her head in wonderment.

"This time, Peter told me before you arrived that

you had sent the family a telegram and were returning to Berlin." He leaned so far in he could have touched her lips. "Are you staying?"

"I'm not sure, Grigory. I trust you implicitly, but I don't want to share right now what happened in the States." She had recognized her failure with John, her lack of honesty. She knew she loved John, but with Grigory sitting next to her, the emotions once again began to twist a knot in her stomach.

He leaned in again and moved from her face a strand of hair that had slipped from under her head band.

"Are you staying in Berlin, Grigory?" She had to know.

"No. But I could come back. Should I?" He rested his chin on his hand. He wanted her to stay forever. Tired of this fire in him for her, he didn't want to look for substitutes. She had to give him some mercy and stop strangling the life out of him.

She was silent.

"Katarina, I'll be back, but don't go back to the States anytime soon."

"I will be here, I think, this time for longer. Why, it's possible I will never go back."

Something bad must have happened, Grigory now thought, but he would wait until she was ready to talk. He had promised himself he was not going to sit in front of her home again, waiting for her. He wasn't going to stop when he thought he heard her name or smelled a perfume that reminded him of her. There were times he would stand in the rain, hold his face up to the sky, and pray for her face to wash from his mind. She was his distraction in the middle of dangerous assignments. He had hoped so many times for the feelings to be gone and dead. But here she was, blowing into his life again, like a storm. A storm he didn't have the sense to run from.

The waiter brought their order of two glasses of red wine. He leaned back in the booth and looked up at the ceiling, wishing he could press his mouth on hers. "I must be going now," he blurted. He raised the glass and drank it down in gulps. "I will be back. I just have a few loose ends to take care of."

Katarina caught his arm as he turned to leave. "It's so good to see you." Tears welled up in her eyes.

"Don't walk away this time, Katarina. If we part again, it will be forever. I can't have you in my life like this anymore. It's just too painful."

Forgetting all about Anthony, she sat there for a long time lost in thought. She knew wherever Grigory was going, when he turned up, it would not be pleasant for the other party. That she knew about him. Her thoughts turned to John, and she hoped he was coping with her absence. She was responsible for ripping his heart out and changing his life forever. She slightly laughed to herself, considering that Lydia would make sure he was cared for. She had stood by him all these years, and Katarina always felt she did not have her approval. Lydia only tolerated her because of John. Switching gears again, she wondered how Francis had known John was in Hawaii. A chill swelled at the base of her spine. Her life seemed to be one big game of espionage.

Chapter 21

Two weeks had gone by, and everyone had settled into a routine. Helena brought Alexandra over, but they were only frigidly polite. Once again, Gertrude took Natalie almost as her own. Katarina spent a great deal of time going on house calls with her father. He could never say no to his old clients and neighbors.

Everyone seemed to have their own life and schedules. She had yet to hear from Grigory, and the only word she had heard from John was that he was seeking a divorce and custody of Natalie. She refused to accept her fate and begged him to reconsider.

She had just taken out one of the horses to groom when Gertrude appeared in the stalls, her eyes red from crying.

"Gertrude, is Natalie okay?"

Tears spilled from Gertrude's eyes. She screamed at Katarina, her voice one of despair. "You have everything—your two brothers idolize you and never find any wrong in you, your parents adore you, and you continue to commit sin after sin, and yet they all still stand behind you. You have children you don't want, and the one thing I have, you try to take away from me! You are to blame for introducing Hans to this lawyer woman, and now he is in her clutches. You brought that whore into his life, but I guess one whore knows the other!" Gertrude's rage, her grief, her hate for Katarina bubbled up all at once to the surface. She slammed her hand across Katarina's face.

Katarina backed away. She could barely breathe, and her face was stinging.

"Hans tried his best to lie. I followed him, after weeks of his not coming home, telling me he was staying in town, and I saw him greet her as she came out of the building. He held her and kissed her in a way he used to do with me. It was you who encouraged them."

"Gertrude, stop! I promise I did not encourage them. I knew nothing about this." Katarina suddenly felt so sorry for Gertrude, pale and broken, now sitting on a bale of hay looking wretched.

"I will never give him a divorce! I know she looks like your Anna. I heard Anthony talking to your mother of the incredible likeness. My heart stopped at that moment, because every cell in my body told me he would see her and fall in love with her. She is not Anna!" The tears poured out, her shoulders heaving.

Recognizing the symptoms, Katarina feared Gertrude might go into convulsions. She sat next to her and pulled her into her arms. "Gertrude, I promise, I had nothing to do with this." Katarina for a moment was filled with sympathy and wanted Gertrude to believe her. Her sister-in-law's breathing finally slowed, and the crying turned into a whimper.

When they saw Hans standing at the stable doors, Gertrude stood up, straightened her dress, wiped her eyes on her sleeves, and glared at him.

"Gertrude, come into the house. Let's talk." Hans looked as if he had not slept for days. His shirt was wrinkled, his face unshaven, and he had a look in his eyes Katarina did not recognize.

Gertrude stared him down. "You will not be getting a divorce from me. I will take my son and I will own every business your family owns and leave you without a dime by the time I drag her through court, and the world will see what she is…a whore!"

His voice roared like a lion. "You will not threaten me! She is not what you call her. I *will* have a divorce, and you will not be left in the dust but provided for handsomely."

She looked from Katarina to Hans. "You have no clue what I'm capable of. I will get my revenge."

He stepped up to her and grabbed her by the arm. "You will stay away from Christina, and you will not blame Katarina. This was of my doing only."

Forced laughter burst from her. "Hans, I am not afraid of your power or money, and your parents will be on my side. They may accept your child, as they love their grandchildren, but I think your mistress will tire of spending holidays alone or when there are family functions, business trips, and things your family will expect you to do with us as a family. I think she will also tire of you, plus don't forget she is young and vibrant, and her head will turn. After all, what does she want with someone who is so much older than she is and getting older by the minute?"

She left the stables, her head held high as she had the last word. Hans just stood there wringing his hands, burning with indignation.

"What the hell, Hans?" Katarina demanded.

He sat down on the stool near the stall door. He ran his hand through his hair. "We went to Rome to finish a contract. I tried to just look at her as our lawyer only, but I would look at her and my heart would burst."

"Hans, she is not Anna. Gertrude is right on this." She pulled up a stool near him, prepared to hear him out.

"I know she is not Anna. My Anna was timid, sweet, shy, and Christina is tough as nails but with the gentleness of an angel. I went to Anthony for counseling, and I kept hearing from him the importance of marriage and that I had to stay away from her."

Katarina was shaking her head. "Well, that was not smart. Anthony is not going to tell you anything different. He is our brother, but church, Bible, and priesthood come first with him."

She smiled at him and patted his shoulder. "I am the worst person to give advice. I have so many sins under my belt that not even Hell will let me in. I'm going back into the house to see what havoc Gertrude might be causing."

Hans nodded, leaned his head against the stall door, and let out a loud sigh. To his surprise, a horse's head came though the opening, sniffed his hair, and retreated back inside. "Even the horses are mad at me," he grumbled.

Hans couldn't let Christina go, as he thought back to their first night together. They were on a business trip. He came to her hotel suite; there was something on a contract that needed adjustment. She was dressed in a simple violet silk blouse with black slacks, and she was barefoot, her blouse unbuttoned enough to reveal the top of her breasts. She offered him a glass of wine, explaining that, after a long day, she always had one before she dove into another stack of paperwork. She sat cross-legged on the floor as she went through the documents, her glasses slightly resting on the edge of her nose. It hurt him to look at her. His thirst for her caused his whole body to ache. When she rose and clinked his wine glass, with a perky, "All done!" he acted on his compulsion to kiss her. Their eyes locked, and she let him walk her backward to the sofa, gently kissing her neck as he sat her down. The wine glasses were placed on the end table, and then their mouths met. She tugged at his shirt, and he helped her lift it over his head, and with ease she crossed her leg over his to straddle him. The kissing continued—fast, aggressive, breathless. He moved her from his lap, took her hand, and led her to the bedroom. They made love with an intimacy of having known each other before. She felt every muscle her hands glided over. He kissed every inch of her body, bringing her to the culmination of passion. With his eyes closed, his mind heard Anna's sighs.

When they came back to Berlin, he immediately found them a penthouse to rent on Ku'damm. It started slowly, first two nights a week, then five, but weekends were spent at home with his son.

Hans rubbed his eyes in despair. Gertrude just had to absorb the situation and realize how horrible it would be for her to stay in a loveless marriage. It had to work out in the end. He rose and stretched his body. He saddled one of the horses and rode to rid himself of the cobwebs in his head, and then, without going back into the house, he drove to the penthouse.

Chapter 22

August

Peter and Grigory were in the room with a British Intelligence agent.

"Peter, do you think the information is correct from your sources in Russia?" Grigory asked.

"I'm positive. Khrushchev and Ulbricht are working on the final details. We know our men are correct—they tracked the Russians' preparatory work on security, and the military forces they will use to encircle Berlin."

The agent walked back and forth, rubbing his chin, then turned on his heel with a direct statement for Peter. "The Russians are playing games with the Americans, and this young President Kennedy does not want war. They have no idea how deceptive the Russians are and what they have planned for Europe. No idea." He continued pacing, this time with more intent.

Grigory cleared his throat. "Sir, I was told the Russians have a timetable they want met. Their plan is to stop all movement between East and West, to stop the flow of refugees. They are losing their best workers."

At hearing this, the agent stopped dead in his tracks. "Do they have a date?"

"I'm not sure, sir, but I plan to meet with some

informers in the East. They might have dates and information. I'll do what I can to get more."

Peter's mind was at work. "We know a border closure has been approved, and we are starting to see repositioning of troops with Soviet military. Norway spoke with Ulbricht, our source tells us, and if there is a closing, they would not help the East economically with products or food. Ulbricht's biggest worry is that there might be a blockage of goods. East Germans are already restless when they compare food and salary to the West. They rely on a quarter of their economic trade this way. We are still gathering information on the location of their nuclear weapons aimed at Europe. We need to get someone in there now."

The agent was nodding his head. "Peter, we can't wait any longer. We have to get the scientist Oberman out of there. We have been dragging our feet on this. He would know what they're up to, and I'm afraid soon the Russians will have him in Moscow. The more scientists we can move out of the East, the better off we are."

"Do we have informants in the West that we can rely on?" the agent asked.

Peter turned and faced the window. He wished at that moment Hans or Anthony were here. They had made the arrangement a week ago, and Katarina had agreed to it. Now was the time to discuss their part in all of this.

"We have, sir, Katarina Von Rahmel—or rather, now, Malloy—will meet with Novotny for dinner right at the border. It's a café-bar he frequents all the time, so it won't seem strange to anyone to have him there. We can pull her out easily, if necessary."

Grigory stood up, anger flushing his cheeks and his hands clenching. "You can't put her in that position. We all know he has tortured women, picked up prostitutes that have mysteriously disappeared. His lecherous behavior toward women is well known, and he is dangerous!"

Peter knew he had to calm him down. When it came to Katarina, he never saw clearly. "Look, Grigory, we have it all figured out. That is why we asked you here today. You and Anthony will be in the same room with her. You will be dressed as a priest, and obviously Anthony will come as himself. She will be watched at all times. Two priests having dinner…"

"How did you get him to even meet with her?"

"As I said, he is our informer, and he always has one condition, that the information be given to a woman. That's how it works. Sickening, I know."

"Well, that is obvious. There is no good outcome. It's not like Anthony will do anything to help. Do you really think he would kill to save her? I understand that this man keeps bodyguards around him." Grigory's frustration rose to another level.

Peter was now glaring at Grigory, while the agent rested his hand on Peter's shoulder. He said, "Peter, are you sure she can do this? I know you have worked with her and this family before, but it seems that Grigory, here, thinks otherwise."

Peter turned to Grigory. "Trust me. Anthony would kill to save his sister or anyone else that means something to him."

"What about his loyalty to his church? I'm sure they would not be on board with this." The agent's question was almost laughable to Peter. He had no idea of Anthony's past or what he was capable of.

Peter spoke calmly and carefully. "I'm sure they look the other way. He has done many things to save his churches. He's not only a priest but one who believes in democracy. Where Communism takes over, the church does not fare well. It was one thing to keep the Nazis out of the Vatican. Fighting the Soviets would be a different story, particularly with their total disrespect for anything that deals with faith."

Grigory sat back down with dejected resignation. "Peter, where is the café?"

"It sits half in the East and half in the West. It's where Checkpoint Charlie is. Anthony will have Vatican diplomatic papers with him, should their agents come in and demand to see them. It happens tomorrow night. If you had not made it back, we would have put Hans in your place. I, for one, am glad to have you there, and I suspect our female partner will be, too."

The agent got up to leave. "I will say only one thing, boys. Please don't let bullets fly, and no bar fights." He forced a chuckle. "We also heard from your prime minister's office, Grigory, and the Mossad says eventually they will need you back, but they want the scientist out. We agreed to share what information we receive on weapons being placed in the East as well as to get as many Jews as we can out of the East." His gaze landed on Grigory. "We all know you are the best assassin—" he looked back at Peter "—and the best in espionage, but for this assignment, please don't kill anyone if you can avoid it."

The agent shook their hands and wished them good luck. Just before he closed the door behind him, Grigory gave it one last shot. "Sir, I respect what you have to say, but I'm sure you have other women who can pull this off, ones who are professionals in this field. I would highly suggest you do not use her."

The agent shot Grigory a warning look, then shut the door.

Peter sighed with frustration. "Grigory, we do have women, but none are readily available, nor do they look like her, and frankly, no one can charm any man like she can. You know as well as anyone the power she can spin around a man within seconds. If I were you, I would try to cut your cord with her. She could possibly be your downfall as an agent."

Grigory's eyes went hard. "Remember one thing, Peter. December 13, 1949, our motto was Proverbs 24:6—'For by wise guidance, you can wage your war.' We will never let our nation fall. We will hunt those who intend to harm us; they will be eliminated, and everyone who killed our people and anyone who ever tries to take our homeland away from us will be hunted to the ends of the earth."

"I understand, Grigory, but I agree with the agent. You are the best in your field, but when it comes to Katarina, you lose your mind. I'm telling you, you need to let her go. Your Director Zvi Zamar wants you back once we have located all weapons and scientists we need to bring to the West. Something big is brewing."

Peter and Grigory made their way to a place on Ku'Damm to have a meal and go over all they had to do for tomorrow night.

Chapter 23

She wore a red silk dress with spaghetti straps and a black belt separating her curves, above and below. A thin silver scarf cascaded down her arms, leaving her shoulders bare. High heels, bare legs, and a pair of ruby-red earrings finished off the outfit, and she moved like a high-class call girl. She wanted Grigory to drool as she sauntered past him, pretending to study the menu. She nearly lost her composure and almost burst out laughing at seeing him in a priest's outfit. He and Anthony were sitting close enough to view the table where she'd be meeting the informant.

The Russian colonel was of middle age, bald, his nose quite red and swollen, with broken veins from too much drinking. His hands were small, with fat fingers, those of a gnome. Oddly enough, his eyes twinkled when he saw her, but the smile wiped away any pleasant traits the man had to offer. His drink was already down to one last swallow.

Katarina bent down to shake his hand, pressing closer to his face as she introduced herself, giving him a glimpse of her cleavage. He motioned for her to sit down next to him. She clenched her teeth as he ran his finger across her arm, placing the other arm around her waist. He ordered another vodka, as he gulped down the remains of the one in front of him, some of it missing his mouth and trickling down his chin.

Grigory was looking for any sign of panic on her face. He had heard how she'd lost it in the States when she was touched the wrong way. His eyes narrowed. "Are you sure she can handle this?"

Anthony whispered, "She's handling it better then you are right now. You need to calm down before someone notices."

Ignoring his remark, Grigory watched as the colonel's hand shifted from her waist to her thigh, moving her dress up higher.

Anthony pressed Grigory down as he started to rise out of his seat.

Katarina politely moved his hand away and teasingly whispered something in his ear, something that made the man laugh. She wagged her finger at him.

His lips moved to her neck, and it was his turn to whisper in her ear.

Grigory's eyes shifted as he suddenly noticed the person he hated more than any of his enemies. He cupped his hand over his mouth and said through clenched teeth, "Anthony, what the hell is Francis doing here?"

Anthony looked confused. "Francis? Francis Lee? Are you sure?"

"Yes, I know his face. I will always remember his face." They turned their attention back to Katarina.

Francis had slipped out of the restaurant. He had traveled to Berlin with the truthful intent of opening up a hotel. He could have picked anywhere in Germany, but he knew she was here. He wanted to talk to her, help her see that it was over with John and that she needed to come back to Hawaii. Maria knew she'd never truly had his love, and his son, Douglas, could be told the truth. He thought Katarina had no place to turn, that he'd be saving her, but seeing Grigory, the thorn in his side, he couldn't believe that once again this family involved her in yet another of their many dangerous undertakings. He had not expected to see her in the restaurant with the man. He knew this would not end well for them.

The colonel was offering her a cigarette. Katarina demurely declined. He took her hand and escorted her to the staircase leading to his private room, an arrangement he had with the owner of the café. Katarina could barely hide her apprehension, and Grigory and Anthony saw it in her face. They looked around to locate any surveillance, and they spotted two of his guards standing at each side of the stairwell. The colonel moved her up the stairs, his hand placed firmly on her back.

"Anthony, I can't handle those two guys right here without causing a scene. There are stairs in the back. I'll find out where they lead and make my way to the first floor."

Grigory casually left the restaurant, but once outside, he sprinted to the back alley and moved stealthily up the stairs. He made it to the hallway. There were only three rooms, but he heard the voices behind one of them. He put his ear to the door and heard the colonel speak, his voice loud and gruff. "Fräulein, the information you require is hidden deep in my pants, so you must reach for it. I expect while you're there you will show me your gratitude with that marvelous mouth."

Grigory was surprised to find the door unlocked. Katarina must have made sure of that. He entered the room easily and found her pinned against the wall, the colonel clumsily trying to unbuckle his belt while she held her arms up over her head. He placed his finger against his lips, shushing her to avoid detection.

The colonel was completely taken by surprise when the priest grabbed him from behind. Grigory couldn't use a gun for fear of the guards below. He simply gave the colonel a few blows to his kidneys, which instantly knocked the breath out of him and crumpled him to the floor. As large as the man was, he tried to fight back, kicking his legs in a vain attempt to knock Grigory off his feet. When he opened his mouth to scream, Katarina came from behind and bashed a lamp over his head.

They both stood over the still figure, and only a quick intake of breath could be heard.

Katarina's eyes were large with fear. "Please tell me I didn't kill him."

Grigory reached and felt for a pulse. "No, he is just unconscious."

Katarina pointed to his trousers. "He says the information is in his pants. *I'm* certainly not going for it."

"Well, I must say, this is awkward." Grigory groaned as he unbuckled the belt. He reached inside, fished around, and rolled his eyes in discomfort until his hand finally came out holding three rolled-up papers.

"Did you get them all?"

"Oh, please, I sure hope so." His sober expression returned. "Where is the lighter? I suspect there is something inside it."

She looked around and couldn't see it. "Check the

pocket in his jacket. I think that's where he put it."

Grigory searched and found the lighter. He opened the bottom of it, and sure enough, there was a roll of film.

"I wonder what he would have wanted me to do for the lighter?" Katarina winced.

"Well, we'll see that he doesn't bother any women again. Start down the steps and go find Anthony. I think this colonel needs a change in manhood."

She gasped. "Won't he bleed to death?"

"Just go, and I'll meet you out front. But first, tousle your hair and pull one strap down to your elbow. Here, I'll make it really authentic and smear your lipstick." He grabbed her around the waist and pulled her to him and kissed her with the passion of a mad lover. "Now go!"

Katarina swooned and felt as if she'd actually had a sexual experience, only it wasn't with that man on the floor. She walked slowly down the steps to where the two bodyguards were still standing. She winked at them when they looked her way, and then they turned their eyes to the top of the steps. Anthony was on his way to the front entry. They reached it together at the same time Grigory popped out from the alley. The three of them walked away down the street, looking for Peter, who was supposed to be waiting for them. Instead, a limo pulled up, the door flew open, and a voice ordered from the back seat, "Get in. Your ride has been stopped by Vopos for inspection. Peter is dealing with it."

When they saw it was Francis, they were reluctant to get in, but at that moment, the guards came running out of the café, looking in all directions, their hands on their hips and ready to draw their weapons. There was no questioning their next move.

In the car, they all remained silent until they reached the West. Anthony was the first to speak. "Please tell me you didn't kill him."

Katarina turned to face the window, not wanting to show Anthony any expression of what she knew.

Grigory answered with a straight face, "Upon the request of our agent friend, I would not kill the colonel. However, he will be speaking with a higher voice from now on."

Anthony directed his next question to Francis, who had been sitting quietly, staring at Katarina. "How and why, Francis?"

His eyes turned from Katarina. "I'm here on business. There is a perfect opportunity for hotels to be built. The Hilton seems to be doing really well here."

Katarina noticed the clenching of Grigory's hands. Katarina knew there was more to this conversation, and her anger was building as she looked at Francis. She wouldn't even be in Berlin if it had not been for this man's cruelty.

"We are grateful, Francis," Anthony said, "although I'm not sure what happened to Peter and why they would stop him." Anthony glanced over at Grigory, who was pulling at his priestly collar. "Grigory, you can take the collar off now. It doesn't fit your personality at all."

Francis asked, "Where is everyone being dropped off?"

Anthony gave the driver instructions to his church, where he would meet Peter and give him the paperwork.

When they arrived, Anthony and Grigory went

straight over to Peter, who leaned against the church wall, waiting for them. The Vopos had decided to go over every inch of his car, for no apparent reason, he told them. He assumed he was just unlucky. Francis held Katarina's arm in a silent plea to stay for a moment.

Grigory stuck his head back in the car. "Katarina, are you coming?"

Francis looked at him in earnest. "I have a few questions, if you don't mind."

Katarina nodded her head in agreement. "It's all right, Grigory. Just give us a few minutes."

He slammed the door shut so hard the car shook.

"What do you want, Francis? Haven't you done enough damage? What more can there possibly be to discuss?"

He had hoped getting back at her would make him feel better, but when he saw her in the hospital in California, he'd regretted telling John everything he knew. In the end, it had made him miserable. "Katarina, I have no words that will heal. The consequences have been a tragedy all the way around. I never wanted to see you in the hospital."

"So you did come visit. It was not my imagination."

"Yes, it was me, but you were so drugged, I didn't think you would recall. The repercussions from my inexcusable actions have been devastating to you and John, I know."

She leaned over and looked into his eyes. "It has caused serious damage for us, but did you think I was going to come crawling to you for help?"

He looked into those eyes he just couldn't reach. "I

did, and I still want you to. I have the only safe refuge for you, and if not now, eventually you will come back, and I will be there waiting, with our son."

She reached for the car handle. "A mother brought back from the dead? How convenient!"

He grabbed her hand. "Katarina, I know everything you do. I know everywhere you go. Just remember that."

"Don't look too close, Francis. You might not like what you see."

"Remember one thing. You are dealing with a man who is a killer. He might think he is doing it for his new country, but he doesn't give a damn about you or anyone. His life is the Israeli Secret Service."

She gave him one more look. "You are wrong. He will always have my back."

He added a final blow to her fear. "He hasn't done a very good job of finding Fredrick Spitz's brother. From what I've learned about that man, you have cause to fear him. He is out for revenge."

Her throat tightened, and a frightened voice shot from her mouth. "Do you know where he is?"

"Not yet, but I will find him."

He leaned over and opened the door for her, his hand touching hers. He wanted it to linger but pulled back. He thought how easy it was for her to work the colonel over, given the effect she had on men with her flirtatious smile and alluring eyes. She was superior in her role as the seductress, and he, like them all, had fallen for her tricks.

She stood outside on the street and watched the car slowly pull away before she turned to the three men sitting on the steps. "My goodness, what do we have here, the Three Stooges?"

Peter came over and put his arms around her. "You can be funny at the most awkward of times. Come into the church, and let's take a little look at what we have before I hand it over."

They left the church and knew after reading the papers that it was an ominous time for West Berlin. They would be fighting for the soul of freedom against the Russians and East German power. The Russians would not rest until all freedom was taken and under the same kind of rule as Hitler had wielded.

Grigory took Katarina's hand. "Let's leave them to talk."

Anthony was not happy watching them leave.

Peter tried to assuage his worries. "Anthony, you can't stop it. It is a long time coming."

"It doesn't matter, Peter. She is still a married woman. How do I keep forgiving her for the sins she continues to commit?"

"You forgive her because you and all of us owe her, and we love her, and we know she has demons that none of us have."

Katarina turned and looked back at the church, knowing her life would change as of tonight. She had brought along a change of clothing but stayed in the dress. She had no idea where he lived when he was in Berlin. But she did know there was no more room for talk.

They arrived at Charlottenburg, a small side street about four blocks from the castle. He took her bag and led her to the small apartment he currently rented. He moved toward the window and pulled down the shade.

"Katarina, I can take you home, or I can sleep on

the sofa."

Her look was one of passionate surrender, a calm before the storm. When she slipped out of her heels, he knew the answer. He crossed the room and gathered her in his arms. He knew every inch of her face, and kissing her now, he could see it still, even with closed eyes. He stopped and held her face in his hands. He wanted to remember this moment forever, the day he had conquered Katarina Von Rahmel, the love of his life. She smiled at him and slowly unbuttoned his shirt, the clerical clothing of a priest that made him now look vulnerable. He winced as she touched his shoulder. She saw the large bandage. She looked at him questioningly.

"It's fine. I'm not dead, and that is all that matters."

She ran her fingers over the scars on his chest. "They are a part of you," she whispered, and kissed them delicately. She acquiesced to his desire to explore with his hands every inch of her body, and stood back, allowing her dress to drop to the floor. He pulled her in close, as if he could meld them into one, and he carried her to bed. Her body was how he imagined it, her scent one he would never forget. Her hair held a hint of lavender as he ran his hands through the soft strands against the pillow. She caught her breath as his lips moved down her stomach, his kisses and his touch nothing like any she had ever experienced. So gently he feasted on her intimacy, lovingly preparing her for him. They moved in perfect rhythm, her body quivering with pleasure under his. She could feel his breath on her neck, the intensity of their lovemaking as if it were their first and last.

They lay there, both glistening under the sweat,

depleted and satisfied. She could not recall having a more powerful feeling of true love. She ran her fingers across his back.

"Katarina, I love you."

They slept soundly until the early morning light entered through the sides of the shade. He had slipped out of bed and stood watching her—her hair splayed across the pillow, her naked arms resting on her belly. He wanted desperately to make love to her again, but time would not allow it. Peter was waiting for him at the safe house. He was glad Anthony would not be there. He didn't know exactly what to say to the holy man who would condemn him for taking his sister. He knew now he had an even deeper need and passion for her.

She lifted herself out of bed and was pleased to see that the sheets were not drenched from her nightmares. Smelling coffee, she stretched her body in the fragments of sunlight seeping into the room, then stood at the doorway looking at him as he made a breakfast the best he could with the sparseness of the place.

He turned and looked at her, wrapped in the sheet. "Come sit, Katarina. Have some breakfast, and then I will drive you home." She sat at the little table, and he poured her coffee and lightly kissed her mouth, her lips so beautiful, so full, with a tinge of natural color, as well as her cheeks. Even now she was breathtaking.

The phone rang. It was to be used for emergencies only. Peter was on the other end. "You have to get downtown now, Grigory! We will meet you in one hour at Kempskies. Do not go to the safe house. I think we are being watched. We're in the process of moving it again."

Katarina had slipped back into the bedroom and changed into her daily attire.

"Grigory, just go. I will make it home," she said hurriedly.

"I can just drop you off."

"I'm a big girl. I know how to take the train. I will call from the village and have our driver pick me up."

Chapter 24

Peter was pacing pensively, waiting for everyone to arrive. Anthony had arrived early and in deep thought. He hoped Katarina would not be with Grigory—the man with two souls, one that loved Katarina past all reason and the other without compassion or feelings. He worried for their life together.

"Look, Anthony, this is not good for Germany. I can tell you, from what we have read, we should be thinking about getting anyone who is valuable out of East Berlin." The doorknob turned. Always on the alert, Peter picked up his Browning HP Mk 1 from the table. He handed Anthony the Sterling SMG.

"Shoot if they are not our friends. Do not hesitate. Our guys do not come in from the front and try the doorknob."

Peter stood behind the door. Anthony hid in the closet with the door partially closed, his senses heightened; an acidic taste of the morning coffee rose from his stomach to his nostrils. He did not want to kill anyone, and he hated to be put in this position. Terrible memories began surfacing, echoing in his mind, and he tried to keep them at a distance.

The door opened, and before Peter could respond there was gunfire, bullets shattering the hardwood floor as if the assailants were just aimlessly firing into the room hoping to hit someone or anything. He rolled his eyes at Anthony and thought to himself, Idiots! He came out from behind the door, aimed head-on at the two men coming through, and dropped them like flies. The back door swung open. From the closet, Anthony released a torrent of fire.

Peter drew away from his position to help Anthony with those entering from the back. He turned quickly to see two more men pausing at the front door. He fired, and they fell on top of the other two bodies. Anthony seemed pinned down. Then, behind the men entering the back gate, they saw Grigory and Hans, weapons aiming; they took the enemy down in a flurry of bullets.

Hans had been forced to the corner of the courtyard by two Russian operatives intent on reaching the back door. Trapped but unnoticed, he could hear shutters being slammed shut above him, and then a cold silence. He froze, hesitating to move forward. The courtyard looked empty of anyone else approaching, and then he saw it. An arm from one of the wounded men lying on the ground lifted in the air to toss a grenade into the house. A shot came from nowhere, and the man's arm was pierced with a bullet at the same time the grenade was thrown. Someone screamed, "NO!" The explosion caused Hans to bite his tongue so hard it bled. He closed his eyes and prayed that the cry was not from Peter. He did not know Anthony was also in the house.

The grenade managed to take out the Soviet operatives and cut short the life of the man who threw it. Grigory crossed the courtyard, followed by Hans, and as he entered the house, he looked down at the dead man he stepped over, the head severed from his neck. There were shell casings all over the floor. He saw the closed bedroom door and ran at it, kicked it open, and found Peter and Anthony, two men dead at their feet. Another on the floor, obviously not dead, went for his gun. Grigory fired direct shots into the man's head and sent blood splattering. No one spoke or acknowledged what had just taken place, but they each moved expeditiously to gather up their own weapons, as well as the maps and written material on the table that the operatives wanted back. In fact, British Intelligence had the originals, and these were only a copy.

The explosion of gunfire and of the grenade had warned the German police, and the men needed to move fast. With everything in a duffel bag, they walked in different directions and circled back to where they had left their vehicle. In seconds they sped away.

Peter was racing through the streets, Hans in the front seat. "Where are we going, Peter?"

He stared ahead, wild-eyed. "I'm not sure where the next safe house is."

Anthony was not looking well. Hans turned to express his sentiments. "I'm sorry, Anthony. I know this is not what you wanted." At that moment, Anthony had been thinking that those men had died for the stupid ideology of Stalin. He wanted to scream it out, but he left the words, bitter, in his mouth.

Hans ordered Peter to drive to the factory. "We will just have to have this meeting in the mechanics room. Machines are running, and no one will hear a word. Anthony, do you want us to drop you off at the church?"

Anthony shook his head no.

At the factory, Hans noticed Peter's limp. "Peter, there is blood dripping from your leg."

Peter pulled up his pant leg to reveal a large cut. "Bastard Russian, he got me with a knife. I'll wrap it when we get inside."

They were all exhausted as they entered the room, each taking a seat. Peter found the first-aid kit in the closet and ran alcohol over the cut. He was about to wrap it in an old rag when Anthony barked, "Peter, that rag is filthy!" Peter acknowledged his mistake and tore his pants leg and used it for a bandage, as if that would be a better choice. It was clear both Hans and Anthony were frazzled.

Under his breath, Peter asked, "Do any of you know how they found the safe house?" They all shook their head in ragged defeat.

Hans sighed. "I thought we had removed all informers, but it seems they just keep turning up like a bad rash."

Grigory handed Peter the duffel bag. "This, my friend, is what we almost died for. The Russians and Erick Mielke of the East German Secret Police have received the final instructions to start building a wall to keep the East separate from the West. Khrushchev is not afraid to challenge Kennedy, knowing full well that the GDR can cripple the East because of their economic powers. The East knows their best workers, intellectuals, scientists—all of them—are leaving. The shortage of these kinds of trades will weaken them."

Grigory read from the notes in the bag. "Walter Ulbricht has a code name for this wall, Operation Rose, and we are not sure when all this will happen, but we think around the thirteenth. Our underground people are listening to every conversation and phone call they can access. Ulbricht put Erich Honecker, Chief of Security, in charge of most of the operation. He is a loyalist, spent a lot of years in Hitler programs, only to follow the Communist line by the end of the war, and is a big believer in socialism and Lenin."

"We didn't know until today that they had bought a ninety-six-mile circumference of barbed wire. The bastard was smart enough to negotiate with West Germany, and even Great Britain, to pull away attention to this purchase. He even kept it under the radar from Western intelligence agents."

Anthony, still shaken from what he had done, once again using a weapon of death, was dwelling on Titus 2:14—"Who gave himself for us to redeem us from every lawless deed and to purify for himself a people for his own possession, zealous for good deeds." The curse of law, he thought to himself.

And then Romans 3:23-25 came to mind: "Whom God displayed publicly as a propitiation in his blood through faith. This was to demonstrate his righteousness, because in the forbearance of God he passed over the sins previously committed: for all have sinned and fall short of the glory of God, being justified as a gift by his grace through the redemption which is in Christ Jesus."

What was he thinking? He should have laid the weapon down, but then both he and Peter would have died. He knew how, in Hungary, the church and the priests were tortured as they surrendered to their beliefs and would not fight back.

Peter knew Anthony was upset, and Hans noted his silence.

Grigory studied the papers and the map. "I guess the reality here is they're going to build something through the center of Berlin. It looks as if they started this in July. If you recall, one of the informers told us they were working with precision, like the Nazis, using blueprints to divide the people. This sure looks like the concentration camps, doesn't it?"

Peter looked long and hard at the map. "I think our informer was correct about the activity of dozens of trucks moving hundreds of concrete uprights, and he saw several hundred police at the State Security compound in Hohenschönhausen." He turned and looked at Grigory. "Are you up to going out and doing some spying at the border near Potsdam?"

"Yes," Grigory answered without hesitation. Upon reflection, he added, "It looks like the Russian colonel I left unconscious at the restaurant was a wealth of information. I almost regret making him suffer."

Anthony looked tired. He told them he was going home to his parents. On his way out, he bent down to tell Grigory something he wanted no one else to hear. "I told my parents that Katarina stayed with me at the church overnight." Then he walked out, his spirit broken.

****

Katarina left Grigory's place with no intention of going straight home and made her way to the factory. She was not sure what she was going to tell her parents, and not quite ready to face them. She saw Anthony coming down the hall. He had been heading toward the washroom to clean off the blood splattered on his pants.

She ran to him. "Anthony, what happened?" She saw how haggard he looked, and then she saw the bloodstains.

"Wait for me, Kat. I'm going to the men's room

and will be right back, and you and I will go home together." He saw her eyes filled with worry, whether for him or for herself, it didn't matter. "Mother was upset, but I told her you were with me all night."

She opened her mouth to speak. He held up his hand. "Don't."

Leaning against the wall, Katarina saw Christina coming toward her, cool, cultured, and in control, giving instructions to her secretary. Her long brown hair was pulled back into a classic bun, and the striking gray suit and yellow blouse gave her an air of confidence. She smiled when she saw Katarina.

She took Katarina's hand and pulled her into the office and poured her a cup of coffee. Her desk was piled with stacks of folders. "I'm so pleased to see you."

"Christina, I'm so sorry Gertrude won't give him a divorce. But I'm sure in time she will. She'll grow tired of a cold bed."

Christina didn't know how to respond to that remark. Something deep inside told her that it was just a matter of time before Hans would decide he couldn't leave his family. And how odd was it that Katarina had chosen to go against Gertrude. The family dynamics weren't clear yet, but Christina sensed it was a good thing Katarina was an ally.

Hans took a double look as he passed Christina's office and saw Katarina sitting there. He was bringing Anthony a clean pair of slacks to wear home. He didn't want him to alarm their parents. He waved to the two of them, his eyes lighting up when he looked at Christina. It was obvious he was madly in love with her. He disappeared down the hall.

A few moments later, Anthony appeared in clean slacks, still looking worried. "Come, Kat, let's go home." He did not look at Christina. There were no kind words for the woman who was living in sin with his brother.

They arrived home, hoping no one would notice them entering the house. They both wanted peace and no confrontations. Gertrude was just coming out of the library. She saw the look from Anthony and decided to show kindness. "Katarina, we thought you might want to know Lisa and I placed Natalie in school yesterday. We couldn't wait till you got home. It's the boarding school here in Berlin. She'll stay there only two nights out of the week."

"You didn't ask my permission." Katarina stepped forward.

Anthony grabbed her arm. "I think you need to say thank you, Katarina. Mother and Gertrude would only do the best for the child."

Katarina thought better of a face-off with Gertrude. She knew she was outnumbered. "Thank you. I will check it out later." Gertrude pointed to the hall table. There was a telegram from John.

She moved away from the two of them and opened the telegram in private. *Bring Natalie home immediately. Want full custody. Saw a lawyer for divorce. Searching for my son.*

She tried to ignore the stab in her stomach just as their father walked through the door. Upon seeing all three of them in the entry, he chuckled. "Well, is this a greeting just for me?" He motioned to Anthony to follow him into the library, where he shut the door behind them.

"Don't tell your mother I'm taking off my boots in here." A boyish grin crossed his old face. "Anthony, I was at the zoo tending to a lion cub. There was a lot of talk about the East wanting to separate the two Berlins. The refugees from the East have stepped up. The new vet at the zoo managed to pull me to the side and said you were responsible for getting him out. Is this true, my son? I try to not ask you what all of you are doing."

Anthony slumped into a Queen Anne chair. "Father, we are just grateful for you helping the wounded when we can't get the doctor to help, but please don't concern yourself with these things. But I can tell you that we are trying to move people as quickly as possible. Those with skills want out, so we give them new identifications to start over. My contact in Paris is an expert in making false documents."

His father went over to the little bar set up with beverages and cigars. He poured them each a cognac. Anthony felt the warmth slide down his throat straight to his empty stomach. He leaned back in the chair and closed his eyes in the safety of the beautiful library, in his childhood home, and with his dear father at his side.

"Son, just be careful. The Soviets are training them, and those Germans who are following the Lenin teachings are former followers of Hitler. I know Katarina is somewhat involved, but don't tell your mother, ever."

Anthony rose, walked over to his father, and placed his hand gently on his shoulder. "Never worry, Father. I will always protect her, and if not me, Hans will." He said goodnight and left the room.

His father had noticed how fatigued his son looked. He sensed it was not only from physical exhaustion but from spiritual defeat. His son was being taxed beyond his faith. He prayed for him right at that moment.

Katarina filled the bath, climbed into the warm water, and closed her eyes. A quiver ran over her body as she thought of Grigory, his strong embrace, the passion, and above all, his compassionate lovemaking. His love and care for her could not be denied. She had the strong desire to be with him again, but she knew that would not be soon. Now, she was confronted with how to answer John's telegram. As for Natalie, she really didn't care that Gertrude and her mother had taken control over the child. It left her with the freedom she always so desperately needed.

Peter, who had stayed behind with Grigory at the factory, sat for a few minutes before leaving. "Grigory, I will come to your place. It still seems safe. At least no one has found it yet, though not exactly a safe place to take Katarina."

Grigory raised his eyebrows.

Peter moved on to a different subject. "I know you are seeking revenge on Marshal Zhukov, and I also know why—the brutality he inflicted on the Jews, and those he sent to the Soviet Union in 1945, encouraging the rape of the women and children. I know he is back, and you want him dead. We have to stand back on this one, Grigory. You're on your own this time."

"Peter." Grigory looked gravely at his partner. "I have been on my own most of the time, as you well know."

"We have a lead on Spitz's brother. Once we find out more, I will forward you the information, but until then we need to see what the Russians are doing. You know as well as I do that Koner was a ruthless commander who believes in no negotiation with the West. He wants to disrupt air and rail travel, and we know he is in Berlin talking to Reuters with Kellett-Long. I'll try to meet up with that correspondent and see what he has to say about their meeting. I will meet you back at your place tomorrow. I hope by then we will have a new safe house."

The next morning Anthony woke refreshed and restored. He prayed over his Bible for forgiveness for his actions. Before heading to church, he would try to speak with the minister Ernst Lemmer for West Germany. He knew periodically of important information regarding the East, and he hoped they would be able to exchange information.

The meeting proved to be fruitless. The minister refused to believe the East would soon be completely sealed off from the West. No one would listen to reason, and no actions were being taken. He was frustrated as he headed for the church, where he would find peace.

That night, with binoculars in hand, Peter and Grigory left for Potsdam, on the border of Berlin. They both were tired, with little sleep that day. Grigory, before meeting up with Peter, had tried to sleep, but Katarina's scent was still on the pillow, and he could not get her out of his mind. He asked himself if he could leave Israel for her, or would she come back with him. He wanted her to file for divorce. The sleep he much needed finally came, but only for a few minutes before it was interrupted by Peter's knock on the door. No rest for the wicked, he thought.

The night was clear, with a slight nip in the air. They were sitting behind a hill, waiting for an informer.

A rustle was heard from within the woods, and then a boy emerged, walking straight for them. He looked to be about fifteen years old. He did not realize a Vopo was following him. They saw the figure lurking behind him, and both Peter and Grigory ducked back down after starting to rise. They knew the Vopo would kill the boy, and they needed the information he carried. Within seconds, the Vopo had jumped the boy and pulled him down by the hair. With one punch, the boy was struck silent. Grigory was up and over the hill so quickly that the Vopo, now rolling the boy over to get to his backpack, did not see the crazed man coming for him. Grigory yelled for the dazed boy to run. The boy wriggled free as the Vopo turned to see Grigory just a few feet away.

The Vopo was stronger than he looked, and when he grabbed Grigory and threw him against the tree, Grigory was stunned. He shook it off, rose quickly, and like a bull, he butted the man so hard the crack of the man's ribs was heard. He jumped back just in time to avoid an uppercut to the chin. The Vopo backed off and leaned against the tree, trying desperately to catch his breath. Not giving up, he stood up, pulled a gun from his jacket, and swung it at Grigory's temple. Grigory felt as though he'd been hit with a hammer, and the blow left him momentarily dazed. But now he'd had just about enough. He hurled himself against the Vopo and knocked him to the ground. The gun flew several yards away. He turned the Vopo over onto his stomach, which made it even harder for the culprit to breathe, yet he still attempted to get loose and reached for a knife at his belt. The man was not going to give up, so Grigory took the Vopo's own knife and held his head back and was about to slice his throat from ear to ear, but at that moment, he looked up and saw Peter and the boy standing there watching. Instead, he turned the knife around and hit the man with the handle, knocking him out cold.

Peter gave Grigory an amused smile. He asked the boy if he wanted to go back or come with them. He chose to go with them, explaining that his parents were already being interrogated, and his father had instructed him that once he delivered the information to Peter, he was to remain in the West and not come back. They knew then how their meeting had been compromised. Grigory threw the knife on the ground next to the Vopo, and they moved quickly from the scene.

"Where do we take him?" Peter asked.

"To the Von Rahmels. They will give him employment and a place to live. Let's get back to my place and see what this folder contains."

On their drive out, the boy sat solemnly stoic, looking back at the place he was leaving. But the tears were unstoppable, not knowing what would happen to his parents. Peter saw, for the second time that evening, a kindness in Grigory as he put his arm around the boy's shoulder and comforted him. "It will be fine, I promise. You will like where we are taking you."

Back at Grigory's sparsely furnished apartment, they called Hans and explained what had happened, and the decision was made to move the boy immediately to the family estate. A driver was being sent over.

They had a beer and would wait until the boy had left before talking about their mission's results. The boy thanked them, still fighting back tears, and quickly threw his arms around Grigory's waist with more gratitude. Grigory thought of his own brother as he patted the boy and assured him that all would work out.

Peter and Grigory looked at each other with excited anticipation when they finally were alone to open the folder. It held pictures of Soviet tanks, T-34s and T-54s, located only forty kilometers away, aimed at Berlin. They were informed that thirty-five hundred soldiers of the Eighth Motorized Artillery Division were making their way to the demarcation line.

"What the hell, Grigory!" Peter snapped. "A hundred battle tanks and one hundred forty more!"

Grigory took the paper from Peter's hand. "Looks like they want a second ring of defense behind the border frontline. I wonder how many more soldiers. I think you need to have your people share this with the Americans and the French."

Chapter 25

August 13, 1961

At one a.m. a reporter from the Reuters News Agency spewed out that the East German version of the Soviet AKM assault rifle, the MPI-KM, was now in the possession of hundreds of German soldiers. The Brandenburg Gate, the main crossing point between the two halves of the city, was surrounded by East German police armed with submachine guns standing in the German Democratic Republic.

The British and the Americans knew they were deep into a cold war. Peter and MI6 were aware of the US Army Special Forces stationed in West Berlin since 1956, and now their own special forces were deep inside East Berlin. They had become one with the Germans in the East, but their orders were to cause havoc and disrupt Soviet advancement if they decided to cross into Germany. They had weapons planted all over the East and were supplied with the means to disrupt rail lines and factories. Few knew they existed, but Peter knew where he could contact them. He had met many of them when they were in Bavaria, and their weapon of choice was the Walther P38 (MPK). Special forces preferred the MPK because it could take so much abuse. Peter and Grigory both preferred the Welrod, chambered to fire either the .32 ACP or the 9mm.

Grigory kept close a stinger, a single shot .22 caliber. It was his favorite survival gun when needed, kept disguised in hair cream or toothpaste. It was lethal and accurate at close range.

Along with the Americans, they knew that with the wall being surrounded, they had entered into a whole different battle. At a certain point they would have to help their agents in the East with supplies as they would need to restock caches of guns, demolitions, and communication devices. They had already heard chatter in the East to assassinate the mayor of Berlin, Willy Brandt. The Communists wanted him dead. This would be a different war in the years to come, and they needed to be prepared, knowing they had to get certain individuals out before they were taken to the Soviet Union.

Peter was compelled to remind Grigory, "You must know the SIS and the CQB have told us it is not enough to put the opponent out of action. He can kill us another day, and you can be certain he will. We are now told to kill quickly, and be ready for the next. They remind us to be cool-headed and remorseless. You know the SMG and the pistol are our main weapons now. They can be used only by the trained CQB as a lethal weapon. But you"—he grabbed Grigory by the shoulder—"you are way ahead of all of us with the order of instantaneous killing. I understood WWII, but now it's a cold war against the Soviets, the enemy of all that is holy and righteous and democratic. We must prevail, my friend."

It was soon realized that Berlin would be called the "Outpost of Freedom" by the US, Britain, and France. Peter knew the French were in the northwest sector of the city, and the British controlled the central western section, while the Americans were positioned in the southwest sector.

The East Germans were now holding machine guns pointed at the West, and at two a.m. both refugees and those who normally crossed for work were now stopped. The West German people gathered together and threw rocks at the East Germans. The special forces knew what was happening, as well as the British underground forces, but John Dimmer dismissed the notion of the wall going up. The morning of August thirteenth, their lives changed when Peter showed proof that the Soviet army division was moving, and one hundred tanks were heading into Potsdam.

Finally, all three of the West's commandants met at Allied Headquarters in Dahlem, in the American Sector. Peter left Grigory to join the discussion.

On that same day, Katarina woke to her father knocking on the door. "Get ready and have breakfast. We are going over to the East. There is a young horse I want to bring back."

Neither Katarina nor her father realized this was the day their Berlin would be forever changed. The wall was being built, one block on top another, and they would soon learn that the people swimming in the river to cross were shot and all transportation was under siege.

Anthony was devising a plan to get Father Grün out of harm's way. His church was being divided. He was on his way over just before midnight to meet with him, but the moment Father Grün stepped foot out of the rectory, the tanks pulled up. Families were already being separated, some caught in the West who could not get back to their families in the East, and vice versa.

Grandchildren visiting grandparents on either side were unable to return to their homes. The special forces that were in the East were sabotaging the roads in order to prevent entry by the tanks, but to no avail. The Soviet tanks kept coming.

Katarina and her father were horrified as they watched the wall going up and weapons aimed at West and East Germans. Tears were falling from all those watching. They left in stupefied silence, realizing they were watching the end of their freedom as they knew it.

Two grueling days had passed, leaving everyone in a state of suspended despair. Hans appeared for breakfast, and they read the paper together. The US President Kennedy was doing nothing to stop the building; he felt a wall was better than a third world war. Lines were drawn, and people were being moved from those buildings on the line. Many tried to jump from windows to the West. The wall was twenty centimeters thick, the papers said. Khrushchev tested the young President, and he saw no interference from the US when he pushed forward. He informed the West that East Germany would have, on August 16th, a military maneuver including nuclear-tipped battlefield missiles.

Hans turned from the newspapers and informed his family that one of their rental homes in Potsdam was now in the control of the East, and two of their factories would not be reopened—they had been taken over by the Soviets.

A week had passed, and to add to the family's fears, they had not heard a word from Anthony. Dietrich was supposedly working with Hans in West Germany, but Katarina's gut told her otherwise.

Grigory had made no contact either, and she feared that he had been caught on the East side. Peter was nowhere to be found.

****

Natalie was in the garden on the swing as Katarina went outside on this Saturday. Gertrude had informed Katarina that a letter from John, specifically addressed to Natalie, had arrived and they had felt she needed to read it, leaving Katarina out of the decision. Natalie gave her mother a feeble smile. “Come, Natalie, come sit at the table with me.” Natalie reluctantly obeyed. Katarina noticed the child carried her head high and seemed to be maturing faster than most children her age.

“Natalie, your father wrote you. May I see the letter?”

Natalie sat at the edge of the bench, avoiding her mother’s eyes. “The letter is in my room.”

“What did it say?” Katarina asked.

“He told me he loved me and missed me, and that Philip asked for me, and he hoped I would be seeing them soon. He told me they spent the summer at Aunt Lydia’s, and my horse was with Aunt Lydia, as well as Kitty.” Her eyes were almost defiant as she chose to look at her mother then, blaming her for the reason she wasn’t home with her pets, her father, and Philip.

“Next time let me see the letter before you open it.”

Natalie cocked her head and crossed her arms. “Why? It was addressed to *me*, not *you*.”

“I don’t need you to talk back to me. I…” Katarina stopped when she heard her mother nearly upon them.

“Why should you read it first, Katarina?” Lisa spoke with authority. “It was her letter from her father.”

"Mother, stay out of it, please. Natalie should have known better."

Her mother told Natalie to leave so she and her daughter could talk. Her mother seldom called the shots. "Katarina, I gave her permission to read the letter. He is her father. I could not let you throw another one of his letters away. I found the last one in the trash."

Katarina sucked in her breath, preparing to protest or lie.

"Katarina, do not lie to me on this."

Hans walked up at just the right time, and a potential argument was defused. "Mother, do you know where Father is?" He sensed the tension between them and kissed them each on the cheek. His mother rose and went inside without another word, knowing full well that Hans knew where his father was, but he had fulfilled his purpose in the question.

Hans spent little time at the house, with unspoken words between him and his parents, while Gertrude said nothing. "Katarina, would you like to go with me? I'm seeing Anthony, who is helping Father John, who luckily managed to slip over before the wall closed. And I just heard that General Clay is going to start moving the military to Checkpoint Charlie with four M48 tanks and attachments with bulldozers. He saved our asses once before, during the airlift in 1948. Maybe he can do something again. I hope to see him, since he has kept in contact with our family. I understand the Vopos were shaking in their boots when they saw the American tanks, and now the M4 rifles are pointing at them."

Katarina agreed to go along, hoping Hans would

give her any news from Grigory or Peter. The two of them were knee deep in all of this. In the car, Hans told Katarina that Grigory had returned to Israel. She was furious. They had made love, he had made promises, and then he didn't even tell her he was leaving. Hans gave her a cryptic note from Grigory saying he would be back. He also gave her a phone message left at her parents' house asking her to meet Francis for dinner at the Hilton.

"Should I meet him for dinner, Hans?" She was shifting in the seat, finding it hard to get comfortable with all this news.

"I don't see why not. It's a good time, since I have to meet with some financial investors from Italy about our vineyards at the same hotel. First, we must stop and see Anthony and Father John." Hans took her silence as an affirmation and moved on to something that was bothering him. "Kat, have you noticed that Anthony does not look well? Maybe you can persuade him to see a doctor."

They were disappointed when they learned that Father John and Anthony were nowhere to be found. The last anyone knew, they had gone down to where the wall was up against Saint Michael's Church, which was literally halved in two by the wall's line. That would not stop either of them from going to the altar situated in the East's half.

Hans and Katarina left for the Hilton, and to her surprise, Francis was not there. Had she gotten the days mixed up? That would not be too surprising, since she had started drinking earlier in the day, sometimes right after breakfast. She was forgetting many things lately.

Chapter 26

November 30th

Katarina was alone in the stables, just finished grooming her horse and leading him back into his stall when she heard her name called softly. She turned toward the voice, expecting to find no one, as she often heard these voices. But there he was, wearing a shy smile and waiting to see how she would respond. Katarina broke into a run and flung her arms around his neck. They kissed each other's faces in pure joy.

She pulled back and scolded him. "Grigory, where have you been? Not a word from you but one lousy note saying you went back to Israel! It was so final, I thought you left me forever!"

"Ah, you know I would never leave you. I was living in daily agony, not knowing when I would see you again. I couldn't reach out to you—I was in South America. Now I have only three days here."

"Only three days?"

"I will be back around Christmas, and then you and I will take a trip to St. Moritz and have a little vacation together. He ran his fingers through her hair. "Come with me. The car is parked on the street. I still have the same place, and I'll bring you back tomorrow morning." He placed his lips on hers, and she breathed a sigh in his mouth.

She hurried into the house and left her mother a message saying she would be back. Up the stairs she ran like a young girl. No one would guess she was a woman in her late thirties. A quick change out of the riding habit, a small overnight bag stuffed with only the bare necessities, and she was down the stairs in a flash. She ran past Cook and grabbed a cookie from the tray she was carrying to the library. Today she would be happy, in spite of the hell around them.

They raced to his place. Standing in the tiny apartment's meager version of a living room, she felt a little shy, not like the first time they had made love here. He came to stand behind her and nibbled on her neck and ran his hands down her hips. The apprehension dissipated. She heard herself panting as he slowly moved both hands to her sides and slipped them under her blouse, gathering both breasts in his hands, kneading them gently as he pressed his groin against her buttocks. She had intentionally left her bra and panties in the overnight bag, anticipating a moment such as this. He sighed with pleasure and walked her slowly to the bedroom. His hands now placed on her hips, he turned her around and backed her onto the bed. They eagerly undressed each other and made love, a different kind of lovemaking, yet it always felt like it could be their last.

He held her closely afterward, and smelled the sweetness of her skin, folding her silky hair through his fingers and delicately kissing the hollow of her neck. These would be the memories that kept him alive.

She brought her lips next to his ear, and he felt the warm breath as it trailed down his neck. He turned and once again devoured her kisses. The night faded to morning. They had been lying side by side, exhausted from waking and making love throughout the night. As happy as she was, she wiped tears that slipped from the corners of her eyes. She didn't want to be confused by her emotions, so she playfully squeezed Grigory and asked him, "Are you as hungry as I am?"

"You assuaged my hunger, beautiful angel."

They went to breakfast after all. He didn't want to take her home, but he had to leave. She was quiet on the ride back until, just a few miles from her parents' home, she reached for Grigory's thigh and squeezed it hard. "Grigory, please come back to me. Don't leave me wondering this time." He couldn't promise her. It was his desire to return to her, but his circumstances were always unknown. He never knew if he would come out alive.

"Katarina, my sweet woman, I promise I will be back. Then we will have a vacation to discuss our plans for the future." She took in a deep breath but said nothing. She realized right then that she really just wanted him now and didn't want to talk of the future. The future never turned out as she planned.

They lingered in front of the entry gates, kissing and gazing upon one another. She knew he had to go and finally tore herself from his arms. He watched her disappear into the confines of her home. She would be safe there, but he knew he would constantly worry about her as long as Frederick Spitz's brother was still in Germany. He was ill at ease with that thought, and a sudden shiver took him by surprise. It was time to leave—he had pressing matters at hand.

She walked into the hallway, and out of the dining room appeared Christina.

"Christina, what are you doing here?" Katarina looked around the empty dining room, the breakfast dishes still not cleared from the table.

Christina put her fingers to her lips. "Shh." She pulled her inside the dining area.

"Your mother was in great agitation when I arrived. They had the note you left, but you never said where you had gone. I covered for you and told her you had stayed the night at my house, we went to dinner, and you stayed behind for some shopping."

"Christina, you do know that Gertrude lives just outside these doors, don't you?"

"Yes, I know, but your parents had to sign some papers, and Hans sent me over here. I was not thrilled about the prospect, trust me." Abruptly, Christina began babbling a different conversation. "I'm sorry I left you so early this morning. I just didn't want to wake you after our late night." Katarina felt the presence of someone behind her. She turned and was facing Gertrude and her mother.

With clenched teeth, Gertrude charged Katarina. "Did *you* bring her here?"

"No, I did not. She is here under Hans's instructions, for business."

Her mother was now ushering Christina into the library. "Come, Christina. Jona will be here in a minute. He just had to find some other files—maps and things." Her mother looked back at Gertrude and Katarina with a quizzical look on her face.

"Mother doesn't know, does she, Gertrude?" Katarina challenged her.

Gertrude turned sharply toward Katarina. "Of course not! She doesn't know because this will be over soon, and he will be back and there will be no divorce. You know as well as I that when I make arrangements for the four of us, your brother will not slight your parents for her, so I will make sure there are dinners to attend, theater, and time with his son on weekends. She will become bored with his having to leave her alone, and especially on weekends."

"Gertrude, I still want you to realize, I did not arrange their meeting, but as long as he lives, he will always love Anna and now Christina. I am sorry for all of this, but you must see he will not give her up."

"Told by one cheating woman for another!" She turned and walked away.

Katarina went to find her father. It would be good to be kept busy and work side by side with him. She had not seen him slip into the library, but when she looked in, he was in a deep discussion, poring over paperwork with her mother and Christina. It was best not to interrupt.

She felt lost for the first time in a while. She actually didn't know what to do with herself. Maybe it was time to visit her old ballet school and find something useful to keep her busy. She wouldn't mind helping to teach movements. She started up the stairs as her father came out of the library. He looked up and saw her on the steps.

"Pack a bag, Katarina. You and I are going to the estate in Italy, and then to Paris. I must see for myself why Hans is in such a hurry to sell our assets."

****

They drove swiftly through Italy, stopping only long enough to look over the vineyards and the olive trees. Everything was going as expected, and her father made his decision on the spot: it would not be sold. As they arrived at the train station, Katarina wished they could stay longer. It felt natural to be with her father, staying close by his side and discussing everything under the moon. They quickly bonded. There was no doubt how much he loved her, how attached he had become to Natalie, and how good it was for him to have a child back in the house.

Arriving in Paris, they drove immediately from the train to the apartment. Her father loved Paris as much as he did Italy but for different reasons. Katarina and he discussed going to the museums, which he also loved. They sent a message to Anthony to meet them at Café Procope at 13 Rue de l'Ancienne Comedie.

They were sitting inside, in a far corner, when Anthony and Hans arrived. Katarina looked over at her father. "Did you know Hans was here? This is rather unexpected."

Jona looked admiringly at his sons. He so wished Edwin and Heinz had survived the war—his boys, so strong, so goodhearted, Anthony always the rock in the family. Hugs went all around.

"Hans, tell me, why are you here?" their father asked.

"I just got here about an hour ago and went straight to Anthony's. I saw your message before I left that the Italy estate is staying, and I assume so will the Paris apartment. Father, please understand I was just looking at the future, trying to consolidate all our holdings, when I suggested we sell."

Jona sipped his coffee, his blue eyes sparkling over the cup. "I understand, Hans, and when it's time, when your mother and I are gone, *then* you may consolidate."

A glimpse of a smile emerged on his face. Hans knew not to push him. The Italy estate was starting to make them money in first-pressed oil, and the vineyards were producing better than even before the war.

Jona folded his hands and with furrowed brow looked intently at both sons. "So let's raise the question—what are the two of you up to?"

"Father, we are thinking of building tunnels into the East, to help people escape. We needed capital, so I thought selling the Paris apartment would have been a good place to start." Hans was afraid of the answer to come, and he knew what it was going to be.

Jona cleared his throat, ran his finger around the stain on the table from the coffee cup. "I don't think either one of you should get involved. We have done more than enough and sacrificed too much blood with the death of your brothers, and Katarina with her own sorrows." Katarina looked up, surprised by his reflective comment. He had never mentioned what she had gone through, the events of the war, her arrest, and where Alexandra was born. He was always silent on these subjects.

Katarina knew Hans's determination would not stop him, so she pressed the matter further. "Hans, who could you trust? Who could you find to help?"

"There are groups already forming to build tunnels, mostly university students who want to be involved. It is a matter of getting people into the East to help bring people out, and as before, we will have the paperwork ready for them to use, should they be stopped."

Jona shook his head emphatically. "You both are being foolish. You think Ulbricht is not on top of the issue already? Look at how many Germans have tried to escape and have been shot. Your mother is sick with worry over two cousins that might have been arrested simply for keeping in contact with us. They have a women's prison over there, and torture and murder is the norm. The Soviets might be pushing their agenda, but they are also having their revenge on any German they can murder."

Anthony had been quiet up to this point. "Father, we already pinpointed those individuals who need to get out. We are working on how we can build the tunnels. There are groups now trying to get out families left behind and others from the university, who we all know won't survive if they do not toe the Communist line. The holdover thinking from Hitler is still alive and well, and the Stasi want to control all citizens. The Russians have made the East a satellite state for the Soviet Union. Ulbricht is a traitor to his people, and in time he will be judged."

"No more talk!" Their father stood. "I'm going back to the apartment, and I will make sure you have your funds from our family's private account. From this point on, I do not want to know anything."

"Father, you don't have to do this. Leave the family funds. We would rather know that we can still count on you if we need help medically."

Jona looked a long time at his sons before speaking. "Anthony, you can always call me. The funds will be in the bank, and the apartment remains ours." He ordered Katarina to come with him. She wanted to stay and talk to her brothers but knew it would have to wait.

Hans waited until they had left the café before he leaned in to Anthony. Anthony reached into his jacket and handed Hans an envelope. "This is the beginning, and there will be more to come in the days ahead. The passports and papers that the East Germans use are a work of art. I don't believe anyone can tell these are not real." While Hans studied the papers, Anthony looked out the window at all the people rushing back and forth, and he realized that soon it would be Christmas. It weighed heavily on his heart to know that Katarina might be joining Grigory in St. Moritz for Christmas. How would she explain it to the family?

"Hans, is there any way when you see Peter you can ask him to keep Grigory away from Katarina?"

Hans waved a dismissive hand at his brother; Katarina's Christmas plans were the least of his worries. "Anthony, I'm not even sure he will be back for Christmas. I'm telling you, he goes deep under and does not surface for a while. He is a hunter, and he always finds his prey. I know he was here in Paris briefly, and I know Peter wants him in East Berlin. I heard he had gone deep into the East and was almost caught at the Neue Kirche at the Gendarmenmarkt. His mission was to locate and get out two scientists that have disappeared. They know the locations of some of the nuclear warheads that are planted in the East."

Hans leaned in closer. "I tell you this in the strictest confidence. I understand the informer was a woman." Hans raised his eyebrows. "I doubt he would ever let Katarina know he sleeps with women for information. It doesn't matter at this point, because they found her dead in her bed. Seems she was also working both sides and was involved with kidnapping Westerners."

"Do you think he killed her?"

"Peter wouldn't say. I don't think it matters if it's a

woman or a man. His conscience doesn't work the same as ours. I think the only time there is a conscience is when it comes to Katarina. We shall see if he shows for Christmas, but I wouldn't hold your breath. Once he's out of Germany, Peter said he falls off the grid."

Chapter 27

Christmas

Katarina was beside herself. No word from Grigory. She was glad she hadn't mentioned her plans for Christmas to anyone but Anthony. She was a bundle of nerves, and she felt like a fool. Even so, she needed to be with him, especially with the current bombardment of letters from John and his attorney. Unfortunately, her anger and frustration was taken out on Natalie, who now had everyone's special attention. After the most recent outbreak, Anthony was called to Natalie's school, and the Sisters were instructed to never let Katarina visit unannounced or without supervision. That beating was the last straw for Gertrude and her parents. Her father, who never took sides against her, showed his fury. The aftermath of that horrible day hung heavily in the household.

It was Gertrude who had the most disdain for Katarina. She had witnessed the brutal attack on Natalie that day while at the school picking her up for the Christmas holidays.

She had been speaking with Sister Agnes, the Mother Superior, on Natalie's progress, and as with all the Sisters, Natalie had a special place in their hearts. The child was compliant, polite, the best in class work, but became skittish when mentioning her mother.

Gertrude had no idea that Katarina had also come to pick up Natalie and was at that moment walking with her in the garden. Nor did Katarina know that Gertrude was nearby, or that Sister Philomena was watching her through the window. During their walk, Natalie refused to leave with her. Katarina became furious and struck the child so hard she broke open her lip.

Gertrude had just turned the corner and saw Katarina shaking Natalie violently, while sobs wracked the little body. When Katarina shoved her, Natalie's head hit the Blessed Mother statue and the child rolled into a fetal position, her head bleeding. At that precise moment, Sister Philomena came tearing across the garden like a charging bull. Katarina was now on top of her daughter and did not see the large female figure bearing down on her until the Sister yanked her up and slapped Katarina hard across her face.

"What in God's name are you doing to this child?" she yelled, shaken to the core at what she had seen. She bent down, took Natalie in her arms, and wiped the blood from her lip with the sleeve of her gown. Gertrude stood just feet away, her eyes boring holes into Katarina.

Mother Superior and Sister Philomena had been grateful to Katarina and Anthony for their heroic deeds. During the war, they had been responsible for moving twenty Jewish children to a Catholic orphanage in Switzerland. Sister Philomena was at times a liaison for Anthony—covertly leaving messages hidden behind a specific brick on the cemetery wall for his retrieval. They felt tremendous pity for Katarina, knowing of the torture she had faced and of her sacrifices. But when it came to Natalie, there was a limit to what they would tolerate. This was the second time Katarina had visited and left Natalie in an emotional heap.

Sister Philomena was tending to Natalie's cuts and bruises when she lost her composure and broke down in tears. Mother Superior, her voice deep and quivering, reprimanded Katarina. "I asked you last time not to take Natalie into the garden, due to a similar incident. We asked you to visit her in the library, which I see you failed to understand."

Katarina gave Mother Superior a contemptuous look. But when she turned to Natalie, it was as if she saw her for the first time: the child's wretched face blotched with tears, the break in her sniffles, the blood on her lip. Katarina swallowed hard and muttered, "I'm so sorry, Natalie, I didn't mean to hurt you." She reached for the child, who withdrew deep into the Sister's arms. Katarina looked around at each of the accusers' faces. "I'm truly sorry. I'm not sure what happened. Please forgive me."

Gertrude started to say something, but she saw Mother Superior's face soften as she said, "Come, Katarina. Let Sister Philomena and Gertrude take care of Natalie, and you and I will have a talk." She reached out her hand to Katarina. She saw within Katarina the child she had known so many years ago, the young woman who had experienced unimaginable things. She must take pity and find forgiveness, and with her arm around Katarina's shoulder, she led her away. Katarina looked back at Natalie, who waited until her mother was out of sight to sob her little heart out.

Gertrude and Sister Philomena walked Natalie out of the school. She would be going home with Gertrude. Furious that Mother Superior had taken pity on

Katarina, Gertrude was determined to make it known to Lisa and Jona what a despicable thing their daughter had done. Surely her in-laws would see Natalie's mother now for who she truly was.

Natalie was sitting in the front seat staring straight ahead, her eyes still brimming with tears. "Aunt Gertrude, why does my mother hate me? I get this sick feeling sometimes when she looks at me. She looks at Alexandra and my brother Philip the same way, but for me it's even worse."

Gertrude sighed and pushed aside her anger for Katarina. "Oh, dear child, it's not you. Your mother has many issues that consume her soul, things that you and I cannot understand. Just remember, for the rest of your life, you are loved by all of us." Natalie was silent the rest of the way home, content with watching the streets go by.

Gertrude didn't take her to the main house but placed her in their home. She immediately took Natalie to the room that was always set up for her and told her to change out of the school uniform while she prepared her bath. Gertrude carefully placed her in the tub and gently washed her scraped back with a soft washcloth, fighting back the tears when she saw the dark blue marks on her body. As she washed Natalie's hair to get the matted blood out, Lisa entered the room, and upon seeing Natalie's condition, she let out a gasp. Gertrude shook her head not to say anything. After she patted Natalie dry and slipped a clean nightgown onto her, she told her to go climb into her bed and rest up for dinner.

Through clenched teeth, she spoke with her mother-in-law. "This is the last time, Lisa, that this child will be treated this way. We need to have custody of Natalie."

Lisa was exasperated. She and Jona turned a blind eye to this side of Katarina. Their daughter had shown compassion for her brothers, Elvia, the horses, even Christina, but why not this child or Alexandra? She took Gertrude's arm. "Let me speak to Katarina."

"You cannot be serious. With all this and all the other times, you still want to just talk to her? What is wrong with this family? You all need to stop protecting this woman!"

"I will speak with my daughter, Gertrude. You take care of Natalie."

Of course I will take care of Natalie! Have they all not seen that is what I've been doing all along? Gertrude shook her head in simmering discontent.

Lisa left with the determination not to let this pass. She had not mentioned the previous incident to Jona, and that had broken their bond for several weeks. She waited for Katarina to return home—a waste of time and energy, as Katarina in her cowardice regarding confrontation with her family spent the night in town with Hans.

That night she told Hans what she had done. She confessed to him that she didn't understand her motives and was terribly sorry for her actions. Hans took pity on her. He knew she was contrite in her confession, and like Anthony, he could only sit and listen. It was not his place to condemn her.

****

Katarina turned her attention to the maps on his desk when Hans left the room. She saw arrows and the word "tunnel" written in various areas, and the Berlin Wall was indicated in bold ink. When he returned, she asked him what the maps meant. The look on her face told him that she would not allow him to keep this from her.

He briefly explained. They had started to build tunnels into the East. She had known earlier, when they visited with their father in Paris, of the plan. Hans explained that a wealthy industrialist had approached him to help financially with the operation. He was asked to bring out several people of importance to him. That plan would coincide with theirs to get others out who could help with the cause. He and Peter had initially not wanted to involve anyone in their family, but Anthony's help in getting papers authorized was vital to the operation. Now that Katarina knew, she might as well do her part. She could be useful, as they needed as much help as they could get.

Several hours later, Katarina and Hans were driving to Mehringdamm near Templehof. They had a meeting at an apartment. He filled her head with more information. Berlin had become the Grand Central Station of espionage, the playground of secrets and agents of all sorts. Their biggest fear in the West was a third world war. The daily fear was of the Soviets rising in a sudden attack, coming over the wall like ants from a hill. Hans and Peter were now placing ammunition in parts of the East for special forces who were stationed there ready to move on Soviet targets. The British and Americans were on their own; few knew of their whereabouts.

The Soviets had four thousand troops and at least seventy-five thousand soldiers from the German Democratic Republic, while the American, British, and French had ten thousand of their own secret weapons, spies, and clandestine special forces in and around the country. They were trained for unconventional warfare. Some went deep into Germany behind enemy lines. Hans and Peter were instrumental in gathering intelligence information to help NATO forces. They were also there to help move weapons stored in the East, and they were trained to merge into the East's society.

Peter was also deep with the British secret service distributing weapons. Only a week earlier, he'd had Grigory fill vials with metal shavings to disrupt turbines in the factories. They both moved through East Berlin with weapons no one knew about, including a one-shot cigarette lighter. They were living in the shadows.

When Hans and Katarina arrived at the apartment, several people were already there. It was a typical German apartment, small but nicely furnished. A young man was putting pastries and coffee on the table; it was his aunt's apartment, and she was in Greece for several months. Peter came over to them the moment he saw them.

"Katarina, are you sure you want to be here? Lots of discussions on tunnel building could easily become boring." Peter was secretly hoping she would want to go home. He knew that once she was involved, much of her intention would be to see Grigory. In spite of that, he also knew she was vital to their mission. He didn't tell Hans and Katarina that Grigory was mingling in an area where the Stasi police had dinner and lunch, a place called Ganymed, near the canal.

Katarina sat in the back of the room, just wanting to listen. She was confused when Peter spoke about English and Americans living in the East, how they wore German clothing, let their hair grow, were taught the cultural nuances, and even had to learn how to hold a fork and knife; simple mistakes could cost them their lives. Surveillance was everywhere, and blending in with the citizens was an essential part of the plan. They had to be completely immersed in the German way. The tricky part for Peter was to keep the British separate from the Americans, as they had to make sure the caches would arrive in the East and not elsewhere. The world did not know that the Four Powers agreement had elite troops in Berlin—not only the Soviet Spetsnaz but The British SIS (MI6), US Special Forces, and the French Secret Service. One of their missions was to see what the Russians were doing and what their plans were against NATO.

The tunnels were not deep, but it took days to move the dirt, with minimum space and very little oxygen. They feared that when they surfaced on the East side, the guards would be there to meet them with Kalashnikov rifles, or that they would flood them out. The Vopos and the People's Police were continuously walking the border.

Hans went on to explain how it worked. The first tunnel was now operational, and they could move people out of the East. They would place a cache in a drop section retrieved by those who would assist the escape. The assistant would lead the escapee to the tunnel entry, which would be as close to Checkpoint Charlie as possible, in a local establishment, perhaps a bakery with the exit through the floor. They had to rely on the cooperation of everyone involved, and no mistakes could be made. It was a tricky maneuver, but plausible.

Hans had promised Anthony to move three Sisters from the Catholic church where they were in hiding. They had already been imprisoned in Hoheneck Castle, an old thirteenth-century fortress overlooking the town, notorious for inflicting fear on those who lived below, as if Dracula reigned over them. At one point the three nuns had been placed naked in a cell filled with ice cold water. One of the sisters lost her foot to severe frostbite.

After all that talk, Katarina asked if there was any way she could help. Hans knew where she was needed. "You can come with us tomorrow. We need guides to help bring them through. Sometimes people panic in the dark, enclosed space. It's quite rewarding to see these people's faces once they emerge. I will be there myself to receive weapons to be moved to the East."

She slept at Hans's apartment after joining him and Christina for dinner. Christina had vehemently objected to their involvement, arguing that building the tunnels should be enough contribution. This conversation had been an everyday routine from the outset, and Hans would listen, but he would stay on his own course.

Katarina woke to another sweat-drenched morning. In her broken dreams, she saw Grigory demanding that she not get involved. She had left clothing from her last stay at Hans's, and after she washed her face, she dressed. Hans would give her a weapon later. Her father had long ago trained her to load and discharge firearms, including rifles. She would have the courage to kill anyone who would come after her family. After the Nazi prison, she'd sworn she would never be a victim again, and holding a gun in her hand now felt normal.

Hans was at the table, dressed in total black. Christina had already gone to the office, and coffee was brewing. “Katarina, you have to eat something. We can’t have you starving, and you need a clear mind.” She looked out the kitchen window to where the Mercedes was waiting with the driver. “You can change your mind right now, should you choose.”

She didn’t reply right away but went to the task of peeling a hardboiled egg. Hans was moving dishes to the sink, and his back was to her when she spoke. “Hans, I wouldn’t have offered if I hadn’t been sure it is just moving people through a tunnel.”

“Yes, but there are always informers, and the Vopos could be walking above us at the border. We never know what to expect, but we have managed thus far to get twelve people out safely. I think we are quite good at this because we are skilled, but still we have to be careful.”

The tunnel workers were at the entrance, waiting, on this cool and foggy morning. Katarina was glad she had grabbed Christina’s leather coat from where it hung on the wall. “For the cause,” she had said out loud when she ran out the door with it over her arm, and she knew Christina would approve at least that part of the plan. They moved silently through the damp tunnel. She could see the moisture on the walls in the lantern’s light as they moved slowly, stopping to listen every few feet.

Hans and one other worker reached the entrance door they had shoveled through. When they slowly lifted the door, the informer was waiting, his eyes darting back and forth, filled with trepidation, the three sisters standing by as quiet as ghosts. The informer had gone to all the different cafés along the way to get the exact time for the delivery. Hans lifted the bag out of the door, and someone came out of a dark corner and snatched it and disappeared without a word.

The delivery was complete, and Hans's face revealed a tad of relief. The nuns moved quickly down the steps, followed by two judges with their families, a journalist, and two doctors, each with their children. He closed the door behind him and began moving them through the tunnel. Katarina was to stay until the knock of three came, indicating there were no more escapees. The fourth knock would indicate there were more. Hans was behind the last group, nearly half way through the tunnel, when he heard her yell. Katarina had opened the hatch door only to be facing three Vopos with guns pointed at her. They ordered her out. She would not budge—the idea of a prison scared her more than a bullet in her head. Suddenly she was being pulled down and the door fell shut. The sound of bullets came down the tunnel as the Vopos entered and were shooting wildly. They stopped within a few feet, knowing they could not venture too far in the dark, and the fear of what might meet them at the other end sent them back up the stairs. Katarina heard Hans fall to the ground. He was grasping his leg, the blood gushing through his pants. She watched him stand up, and he hissed at her to keep going. At the other end of the tunnel, workers were now down the steps and bringing the people to the surface.

Katarina waited until she saw Hans appear. They would have to go back to the safe house and locate a doctor. A couple of the workers helped him into the car, and Katarina climbed in next to him, prepared to wrap her scarf around the wound. She looked back and saw the three Sisters crossing themselves, their eyes to the heavens, as they and the others were being moved safely away. They felt the earth rumble, and they knew the tunnel had been blown up. Hans just shook his head. "It's all right. We never use the same tunnel twice." He jerked with the pain. "Take me to the estate home, not the apartment," he ordered the driver. He put his head against the leather and closed his eyes.

They saw a car following them, and then it slowly passed. Peter was in it, motioning for them to follow. They arrived at yet another safe house. A doctor was waiting. No questions were asked, and he went about his work in secrecy. They had gotten the doctor's sister out of the East a few weeks back, and he owed them his loyalty. He found the bullet had gone straight through Hans's leg, so he didn't have to dig for it.

"Kat, thank you," Peter said, handing her a glass of water. "All things considered, this went well. Unfortunately, so many organizers, mostly students, have been arrested." He hesitated to tell her his next bit of information but felt she needed to know. "Grigory will be in Berlin tomorrow. You already know my thoughts on the matter. He works in a world you could never be part of. What you did tonight is nothing like what he is up against. How he has survived thus far is a miracle in itself. I must go now."

"I can't give him up," she said softly, watching Peter walk out the door. Her heart was pounding, and she felt her hands go cold. The anticipation of seeing Grigory was her only relief.

Hans came out of the room where the doctor had seen him, limping, looking pale, his pants torn to the knee, a large bandage covering his wound. He grinned at everyone in the room. "Don't look so grim. It's just a misfortune, and we'll learn from our mistakes." He leaned against a chair, closing his eyes in pain, and held up two fingers. “Victory!” he said in a hushed tone.

He turned to Katarina. “Come back to the apartment with me. Christina will be in need of someone to calm her down when she sees this bloody thing.”

“Don’t you think you should go back to the estate? I know the strain is now deep between you and Gertrude, but the care from our parents will be better.”

“No, I just want to go back to the apartment, sleep for a while, and then get back to the office. I can’t neglect our factory and workers.” He sounded exasperated. “Listen to me. Go and signal to the driver to pull the car around.”

She walked down the street to find their driver. She was trembling again at what had happened, and on top of that, the thought of Grigory brought so many mixed emotions. She wanted to close the door to him, to their past, but she couldn’t. She wanted to be angry with him for his lies and neglect, and have him suffer by her refusing to see him, but she wouldn’t, for it would be she who suffered the most. In the end, she always welcomed him back into her life. Yet a cold, distant voice nagged at her, “You will always be alone.”

She waved to the driver to come. He pulled up outside the safe house, and Hans came limping out. He ordered the driver to take him to the office instead of the apartment and told Katarina she needed to go home.

“Listen to me, Kat. Do not tell Gertrude or anyone in our family what happened.” He felt lightheaded and held himself up against the car door. “If anyone questions you about today, Christina will cover for you. If Mother finds out, she will kill me.”

"How funny." Katarina laughed. "Risking our lives like this, and yet both of us are afraid to face our mother."

Chapter 28

She arrived home too late for dinner and silently went upstairs, knowing better than to open Natalie's door, certain she was at Gertrude's. She couldn't wait to bathe and sit in the comfort of the library with a soothing drink.

Later, relaxed and in her robe, she fell asleep in the big leather chair, an empty glass at her fingertips. Jona saw the light on as he passed the library. He entered quietly and, finding her there, placed a blanket around her and put a letter in her lap. The ballet company wanted her to supervise their stage production of *Swan Lake*. He hoped she would take the position to keep her busy and to keep her mind off other problems. He stood over her, recalling how inexplicably beautiful she was when she danced—precise toe steps, the graceful leaps, like an angel, lost to a different world, a better world. He'd tell her later that John had sent legal papers for him and Lisa to take temporary custody of Natalie until he could take her back to the States. He would always be there for her, but it was time she let Gertrude raise Natalie.

She woke up startled by the footsteps. Katarina wondered how she'd gotten downstairs. Her head felt groggy, and if the crick in her neck was any indication of how the day was starting, she might as well hide under the library table for the rest of the day. Then she saw the letter on her lap. She eagerly opened it, and a smile came across her face and changed everything. She threw the blanket off and practically ran up the stairs. She looked dispassionately at all the clothing strewn on the floor. She had an interview today with the school and needed to fit the part. A dark blue Chanel suit with gold buttons, low pumps with dark stockings, and a ponytail with a red bow should do the trick, she thought. Dressed and in front of the mirror, she dabbed lipstick on her lips and cheeks.

Her parents were seated at breakfast; her father smiled as he looked at her. "Where are you off to this early and dressed so elegantly?" Although her mother was still bothered by what had transpired with Katarina and Natalie, she dismissed it when she saw her daughter smiling. She would have to deal with Gertrude's percolating anger later. Seeing their daughter's eyes so bright, as she spilled over about the interview, pleased her parents, and the driver was called to take her to the opera house.

Three hours later, she was standing outside the building reveling in her success. They knew all about her dancing history, and they wanted her to help with the performance and work with the dancers. She would start next week.

Arriving back at the estate, she saw Grigory's car across the street. He was back. She told the driver to tell her parents she would be home later and was with a friend.

She hesitated at the door of the car, still furious with him. She was at a loss for words. It started to rain, a little sprinkle followed by a heavy drizzle. She got in, and he drove, both of them stubbornly quiet.

"I'm sorry, Katarina. I truly tried to get back to you over Christmas." She studied his face, the face she loved. He pulled into a little restaurant and guided her inside with an umbrella over her. He ordered for the two of them. A cheese plate was placed on the table. She realized she had skipped breakfast and she was hungry. She explored the different cheeses and took a sip of the Bordeaux, waiting for the anger to subside. Then she reached for his hand.

"Katarina, I heard what happened in the tunnel, and I wish I had been there to help. I also know you received a position at the opera house. I'm delighted that now you can use your energy toward that instead of all this espionage business. Your passion awaits." He moved over next to her and drew her close.

She whispered in his ear, "I don't care what happened. I just want to be with you." He felt the heat radiating from her body.

"Let's finish eating and go back to my place. I missed you. You were never out of my thoughts." Her eyes filled with tears looking into his. He looked as though someone had ripped out his heart. They were both hurting.

They arrived back at the same apartment. Nothing had changed, as if time had stood still. He removed her jacket and unzipped her skirt. She stepped out of it slowly, and as she rose, she slipped her hands underneath his shirt. She closed her eyes and traced his hard stomach, circling his nipples with her palms. His mouth claimed hers, and she felt her body melt with his embrace. As he undressed her, he was again pleased to see she had kept the disciplined body of a dancer. When he removed his clothing, she too was pleased with his strong physique. He wasted no time. The thrill of his mouth on her breast had her burning from inside as they dropped to their knees. He pulled a blanket from the sofa, and they crawled on top of it and wrapped themselves in it to form a cocoon. She lifted her head to meet his kisses. Their bodies locked together, and she let out a low moan as he entered her. It was a quick and fierce release for both of them.

He buried his face in her shoulder and whispered into her neck, “Katarina, I know you must think I abandoned you, but I didn’t. I was in constant agony thinking how this could cause me to lose you. I’m sorry.”

“I believe you. I never really doubted you. Wanting you and worrying about you tore me up inside.” She saw the truth in his eyes and allowed herself to be loved again. She felt the muscles tensing as he pulled her closer.

She saw his Beretta on the sofa, always within reach. “Did you accomplish what you wanted this time?”

“I accomplished more than I had expected. While on Cote d’Azur, I found a stolen painting from a collector in France who had many paintings in his possession that did not belong to him. He had looted many Jews’ homes when they were sent to the gas chambers. The idiot knew exactly what he had. He had sent a vast amount of money to the Bank of Israel for those who needed to be reestablished from Europe. It’s just a small chapter of history that needed to be corrected.”

She looked at him long and hard and wondered how many assassinations, how many passports, how many safe houses did he have in his life. She shook it from her mind—it was better not to know, as long as he kept coming back to her.

Grigory kept his word. He was in and out of her life through 1962. She never asked him where he had been.

****

Life was good for her now. She had something to look forward to, working at the ballet company on the performance of *Swan Lake*, written in 1876 by Pytor Illyich Tchaikovsky, the haunting story originally credited to a German or a German folk tale. In her own dancing career, she had loved playing Odette, the princess turned into a swan by the sorcerer's curse. The first performance of Tchaikovsky's version of the story was with the Bolshoi Ballet in 1877, later staged at the Imperial Ballet in 1895 in St. Petersburg. Katarina knew just how difficult it was for the same ballerina to dance both the part of Odette and that of Odile. It was once speculated that the ballerina Pelageya Karpakove in the first performance had used a second dancer.

Katarina felt respected and acknowledged, as many knew of her rich dancing history. She admired all the young people who came to her for advice, and several times they pulled her on stage to do small performances. She didn't need to hear music to dance; it was there in her head.

Katarina's suggestions for this performance made it rich and touching as she advised the dancer playing Odette on working her delicate arms to slightly drag against the long feathers and the quick footwork of the dancers, letting the audience feel for Odette and the tragedy of her curse and her love for Siegfried. Katarina wanted the choreography to be of elegance and style, the couple dancing to look as if they were sharing the same breath, the lifts and their balance so perfect it would be one of the best performances ever.

It had been discussed to change it to a happy ending, performing only three acts, as some ballet troupes did. In 1950, Konstantin Sergeyev had staged *Swan Lake* for the Marinsky Ballet, under the Soviet regime, with the tragedy removed and Odette and Prince Siegfried living happily ever after. But the point of the story was the beautiful tragic ending including the fourth act, Katarina felt. She always wiped her tears as Odette tried to overcome the betrayal within the story and Siegfried and Odette ascended to Heaven to stay united in love.

One morning, Katarina came early to the stage. She wore a cotton skirt over tights, and a loose blouse. She removed her shoes and slipped into her ballet slippers. It had been years, and now she had the stage to herself. She heard the music in her head, as if the orchestra was in the pit at that very moment. She didn't see some of the dancers and the choreographer gathering backstage to watch as she performed the difficult succession of thirty-two fouettés, her raised leg never touching the ground, giving her propulsion. "Fouetté" is French for "whipped." This whiplash movement gives the dancer the brilliance of the quick up-and-down fluttering like a bee's wings. As she did each turn on point, she came to point exactly, raising the working leg as it shot out to the front and swept around to the side. How perfectly the working leg whipped in! Katarina was dazzlingly skilled in this technique. So many avoided this part of the performance if they could.

When she stopped, there was applause from the wings. The principal dancer came running to Katarina with a warm embrace and gracious compliments—she was truly the broken swan. Her heart swelled. To be dancing at her age was unexpected, as the career of the ballerina is a short one, but it was still part of her, as natural as riding horses. She was asked how she could show so much sorrow, performing in silence without any music. Katarina said she only had to recall heartbreak and betrayal; it was easy. She would not tell them it came from deep inside her own soul.

When *Romeo and Juliet* opened in 1938 in Czechoslovakia at the Mahen Theatre, she and the maestro had traveled there to see the performance. Later she had performed that ballet in front of Hitler, knowing at the time the fall of Germany was at hand. She'd felt like dying after that performance.

It was late in the evening when she left the building after working with the *Swan Lake* production. Anthony was waiting outside. "I watched you dance, Kat, and my heart ached for you. So many years lost." Anthony still blamed himself for her injuries.

"I think I was pretty good. I showed the young ones what this old broad can still do on stage. But in all honesty, my knees and legs are killing me! I'm afraid my body can no longer withstand the rigors of this profession. It is for the young." She linked her arm in his. "By the way, what are you doing here?"

"I'm here to give warnings to my young seminarians to stop helping with the tunnels, and for Hans to take a break. He is haunted by Peter Fechter's death, an eighteen-year-old shot on the wall, and they let him bleed to death. Hans saw the guards fire at him.

He was helpless and…"

"Anthony, let me enjoy the moment, and besides, I'm starving! Have you eaten?"

"Aw…" He paused to consider her happiness. "Do you want to stop somewhere or go home? I'm sure Cook has some good leftovers."

"Actually, I've been staying with Hans and Christina till this production is over. It's just easier."

He raised an eyebrow. "I would venture to say that it's also easier when Grigory comes into town. But there I go again… It's just one more thing to pray for."

Time slipped by. There was rousing feedback in the newspapers and from those who saw the production of *Swan Lake*, and the applause was thunderous when they introduced Katarina on stage as a consultant. Promises were made that she would be notified of future projects. She felt a heavy sadness that it was over.

Chapter 29

September 1962

Katarina was back home with her parents. She felt out of sorts, not having the daily routine of dance. Making house calls with her father filled some of the days. There were few veterinarians left in Berlin, and his knowledge of large animals matched no other.

Katarina's highlight was when Grigory returned to Berlin. With his visits always brief, they made the most of their time together. She wanted so often to ask him questions, but he refused to hear them. There were always bruises or cuts on his body that he would not explain.

There were fewer letters from John, especially since he had given her parents temporary custody. She still had time with Natalie, but knowing she was always in good hands was one less thing to worry about. Natalie preferred being with Gertrude and her grandparents. The hard-headed child defied her at every turn. What bothered Katarina the most was how Natalie would shudder and back away from her, even with the simplest conversation.

In addition, her mother had taken three messages that Francis was in Berlin and would like to see her. He was staying at the Hilton. Her mother and Gertrude had continuous contact with him and had received pictures of Douglas. This frustrated Katarina to no end.

Hans was still coming home on the weekends, when his son was home, but the rift was still wide with Gertrude, who would not concede to a divorce. On this Monday morning, Hans was wearing a path in the carpet, walking back and forth in frustration after his mother had told him the latest news. Her cousin had been confined to prison for communicating with her, and she was now in hiding inside the church in a hidden room, the very same room where they had hidden the Jews so many years ago until Anthony and his family could finally move them.

The brothers were making plans to get the cousin out, and possibly more, if they could. Anthony had diplomatic papers to inspect his churches. He had created a document with a picture of his mother's cousin, portraying her as a maid assigned to clean what was left of the few churches the Russians had not destroyed in their effort to create an atheist society. Hans was currently building two more tunnels. Katarina listened in on the conversation. This time she would not volunteer.

She was worried about Anthony taking on this rescue. His breathing was labored at times, and his color was off. He would not go to a doctor, even upon their insistence. He blamed it on the lack of sun, something a vacation could cure. When Anthony walked out of the room, Katarina changed her mind and asked Hans if she could come with him when it was time to bring the cousin through the tunnel. He agreed, and the plan was set for the following evening.

****

In priest attire, Anthony crossed over to East

Germany and had reached his church and his contact. Father Schönberg had been trying to hold the church together, but it was impossible since the East Germans had decided to board it up because it was too close to the wall. He too, wanted to leave the East, as he had no purpose there anymore. Relieved to see Anthony with his traveling papers in hand, he busied himself with packing up things to remove from the church.

Anthony opened the hidden door, stuck his head in, and spoke in a soft reassuring voice to the figure huddling in the dark corner. "Lizzie, you're safe. It's me, Father Anthony." Slowly, she walked toward him with a slight limp, and in the light, he noticed first her long hair. "Oh, dear, I'm sorry, but I have to cut your hair so that it fits under the hat. It's better if you appear as a male until we get you safely out." Her face gaunt, she was a good five feet six inches, lanky, with dark circles around her muddy brown eyes. She looked as if she hadn't eaten in weeks. He noticed the scars on her arms and the marks on her wrist, indicating that she had been tied.

A small tear escaped when she watched her long brown hair fall to the floor. Anthony managed to leave it at the top of the collar. She quickly changed into the clothes left for her. The legs were a little short, but she would pass. Before leaving the church, she memorized her new name.

She held her papers of identification tightly underneath her shirt as she followed Anthony through the streets. He spotted a Stasi at the location where he was to place her, but no other military personnel nearby. A car was blinking its lights on the West side.

The Stasi had rounded up at gunpoint those who

had already gathered at this designated location. Anthony didn't know what to do. Taking Lizzie back to the church and waiting it out seemed like the only alternative. He grabbed her hand and backtracked. When he turned a corner, hands came down on both of their shoulders. Lizzie let out a small cry. Anthony turned to fight.

The unidentified man's face was covered in black, and he had his automatic rifle by his side. He was clearly not the enemy. "Father." He spoke in a low rushed voice. "Come. We screwed up with the tunnel! It came up in an alleyway and not in the butcher shop. The dimensions were off. Those people you saw were caught, but the early ones are somewhere safe, waiting for new instructions." The man moved them along quickly to another tunnel that was passable but not as large as the other.

Anthony saw Hans come into view, waving frantically for them to hurry. He, too, was disguised. Lizzie was first to enter the five-foot opening and go down the steep steps into the tunnel. Anthony held back. Hans waved for him to come. The man who was still with him said, "Father, you need to take the tunnel out. I'm not sure you were not compromised. The Stasi is already at the church."

"My fellow priest is there!" Suddenly Anthony pictured the priest, panic-stricken and helpless. "They will arrest him if they think something is wrong." His own voice filled with apprehension.

"We got him out. He will be coming through also. He's on his way. Father, you have to move quickly, please!"

Lizzie was moving through the tunnel, Anthony

not far behind. Katarina had also entered the tunnel from the West with a cache of weapons and explosives in a duffel bag, should Hans need them. Hans waited at the base and received ten more people, as well as Father Schönberg. Hans pulled the opening closed and locked it. Garbage cans were placed over the entrance by those who agreed to help. Katarina burst out laughing, and Hans joined in, when they heard one of the refugees complain that if she had known the tunnel was so small, she would have tried to lose weight. The woman's hips were nearly touching the walls.

They were all exhausted when they reached the exit and climbed to safety. The West German police had arrived, since the East Germans across the way had decided to shoot a few rounds toward what they thought might be an entrance to a tunnel. Everyone froze in place when the police looked their direction. Far enough away, the officers couldn't see the duffel bag full of weapons, but they did recognize that there were two priests with the group of people. They turned their backs on them when another officer drove up and caught their attention. The group walked away as if they were on a casual stroll with the ministry.

Katarina had dirt all through her hair and smudges on her face. Hans was covered with dirt as well and was wiping his face off with a rag when he said to Anthony, "I'm so sorry. I think we were given deliberately false measurements so we would come up in the alley. We didn't want to take a chance with you going back through the border—they could have been waiting for you. Once the Stasi appeared at the church, we felt it was better to get Father Schönberg out as well."

"Who was watching the church to let you know?"

"Who do you think?" Hans cracked a smile. "He's in the East working with special forces who are living there. He needs to extract information for Israel on those who still want to arm his new homeland."

A police officer came over, one who privately helped the university group build tunnels. "Hans, we counted eighteen people who got out. We will take them to a safe house and give them new identification. We also found your traitor. Keep your hands clean this time. We'll take care of him."

Katarina placed a blanket around Lizzie. They were waiting for the cars to come pick them up. To Anthony, Katarina said, "She is so frail. We need to let a doctor look at her."

"Dr. Klein is meeting us at home," Anthony assured her. "Hitler's legacy lives on. She was in the women's prison, Hohenschönhausen, tortured, and saw others murdered. And at what I'm about to tell you, do not get upset. A colonel inspected the facility, and it was Oliver Spitz, Frederick's brother. He wanted the torture increased for answers, and if there were no answers, his orders were to execute the prisoners. He confronted Lizzie on our family, and she was forced to talk. She got out because of Grigory. I don't know the full details." Anthony felt terrible having to tell her this and could not contain his frustration.

Katarina bent over, feeling the pores of her skin erupt in sweat, her stomach instantly queasy. She thought she would vomit right there on the spot. "God, Anthony, do you think he would have sent Alexandra there?"

"I'm not sure, but I *am* sure he would have made her a true Communist and taught her to hate her family.

But rest assured, Hans and Grigory will eventually find him, and he will be dealt with." She wanted to learn more about Oliver Spitz; she hadn't even known his name before. She only knew he was her dead husband's twin, raised by the mother in England or Scotland—they were not certain which.

Before she could ask any more questions, the car pulled up, and Lizzie was on her way to safety, food, and a warm bed, Anthony by her side.

The taxi pulled up to take her and Hans to the apartment. He looked concernedly at his sister. "I guess Anthony told you about Oliver Spitz." She nodded.

"I'm sorry the devil is still out there. I promise we will try to find him. We think he spends a great deal of time in Russia, and because of that it will be harder to locate him."

"When are you going back to the East?"

He sighed heavily just thinking of the idea. "I'm not sure. We got this close to being caught"—he held up his thumb and forefinger to illustrate a half inch—"and that is much too close. And if we had left Anthony behind, well…" He was tired, she could tell. "I will tell you, I worry about the student group. The Stasi will be on the lookout all the time. I'm not going to keep building once we have accomplished getting out the people we need, but I will give the students financial help. I think a few more tunnels and we are done."

"I hope so, Hans. We came too close to nearly losing our brother." She held up the same finger gesture to make sure he knew she understood. Then her mind drifted to Grigory.

Chapter 30

Berlin 1963

Christina again woke up not feeling well. Hans had taken a few days off. He was tired of building tunnels and working to move refugees out of the East, and the factory was taking up so much of his time. A leisurely week in Italy was the answer, he'd said, and now as she rolled over in the bed, a slight breeze brought the scent of lemon through the window, and the crisp linens smelled of lavender. Fresh flowers were on the table.

Her feet hit the tile floor hard, and she barely made it to the bathroom. Initially she had thought that Giuseppe and Marie's rich Italian recipes were the culprit. The day before, the doctor had said otherwise, and she told Hans that evening that she was pregnant.

She left the bathroom and quietly made her way downstairs to find fresh orange juice and coffee with hardboiled eggs, salami, cheese, and pastries on the table. As she stood looking down at all the food differently, knowing that now she must eat for two, suddenly she felt his hands on her hips and a kiss on her neck.

"Good morning, my love." His eyes were sparkling with joy. He led her to the table and placed a plate of food in front of her. She sat with her hands in her lap and watched him. This was part of Hans's childhood;

he knew this kitchen well. He sat opposite her, eating bread and cheese, his eyes fixed on hers.

Christina did not want him to know she was in misery, especially when he had only a few remaining days of relaxation away from his hectic work schedule. "Hans, when we go back, what is going to happen? I'm three months, the doctor said. We could just move here, and I can find out what is needed to practice law. My Italian is not bad, which is one of the reasons your firm hired me."

"Well, I will have to demand that Gertrude give me a divorce, but you know it's complicated. She can be fragile at times, and then there is my son, who has already taken his mother's side against us."

She managed a smile and reached for his hand. "All right, let's just enjoy the rest of our stay, maybe do something fun and visit Milan." He came around the table and kissed her cheek. "And there is a baby store that's supposed to have exquisite clothing and blankets."

"If that is what you want to do, I will make the arrangements and check us into a luxury hotel."

The week went by quickly, and they made it a wonderful memory. It was magical, but then it ended, and it was time to go back to Berlin. Christina wanted so much to stay, but that was not possible. They would come back after the baby was born.

They arrived back in Berlin; she went to the apartment and he went back to the estate. He needed to tell his parents and Gertrude of the pregnancy. There could be no hiding it. The house was dark as he entered. He heard the rocking chair move and saw the lamplight come on as Gertrude revealed herself. Her eyes were red from crying. "You took her to Italy?"

He let out a long sigh. He wanted to approach her with the empathy he carried in his heart, only he did not love her. "Gertrude, I think we are now at a crossroad, and I must tell you I will not give her up. She is having a child."

Her body slumped in the chair. This was not going to happen! Suddenly she stood from the rocking chair and came close to him, intense as she said, "It won't happen, Hans. Your parents won't accept the child or her."

"Gertrude, we have been separate people for a long time, and Father knows about Christina."

She was now seething. "Don't say her name in my house."

"No, Gertrude, it's my parents' home. I wanted us to move, but what you went through after the war kept us here. I asked you to move to Italy or Paris with me, but you wouldn't. I'm sorry for what happened to you, what the Russians—"

"Yes, they raped me and left me to die, Hans. You found me and saw the condition I was in. I was raped because I went looking for you and your sister. It's her fault! If you hadn't gone looking for her…"

"I'm so sorry and always will be. I asked you to go to counseling, but you left our bed after our son was born. You couldn't stand to be touched any longer. I heard your cries at night. I could do nothing for you."

"You knew I couldn't have children after what they did. We were blessed to have had our son. You have no idea—their faces, always there—I can still feel their hands all over me, ripping at my clothing! So many others…I was one of the lucky ones, to have survived."

Her voice trailed off. "And if it had not been for Grigory killing all three of them, I might have lived in continuous fear, as your sister does now."

She was on the verge of hysteria. He had seen it before. "Gertrude, you have a good life here, and it was your decision to isolate yourself from me. You didn't even try to work something out. Our lives could have been different. I did love you when we married, but you knew Anna would always be a part of me. You told me you could live with the ghost."

"I did, but now the ghost is alive again. I tolerated your little indiscretions, but you fell in love, and you let her trap you."

"She didn't trap me."

Several minutes passed as they stood there wallowing in words but with nothing else left to say.

"Good night, Gertrude. I will draw up the divorce papers. You will be left in a life of luxury, and you can remain in this house." He didn't look back when he walked away, but he felt an incredible weight of sadness. He wished this could have turned out differently.

Gertrude watched him leave and walk across the grounds to the main house. She would let this go until tomorrow, when she would tell the family what this woman was made of, the whore she was, trapping a married man. She lifted the phone and called the office, leaving a message, supposedly from Hans, for Christina to arrive at the house in the morning. Hans was staying at the main house and not going back into town. She checked on Natalie. She stared long and hard at the sleeping child, the child she wanted, the girl she longed for, her sweet Natalie.

****

The next morning, Gertrude arrived early for breakfast. Making sure Lisa and Jona were there, she instructed Cook to feed Natalie in the kitchen. She was just entering the dining room when the doorbell rang. Hans was coming down the stairs dressed for work, and the butler opened the door. Hans stood there looking in confusion from Christina and then to Gertrude. Lisa came from the kitchen. "Why are the three of you all standing here? Come have breakfast." She ushered them into the dining room.

Katarina had just come back from riding when Lisa saw her. "Katarina, take off your riding boots so you do not track the mud in, and join us in the dining room for breakfast. We have guests."

Katarina had a bad feeling upon seeing Christina. She walked over and gave her a hug and whispered in her ear, "What are you doing here?" Christina explained about the message from her secretary.

Gertrude smiled at them when they sat down. Katarina knew for certain that something dreadful was about to happen because Gertrude was never this polite around present company.

Gertrude moved to sit in her rightful place next to her husband. "Christina, so sorry you had to come all this way, but my husband is exhausted from our late night of enjoyment together. So seldom do we have our special time, since he is so busy these days." Christina took a long and arduous breath and set her eyes on Hans.

Hans was beside himself and stood up to speak. "Christina, first of all, why are you here?"

"I was told to come," she answered.

Hans looked over at Gertrude, a smile playing on her lips. She turned to her in-laws and stated, loud and clear, “I think, Lisa and Jona, you should know that Hans is sleeping with your company lawyer, who is also carrying his child. He wants to divorce me.”

Lisa placed her hand over her mouth, and when Jona lowered his head, Lisa challenged him, “Jona, did you know?”

“Yes, Hans told me a while back, and he called me from Italy and told me about the baby.”

Katarina moved to Christina’s side. Lisa looked at her son. “Is this true, Hans? It is not like you to do something like this.”

Gertrude laughed. “Not *like* him? Have you ever asked him how many other little trysts he’s had, always coming back to me?” She directed the question at Christina, not at her mother-in-law.

Hans glared at Gertrude with contempt and spoke only to his parents. “I won’t be coming back this time, Mother, Father. You can accept Christina and your new grandchild or not. I’m not leaving her.”

Gertrude leapt from her chair and screamed, “You can’t! You have a son to take care of, not some illegitimate child! There will be no divorce, do you hear me?”

Lisa stood and motioned for all to sit and calm down. “Do not say another word.” She focused on Christina. “You are a lovely girl, Christina, but I don’t think a divorce will happen.”

Katarina spoke up. “Mother, please, there is a child involved now.”

“Katarina, you need to stay out of this. You have your own skeletons, which I do not wish to bring out.”

Katarina was momentarily stunned; her mother had never spoken harshly to her.

Jona moved to stand by Hans. It looked as if battle lines were drawn. He was and intended to remain the lord of the house, and he said directly to his son, "Take Christina home. I will talk to Lisa and Gertrude." And to Gertrude's horror, he kissed Christina on the cheek and offered her his kindest sentiments. "Christina, we look forward to a new grandchild."

Hans took Christina's elbow and led her out of the house. Katarina took a tray and placed her coffee and pastries on it and left. She felt like the prodigal child, but for once she was not the one causing the scene.

Gertrude picked up a coffee cup and threw it at Katarina, missing her by inches. Katarina turned and just shrugged her shoulders, and Lisa tried to calm Gertrude as she blamed Katarina for introducing her husband to the lawyer.

In the car, Hans and Christina looked out their respective windows. Deep in thought, he heard her say, "Your wife is insane, and she will try to destroy us."

He saw the vulnerability in her eyes and reached for her hand. "Christina, have no doubt I'm here for you, and if she doesn't give me a divorce, that won't change anything."

"It will for me, Hans. She will then always have the upper hand."

****

Katarina changed out of her riding pants and sweater. On the ride earlier, she had been filled with happiness because of the message she'd received containing only two words, "I'm back." She knew he was at the apartment. She thought this was a perfect opportunity to use Hans as an excuse to leave. Naturally, a sister must console her brother. She also would keep her appointment with Francis; this was his fourth attempt at meeting her. Two birds killed with one stone and one lie.

She stopped first at Grigory's apartment and dropped off her suitcase. He was not there, so she proceeded to the Hilton. She eyed Francis in the lobby, taking note how handsome he was, how he stood out amongst the others. She looked down at her own outfit, with its line of gold buttons trailing down the full length of the navy-blue dress. She had picked it out with the intention of letting Grigory take his time unbuttoning each one, removing first the blue belt cinched at her small waist. She tucked away the moment of pleasure and remembered that she was about to be in the presence of a man she hated but at one time thought she loved. She would not allow herself to think of their child together.

What a spell she still had on this man. As they approached each other, Katarina could see Francis could not help but marvel at her beauty.

"Hungry, Katarina?"

"No, not really. What do you want? Have you not done enough damage in my life?" She was annoyed by his casual question.

"Well, it looks like you always come out on top. Let's face it, you will always find a way to come back here to your beloved Germany. Why, look, even I'm here. So, if you're not hungry, come to the bar."

She followed him to a lounge area, where he ordered two drinks, taking the liberty to choose for her. "I believe you're still fond of red wine," he said with a combination of cordiality and curtness.

"Why are you here, Francis?" She wanted to know sooner rather than later.

"I have all the documents in order to build a hotel here. It seems they are in demand."

"I'm not sure this is a good place for you to have a hotel," she said, waiting for the other shoe to drop.

"Well, if you are concerned that your son might come and seek you out, don't worry. You know we agreed to let him believe you died in a car crash. However, I promised your mother that I would let her know how her grandson is growing up." He saw an errant strand of hair that crossed her brow, and he was tempted to move it away.

He saw tears gathering in her eyes. "I wish you wouldn't communicate with my family. It's wrong, you know." He always fell to pieces when she cried. "Look, Francis, I never meant to hurt you or John, and I'm truly sorry. My life is better. I'm more at peace."

He knew she was lying. She would never be at peace. The despair that dwelled just below the surface of her vibrant eyes would always be there. They sipped their drinks, and once again she was compelled to make her case and then move on to better things—Grigory.

"If this meeting was just to remind me that I am dead, you've wasted your time. Raise the little boy well. I could not be a good mother to him. It's clear now that I can't be a good mother to any of my children. I have to go, Francis."

He handed her a card. "Take this. It's my private number, if you ever need me. With what's going on here, there might come a day when you will need a safer place to hide. West Berlin is not a good hiding place for you."

"I wouldn't be here now if you hadn't..."

"We've been over this too many times, Katarina. How many more times can we say 'I'm sorry'?"

She left him with an aching sense of loss. But he had accomplished his purpose, and he knew she would not throw the phone number away.

Chapter 31

She took a taxi back to Grigory's, exiting the cab just in time to see him outside the building. She let out a slow whistle. He turned and saw her standing in the street. It was like a scene from a movie, running toward each other, the prospect of joy spreading across their worn faces. He had a bag of food with him. They kept the kisses light and held hands up the steps.

"I'm impressed. You went dinner shopping."

He unlocked the door to the safe house. From habit, he glanced at the wire rigged at the bottom of the door to alert him if someone had entered the apartment. He stepped back, placing his hand across her path. "Did you already go into the apartment?"

Her eyes widened. "Yes, should I have not?"

"Just being safe." He kissed her forehead, but he still entered with his hand on his Beretta.

It had been only two weeks this time since they were last together, but he still worried that she would grow tired of the arrangement. He tried to talk to her about coming back to Israel with him, but she continually changed the subject. She saw the angst in his face now and smothered him in kisses to make it go away.

She was removing the items from the bag, the bottle of wine first, when she decided to tell Grigory where she had been earlier. "Grigory, I met with

Francis at the Hilton. Not sure exactly what he wanted, but he apologized for his actions again and reassured me that my death was still the best reason to give Douglas for my absence."

His eyes turned dark. "Is that *all* he wanted?"

"Yes, that is all he wanted." She didn't tell him about the phone number that was tucked in her purse. Her sigh was wistful as they sat down for dinner, and he poured the red wine from France. He had picked up *wiener schnitzel* and red cabbage with red potatoes, and bread pudding for dessert. How comfortable they had become now, having dinner before sex.

They snuggled into the sofa after eating. "I heard you were in East Berlin and saved Anthony and our cousin from a deplorable situation," he said.

"Not quite saved, but I was there and just helped out. Don't worry about it. It was simple." She looked into his eyes and wanted him to believe her. "You also now know that Oliver Spitz is alive and well, right?"

"Yes, and I will make every attempt to make sure he joins his brother, so don't you worry. And this time I will make sure he's dead." Moving on, he presented a lighter subject. "I was in your favorite place in Paris when I went to see Anthony and other contacts. I heard you went to the spring fashion show and how much you loved it. Why don't you just move to Paris, and then we can work on you coming to my homeland?"

"I don't think I fit in any longer. '*Le comme il faut*,' always about appearance." She sat back and crossed her arms, knowing where he was heading with this thought.

Grigory pulled out his backpack and spread some books on the floor. "Anthony gave me these to give to you. Ann Proust's moral satire, and a book on Rembrandt and Montaigne."

"And did you know that Alexandra is staying at the University of Berlin, and her cousin Sarah will be going to the Sorbonne? My family is euphoric." She flipped through the pages without really looking.

"Katarina, you're avoiding the subject of coming to Israel and getting a divorce as we discussed last time. Life is unpredictable enough, and I want to know you are safe and at my home. I want to marry you."

He could see she was getting upset, but he still couldn't understand why. "All right, let's change the subject once again. I don't want to ruin the evening talking about your past relationships."

"Well, first, that was a little harsh…my past relationships?"

"Isn't that what's keeping us apart? It's so frustrating! If you love me, why won't you divorce?"

"It's not like you're going to be home every night for dinner," she said with an edge.

"I would, in time, if you came back with me." His need for her was genuine, and it tugged at her heart.

"I'm sorry. I'll consider it," she said without thinking but wanting to end the sobering conversation as quickly as possible. "So you spoke with Hans, I'm sure, since you've been here. What is the latest?"

"We have an important mission coming up, which Hans believes will require your help. You know I objected, but Hans feels you're up to it."

"Is this for you or Hans? He has been moving people through tunnels without my help. Why are *you* asking me instead of him?"

"We need to get a scientist out," he said, avoiding

her question. "He has information on the nuclear sites, and he is always watched, but we can set him up in a café for you to meet with him. It won't be far from Checkpoint Charlie, and we can pull you out fast. You will start with visiting the Fischers, our informers, who will direct you to the café to meet the scientist, and from there, he will give you what we want and proceed to the tunnel. We will get him out, but we don't want the information on him if he is stopped on the street."

"Why are you not handling this yourself?"

"I will be there, but not seen. I think I have been compromised."

"Who am I to the Fischers?"

"They used to be involved with the Berlin Opera House in the East, and you are simply visiting with your old friends who know you through dance."

"Grigory, you do know the East says the escape helpers are equal to the Nazi resistance fighters and need to be caught and sent to hard labor?"

He cupped her chin. "I promise you will be safe."

"When do we meet with Hans? And I'm sure Peter is right in the mix."

"This won't take place for two more days, so you can change your mind at any time. I know we must get our scientist out on the first escort truck. The tunnel is only a hundred meters long, seven meters deep, the excavation finished just yesterday. We don't have a second tunnel, so it has to go like clockwork. Our helpers will reach out to you and those scattered in other cafés when it is time to move, and at that time, you will go back through Checkpoint Charlie. You only have a certain time slot for visiting, and the Americans will give you a time to be back."

They were in each other's arms that night, and she couldn't sleep, too lost in thought. Her fear of Oliver Spitz was very real. Sure, Grigory would find him someday. But he very well might have signed her death certificate by sending her back to the East on this mission. Was she less important than the scientist? Had he hardened that much, to sacrifice even her? And why did *he* tell her about the plan and not Hans? Her fear was warranted, and no one seemed to care. She had to think of something that would give her more protection.

****

Without anyone knowing, Katarina retrieved Natalie's identification papers from the files kept in the library. She woke Natalie the morning she was going over to the East. She had to convince Natalie to go shopping with her, and she added that her grandmother would be joining them. Of course the girl balked, but Katarina enticed her with the idea of buying something special for her father, and that seemed to do the trick. Agreeing to bring Natalie back in time for practice was a condition that also had to be honored. She was in a horse jumping competition the coming weekend, and it was imperative that she be ready. Gertrude was out in the garden when Natalie informed her of their plans. At first, she was hesitant, but after thinking about it, what harm could be done as long as the grandmother was present, and Natalie seemed to be relaxed about going on a shopping spree. Katarina moved quickly and rushed her through the house and out to the car where the driver was waiting. She instructed the driver, and they were off.

"What about Grandmother Lisa?" Natalie asked.

"She will join us later," Katarina said sweetly.

"Look what I brought for you." She handed her a book from her bag, *A Girl's Guide to Grooming*, written by a French author. "Look at these cute hairdos. I used to wear mine like that when I was a dancer."

The book kept Natalie busy until they arrived at Checkpoint Charlie.

"Miss Katarina," the driver asked with concern, "are you sure this is where I am to leave you?"

She would not look in his eyes and ordered him to go back to the house. They stood there at the gates. Natalie looked all around for the shopping area and was worried at what she saw. "Mother, this is a bad place. Grandfather says we shouldn't go here, because they have guns."

Katarina took Natalie's arm, held it tight, and moved forward. "Listen, Natalie, I'm just going to make a quick visit to an old friend. I want you to be completely quiet and not say a word to anyone. It's very important. I promise we will go shopping right after."

"No, Mother, those are evil people. I don't want to go."

"If you don't come and be quiet, I will leave you here alone and let them arrest you."

Natalie's eyes swelled with tears, and her voice was a whisper. "I will be quiet, Mother, but I *will* tell Grandfather." Katarina hid her anger and would deal with that later.

Katarina moved through Checkpoint Charlie, showing addresses where she would be visiting, and they informed her when she had to be returning to the gate. After their bags were inspected, Natalie received a smile from the Vopo. They walked hand in hand past the guard and crossed over to the East. They were immediately approached by the Fischers, who were quite puzzled to see a child with their contact.

She stood there for a moment, looking at them and feeling claustrophobic, her smile quivering. She whispered, "I don't think I can do this, I have to go back."

Frau Fischer, a tall, straight-backed woman, bent down as if to embrace her and whispered, "Fräulein Katarina, you can't go back. If you do, you will arouse suspicion on yourself and us." She walked her away with her arm around her shoulder. "We only need walk a few blocks."

Herr Fischer, who looked as if he did not miss a meal, walked next to Natalie and, noticing the book in her hand, asked her what she was reading. They had small talk as they walked.

They stood outside a building and continued their conversation. Frau Fischer gave Katarina the instructions to the café just a few doors down and explained that she would take Natalie to her apartment, where they would wait for her. Katarina had wanted Natalie with her for a diversion but was convinced that it was better this way.

Katarina found Herr Fritz immediately, in a corner, peering over his spectacles at a newspaper, looking like Albert Einstein. She walked slowly over to him and greeted him in a soft manner. He invited her to have coffee, and she sat next to him as if they were old friends. The coffee was nearly undrinkable, and she had to keep from making a sour face.

"Herr Fritz, are you ready to leave? I will walk you to the corner where the transport bus will pick you up."

"Yes, but first"—he handed her the newspaper—"look at this article, the one at the bottom left of the page." As he reached over to underline a sentence of particular interest with his finger, he dropped a folded-up paper on her lap. She wrapped her hand around it, and when they rose to leave, she slipped it into her pants pocket. She would need to transfer it to a safer place.

"Excuse me while I go to the ladies' room."

She found the restroom and quickly stuffed the paper in her bra. She had created a small pocket in the bra lining for things just such as this.

In the meantime, Hans was in a panic, dealing with issues in the tunnel. Water was excessively leaking from the ground, making the path slippery and forming puddles. Couriers had already crossed to give notice to the refugees of where to meet. The refugees were scattered in different areas and the couriers knew exactly where to meet up with them, either a park, a café, or a butcher shop. The end of the tunnel came up a block from a derelict factory. If there were guards or Vopos walking in the streets, no one took notice.

Katarina walked casually out of the café with Herr Fritz. They stopped a few blocks away, and she wished him well and said she would see him on the other side. As she started her way back to the Fischers' apartment, her knees nearly collapsed from under her as she walked right past a Vopo who turned and gave her a second look.

****

Hans and Grigory opened the panel and slid it open. The water was coming into the tunnel even faster. They raised a small mirror out of the opening to make sure there were no guns waiting for them. The coast was clear.

Two sets of refugees from two different cafés were making their way to the tunnel. One of the couriers hurried his way to Hans to let him know that the Stasi were on their way to the Fischers' apartment.

One of their own informers in the East had alerted him of the situation. Grigory stiffened and gave Hans a stern look before he turned and pushed past the line. He had talked her into this and would move quickly to find her and bring her back through the tunnel. He spotted Herr Fritz heading their way, and he felt a sharp pang of guilt in his stomach. Herr Fritz grabbed his arm and put a gold pendant in his hand. "Thank you. This has brought me much luck." Grigory had no time to argue and stuffed the shiny gold piece in his pocket.

He found a bicycle leaning against a wall, and he stole it to make up time. He had to reach her and stop her from entering the apartment. He was sweating profusely, the adrenaline pumping a fierce energy to his muscles. He saw her turn the corner to the Fischers' home, and in a flash he had disposed of the bicycle and was walking by her side. Startled, Katarina sucked in a yelp and had to adjust the look of surprise to a welcoming smile. He felt in his jacket for the papers of identification should he be stopped. Even with that security, he knew he must get off the street.

"How nice of you to join me," she said with forced cheerfulness.

"The Fischers have guests arriving." He led her away from the apartment by her elbow.

"Oh, my God! Natalie is there!" She could barely get the words out.

"What the hell are you talking about?"

"I thought she would take away any suspicion…I needed…"

He turned her again toward the apartment building. "Let's just keep walking and hope you get there before they do. The Stasi won't arrest you. It would cause a diplomatic disaster. You were only visiting a friend."

"What if they are looking for *me*?" She stopped and looked at him.

"Well, I can't waltz on in there. Only you can."

He waited on the corner and watched her approach the building. Something made her stop and look across the street. Grigory's eyes followed hers as both of them saw Natalie sitting on a swing in the park. Katarina walked quickly to the playground while Grigory hid in a doorway.

Natalie jumped off the swing and met her mother half way. Katarina bent down and held her. The child was crying.

Grigory leaned his head back against the building in pure relief. He had to make his way back. She would be fine now, and they would meet in the West. He would not mention this change of plan to Hans.

Katarina and Natalie made it through the check points without incident. The child's crying annoyed the guard, and he let them through without further talk. After she hailed a cab, Katarina told Natalie to stop crying and tell her what happened. Natalie explained how the Fischers had her hide under the sink when they saw the Stasi pull up outside. They told her when all was quiet for her to leave and go across the street to the park. She didn't see anything, but she had heard the voices.

The anxiety Katarina felt at that moment was not worth her ever helping again. What if she had not seen Natalie at the park? She felt like a stupid frightened rabbit. She hated Grigory at that moment.

Grigory was the last to exit the tunnel. Hans grabbed his shoulder. "Tell me she's out!"

"Yes, by the skin of my teeth this time." He said nothing about Natalie.

"Where did the blood come from?" Hans asked, fearing the worst.

"I encountered an obstacle," Grigory said dryly.

He and Hans moved toward the entrance of a building where they could talk away from the others. The refugees were in good hands. They were on alert when they heard running footsteps. It was just someone on the street. Hans looked down at his trembling hand. "I always feel nervous. Even over here we could be killed." He groaned. "So tell me about your obstacle."

They moved away to be sure the man standing against the building could not hear. No one could be trusted, but they had nothing on them to cause too much concern. Katarina was carrying the information they needed.

Grigory explained that he had been followed by a man with a knife, and when he had grabbed him and put his own knife to the man's throat, the bastard nicked his leg.

What really happened was this: He was heading toward the tunnel when he was aware someone was following him. The air was alive with added fear since the episode with Katarina and Natalie. Grigory hid in the shadow of a doorway and grabbed the man following him in passing. His knife grazed Grigory's leg, and he dropped it when Grigory pinned him against the wall, his own knife at his throat, ready and willing to take his final breath from him. Grigory pushed harder against his throat, the man whimpered, and he felt his body let go. He realized then that the man was merely a teenager, and the look of terror on his face was not one of a killer. He turned the boy around and looked into his eyes. "Tell me why you were following me."

The boy blurted out, "I need money for my family. We are starving."

"And you would have killed me or even died for whatever you could find in my pockets?"

"I…I…"

"Listen to me, young man. I will spare you only for one reason. You must survive this hell you're in, and when you are older, join the others who are working for freedom. Then, if you should die, you will die with dignity!"

He let go of the boy, who slumped against the wall and hid in the shadows. He looked back and saw the wretched boy crying. He pulled from his pocket the gold pendant the scientist had given him. He tossed it to the boy and said firmly, "Remember this day."

Hans always had to know. "Grigory, what did the man want, and did you leave him alive?"

"Let's just say this. He was not there to invite me for a drink, and I doubt we'll ever meet again."

Grigory would not let Hans know that his heart had softened.

The fog was coming in and the streetlights dimming as a taxi pulled up only a few yards away. Katarina was speaking with someone in the back seat. Hans could not imagine who she was sharing a taxi with. Grigory looked on, wondering what surprises his lover had in store for them next.

Katarina was giving Natalie instructions to say not a single word about going to the East.

Natalie was crying. Katarina had once again lost her temper to the point that the taxi driver had actually stopped the car and insisted that she stop berating the girl.

Katarina gave the driver money and told him to take the child home. Her parting words were said with a steely gaze. “Not a word, Natalie, or you will never ride horses and attend competitions again. I am still your mother, like it or not!”

Hans and Grigory stood waiting. Grigory was rubbing his tense neck. Hans reared back when he saw Katarina’s hand coming toward his face. “Don’t ever ask me to cross over again! You either, Grigory! I will help you with tunnels, but never again will I cross over and be so exposed to danger!”

There was a panicked recognition from Hans. This was the face he had seen when Katarina had tried to strangle her torturer and ordered him killed. She had never been this angry with him before, and he was confused as to why it had surfaced now.

Grigory knew why but just kept rubbing his neck. “I’m sorry. It was a successful mission, thanks to you. You slipped in and out without any problems. As it is, Kat, you are safe,” he carefully reminded her. Grigory’s voice was low. He placed his hands on her shoulders. “We need to move out of here now and become invisible. Did you give Hans the papers?”

She spoke with strange calm and handed them over. “Here.”

"You did a good thing, sister," Hans said with a sad face.

She knew she had been too hard on him and had taken out her fear for herself and Natalie on this man who had done so much for his country. She walked over and took his arm. "I love you, Hans. I will help you in whatever capacity you need me."

He watched her walk away with Grigory and disappear into the heavy fog. A strange feeling enveloped him. In the heat of the moment, he had forgotten to ask her who was in the taxi with her.

As they walked, Grigory said not a single word about Natalie.

Katarina said nothing else either, except, "I would like to go to a hotel, not to your place. I could use a nice bath and a great dinner."

"So it shall be." They checked into the Hilton.

They had a leisurely dinner and retired to bed early. He woke up during the night and found her sitting in a chair, a glass of wine in her hand, her hair loose around her face. She was staring at the blank wall as if it were a movie screen showing scenes from her life. The tears fell in slow streams, but her expression did not change. He wanted to bring her back to bed but thought better of it. He knew where she went in her mind, and she needed to work through it alone. He checked on her later, and her eyes had closed, and she was breathing evenly. He placed a blanket around her and let her be.

Tomorrow would be hell, as she was certain that Natalie would tell her parents all about it. There was no loyalty between them.

Chapter 32

Natalie sprang from the taxi and raced into the stable where her grandfather and Alexandra were tending to the horses. She ran into Alexandra's arms and buried her face in her chest. She had cried all the way home and there were no more tears left, but her face said everything.

Her grandfather, Jona, let go of the brush in his hand and bent down to get his granddaughter's attention. "What is wrong, Natalie?"

"My mother took me over to the evil side, Grandfather, and I was so scared when those mean people took away Mother's friends."

"I don't understand, Natalie. You left a note saying you were going shopping and to dinner with your mother."

Natalie bit her lip, realizing she didn't want to say more. She had said enough already, and her mother would be even more furious if she told them they hadn't gone shopping, and about the gift they didn't buy for her father, and when she had looked out the back window, she saw her Uncle Hans and a man she couldn't see through the fog. Instead she looked at Alexandra and touched her face. "I hope I grow up as beautiful as you, Alex."

Alexandra looked at her grandfather, and he knew she would not say anything to anyone else about this.

She would let him handle it. So she said, “Come with me, Natalie. Let’s go upstairs and change into something comfortable and maybe have a big bubble bath. I promise to stay with you.”

Upstairs, Alexandra drew the bath. From the doorway, Natalie said, “Alex, can you help me pull off my sweater? My side hurts.”

There was an audible gasp when Alexandra saw the large bruise on her side. She was afraid to ask her, but she must. “How did you get that?”

Natalie’s voice had a slight tremble. “I fell in the barn.”

Alexandra looked at her long and hard, giving her a chance to cough up the truth. “Okay, Natalie, we will let it lie, but I know differently.” She could feel her chest filling with anger, and then she just wanted to cry. She had not received physical abuse from Katarina, but her mother never failed to abuse her verbally and with her actions otherwise. There were several close calls, but she had been lucky they were interrupted by someone else. Alexandra had no more tears left for this woman.

“Alex, please don’t tell anyone.” Natalie’s plea softened to a whisper. “I don’t want my mother angry with me.”

“I won’t, Natalie, just promise you won’t ever go on any more excursions with her ever again. You go to our grandparents or Gertrude if she asks you to leave again.” Natalie promised.

****

Katarina opened her tired eyes to Grigory sitting opposite her, just watching her. She was happy to see him still there.

"I'm so sorry, Grigory, for lashing out at you and Hans."

"Sweet Katarina, we should apologize to *you*." He lifted her up from the chair and held her tight. "I love you, Katarina, and nothing will ever happen to you as long as I'm alive." He kissed her forehead and moved toward the bedroom. He spoke to her over his shoulder while putting on his pants. "I'll take you home, and then I have to pick up Fritz and take him to Israel."

In the kitchen, he handed her a cup of coffee.

"Just take me back to Hans. I would rather have him take me home. He can calm my parents down if there is an issue."

When they arrived in front of Hans's apartment, he held her face and kissed her softly. "Will you be all right?"

"I will, when you return."

She looked back at him as he pulled away from the curb. She adjusted her face. No more tears, she thought.

She had not seen the new larger penthouse that Hans leased for his growing family. When Christina answered the door, she smiled at seeing Katarina and pulled her through the house. Her stomach had expanded, and she was glowing in her pregnancy.

Katarina was shown into the guest bedroom. She saw some of Christina's slender clothing pushed to the side of the closet. She peeked into the living room and saw Christina bringing out a cheese and sausage platter with cups of soothing hot tea. "May I wear some of your clothing? I have been in the same outfit since yesterday."

"Of course. I certainly can't fit into anything these days."

The penthouse had a shower. She was used to bathing in the tub, but the water beating on her sore back felt wonderful. She stood there for a while, basking in it.

Clean and enjoying Christina's nice blouse and slacks, she walked into the living room at the same time Hans entered from the kitchen. His face lit up. "I'm so glad you are here, Kat. I was not sure where you went, so I told Mother you were here."

"Grigory brought me."

"I figured." He tried not to sigh.

Christina was spread out on the sofa, resting her aching legs. Hans walked over and placed his hand on her stomach. Katarina saw the love between the two of them. She hoped deep within her soul that Gertrude would grant a divorce, but at the back of her mind she suspected it would not happen.

Hans went into the bedroom and changed his clothing, returning much more relaxed.

Christina approached the subject with, "How many more tunnels, Hans?"

"I think only one more. Our refugees are more political than what the students are dealing with, the Girrmann Group. We also don't have enough couriers to go in ahead of us into the East to help the refugees find their way to us."

Katarina was slowly sipping peppermint tea. "Are the Americans helping at all, Hans?"

"Not really. President Kennedy is walking a fine line. He doesn't want another war, but he does recognize that the Soviets want to move on Berlin. We don't in reality have enough troops or German police here to take on the Soviets, so we shall play their game as long as we can. But when it comes to push and shove, I think Kennedy will do something. In the meantime, we will continue to have censorship of news outlets, including radio, except for what they can hear from Radio Free Europe. The Soviets have pretty much made East Germany a Communist satellite. We have only one more tunnel and a few more doctors and judges to get out, but it will be about a month from now. It's time now to pay attention to my wife and business." He picked up Christina's feet on the sofa, placed them gently in his lap and rubbed her swollen ankles.

"Beautiful legs," he teased. Katarina and Christina laughed.

"Kat, your brother has gone blind."

Katarina asked Hans the one burning question she had not asked Grigory, "Will Grigory be back for this last mission?"

"Yes, he will assist."

Katarina thought that might be the last time she would see Grigory for who knew how long, and it also occurred to her that after each mission, there was always a sense of pride knowing how many lives they had saved. "I know how much this means to Anthony and to you, so if you need me to go in as a courier, I will."

****

Her hands were on her hips. Hans observed her watching her father train a new horse. He asked himself if he had been right to accept her help on their last tunnel run. But he convinced himself that this time everything was arranged as in an assembly line, with more precision than any mission before, and they felt this would be their best refugee rescue in terms of efficiency, although the outlay of money was not as much as usual. Still, it was their last mission of this kind, and Hans felt strongly that it would be a success.

Katarina was laughing, her mood bright, and it occurred to Hans that it had taken her days to recover from prior missions. So why would she want to put herself in that situation again? He saw both hands leave her hips and swing up to her head, as she started to laugh. Their father was at his last wits with this horse. It would not move no matter how much he tried. This animal was stubborn like his sister, Hans thought, as he slid his arm around her waist. “Hello, beautiful sister.”

She dropped her laughter to a sweet smile. “And where have you been, handsome brother?” He was trying to reach an itch on his back, and Katarina moved behind him and set her nails to work. “Here? No, here? How about here?” When she finally located it and satisfied her brother, she told him that Anthony was up at the house.

“Let’s go inside,” Hans suggested, waving to his father as they left.

She checked the mail, relieved to find nothing from John. Silence was golden, for the time being.

Anthony was muttering to himself, trying to figure out the new coffeemaker. He wore glasses, and it was the first time Katarina had seen them on him. His eyes were even more intense behind the large lenses. He glanced over at them watching him in amusement.

“I can’t figure out these new gadgets. Why can’t Cook just leave the old ones out, and what was wrong with them anyway?” He offered a chuckle mixed with irritation.

Katarina peeked around Anthony. “Oh, you are in so much trouble. What’s that behind you?” Tracking in mud was a puppy about three months old, a tri-colored German Shepherd. Anthony picked him up as if he was already a member of the family and kissed his nose.

“I saw them being sold, believe it or not, on the side of the road. I couldn’t help myself, but he’s coming back with me unless he stays here or with Hans.”

Hans raised his hand in protest. “Not me, dear brother. I have a baby coming.”

Anthony put the puppy down and watched him track the rest of the mud across the kitchen floor. “I’ll take care of it later.”

With Katarina’s help, coffee was made, and three cups were poured. Hans was running his finger around the rim of the cup like his father often did just before he said something important. “Anthony, we are ready in two days.” Hans saw the playful light in their eyes change to a dark shade of serious. He hoped both of them were up for it.

Anthony cleared his throat. “Hans, it’s good this is your last run with Grigory. How many more people can that man kill without losing his soul altogether?”

“Anthony, consider this. Grigory is a soldier of the purest kind. He can’t afford the luxury of sympathy or compassion. He is fighting for all those who could not be saved in the camps, for his new homeland, for the innocent. You can’t fault him. I know he suffered terribly when his brother Nicholas died, and then witnessing his sister and parents murdered. We all know, at this table, how hard it is to live with death.”

Katarina shuddered, remembering Nicholas dying in her arms. It seemed so long ago, and he was another reason she should continue to join the forces. Like Grigory, his brother had saved her life.

They heard feet shuffling toward the door. “Oh, good saints in heaven, look at the floor! Where is all that mud coming from?” It was Lisa and Gertrude. Gertrude gave Hans a hard look and turned and left. In the corner the puppy was chewing gleefully on Cook’s garden shoe.

“Mother, he’s mine,” Anthony replied with a smile.

“Fine, then you take that shoe from his mouth, and give him one of your shoes instead.” His mother smiled through the order.

It struck Katarina at that very moment that the last time Anthony had loved a pet was right after the war, and the Soviet devils came to the church and killed the mother and all her pups. She would never forget watching him gather the lifeless creatures in his arms and scream to God in agony.

“Just clean up the mess and take it out to the barn. Your father will love helping you raise a new puppy. I don’t think it belongs at the church with you.” Anthony caught Katarina’s eye, and they had a moment of mutual understanding.

He lifted the puppy in his arms, and while he was kissing his mother on the forehead, the puppy licked her face. “Mother, it’s God’s creature, so I will take it if Father says no.”

She raised her eyebrows and smirked kiddingly, “Now tell me, when has your father ever said no to any stray that comes to this house?”

She left the kitchen looking back at her three children that she loved with all her heart. She and Jona were getting older, and she prayed that, before they died, all of them would settle into a peaceful life and take over this house and all that came with it. They had their faults, stubborn and brave, but they were her children, and she knew what was in their hearts. Her main worry would always be Katarina. As much as she ran from life, she always returned to her family. It was the one constant she could depend on.

Chapter 33

Hans gave the instructions in a brisk manner, too tired to elaborate; they had heard it before. If they were nervous, they showed no sign of it. But there was still time. Their mission was twofold. Peter had one more cache to deliver to the East, and their underground spies needed to hide even more. They would attempt to derail as many infrastructures as possible to slow down the Communists. Along with the American forces, they would be ready to take on the Soviet Union if they tried to cross into the West. Bringing to safety the people who were forced into creating weapons of war was the icing on the cake.

Hans and Grigory held back, securing the tunnel. Katarina accompanied Peter, who directed her to the café where she would find the refugees. He would be meeting with the operatives, and she was to guide these men to the tunnel at the synchronized time.

Peter was in his element, just like Grigory; nerves of steel and bent on success. Katarina hesitated when she and Peter parted ways, suddenly anxious without him near her. In a rare moment, she lifted her head and whispered to Anthony's God for his protection. Dressed in drab gray pants, thicker than she was accustomed to wearing, and a black sweater that hung loose on her frame, she would fit in with rest of the civilians. To further her disguise, she wore a simple colorless scarf tied underneath her chin, and a light black overcoat flung over her arm. She chose to wear riding boots that she could remove quickly. The sweat trickled down her back when she walked the streets of the East sector right out in the broad daylight. The people passing looked sad and worn, their heads mostly down, not wanting to look anyone in the eye. She saw cars slowing as they drove by pedestrians, looking directly at them, as if on alert. They had to be Vopos or Stasi, she thought, so she slowed her walk, not wanting to draw attention to herself.

A man watched her, still amazed by her beauty. Even in unattractive clothing she carried a seductive air about her as she smiled slightly to those who passed her. It was a shame, he thought, what could happen to her on this side. He would let her take her little friends to the spot. Then it was his time to introduce himself.

She found the café and located three older gentlemen sitting in a far corner, one wearing a red scarf turned backward around his neck, indicating they were her contacts. Realizing how tense her shoulders were, out of the blue came the most ludicrous thought—she wished Grigory was there to massage her shoulders with his warm and powerful hands. The hint of pleasure on her face brought a smile to the worried men when she sat down next to them. She ordered some water and regretted it after tasting what was brought. No wonder the coffee here tasted so bad—the water was simply awful; she kept her opinion to herself. She made small talk with these intelligent men who worked on the missile program and were being transported back and forth to the Soviet Union. They had first-hand knowledge of the weapons being relocated from Poland

and Hungary. If the Soviets attacked, they would strike from all directions.

Grigory was at the entrance of the tunnel, receiving the arriving refugees. They had expected about twenty, all high-profile citizens. He was not leaving until Katarina showed.

Katarina felt uneasy leaving the open air and ushering the men through the broken-down factory. They were heading toward the back to a set of stairs that led to the basement, where the entrance to the tunnel was waiting to deliver them to freedom, when out from behind a pile of rusty pipes stepped two intelligence officers with guns drawn. The three men stopped, frozen in fear. Katarina saw another man removing explosives from a case. They were already preparing to blow up the factory, and the tunnel with it. She backed into a hall that led to a warehouse. She thought she could run for it, until she heard breathing behind her and felt hard metal pressed into her side.

He yanked the scarf from her head and pulled her by the hair into the dusty warehouse. She could barely breathe with the gun now jammed in her ribcage. If Satan had a smile, it would be the one she now saw when Oliver Spitz turned her to face him.

"So we finally meet again," he said, his voice familiar. "I thought I almost had you at the Fischers'. You may add to your list of fond memories that couple who are now in prison because of you."

She gasped and wheezed at the same time.

He was nearly identical to Frederick in voice and appearance. Only his skin seemed tightly stretched, with a bloodless pallor as if he were walking dead. His eyes lacked luster, and his teeth were chipped from grinding them in his sleep. The narrow scar above his left eye had widened since she had seen him last. He held her against the wall with his body, crushing the breath out of her, his chest heaving up and down, the stench of his breath just inches from her face. He ran the gun down her side, and then he stepped back, tracing her body with his eyes. "Take off the jacket," he barked. She stood frozen in place and could not get her arms to move.

"I'm bored, Katarina." He sighed wearily, reaching down into the top of her pants, enjoying the fear in her eyes. "Come, come, do I not remind you of your husband, my brother?" His fingers clawed at her pubic hair. "Katarina, I'm sure you wouldn't mind if my officers outside the door have a little piece of you after I'm done." He tried to rip through the pants with one hand, but the fabric would not tear. Exasperated, he clumsily attempted to pull his hand out, and his fingers caught in the elastic of her panties.

"No!" she yelled and pushed him back with such force her power took him by surprise. The gun flew from his hand when they fell to the floor. Katarina, now on top of him, slid down his body and released his hand from her pants. His head had slammed against the concrete with the fall; he was temporarily stunned. She lunged for the gun, but he caught her by the legs and pulled her back. He threw his body on top of her; his breath reeked of bile. He took control of the gun again.

"I almost had my niece. I would not have killed her but would have trained her and turned her against all of you." He ripped through her blouse with the gun and lifted one of the bra straps from her shoulder. "You took my brother's life. I could kill you now, or send you to the prisons in the Soviet Union. Which do you choose?"

She screamed as loud as she could for help. He slapped her hard across the face. The guards outside would be thinking he was raping her, as they knew of his history with women. Her yells would be useless, but he knew he would not shoot her, either. She was a valuable commodity, and he knew Grigory would come for her. They had been trying to capture him for the longest time. He had killed too many of their important men and was continuously interrupting their missions. For himself, though, he would like to see her tortured, a pleasurable thought for a demon like himself. He yanked on her zipper, and she gouged his face with her nails. She let out a primal scream as he tugged away at her pants. "Shut up!" he yelled and pummeled her face with his fist. She was bleeding from her nose and nearly unconscious when he rolled her over on her stomach.

He touched the blood on his face and licked his finger. Then he rose to his knees and began pulling her pants down. "You're dead now."

Grigory and Peter had gone looking for Katarina. She was already past the time to have returned. They heard the scream, then the second one, and Anthony came running, Hans at his side. Peter instructed both of them to stay. He and Grigory would be back.

They climbed the stairs to the ground floor and saw two men kneeling over explosives. To their right were the three refugees lying face down, a Stasi standing over them. Peter and Grigory worked their way toward them behind the stacks of barrels. Peter reached the first Stasi and with a vise grip in hand, he smashed the man to the ground, snapped his head, and the man's eyes went blank. The three refugees stayed perfectly still. At the same time, Grigory easily slit the throats of the two men working on the explosives. Barely a sound was made as he carefully dropped them to the floor. He signaled he was moving toward the area where they had heard the screams.

The two men guarding Spitz were now laughing, hearing Katarina's whimpering from inside the door. One was whispering in German, "I hope he leaves something for me. I don't like sex with dead women." Grigory had no problem shooting both men in the head, a silencer on his gun. He stepped over their bodies and carefully opened the warehouse door.

He felt like a caged animal when he saw Katarina's legs fiercely kicking as she was being dragged away. He couldn't let Spitz reach the outside, where she could be lost to them. He heard her fighting back, and when he got to a place where he could see them clearly, he saw that her blouse had been torn from her and her face was bloody. From behind a large piece of machinery he let himself be known.

"Spitz, you have no place to go. You are surrounded, and your men are dead. Let her go and we will let you walk away."

"Like hell you will!" Spitz kicked Katarina in the head and fired a volley of bullets in Grigory's direction.

There was silence from Katarina when Grigory called out to her. An unstoppable rage was running through his veins. He pulled out the Beretta from the back of his belt. Peter was heading out a side door to get to Spitz from the outside, but he was forced to retreat when he saw men unloading a truck full of explosives. He feared if he shot them down, Spitz would hear the gunshots and kill Katarina right on the spot.

Spitz looked down at Katarina, face down, the blood spewing from her nose to the floor. He knew Grigory took no prisoners, and she was now his only hope. The guards must have been killed or they would have been there by now. He had to think fast. He turned to pick up a concrete block to throw across the room for a distraction. Katarina tried with every fiber of her being to ignore the pain as it seemed her life was being extinguished. She saw a screwdriver on the floor, and with the last of her strength, she reached for it and plunged it into his calf. Spitz yelped like a dog whose tail had been slammed in the door, and in his pain and rage, he threw the concrete block at Katarina's back. He grabbed her by the arm, and with his leg dragging, he tugged her toward the back door, the gun aimed at her head. Grigory was shadowing him on the other side of the rubble.

Like a bull with his head down, Grigory rammed into Spitz, firing two shots in his side as they fell. Taking no time to evaluate the damage, he turned his attention to Katarina, bloody, bruised, nearly deprived of life. Peter came running in from the front entry and saw Spitz on the floor, the blood oozing from his side, and Katarina's body like a rag doll on Grigory's shoulder. "There's more out back. We must hurry!" Peter urged, covering them as they ran to the tunnel.

Peter ordered the three men still lying on the floor to get up and follow them. Katarina made no sound, nor did she open her eyes. Grigory feared she was dead. A guttural, animalistic noise rose from his belly and flew out of his mouth as he ran.

Peter and Grigory heard the gunfire hitting the machinery just above them, the sparks falling down on their heads. They were just feet from the stair entrance to the tunnel when a riddling of bullets chewed into the machinery and the floor around them. One of the bullets skimmed across Grigory's thigh. With the surge of adrenaline pulsing through him, he didn't feel it. All he could think about was getting Katarina to safety. He tore down the stairs while Peter opened fired on the shooters from the top of a ladder. With three less guns to worry about, he ran toward the tunnel.

Anthony knew something was wrong, and he ordered Hans to radio for a doctor as soon as he reached the West. He let out a gasp when he saw her condition, her face unrecognizable, covered in blood. More Stasi were coming toward them, and they heard Peter curse, asking for a weapon. His gun was empty. Anthony grabbed the gun from Grigory's hand and said, "Go, get her out of here!"

Over Peter's shoulder a Luger fired, and down went two men. He turned and saw Anthony, his eyes filled with rage. Together they scrambled through the tunnel and caught up with Grigory, struggling to get the two of them through the tight muddy hole, hunched over with her body dangling from his back. The three refugees were moving as quickly as they could up ahead. There was nothing Anthony and Peter could do but follow helplessly behind. Anthony, terrified that because he had killed again, God might take Katarina in return for his sin, reached for his sister's arm and prayed out loud. Memories of losing his own family filled Grigory's head, and before he knew it, he was repeating the prayer over and over with Anthony until they reached the West side.

They heard the explosion at the other end, just as they were climbing the stairs out. Hans was smiling when he saw the three refugees come out first, and then he lost it when he saw Grigory and Katarina.

The doctor was immediately beside Katarina. He shook his head, a hopeless look on his face. Anthony started to move forward; he had to say prayers over her. Grigory stood next to him, repeating the prayer from the book of Isaiah, "Do not fear, for I am with you; do not be dismayed, for I am your God, I will strengthen you and help you; I will uphold you with my righteous hand." Hans's eyes filled with tears as he reached for Anthony's hand.

Peter shook the doctor's shoulders. "Stop shaking your head as if she is dead!"

The doctor turned to him. "Her pulse is weak, she is barely holding on, and the bullet lodged in her has to be removed quickly."

"Bullet?" Peter and Grigory said the word in unison. They had not known she was shot.

The ambulance arrived. There was no taking her to their home—the damage was too severe and required hospital care.

Katarina kept hearing her name called from far away, and through the horrific pain, she fought to see who was calling for her. Then she saw lights flashing above her and heard Anthony's voice: "Save her, for God's sake!" She drifted in and out of the darkness.

At the hospital, Katarina was taken straight to surgery and met by a team of doctors. They removed the bullet and stitched her head at the same time; the doctors bent over her in urgency. The gaping wounds on her back and arm would have to wait.

Peter looked down and saw blood oozing from Grigory's pants leg. No one had realized, not even Grigory, that he had taken two bullets. His only focus was on Katarina. He was immediately placed on a stretcher. "Peter, please make sure I'm informed about her as soon as you hear."

Anthony and Peter stood outside Katarina's room, while Grigory lay next to them on the stretcher. A nurse was cutting away at his pants while his room was being prepared. Waiting to hear about Katarina's fate was unbearable. Anthony stood in silent prayer while Peter went to the restroom to scrub the dirt and blood from his hands.

As he was being wheeled into surgery, Grigory heard the doctor talking to Anthony. "We are hoping she will make it. The next twenty-four hours is crucial. We're highly concerned for the baby. She is about twelve weeks, from what we can tell."

Grigory grabbed the doorjamb and stopped the stretcher from rolling into the surgery room. As the nurse stood back, startled, he looked over at Anthony. "Did you hear that correctly?"

"We can talk about it later," Anthony said, dropping his head once again in prayer. Now he had two lives to pray for.

As Grigory was being put under, the words ran over and over in his head, "She is pregnant with my child. Why didn't she tell me?"

Katarina's parents arrived with Elvie and Dietrich. Hans embraced his parents and told them what he knew. They saw blood on both Hans's and Peter's clothing. In all the commotion, they had not noticed.

Both Lisa and Jona closed their eyes and wept.

Hours later, Peter left his family to get back to headquarters. He knew there were those who wanted to know about the delivery of the cache, and he would need to type up a report to Hanover and Berlin. All in a day's work, he thought as he walked out into the dark and stood looking up at the moon, asking God to spare Katarina.

****

The next morning, Anthony was sitting in the hospital room with his rosary, looking down at his sister. Grigory had hobbled out of his own room and was sitting on the opposite side, his head resting on her bed next to her arm. She was hooked up with tubes and had an oxygen mask on her face. Several of her ribs had been broken and breathing was difficult. But she was breathing, and that was all that mattered.

Grigory and Anthony slept in the hospital over the next few days, and Lisa and Jona came in and out of the room, checking on her progress. She was in a coma, and everyone was waiting for her to wake. Her eyes were bruised, and one was swollen completely shut. Grigory begged her in whispers to come back to him.

Anthony saw the slight movement of her fingers on the fourth day, and then her lashes fluttered. Both men began talking to her at once. Anthony wiped her forehead with a cool cloth. "Wake up, Kat. You have never let the darkness overtake you. Wake up now. Your family misses you."

There was only a hoarse whisper when she opened her eyes. "Baby?"

Grigory leaned in. "The baby is fine. You just concentrate on getting better." He took her hand and kissed it. She closed her eyes and said nothing more.

The nurses and doctor shooed Grigory and Anthony out into the hallway just as Hans arrived. Anthony shared the good news about Katarina waking. The three men sat together in silent relief. Anthony looked at Grigory's bruised and stitched body and leaned in and asked in a low voice, "Grigory, I have to ask…did you kill him?"

Hans was also curious; they had not talked about the incident.

Grigory spoke with hesitation, the memory foggy in his head. "I'm not sure. I was so concerned about Katarina, I just took some shots at him and hoped he was dead. I know for certain that I put two bullets in him. Peter and I were concerned about the Stasi outside. We just wanted Katarina out. If the Stasi had blown up the tunnel before we got there…I'm not sure any of us would have survived."

Grigory turned to Hans. "What did you tell the German police?"

Hans suddenly hushed when they saw Gertrude coming down the hallway with Alexandra and Helena. Hans stepped in front of Gertrude. "Gertrude, it's best that you leave."

Her look was defiant, and she stood taller when she spoke. "I'm here for Alexandra and Helena. Alexandra has the right to see her mother by name."

"Look, Gertrude, this is not the place for your venom. I heard you tell Mother how she deserved to feel pain after the pain she caused Natalie and all her children. How could you say that, when she has been so close to death?"

Alexandra didn't want the argument and stepped

forward. “Uncle Hans, just let me go in and see her. I won’t stay long, and I’ll just give her small talk. She didn’t deserve this. We all know that.”

They waited soberly outside the room, the tension still in the air, while Alexandra went in and sat next to her mother, taking her hand and talking about her job, the horses, and other everyday topics. She came back out and went to Helena’s arms in tears. “She didn’t deserve this…and I read on her chart she is pregnant.”

Gertrude’s eyes narrowed. She looked first at Hans with a scorned woman’s accusation and then set her gaze on Grigory. “You both deserve to rot in hell!” In a huff, she walked past them toward the stairs.

Alexandra mouthed her apology to them as she left to follow Gertrude. Helena sat silently with crossed arms, staring at the cross hanging on the wall directly over Grigory’s head. She wanted to laugh.

Chapter 34

Katarina wanted desperately to get out of the hospital. Back home, her parents were waiting for her arrival. They would take care of her and start the healing process.

She was frustrated. Grigory had to leave. They had talked briefly about the baby, but once again his country was more important than she was. Hans tried to explain how Grigory had saved her, how they both could have died over there, and how much gratitude he deserved for his heroics. It seems they were always trying to explain Grigory, as well as Katarina. The odds were against them. In the end, she talked Anthony into speaking with her parents about her returning to Paris to recuperate. She wanted out of Berlin.

Hans closed the refugee rescue project down and donated money to the university students for their efforts instead. It was becoming too dangerous, and Christina was in tears all the time with the baby almost due. The last mission was the final straw, and the one before that should have been it. The Von Rahmels finally realized they had contributed enough.

Wolfgang Pilz, the scientist they had moved out of Berlin, suddenly disappeared without the British able to take him back to London. He knew of Egypt's rocket program, which could harm Israel down the road, and had evidence regarding the development of chemical biological gas-filled warheads in Russia. Oddly, he had mysteriously disappeared at the same time Grigory did.

Peter did receive information that Grigory was instructing the use of weapons and sabotage technique in Africa. He would be gone for several months, leaving Katarina to deal with her pregnancy on her own.

Before he closed up the apartment, Grigory had stood in the bedroom for the last time, looking down at the unmade bed, her nightgown still there spread across the crumpled sheets. He buried his face in the pillow to inhale her essence for what could be the last time. Lost in his memories, he twirled around when he thought he heard her laughter. He swore he would be back. He would take her to Israel with his child.

****

Katarina was driven to Paris by Hans, and Elvia was to join her later. Hans stayed for a week, giving the house help vital instructions for her health. Anthony was there every day, making sure she ate, and eventually they progressed to small walks. The nightmares came on a more frequent basis, and because she was pregnant, alcohol could not save her. She healed slowly in body, but not in mind. The earlier tortures were now replaced with a more recent one, and Oliver Spitz was the main character. The fact that no one could verify his death left her, once again, in a constant state of fear.

****

December 1963

The birth came in the middle of the night. Christina was there to assist the midwife. She had already given birth to her own son, and she was relishing motherhood.

Her spirit filled the room, and she was as excited for Katarina as she had been for herself, yet there was an underlying sense of doom beneath her joy. She had not told Katarina that Gertrude had begun threatening Hans with her suicide if he didn't come home. Hans and she both carried the guilt daily. It was a dark cloud that hung over their lives.

The following days held visitors and gifts for the new baby boy. Flowers arrived from Francis. The man was relentless. If only she had an ounce of love for him.

She named the baby Benjamin Leibowitz. Very few had known Grigory's last name before he had it changed after the war to fit in better in Israel. His old name was Tadeusz, a life he left behind after the death of his family and his village was burnt to the ground by the Germans.

Soon Hans's fears came true when Gertrude carried out the threat and attempted to take her life. It was thwarted when Lisa found her in time, before she had bled to death. This was the end of a happy life for Hans and Christina. Christina knew deep down inside he could not stay with her, so she made it easier on both of them and decided to move on without Hans. The arrangement for their son, Rudy, would keep him involved with the Von Rahmel family, and she was given the rights to any of the homes to use at her will. Lisa and Jona wanted the child there for birthdays and holidays when possible, and they would work with Gertrude on the matter. The important thing was to keep their grandson in their lives. Rudy, a Von Rahmel by right, would not be a secret to the world.

As it happened, it was in Paris that inexplicable joy entered Christina's life. Her law professor was in Paris, opening a new branch of their law firm. She was asked to come aboard, and she left the Von Rahmels' business to enter international law out of Paris, a dream she had always hoped to fulfill. She avoided seeing Hans, as her life had changed and she had grown very close to her professor. Hans would never recover from losing her. He would continue having insignificant affairs, but Christina was his heart.

When Christina announced she was engaged to her professor, Katarina was happy for her, knowing she had to move on, just as she herself should move on and divorce John if she wanted Grigory to stay in her life. But in her anger, she had ripped the divorce papers up when they arrived.

Chapter 35

He looked down at the dead man, whose eyes gazed sightlessly straight up, the mouth open in surprise. He'd grown used to all that. Grigory was finishing up last-minute details, meticulous in precision.

The fat man's breathing had been heavy when he caught up to her, and no wonder—he was in grotesque condition, his belly hanging over his belt like a balloon half filled with water. She had tripped over the body that Grigory just minutes earlier had slain, and fell right into the fat man's arms, her dropped gun bouncing off the dead man's chest. He was confronting her, holding her arms and making demands. She zeroed in on the Beretta next to the body. In one swift move, she kicked the fat man in the groin, grabbed the gun, and shot him in the head.

"What the hell, Mira?" Grigory grabbed her by the arm. "He was to be extracted, not killed. I had no choice but to kill his chauffeur, but now look what you've done!" He felt frustrated; she was too quick not to think things through without concern for the consequences.

"Help me clean this mess up."

They both pulled the bodies behind a line of trash cans and took their wallets to make it look like a robbery.

She noticed he was limping. She looked at him

worriedly as they made their way back to the hotel down a side street. In her black tights and clinging black sweater, the outline of her curves reminded him of Katarina. Coal black hair tucked inside the black beret made her green eyes appear like a cat on the prowl. She was clearly angry.

"Grigory, stop being upset with me. The man was a pig! I almost had to sleep with him to get the information, until that damn phone call came in, and he ushered me out of the room."

He stopped in the middle of their walk and looked at her with something he wanted to say but decided not to.

They arrived back at Le Dixseptième, an old fourteenth-century hotel in Brussels. Mira ran ahead of him, excited to be there. He was still limping when he made it to their room. She had already ordered a bottle of wine with a plate of appetizers. He sat down in the chair and contemplated her. His tone was serious.

"Mira, this is why I like working alone."

"Yes, but you have no charm and would not have gotten the information out of his briefcase, as I did." She tossed him the roll of film. "While he was tending the bath, thinking I was to join him, I took the pictures. I doubt you could have done the same, unless of course the man was homosexual, and even then, you're much too manly to participate in such a waste."

She smiled as she walked over to him. "*You* prefer women. *Real* women." She stood before him looking into his eyes. "Take off your pants, so I can see what is wrong with your leg."

He sat looking at her, reluctance in his demeanor.

"Oh, please, just how many times have we seen

each other?" She leaned over and her lips touched his.

"Not now, Mira."

She knew better than to argue with him, and even if he wasn't in the mood, she would make him get there. She always went after what she wanted, and she always wanted him.

She stepped back and stripped down, leaving her clothing on the floor. He watched her walk into the bathroom. She had the most exquisite ass. "I'm going to take a bath. Join me if you'd like."

There was a knock at the door. He pulled out his weapon and asked through the closed door who it was. "Room service." He grimaced in pain, took deep breaths to steady himself, and opened the door to the bellhop and his delivery.

In the bathroom, he removed his clothing, exposing a deep blood-encrusted gash, an old wound reopened in his struggle with the chauffeur. Incompetent oaf, he called himself. Peter would've laughed.

She looked at him now, as she soaked in the warm water. How many times had she enjoyed his powerful energy when they made love, his hands covering every inch of her body without restraint. She rose from the bath and wrapped her wet body in a towel, then ordered him to sit on the edge of the tub so she could carefully wash the wound.

Pulling him to the bedroom, she pushed him back on the bed, and the towel dropped to the floor. She stood looking at his nakedness, then threw her body on top of his.

He could feel her back arch from his touch, as his hands began to explore. They had used each other many times in his effort to forget Katarina, who had not even tried to divorce John. She had refused to move to Tel Aviv to his aunt and uncle's home. His son was now three months old.

Mira never asked him anything, and he never inquired about her. She was the darker side of him, their lovemaking rough and uninhibited, lasting until they were physically depleted. His mouth was now crushing hers with a growing ferocity, pinning her down, trapping her like a wild animal. He wanted to possess her. Knowing she could take him down at any time was part of the thrill. She was a trained assassin, his rival. He was gripping her hair and pounding her with his thrusts. Savagely.

Mira understood him as a tormented man and expected nothing from him. There were times she wanted more, but she would quickly dismiss the thought. They were who they were, and they remembered that the next morning when they awoke to their nakedness, the bottle of wine empty by the bed. They dressed quickly, spoke little over breakfast, and parted ways…until the next time.

****

Grigory arrived back in Israel, at the house by the sea in Tel Aviv. His parents had bought the house and would have grown old there if not for their sudden deaths. Now, his aunt and uncle occupied the main home while he took over the guest cottage, his preference and ideal for his comforts. Aunt Esther had a room decorated for a nursery and was quite thrilled with anticipation of a little one. She would welcome him home with arms full of love, and his uncle, content with working on sailboats, would ask Grigory to assist him. This was his home and where he wanted to raise his child.

Aunt Esther was having tea on the porch with someone when he walked up unannounced, and with his first hello both women jumped, almost tipping over the teapot. She ran to her nephew and squeezed his face in her hands, kissing both cheeks with vigor. She looked behind him for Katarina and their child, but he was alone. She tried not to show her disappointment.

"Darling, this is Alise Ronning, my friend from Sweden." They nodded a hello, as Grigory had remained standing on the steps. "She is working here as an archeologist with our museums. We met when I was doing the cataloging there. But come sit with us, Grigory, and have some tea."

She was a dark blonde with lighter streaks of silver blending through her hair. He noticed first the long eyelashes—thick and luxurious, they popped out like a kitten's. Her frame was delicate, with small wrists, a wisp of a woman, perhaps five feet three, he surmised. Her reading glasses were propped on her head, and if he hadn't known better, at first glance he would have thought she was a teenager. In fact, she was twenty-eight, and much too young for him, he thought, but she was appealing all the same. She offered her hand and formally introduced herself.

His aunt hurried to the kitchen to bring out some pastries and left the two to talk.

"Are you here for long?" Grigory began, as the woman seemed reluctant to start the conversation.

"I have a year here," she answered. His intense eyes made her nervous, and a blush of soft pink bloomed on her cheeks. Grigory was amused.

"Your aunt tells me your wife and child will be

joining you."

His body stiffened. "He will eventually come, but I doubt she will, and for the record, I'm not married."

His aunt returned with a question that had popped into her brain while in the kitchen. "How long will you be here, Grigory?" She plucked a small bite of pastry from the tray and held it in front of his face. "Here, have one, my boy."

"I'm not certain how long," he said, chewing through the answer. Before she could force another one down him, he stood and said, "Aunt Esther, I'm going upstairs to freshen up, and then I need to rest for a while."

As he walked away, he looked back at his aunt's guest. "Miss Ronning, I hope to see you again."

For some reason, he made her feel uneasy. "I doubt we will, since I have a very busy schedule, but thank you."

He gave a light smirk. "I will see you again, count on it." He walked into the home and left the young woman slightly unnerved. He liked it that way.

His aunt, who was now grinning, said to Alise, "My dear girl, he always gets what he wants, and if he wants to see you, I can promise you he will."

Alise stuttered, "Esther, he is deeply involved, from what you have told me, and I don't find it comfortable to be in the middle of that."

"Well, I believe that woman has broken his heart too many times, and he is trying to cut the rope…but he wants his son. He will work it out soon. Katarina needs to also let him go. The man needs to be happy just once in his life."

****

Two days later he was at her doorstep in Paris. Grigory had not seen his son, heard the child's cry, or held him in his arms. When Katarina opened the door with Benjamin on her chest, he was startled by the eruption of emotions. He had not seen her since Berlin, and there she stood, the most beautiful woman of his life, greeting him now with his flesh and blood in her arms. She pulled him into the hallway and planted a long kiss on him, the baby in the middle. Then she handed him his son.

She allowed him only a few seconds to behold his child, long enough for Grigory to decide that he favored his brother, Nicholas. She motioned for him to follow.

"Katarina, he is so handsome." The little bit of hair that was coming in was stark black, and he had eyes identical to his mother's. No other child of Katarina's had those marvelous eyes, but his son did. The little boy giggled and reached out to touch Grigory's face. Katarina stood and observed.

"He is a miracle," he said softly.

She took him from Grigory, and said sternly, "Yes, and it's also past his sleep time. Come into the nursery and put him to bed."

Grigory stood watching his son fall asleep for a long time before he went to find Katarina. He couldn't resist her, and it seemed natural for both of them when he picked her up and carried her around the house kissing and laughing until he found the bedroom. No words needed, they had both missed each other terribly.

As always, their lovemaking was bittersweet, and he fell quickly under her spell. And as always, they vowed silently to never leave one another. They heard the baby cry, and Grigory instinctively got out of bed.

Katarina pulled him back, saying, "He has a nanny. You will see him at breakfast."

Grigory awoke to the reality of life—he had a son. But as he looked at Katarina, her fine long legs outside the sheets, her hair disheveled from the night of lovemaking, he realized also that he didn't have a wife. He quietly slipped back into his jeans and pulled the sweater over his head and tiptoed barefoot down the hallway toward the sound of Benjamin's cooing and the smell of coffee.

"Hello," he greeted the startled nanny, who held the spatula up as a weapon upon seeing this barefoot stranger in the kitchen. Grigory laughed inwardly at her response. "I'm his father. Sorry if I startled you." He presented a first-rate smile.

"No, no!" She laughed at herself, lowering the spatula. "Please visit with your son. I will pour you a cup of coffee."

Grigory held the baby in outstretched arms, studying his face. "His eyes are spectacular, are they not?" he bragged to the nanny. The boy was a lively little creature, squirming and kicking, yet his eyes never left his father's, and Grigory knew with certainty that he was indeed his child. At that moment he was pained that his parents would never know him.

Katarina entered the kitchen in a flowing green silk robe. She was the picture of a pampered woman, sitting at the table with a cup of coffee in her hand, relaxed in knowing that the nanny would handle the necessities—diaper changes, feeding, all the motherly things she could not find joy in doing. The nanny tiptoed around her like she was a porcelain doll.

They planned an outing, and Grigory insisted that

they take the baby without the nanny. He wanted to push his son in a stroller, as he had seen so many other proud fathers do. Katarina thought he had lost his mind.

Later that morning, they took a taxi to the district of the Romanesque church of Saint Germain des Prés. Katarina saw an outfit in a shop window and ran inside to browse while he stood outside with the boy; those passing by smiled at him and the baby, with an occasional pat on the child's head by the elderly. At first, from years of training, he eyed everyone with suspicion, until he finally relaxed into the role of a father instead of a professional assassin.

Katarina came out of the shop with several outfits, and they made their way to Rue de Rivoli for a café.

Grigory started the conversation he had saved for the right moment. "I saw your wardrobe back at your place, and it's a lot of clothing to take back to Tel Aviv."

Her body stiffened. He noticed her reaction.

"Trust me, you will love it there, and my aunt is so looking forward to the two of you."

"We can talk about it later," she said flippantly. "Anthony is meeting us tonight in the Latin quarter to see the French classic *Les Enfants du Paradis*. It is a drama very similar to our lives."

"My French is limited, as you well know," he said with a slightly agitated tone, and then changed it when she looked at him crosswise. "Couldn't we just dine alone, instead, and get to know each other again?"

She laughed. "I think we did that last night."

"Yes, but we have always known each other that way. What I'm talking about is getting to know each other now that we are away from Germany…and our causes. Let's make it special, go out without worries or deadlines in the beautiful city of lights. Make up for all the times we didn't have together."

Katarina wanted to be with him but on her terms. He would need to live with her in Paris to make it work. He would have to stop hunting. She agreed to their special night out.

He had seen her dressed to the nines before, but not for him. She walked out of the bedroom in a black taffeta dress covered with a thin layer of black lace entwined with silver threads, and her skin shone through the lacy sleeves. Around her graceful long neck she wore diamonds, and on her wrist an emerald-and-diamond bracelet. He hated the bracelet, remembering it was a gift from Francis. He had brought along a fine Italian suit that he had worn on only one occasion, and together they were a striking couple.

In the restaurant, popular French tunes surrounded them, and they were led to a corner table where they would face one another. Grigory felt an immediate need to have his back to the wall, a habit from so many years of covert observation. He could not let her see his discomfort and ordered wine to calm his nerves. He wanted this night to be perfect, as he was certain he could woo her to his world, if he had a chance. There were always so few chances.

She was genuinely happy to be with him, this man she had wanted for so many years. She had no desire to share him with a country or other people. Her selfish side was always just below the surface.

The restaurant was not far from the apartment, so they decided to walk back. As it claimed, Paris delivered its love promise, and the soft twinkling streetlights led the way. They walked slowly, hand in hand.

He spotted a bench and walked her over to it. They sat for a moment, relishing the fine dinner they had just eaten. They had skipped dessert in lieu of more wine. The evening presented a perfect setting for honesty. He turned to her and gave her his final plea. “Katarina, come back with me. I don’t have much time before I have to return to Israel. The paperwork has been done from my side to bring you and Benjamin, and there won’t be any problems with your entry.”

His sincerity was undeniable, and she listened, knowing full well her answer had been decided months ago.

“We finally have the freedom to walk away from everything,” he said.

She looked away. He didn’t know that she had not signed the divorce papers.

“I can’t leave. I don’t want to live in Israel, and I don’t want to be away from my family.”

He looked up to the sky and closed his eyes. The woman was as stubborn as he.

“Katarina, you can always visit your family.”

“Well, then, what will be your sacrifice? Will you give up what you do?”

Anger flashed in his eyes. “Why won’t you do this for me?” he pleaded.

“I may, in my own time, but not right now.”

She tugged on his coat sleeve and made him look at her. “Please stay, make a new life here with me and Benjamin.”

“Katarina, I can’t. This is not the place I want to live in. There are no roots here, and we fought too hard for our own homeland."

She pulled away and pouted like a child. "Well, then, how much love is left for me?"

"You have all my love. You always have. There is no reason for you to ever question that."

She rose and walked slowly away.

He stopped her. "I need to ask you. Have you bothered to retain an attorney for a divorce? Let's call a spade a spade. You want me to leave Israel and live with a married woman who has my son?"

She was fuming now, anger surpassing the sadness. "I have not retained anyone. I can't hurt him any more. The man has been nothing but kind to me, no matter what I've done. I have his child thousands of miles away, and he wants Natalie back when he retires."

"Why would it matter? It's not as if you ever spend time with her. You are content with your parents raising her. I'm not sure I want my son raised by your parents."

She had nothing to say to that. It was the truth. They reached the apartment and entered it in a stiff silence.

"Katarina, I'll sleep in the guest room." His statement said it all.

"Please don't." The panic rose in her voice. "I need you."

"Truth is, you don't need anyone. I'm coming to realize that you'd rather fight your ghosts and demons on your own." He paused and looked down at the ground, assuring himself of what he was about to say. "Let me be perfectly clear, and do not doubt me, Katarina. I'm taking my son back to Israel. I would not oppose me on this if I were you."

He made his last stand. No more bantering, no

stupid excuses, and no more lies. This was her last chance, and he hoped she would take it. Either come with him or fight for her son.

The next morning, he slipped into her bedroom and left a note lying next to her on the bed. He watched her sleep. Her arm was draped over her eyes. No doubt she was hiding from her nightmares again. He chose not to wake her. With a kiss on the baby's forehead and a promise to be back for him, he was out the door.

She woke to an empty bed and found the note where he should have been. She pulled her knees to her chest and cried after reading the words. She didn't want to lose him, but she couldn't leave, either. This was what she'd thought she wanted, all her life, and the one person who loved her through everything, her faults, her insane world, who looked the other way and forgave her—yet she could not sacrifice for him. She picked up a vase and threw it at the door. The crash of the glass represented the shattering of her life.

Chapter 36

She found herself in the rectory, sobbing. Anthony was saying Mass as she waited for him. She was sitting on the floor cross-legged, rocking back and forth, as he entered the office. She looked bedraggled and frightened, as he had seen her too many times in the past. He lifted her off the ground and embraced her.

He moved her to the chair, trying not to show his despondency over her plight. He was already burdened with his own shame for killing again, and seeing her like this brought that sin and his current quandary closer to the surface. He was in hot water for protecting the abused women, moving them out of terrible situations. Critical of his own church for some of the priests' illicit behavior toward younger women and children, he had written several letters to the cardinals and bishops, for which they sternly silenced him. He was threatened with excommunication. The thought of leaving the church plagued him daily, yet he could not turn the other cheek on matters such as these. It was all beginning to take a toll on him in body and spirit, and each day he felt weaker in both.

He questioned many things, but he never questioned his love for his God and his church. He would not forsake them, just as he would never forsake Katarina. Yet as he sat there watching her cry, he knew his and Hans's promise to protect her was not enough.

"What has you so upset?"

Katarina held her hands in front of her face, still crying.

"I can't help you until you tell me what's wrong, Kat."

She sat up straight. He wiped her cheeks with his handkerchief. "He wants me to go back to Israel with him. He wants me to divorce. I can't go to a country where we as Germans tried to eliminate a whole race."

"I don't think that is the issue. You just don't want to go. I could say I admire your tenacity for not wanting a divorce, but what is the real reason for holding onto a marriage when your husband wants out, and you stay here as if you can be married and have separate lives? And then there's Grigory, a man who has loved you all the while. I don't think I can advise you or even help you."

"You can't help me?"

"I want to, but I can't tell you what your heart wants. But I can tell you what I see, and I worry about Grigory's job for obvious reasons, and I don't believe you could find happiness in Israel with all its differences and strife."

"He wants his son," she said laconically.

Anthony leaned back in his chair. He closed his eyes and said a small prayer for her. He knew her answer before she spoke.

She kept her head down, not wanting to see his face. "I'm going to let him take Benjamin. I can't raise him on my own, and you know I'm not good with children. I never should have had children. It seems once they start to speak, they scare me."

"Kat, you leave your children so easily. I don't

understand this part of you." He pressed his palms to his eyes and sighed so loudly Katarina thought he was about to yell at her. "I am not one to judge."

He looked over at her, the sister who had been through hell and back and managed to bring beautiful souls into this life in spite of it all. "God works in mysterious ways. That, I do believe. Now, what is it you want from your big brother?"

"Anthony, let us baptize Benjamin. I don't want Grigory to know, but it's important for all my children to be baptized."

All those refusals to attend church, to eliminate deep prayer from her life, and she still wanted her children blessed. She herself had been baptized as a child. He remembered the first baptism with Alexandra, in the concentration camp, when he was certain she and her child would die. And here she was, right in front of him, still alive after that and so much more. He knew then that her belief was even stronger than she could imagine. He also knew that as wrong as it was to give up her children, it took an inner strength to admit her inability to care for them, and that, in all its perplexity, somehow lessened the pain.

"Bring him today around three, and we will have your beautiful child baptized." His warm and loving smile made Katarina cry for a very different reason…her brother truly loved her.

"What would I do without you?" She had told him that often, for too many years.

When she left, he slumped over in the chair. He was experiencing again the pain that caused him to hold his breath.

****

In the quietness of the church, Christina and one of her associates came to witness Benjamin's baptism. As Anthony spoke, Katarina looked around and felt that the saints etched in the stained-glass windows were all silently judging her. She heard them whisper "sinner" in her ear. She didn't belong in a church of God. Her life had been a book of sins, each chapter glaring, deceiving. As she looked at the Blessed Mother statue looking down at her, she felt suffocated and found it hard not to run out the door into the sunny day that would wake her back in the world where she belonged.

Her thoughts dissipated when she heard a soft gurgle as Father Anthony poured water on Benjamin's head and whispered, "You will be loved."

****

Grigory returned to Tel Aviv. He told his aunt and uncle that he would be bringing back Benjamin on his own. His aunt was not surprised that the mother wouldn't come there to live, but she was surprised that she would allow him to take the child.

****

Alise was at the house helping Aunt Esther, who had twisted her ankle and couldn't manage going upstairs to prepare the nursery. Grigory found Alise in the nursery, folding blankets and putting away clothing for the baby.

She jumped when she heard his voice. "Looks like someone painted the room."

There he stood, even more handsome than she had thought in their brief first encounter, but now the sadness in his eyes was more prevalent. "Well, I just thought that since it is a boy, he didn't need a pink room, so I painted it the color of the ocean—blue. I couldn't stop myself and added the dolphins and whales on the wall, too. I hope you like it."

"Thank you, that was very considerate." He looked at the finely drawn playful sea creatures and smiled at the idea of someone taking the time to do that for him. He looked at her differently now.

"This required a lot of time and effort. Would you let me take you to dinner in return for your kindness?"

She blushed again. Knowing that the mother of his child was not coming, she felt compelled to say yes, but she hadn't gotten the word out of her mouth before he asked her another question.

"Are you involved, Alise?" He looked at her quite seriously.

She gave a soft laugh. "No, I'm not involved with anyone." She felt nervous, as she'd never had a man of his intensity look at her the way he did.

"I will come to your home and pick you up at six."

"But I didn't answer your question yet," she said.

"Yes, you did, with your eyes." He smiled at her and cocked his head, giving her a tiny space to disagree.

"Hmm, well, let me give you my address."

"No need, I already have it."

"Of course you do," she answered, throwing up her hands in surrender.

That evening he showed up at her doorstep in a crisp white shirt, casual jeans, and a blue blazer. He somehow knew that she would be dressed in nice but simple attire. She was not a pretentious woman, and her casual style was quite appealing, and quite a change from Katarina, who dressed to impress everyone. He was pleased with himself and with her when she answered the door in a green skirt, pink blouse, and a small string of pearls resting at the top of her cleavage. He did not know she had researched Katarina Von Rahmel and learned of her exquisite beauty, designer wardrobe, and ballet career. How she could possibly compete had bothered her as she was dressing, but then she decided it was only dinner and nothing more. But still, she added her only pair of sexy sandals to the outfit.

He placed his hand on her back and guided her out of the house. A small shiver raced down her arms when he touched her. When he helped her into the car, he caught a slight rose scent in her hair.

The dinner was so easy, no strife, no anger or sorrow, just sweet conversation. They talked of her family and six siblings. She adored her parents, who were still alive and well and very much in love. She was not afraid to laugh openly, and she spoke with ease. When she felt she had rattled on too much, she politely apologized and blamed it on her nerves. She had not dated for some time and was consumed with her work, but she explained how lovely it was to be out with him.

He enjoyed watching her eat as much as she enjoyed eating the delectable dishes he had selected for her. Her eyes were alive with a softness that he had not seen for a long time in a woman. Katarina's eyes, as incredible as they were, were always filled with a trace of anguish, and those he had bedded carried no feeling whatsoever in their eyes. He figured it out before the dinner was over—what he liked about her. She was as guileless as a piece of fruit hanging on a tree.

She encouraged him to talk about himself, his life, his family. He wasn't as ready as she to share, nor did he want to burden her, but with her gentle coaxing, he was able to remember some joyful times before the war and before Katarina.

After another glass of wine, while sharing a bowl of ice cream, she finally asked when Benjamin was coming and if he was certain the mother would not be with him.

Relaxed and without fear lurking, and in the comfort of familiar surroundings, he gave her a brief history of his relationship with Katarina. He told her that he had loved her for many years, but it was time to move on. He admitted to Alise, as he looked directly into her eyes, that Katarina was in his blood and would remain there. But he assured her also that Katarina had drained him of hope for any future together, and he would move on without her.

She swallowed hard and realized what he had said. If she were to get involved with this man, she would always be second in his life. She wasn't quite thirty yet, and her experiences were few and with unsophisticated men. This man would make her a woman, and she was both excited and scared at the prospect. They ordered another glass of wine and talked until the restaurant closed.

They stood at the door of her cottage and expressed how delightful the evening had been for each of them. Grigory leaned in against the door frame and ran his finger down the bridge of her upturned nose. He lifted her pearl necklace and slid his fingers down to where it looped at the top of her breasts, and then he leaned in and kissed her. The kiss was soft and tender.

When she opened her eyes, she heard herself say, "Would you like to come in?"

"Not tonight sweet girl…not tonight."

She said goodnight, and as much as she wanted to watch him walk away, she closed the door and leaned against it, waiting, just in case he changed his mind.

Grigory stood at the edge of the sidewalk, thinking he should turn around and go back.

****

He was wondering if Paris would ever be the same for him when he walked toward Katarina's apartment. He braced himself for what was coming.

He was surprised to see Christina open the door and more surprised to see the sadness on her face.

"I'm so sorry, Grigory. We have everything packed, but she doesn't want to see you."

"Where is she?"

Christina hesitated. "She is at the café down the street with my brother, who is visiting. I think it's best if you take Benjamin and go. Just leave, Grigory. Don't put yourself through any more pain. I love Katarina, but there is a side of her I do not understand."

"I'll be back. Please have Benjamin ready to leave." He turned on his heel like a soldier who had just been given his orders.

He slowed down his pace as he approached the café and prepared himself for her reaction. Music was coming through the door. He peeked in, took two steps inside and stood against the wall, where he watched her slow-dancing with a man. The man held her waist tight, and she was tilting her head back in laughter at something he said. He felt the heat rise to his cheeks and his hand ball into a fist. The strap of her dress had fallen slightly off her shoulder, and she had not bothered to move it back into place. He remembered that dress. This bothered him greatly. The man kissed her cheek and pulled her closer. Grigory closed his eyes and opened them again, hoping he was hallucinating. The cold reality struck him that it was over. She had no problem moving on. The last thread of hope that she might change her mind was gone.

He walked back to the apartment with a slow stride, his head bent in sadness.

As he gathered up his son, Christina sat nearby, fighting back tears. She had wished for Benjamin to grow up with her Rudy, but now that would not be. She kissed the baby goodbye and chose not to follow him out. As he left, Grigory opened the door and found Anthony solemnly standing on the porch. His clear blue eyes were already filled with tears. He walked with them to the street. Grigory handed Benjamin to Anthony to hold for a last time. He respected this man so much, his pure heart, his determination in everything he did, including trying to help his sister. They both stood as if frozen in time, kindred spirits brokenhearted for the same woman.

"Anthony, please come visit any time. I will make sure he knows of his family, and maybe Katarina will come to her senses."

Anthony handed back the baby, and with pure honesty he said to his friend, "Don't count on it, Grigory. Just raise this child as a good human being and move on with your life. Remove her from your heart. It's time for your own happiness. I can't save her, and neither can you. No one can."

They shook hands and parted ways. The goodbye had been sealed with Anthony's final words. *No one can.*

Chapter 37

Grigory arrived back at his home, hoping Aunt Esther was there, as he had not given her an exact day or time, not knowing what to anticipate. He found Esther and Alise in the garden. They heard the cry of a child, and Alise was the first to run to him. She reached out for the infant and took him from his tired father. Grigory gave her a smile of approval, and she took the baby to his room.

He followed her, watching her natural control of the situation unfold. He was relieved to have help.

"What are you doing here in the middle of the day, Alise? You usually work long hours. Did you find the Holy Grail and call it a day?"

"Ha! I took a sabbatical to help your Aunt Esther. She still has difficulties with her ankle, and besides, she was fretting knowing you were coming home soon with the baby and she would not be able to help as she wanted."

Seeing the baby in the capable hands of Alise, he went downstairs to check on his aunt, who was standing at the base of the steps, looking up in exasperation.

"Grigory, I don't think I can walk up the stairs. Please bring him back down as soon as you can. Welcome home, dear nephew."

He guided his aunt back into the sunroom and asked with concern, "Are you sure you can handle him,

Aunt Esther, while I'm gone?"

"I will be fine. Alise can help me. I've asked her to stay here. With all these rooms upstairs, why should she pay such high rent? Surely, you don't mind." There was a suggestion of impishness in her smile.

"I think she will be good for you…for us…for the baby." He finally got the words out.

Settled in the living room, a nice alcoholic drink in hand for both aunt and nephew, Alise came downstairs with Benjamin. She had given him a bath and dressed him in blue cotton pants and a sweater, his hair combed, his little cheeks filled with a fresh peach color.

Esther reached out for him, and he was placed in her arms. Benjamin seemed to be adjusting to all the fuss over him, and with a bottle in his mouth, he was a happy baby in his new surroundings.

Esther looked at Alise and Grigory. "You two go out for dinner. Your uncle and I will take care of this little one."

Grigory looked at Alise and asked, "Are you hungry?"

"I'm actually starved."

They went to a small café, and as before she felt a bit hesitant around him. It wasn't so much his words, or even the way he carried his body, but his eyes, the way they looked at her, so intense, as if he were taking in all of her senses. They talked about her staying at the house and when she thought she would go back to work. He asked her if she would take care of Benjamin until he found a nanny. She found herself agreeing and glad that he never once mentioned Katarina.

This time when they came back from dinner, she knew it would not be a simple parting of the ways, as it was last time. In fact, he led her by the hand to the cottage and was about to open the door when he realized that she should be asked first. "Come in, let's have a glass of wine." Not quite a question—he was used to getting his way.

At first, she hesitated, until he pulled her in to his chest and pressed his lips next to her ear. "Please come in."

He felt a strange desire for this woman who seemed incapable of hurting anyone or anything. A woman with an old soul, who cared deeply enough for his aunt to help her through the daily routine, and who took his baby with the eagerness of a new mother. She was patient like his own mother, kind and gentle, and eager to relate. Yet beneath her youthful skin was a woman waiting patiently for the right man to bring her to the height of passion. She was ripe for the picking, and he could harvest her as his own. She was nothing like any woman he had ever considered, and so different from Katarina. Perhaps this was the change he needed. After all, his life was moving in a different direction now that he had a child, and it was uncertain how long he could keep up the pace in his work.

These thoughts were going through his head as he sat next to her on the sofa, sipping wine in quiet contentment. He would take his time with this one, he decided.

She let him take the glass from her hand, and when he turned his body toward her, she knew she wanted his kisses. He tasted like wine, with a trace of a fine salty sweat like the sea. She felt his hand move across her breast and around to her waist, pulling her body in to his. This was not a man accustomed to light foreplay, not someone who would start something he couldn't finish, that she knew. There would be no teasing him; getting nearly there and ending the night in a flush and hoping later for a second chance. He would take her, and she would let him. She unbuttoned her blouse as he watched, and then the lovemaking began.

****

He lifted up on his elbow, his chin in his hand, and looked down at the beauty in his bed. They had expended their energy on making their first time together last longer than a simple roll in the hay. She smiled up at him with a look of completeness and joy. Grigory had no idea who or what prompted the next words that came from his mouth and from his heart.

"Marry me?" he murmured in her ear.

She raised her hand to his cheek and studied his eyes before she asked, "Why?"

"Because I want someone to love me. I want to feel what we just experienced, more than once. I want to be happy for a change and have a pure relationship without complications. I want someone to love my son."

She understood what he was saying, but she needed to know. "Do you love me?" she asked.

"I know that from the moment I saw you, a feeling stirred in my heart for you. I'm not sure what love feels like anymore, but I know I want you in my life. You must know, first of all, Alise, I'm no angel. My world is one so different from yours, one I would not expect you to understand."

"And what about Katarina?" She had to ask or never forgive herself for not asking.

"She has been my only love. But it has worn thin, and it's time to let her go. I promise to give you all of me, and I will not be unfaithful."

He saw the need in her eyes. She felt the need in him. They sealed his promise with a kiss, and he waited for her answer.

"I will marry you, but I need one more promise from you. You will never go back to her."

"I promise. It's over."

Chapter 38

1964

Katarina waited for months to hear from Grigory, as if in her confused mind he would realize that he could not live without her and would return with their son and succumb to life as a family man and they would live happily ever after. When she approached Anthony with this ludicrous idea, he explained to her that in their last discussion together, Grigory knew he would let her go. She refused to listen to him, knowing full well that it was just a matter of time before Grigory would be crawling on his knees back to her. It had always been so.

Since then, Anthony had gone to Israel, seen the baby boy, and brought back a picture of him. When Katarina quizzed him about Grigory's life, he spoke of nothing important. She knew he was keeping something from her. In the meantime, she had found solace in the company of Christina's brother.

One day she had an unexpected visit from Francis as he was passing through Paris. Naturally he had sought her out, and they arranged to meet for a drink. When he was told she had given up Benjamin, he left her in sadness. He had hoped she would have kept one child. Still, he would not break ties with her, although he felt he should.

As always, Katarina eventually found herself missing Grigory so much she became restless in her skin. Given the erratic pattern of their life together, she thought by now she would have at least heard from him, whether in a call or by his sudden appearance without warning. She found herself growing weary of waiting. She could not stop herself from dialing his aunt and uncle's phone number.

A woman answered.

"I would like to speak to Grigory. Is this his aunt?"

"I'm Alise, his wife."

There was dead silence on Katarina's end. Alise knew immediately who was calling, and she would not let Katarina have the upper hand. She had made up her mind after they married that she would fight Katarina and never let her disturb their lives. Benjamin was now her child.

She spoke with unwavering clarity. "Katarina, I know it's you. Please do not call here again."

Katarina found her voice. "I don't believe you. He would never marry someone so quickly. Please let Grigory know that the love of his life, Katarina Von Rahmel, called."

Alise felt her hand shaking. "He doesn't love you any longer, so please go back to your life and leave us be." She hung up the phone, and it immediately rang back, again and again until, between the calls, she took the receiver off the hook and let it lie there lifeless.

Grigory walked in, minutes later, with Benjamin. They had gone to the beach. He noticed right away that she was pale and trembling.

"What's wrong?"

"I just stubbed my toes so hard it brought tears to

my eyes." Her laugh was unsteady.

He walked upstairs with Benjamin, who was reaching out for Alise. "I'll take him upstairs and put him down for a nap. When I come back, I think I should kiss the pain away." She nervously smiled at the mischievous look in his eyes. He was her man now.

****

Katarina was fuming when her brothers joined her at the café. She looked directly at Anthony and demanded, "How long have you known, and who is she?"

Anthony inhaled a deep breath. Hans looked at him sympathetically.

"There was no point in telling you, Kat. It was clear that you had moved away from him, and he deserved to find happiness."

She now looked at Hans. "Did you also know?"

"Yes, I knew. Look, you need to move on. I just think you both are poison for each other. Think about it—your life together has been lived only through drama and sorrow. The truth is, he found a lovely girl who loves him and Benjamin. She brings no baggage."

"Good heavens, please don't tell me you, too, have met her?" Her eyes pierced his in anger.

"Yes, Anthony and I both met her. I was in Israel for Father, looking for individuals who were board members of the Berlin Zoo. I asked Grigory for help. We traced one person who is a living relative."

Tears were now running down her face. "You both could have told me, not let me live with wondering what happened to him. You know I can go back for Benjamin at any time. I have the right to my son."

Anthony's voice was stern. "That is pure revenge

on your part. You want to hurt them. He will never let his son go, and you won't win that battle, with as many children as you have left behind..."

She looked at Anthony with anger. "You of all people are judging me?"

"I'm not judging. I'm giving advice and hopefully clarifying the situation for you, as your sensibility is clouded."

She stood up and glared at her brothers. "Both of you don't talk to me anymore. I'm going to Israel, and I'm going to confront him and his new *lovely* wife!"

Hans grabbed her hand. "It won't end well, Katarina. I'm just warning you."

"I guess I will have to see for myself. You have forgotten my capabilities."

****

She arrived in Israel, found a five-star hotel, and set up camp. She would figure out a plan and strike at just the right moment. She was used to waiting.

She took long walks in front of his house. Hidden behind rock walls and trees, she saw his new wife go in and out of the house, leave the premises and return again. For the life of her she could not imagine what he saw in this tiny waste of a woman. Sure, she was younger, but that had never been Grigory's forte. For several days she observed them. She could not deny the affection Alise had for Benjamin. Sitting outside on the porch with him in her arms, she looked as natural as any other mother with her child. She could see the love Alise had for Grigory, and it hurt her to see the love he had for her. It was when she saw Grigory walking back into the house with just her, his arm around her waist, and he lifted her chin and delicately kissed her lips with a look of contentment on his face, that she knew he was happy and in peace. But this was supposed to be her life now, and she would not let that thought go.

During her spying spree, she followed Alise and watched her stroll into a café with Benjamin. Through the window, she saw her being seated at a table. Once she was settled in, Katarina approached her, towering over her, strong and defiant. Alise looked up to see the face of the woman she feared. Benjamin, too, looked up at Katarina but no longer recognized his mother.

Katarina was breathing deeply with forced control. She wanted to slap this woman. Instead she reached down to pick up Benjamin. Alise grabbed her arm. “Do not touch my son,” she said.

Katarina’s eyebrows rose, and she was instantly incensed. “You really didn’t say what I just heard. ‘My son?’ You, little girl, must realize your mistake in that remark.”

Alise pulled her courage together. “Stay away from us. You are no longer part of him. He is done with you. He is happy for the first time in his life.”

Katarina hissed, “I doubt that. His only happiness is with me. I’m in his soul, and you should know that.”

Alise felt raw and vulnerable looking at this determined woman; her biggest fear had now come to life, standing before her in all her self-righteous beauty, this woman she knew could shatter her life. She had many times heard him say her name in his sleep, and when he left for days at a time, she prayed it was for work and not going back to her. But he would always return to her, loving her more, extinguishing her fears until the next time he left.

Katarina stepped back from their table and took

another look at Benjamin. “I’m leaving for now, but I will not be leaving Israel until I see him.”

Two days passed, and Katarina heard nothing from Grigory, even after she got a message through to him by mail, putting the return address on the letter as though it were from Anthony.

She took a chance, after having many drinks, and called late one night. He had just taken out the Beretta and placed it in the nightstand drawer. Alise was sound asleep. It had been a grueling day. He heard the phone ring and quickly moved to the living room and answered it.

“It’s me.” He heard the voice he knew so well from the past. He held his breath. He had read her letter earlier and burned it in the fireplace, taking note where she was staying. In fact, he had gone by the hotel, but his conscience had stopped him from entering. He knew it would only be heartbreak. He could not allow himself to think of her, and also, of course, he had promised Alise.

He caught himself whispering her name, when he knew he should have hung up the phone. “Katarina.”

“Yes, it is me, my love.” Her speech was slurred.

“What do you want?”

“Your marriage is a sham, and you know it. You love me. I saw her. How could you even think of marrying such a little mouse?”

“You made it quite clear that your life would not include me or Benjamin.”

She started to cry and plead for understanding. “Why would you do this, Grigory? We have always made our way back to each other.”

He swallowed hard, knowing she spoke the truth.

"Katarina, go back to Paris. It's over. I have found a good life now." He didn't want to stay on the phone listening to her voice drawing him back.

"Please come to the hotel and talk to me. Please."

He hung up and turned to see Alise standing sad-faced at the door.

"You will go to her. I know I can't stop you. Go, get her out of your system, Grigory, and then come back to me. I know you will make the right decision." She could not believe where the strength to say that came from. She felt faint.

He knew he had to go. He kissed Alise softly in passing and said, "I will be back."

She watched him leave, and with eyes closed, she prayed that he would.

He arrived at her hotel room and knocked, his forehead pressed against the door in sudden fatigue. She slowly opened it, and his breath caught in his chest. How many times since he left her had he questioned his decision. But even her brothers had told him that what he was doing was for the best. Alise gave him confidence and a constant love he needed. She would be a mother to his child without question. Why couldn't this end?

He stepped into the room and tried with all his might to keep his focus on the reality of his life now with Alise. His eyes dropped from hers to her hair where it hung loose around her shoulders. She stood posing for him, letting him see what he had missed, what he had earned, what he could still have. Through the thin silk nightgown, he saw the curvature of her full hips, the outline of her breasts and her magnificent legs.

After she let him take her all in, she slowly moved

toward him. She clasped her hands behind his neck and pulled his lips to hers. He could taste the wine. His mouth slipped from her lips to her shoulder and he smothered his face in her hair, all the while afraid to put his arms around her. She pulled him close and pressed her body against his. He felt his desire for her, but still could not bring himself to take her to bed. She moved his mouth back to hers and devoured him. He was lost in her, completely lost. He placed his hands on her hips and moved her to the bed. He looked down at her, and in her eyes he saw a ghost of what she had been and was no longer. They were as alluring as ever, but cold.

He stepped back. "No, you can't do this to me again. We are done."

She looked at him, stunned and dismayed by his words. "You couldn't have stopped loving me!" she cried, the tears gathering quickly, her body beginning to tremble. "Grigory, please." She opened her arms to him and begged.

He saw the pain he had known for so many years, and he wanted to fall into her arms and let them comfort each other, but he couldn't because he knew if he did, he would not leave her. She walked toward him, and he couldn't move his legs. She held his face and kissed him again, saying his name over and over in his mouth. He didn't realize he had lifted his hands and was combing his fingers through her hair while his lips crushed hers willingly.

In a flash, Alise's sweet face appeared, and he heard her words. *Get her out of your system.* He wanted that. He wanted that so badly. He could not live the rest of his life with this madness. He yelled, "Stop!" and pushed Katarina away.

"Go home, Katarina. You made your decision earlier, and you have Christina's brother to go home to."

She was crying again. "He means nothing to me. I just tried to forget you."

"Then you need to try harder. I'm leaving. I have a wife waiting for me. Married, Katarina. I am a married man now. It means more to me than I thought."

She saw tears in his eyes and a look she didn't recognize. A look of conviction.

He opened the door, and turned to her with his final words. "Try to find some happiness, Katarina. I will always love you, and I will always make sure you are okay, and in time I will explain to Benjamin who you are. You will not be forgotten."

She watched in disbelief as he closed the door. She was genuinely heartbroken; she had believed he could never truly let her go. She would make sure to keep him in her life, married or not. She needed him. She needed to love him, and she needed him to protect her. He was the only one who knew her demons, her memories. No, she would not let him go. Never. He would be back. She was determined to have him love her again.

Grigory walked the streets of Tel Aviv and continued walking even when it began to rain. She was the only one who could bring him to tears, and he wondered if he would ever really get her out of his heart. Perhaps never, he thought. Just like Francis and John. Neither of them, in the end, could give her up, but he vowed that he would. He returned to his car and drove aimlessly until he stopped and gathered his energy from the sea. From there he went home, newly restored.

Alise had paced the house until she was exhausted, and finally settled in bed, propped up on a pillow, talking to herself in the dark. She heard Grigory coming down the hall. She watched his silhouette as he stood in the doorway, bracing himself with his arm, looking as if he was thinking. She gave him a moment and then turned on the lamp. She sat motionless, waiting. He could see she had been crying. He stood a little longer and just looked at her, this beautiful human being who loved him. He opened his arms, and she threw herself into them. He loved her. He came back.

Chapter 39

A season passed, and life went on for Katarina in Paris. She went back to Israel one more time and watched Grigory's house day after day. The perfect family, she thought. When she saw the three of them out together, she noticed he would glance around, a slight anticipation on his face; she knew he sensed her. She left in a disturbed surrender.

For a while, she spent days alone in the Paris apartment, crying, drinking herself to sleep. She often asked for Hans to visit, but the only person who could calm her was Anthony. She traveled extensively, hoping for a geographical cure. In Greece, she wandered the islands with Christina's brother, Ralph. He also came with her to their Italy estate and stayed a month. She enjoyed his company but felt nothing for him in the way of love, although she knew he was falling in love with her. His presence helped distract her from thoughts of Grigory. She went to see Natalie and Alexandra, and from there they went to visit their cousin at the Sorbonne. Alexandra never left Natalie alone with Katarina during those visits.

At one point she considered going back to John, but the guilt overtook her. She felt he was capable of forgiving her, but the memory would linger, and she knew he could not help but look at her differently after giving up his child. And she had to admit that she had no interest in helping him find the child. He no longer asked for a divorce, possibly because he had no intention of remarrying. She seldom heard from him. Natalie, however, received weekly letters.

Anthony prayed for her every day on bended knee. He knew the excessive traveling was a temporary fix, and running away instead of coping would soon get the better of her. He encouraged her to get busy and start the ballet school she had often talked about. She signed papers to begin the process and spent hours planning, but she procrastinated to the point of nothing happening.

Every morning when she woke, she thought it would be different. Some days were filled with ease and a temporary reprieve from the sadness, usually when her brothers took her to dinner and the theater. She felt vulnerable every time she went back to Germany, spending the bulk of her time with her father. They never ventured close to the Berlin Wall. She found herself constantly looking over her shoulder, and the division of her country would always remind her of the dreaded past. It was painful being there without Grigory watching over her. She stayed just long enough to enjoy her parents and left as soon as she could to go back to Paris, where she could breathe evenly again. So she thought.

On a night when she felt the most despair, she cut her wrists, and through the daze in her mind she knew he was there. His head bowed as she placed her hand on it, and they didn't speak. Grigory would always be there.

Anthony had Francis come to his church to discuss Katarina's condition after the suicide attempt. Francis was equally concerned and reassured Anthony that he would be there when the time came. Soon after, he sought her out and pulled up beside her in his limo, as she was leaving a café. He asked her to get in. She hesitated at first, but she did. By then she had realized how few people cared for her anymore, how many bridges she had burned, and time with Francis, someone who had forgiven her and accepted her, was something she needed.

The brothers went one last time to Israel and met with Grigory and their nephew. They saw that his life was good with Alise, yet Grigory still kept tabs on Katarina. Somehow, he had been there the night she followed through with her threat to kill herself. Once again saving her life, he was unable to completely cut the cord between them. Hans and Anthony were grateful to this man, and they were glad he had found his own peace. They wished their sister could do the same, not just for herself but for all those who loved her.

In a series of confessions, Katarina told Anthony as much as she could, and how in the end she would not forget that God had forsaken her when she had cried out for him while being tortured in the prison with her baby. She was consumed with bitterness and could not find her way clear to attend church. Anthony explained the power of guilt, which he too had to learn to harness. He eventually felt that his Lord understood the ways he had strayed to help others and to protect his family. He tried desperately to convince her that God never left her side and was forever present. Katarina refused to believe.

Anthony came to realize that Katarina was the

child he'd never had, that she was the most important person in his life, second only to God. When she was born, he'd promised to protect her and love her always. The hours he spent speaking with her from his heart were not in vain. The light at the end of the tunnel was beginning to shine through.

Eventually the confessions released some of her pain, followed by periods of lightheartedness when Katarina and her brothers got together. Anthony saw genuine laughter return to her when Hans told his jokes, and when they shared stories of their father's frustration over training his horses, as if they were his unruly children. On such occasions they talked of only good things, and the chapters in between the horrifying events were revived as they began to slowly erase the memories of the war. During these moments, Anthony saw his sister's eyes brighten with innocence; the Katarina he had missed was still alive.

Early one evening, after one of their frequent dinners, Anthony was in such a hurry to get back to the church they had skipped their usual dessert and the long walk that followed. He was not feeling well, and hadn't been for several years, but whatever was happening to him peaked that night. Hans and Katarina accompanied him.

They hugged goodbye and reminded him that they were going to the opera the following week. Hans, as always, gave his brother a playful light choke hold. Usually Anthony would horse around with him, but this time he gave only a weak chuckle. Hans and Katarina looked at each other with concern as they waved to him at the top of the stairs. Walking away, they turned at the exact same time and saw him stumble and fall down the steps. They raced back and caught him just as he landed at the bottom.

Another priest came running out of the church when he heard Katarina's cries for help while holding Anthony, unconscious in her lap. She was shaking him and pleading with him to open his eyes, to wake up, while Hans knelt, weeping, at his brother's side. Raindrops fell in soft sprinkles, as if the angels above were crying with them.

Nearly in hysterics, Katarina was pulled away from Anthony's lifeless body by a police officer while the priest checked for a pulse. Placing his hand on Hans's back, the priest shook his head in deep sorrow and said resignedly, "I'm sorry, my son, he is no longer with us."

Hans looked down at his brother's face; undisturbed and peaceful. He took his hand, held it to his chest and closed his eyes in prayer. Katarina went back to Anthony and cradled him in her arms. Hans eventually let go of him and tried to help his sister do the same. He had to pry her away as the priest gave their brother his last rites. The police officer, who had confessed to Anthony many times, was also in tears for this man whom he had grown to love as a friend. When Anthony was taken away, Katarina crumpled to the ground and began pounding her fist hard on the steps. She begged for his God to bring him back. There was no comfort she would receive. Hans had to wait patiently with his own tears until her wretched sobs had subsided.

Back in Brighton, England, Peter was in the shed putting together rods, preparing for his annual fly-fishing trip to Spain with Anthony. His back was to the door as his wife came to stand there and whisper his name. "Peter, turn around."

He turned to see her, her bottom lip quivering, her red-rimmed eyes the saddest he had seen them in a long time. He dropped the rod and ran to her. "Claire, what is wrong? Is it one of the children?"

"I'm so sorry, it's Anthony. Your cousin Hans just called…Anthony died a few hours ago."

As if someone had just punched him in the stomach, Peter staggered backward to a chair. He began sobbing inconsolably. Claire rushed to his side and held him.

"Not Anthony! He was everyone's conscience! He is the one who had perfect submission and humiliation before God. He always held the power of reasoning. He put love into all of us."

Claire gently wiped the tears from his cheeks, and with her soothing voice said, "Peter, he has wings now. He is above all of us. He lived his life well, faithful to God."

"He was more than a cousin…he was my brother. He was my strength." He turned back to the table and picked up the fishing rod, remembering all those special moments wading in the flowing rivers, the peace they'd shared, the profound talks of life as they walked along the mountainside. "Claire…I'll be in soon."

She reluctantly left his side, and as she closed the door, he let loose a guttural sob followed by an ancient warrior's cry pouring out from the depth of his soul for a man he loved with all of his being. Claire knew that she could not bring him comfort and stood helpless behind the door, crying with him.

In Hawaii, Francis read the telegram saying that

Anthony had died. He leaned his head back in his chair, closed his eyes, and whispered to himself, "She will be back."

Natalie wrote her father of Anthony's death. She told him not to carry any hope that Katarina would come back. She would be seeing him soon, but without her.

****

On the day of the funeral, Katarina, dressed in black with a full veil, stood at a distance, next to Hans. Her grief was bottomless. She looked like a wounded animal, unable to hold her perfect posture, the pain of losing Anthony simply unbearable.

After the funeral, a woman came to her and took her hand. "You were there when he put me on the train to Paris," she said, pausing to give Katarina a moment to recognize her from behind the tulle netting. "Father Anthony saved me from a life of abuse. He made sure I was granted a divorce, and he found me a job. Not only me, but so many others. I feel he will watch over you as he did us."

Alexandra tried to bring her back to the Paris apartment in a humble attempt to be a loving daughter during this dreadful period. Katarina only smiled and said she would be there later. Elvia whispered something lovingly in French in her ear, and her parents hugged her in silence. The others were merely a blur.

She stood at the grave for a long while after everyone left, until she dropped to her knees and with her bare hands began digging into the loose dirt. "You can't leave me, Anthony! Please don't leave me."

From a distance, Grigory had been watching. He restrained himself from reaching out to her and remained hidden. He knew that, with this amount of grief, he could not leave her. Anthony had been her guardian angel on earth, and now he was gone.

Katarina lived every night with ghosts swirling around her, and always Anthony was there to smite them with a mighty sword. She held on to the last picture taken of the two of them eating in Lucca, a fond memory captured on film with the help of a tourist at the next table. The picture of him holding her as a baby and kissing her forehead was always on the pillow next to her. She would make sure he never left her.

Grigory looked in on Katarina one more time before he left Paris. He followed her as she walked to Anthony's church. She stood for a long time at the foot of the steps, finally bending down to touch the spot where she had last held Anthony in her arms. Then, to his surprise, she slowly entered the church.

She was sitting in the last pew, her eyes focused on the altar, still as a statue. Only her lips were moving in a muted prayer, the tears trickling down her cheeks. In a ghostly silence, Grigory watched her, until the room gradually dissolved around him, and in a soft haze he heard Anthony's distinct voice whisper in his ear, "I'll take care of her now." He took one last look at Katarina and quietly slipped outside into the sunlight now dancing through a gentle rain. He felt a smile cross his face as he walked away and left the love of his life in the hands of God.

Author's Note

It was when I published *The Star and the Cross* and was interviewed by Tiffany Murphy, anchorwoman for Fox 6 KFDM, that I knew the sequel needed to be written. With genuine curiosity, she wanted to know what happened to the people and was looking forward to reading the next book. Many others also asked eagerly for more. Years ago I wrote the outline to continue the story of the Von Rahmel family, so when I saw how the first book was received, I wrote more.

I hope that as you have read the sequel you gained a sense of understanding about the Von Rahmels and the challenges they faced. I felt honored to write about this family and their struggles and the way they handled life. I wanted to portray their strengths, their beauty, and their human characteristics as they all flew on their own wings to live out their lives, and at the same time, they stood up against Communism, stood up for women's rights, freedom of press, Christianity and faith, and fought wholeheartedly for justice.

I'm not sure any of them completely crawled out of the darkness, but they all had great spirits. They loved fiercely. Some walked with their souls tormented. Others were left free, and some were lost to us forever. We come away hoping and wishing the best for all of them as they are revealed in these chapters.

With much encouragement from many, I moved from Austin to Banner Elk, which I call a Hallmark town—mountain beauty, great food, skiing, hiking. It was on my hikes I formulated the story in my head, watching the snow filter down from the heavens and my breath turning to crystals. This is where my characters came to life. I rooted through old pictures and documents and letters, and as I did with the first book, I discovered many family secrets once again. I truly hope I did them justice, combining facts with my memory and imagination as I formulated their history.

I am blessed with special people as my biggest supporters: Shawn, Libby, Rod and Tiffany Murphy, Greg, and my husband Gerry. Your help and encouragement has lifted my own wings.

I see my life as ripples on the water, from a stone thrown by another.

A further word from the author…

I live in the mountains of North Carolina, where every day is a new adventure as I am surrounded by wildlife and all that nature offers. I spend hours with our horses, dogs, and cats.

I have been blessed with a wonderful marriage, a second chance in life, and my husband encourages me every day to keep writing. Besides my fantastic husband, I have the best group of friends, and all are dear to my heart.

I grew up all over the world as a child and worked with the airlines for 39 years, living in Paris and Rome and flying international flights. I loved being a flight attendant.

If I'm not painting, I sit and think of the next book to write. The future holds many stories and children's books.

Thank you for purchasing
this publication of The Wild Rose Press, Inc.

For questions or more information
contact us at
info@thewildrosepress.com.

The Wild Rose Press, Inc.
www.thewildrosepress.com

To visit with authors of
The Wild Rose Press, Inc.
join our yahoo loop at
http://groups.yahoo.com/group/thewildrosepress/

CPSIA information can be obtained
at www.ICGtesting.com
Printed in the USA
BVHW042015131019
560992BV00006BA/22/P